LYING IN RUINS

JAMI GRAY

Publisher: Celtic Moon Press Revised edition, 2021
ISBN: 978-1-948884-52-5 (ebook) ISBN: 978-1-948884-53-2 (print)

First edition, June 2017, Escape Publishing - HarperCollins Australia
ISBN: 978-1-48924-565-6 (ebook) ISBN: 78-1-52525-434-5 (paperback)

sign up for free reads from jami!

Join Jami's newsletter to be the first to hear about new releases, free books, special prices and other nifty events.

Sign up at: https://www.subscribepage.com/jami-gray-books

what readers say...

About Arcane Transporter:
"Taking a refreshing approach to fantasy magic, this fast-paced, economical thriller is told from a highly likable perspective." —Red Adept Editing

About PSY-IV Teams:
"This story is an emotional roller coaster, from betrayal, anger, fear, love..." —InD'tale Magazine

About the Kyn Kronicles:
"...a fantastic paranormal action novel is quite possibly the best book I've read this year. I could not put it down, and had to exercise serious self-control to keep from staying up all night to finish it." —The Romance Reviews

About Fate's Vultures:
"...if you like your characters with a bit more bite, with secrets, with hidden agendas, and all those sorts of things, and your worlds are a far more deadlier place, then this is for you." —Archaeolibrarian

also by jami gray

ARCANE WONDERLAND

Last Call

Bitter Spirits

Rune & Tonic

ARCANE TRANSPORTER

Ignition Point (*Prequel Novella*)

Grave Cargo

Risky Goods

Lethal Contents

Collision Course

Blind Spot

Terminal Drift

THE KYN KRONICLES

Shadow's Edge

Shadow's Soul

Shadow's Moon

Shadow's Curse

Shadow's Dream

Shadow's Fall

Tangled in Shadows (*Short Story Collection*)

FATE'S VULTURES

Lying in Ruins

Beg for Mercy

Caught in the Aftermath

Fear the Reaper

PSY-IV TEAMS

Hunted by the Past

Touched by Fate

Marked by Obsession

Fractured by Deceit

Linked by Deception

BOX SETS

PSY-IV Teams Box Set I (Books 1-3)

The Collapse: Fate's Vultures (Books 1-4)

The Kyn Kronicles Box Set (Books 1-6)

Arcane Transporter Box Set I (Books 1-3)

Arcane Transporter Box Set II (Books 4-6)

For my Ian, who handles having a mom who asks strange questions by providing brilliant answers so she can finish the damn story.

For my Brendan and his endless patience in advising his mom on the best weapons for any given task and his willingness to block out fight scenes with the same weird mom, despite our height differences.

For my Ben, who manages to keep the other two males in our household, plus the Fur Minxes, the actual house, and life in general, stable so I can disappear into my imaginary worlds without guilt.

Without you three—this and every other book I write, would never happen.

acknowledgments

Besides my family, there are three very important people who deserve recognition as their endless support plays a major role in my success, my writing group:

Dave—You, sir, rightfully claim your throne as a cherished friend and king of plot twists. When the battle of creativity becomes strewn with word carnage and the dark cloud of 'This-sucks' looms on the horizon, your encouragement rallies the troops and leads them to victory. Whether we shared the agonies of pen and ink or not, I count myself blessed to have you in my life.

DeAnna—Your dedication to the craft amazes me and leaves me stretching my muscles trying to keep up with you. I know there will come a time when I say with utmost fondness, "I remember her when ..." From one writer mom to another, I promise those small humans will eventually let you take a breath without providing commentary and be able to sustain life on their own. In the meantime, we'll keep making a run for hidden coffee shops where we can freely discuss adulting and ponder our creative dilemmas.

Camille—Woman, you are the coffee in my morning and the chocolate in my addiction. Only you could match my dark, twisted humor and best it without breaking a sweat, all while providing endless topics of intriguing conversation, and laughter when I need it most. Not only do you have mad skills as a writing partner, but you kick-ass as a best friend. And yes, some day, we will be the leaders of the pack.

And, as always, I bow to you, my readers, and offer my humblest thanks. Telling stories is no fun if there is no one to listen to them.

one

With her shoulder braced on the doorjamb of the ramshackle shop that served as Pebble Creek's delivery and message center, Charity took in the blood-spattered room and decided she picked the wrong damn day to visit.

"As soon as the last Raider was down, I headed back and found this." The comment came from her old mentor turned friend, Boden. Modeling the latest in crimson-stained field medic bandages he stood on the other side, his expression as grim as his voice.

This encompassed the fly-infested carnage that filled the confines of the room with the stench of hard death. A scent the spring air couldn't cut, even as it found its way in through the broken frame that once held a door and the shattered remains of the front window. Sunlight and dust motes danced among the pieces of glass strewn through the grisly mess, igniting tiny, bloodstained fireflies. As far as Charity was concerned, it was a too familiar scene.

Years before her birth, the winds of change swept over the world and laid waste with gleeful abandon. They ripped apart the wonders of modern man even as man-made super viruses tore through heavy urban populations and vital crops, leaving decimation in its wake. Under the devastating onslaught, it wasn't long before logic fell to its knees under the unbreakable grip of desperation, fear, and panic as city centers raged and burned.

Never one to be left out, Mother Nature joined the caustic mix, drowning coastlines and recreating the landscape and borders with the tools at her disposal. Each event cascaded into one overwhelmingly brutal lesson for humanity's children, a lesson they refused to acknowledge until it was too late to do anything but survive. And even that became a brutal, vicious game.

A game that resulted in grisly scenes like the one Charity now stood over. Part of her wanted to turn heel and walk away. She had enough things to worry about and adding this cluster to her To-Do list wasn't ideal. But instinct whispered that this was tied to her personal agenda, and instead of leaving, she stepped inside.

There wasn't much to the room. A long counter with a good size opening in the middle split the space in half. She counted three, maybe four bodies. It was hard to tell if the leg sticking out from behind the counter was still attached.

"Had to have happened during the raiding party's assault." She shifted, trying to ease the ache from the shallow bullet graze in her shoulder. A remnant from her role in the brief, but furious, firefight from earlier.

"Appears that way." Boden's agreement carried equal parts of disgust and anger, even as it edged on a growl.

"I'm not a big believer in coincidence." She recognized the dead man sprawled on the under the counter against a water-stained wall, and surrounded by blood-soaked papers and packages, most likely part of today's delivery. Crane, the man she was here to see. *Guess their meeting was cancelled.*

That comment earned a grunt from Boden. "Funny, neither am I." He dug a thick finger under the bloodstained strip of cloth covering his weathered chest and scratched. "Especially when they come in pairs. First, Raiders don't generally come this far up the pass, especially during early spring. Too much hassle, which is why Crane picked this spot to set up shop."

This spot was Pebble Creek, a virtual stronghold situated in a narrow natural valley between two ridges in the southern area of what used to be the state of Idaho. A place that should be too far north to tempt the desert dwelling Raiders into crossing the ravaged bones of what once made up Nevada, Utah, and Idaho. After the Collapse, humanity's remnants hunkered down in a few key urban areas, or huddled in strategic rural communities like this one, in the flimsy hope there was safety in numbers.

Charity waited for Boden to elaborate, but when he remained mute, she prompted, "Second?"

"Second," he said. "Crane was ambushed." He waved a hand at the corpses littering the floor. "Indicates they were targeting him, not our supplies or shipments."

From her position in the doorway, she eyed the undisturbed stack of boxes lining the back wall. "Which means the attack at the front gate was, what, a smoke screen?"

"Probably."

She sighed. She rode into Pebble Creek an hour ago, hoping to claim some of Crane's time and maybe get a solid lead on the trail of breadcrumbs she was sent to follow. When she reached the main gate, she was waylaid by Boden, who was informed of her arrival by one of the guards on watch.

Boden explained that Crane was in the middle of something, so they passed the time playing catch up. They were headed to the café to grab some coffee when the Raiders hit, and everything went to hell. Just her luck the damn scavengers decided to descend en masse in some crazed version of a suicide attack. Suspicions nibbled on the ragged edges of her mind, but she still asked, "Why Crane?"

Boden arched a brow. "Got time for a list?"

Right, this was Crane they were talking about. Narrowing down the reasons why someone would want Crane dead was nigh to impossible. He could be accused of being many things —arrogant and a dick were the first two that came to mind— but he was far from stupid. Especially when it took a special kind of ruthlessness and intelligence to hold a territory free and clear while surrounded by the two biggest power players on what was left of this side of the Mississippi. Crane might be unlucky as shit since he was dead, but he was far from stupid.

Time to figure out what the hell happened and screwed her plans to hell.

From her position just inside the doorway she and Boden shared, she studied the gruesome scene and did her best to ignore the slow pitch of her stomach. Closest to her was a body that lay halfway through the doorway, a crimson pool seeping from under it, the side of his skull dented. She crouched down and flipped the body over with a soft grunt, revealing a gaping gut wound and bloodstained knife on the floor. Bloody smears along the pitted floor marked the Raider's trail from Crane's propped position to the door.

A handset from an old rotary phone lay just beyond Crane's curled fingers, the heavy base tipped on its side, marked by stains of reddish-brown. She'd bet good money Crane used the heavy base as a weapon, before sinking his knife into the Raider's gut.

The phone's cord dangled across the counter probably plugged into a jack on the other side. While very few landlines survived the Collapse, most were attached to key spots, like Pebble Creek, but the positioning of the phone's receiver made her wonder. "Did he get a call out?"

Boden remained in the doorway and studied Crane, a frown darkening his blocky face. "Don't know, maybe."

"That the only line available?"

He nodded.

Huh, who would a dying man call? Setting the question aside for later, Charity carefully stepped inside the room. She managed a whole step before a big palm landed on her uninjured shoulder and held her in place.

Instinct took over and she wrapped her fingers around Boden's wide wrist, zeroed in on key pressure points, and tightened her hold until his fingers finally spasmed and released. She gave Boden an arched eyebrow.

Correctly interpreting her expression, he warned, "Don't go getting your panties in a twist, little girl. Just want to be sure you're good with getting up close and personal with this mess."

Trust her old mentor to remember how much she abhorred all things gore. Granted, she spent years working on her aversion, until she could now stare at the most gruesome scenes without betraying a flinch, but it didn't stop her guts from twisting into nauseating knots. Not that she would let the minor discomfort get in her way. "It's a good thing I adore you, old man, or you'd be curled on the floor trying to stuff your guts back where they belong."

Undaunted he simply grinned and shook out his hand. "That threat would carry more weight if you had used that knife I gave you, instead of being polite."

She couldn't argue that one. The grizzled warrior who spent hours training her was one of an elite few who held her loyalty and were safe from her preferred method of making her point. "Maybe I just don't want to nick one of my blades on your thick skull."

He snorted.

Done stalling, she turned and worked her way across the

floor, being careful to avoid messing up the scene. Which turned out to be harder than it sounded, thanks to the multiple bodies and scattered brass bullet casings. She stepped over Crane's legs and ignored the unseeing gaze and frozen grimace of a second Raider who barely looked old enough to shave but now sported more holes than Swiss cheese.

Reaching the opening in the counter, she scanned the back half of the room. A tattered couch with a couple of duct tape mended cushions crouched against the back wall. Next to it were two salvaged metal filing cabinets that shared space with boxes. A battered metal desk sat to the right, with a broken and bent lamp on top. The other items that once graced the desk's surface were now scattered to kingdom come. To the left, under a narrow window wearing a spider web of cracks, stood a cluttered bookcase made of cement blocks and sheets of warped wood.

Leaning over the counter, she confirmed the protruding leg was still attached to a third Raider who was face down behind the counter. Death was courtesy of the dent in his head, or—*was that a letter opener?*— still pinned in the base of his skull. Most likely it was a combination of both.

Needing a moment before, as Boden said, 'getting up close and personal' with Crane, she focused on the far wall covered with a large map of the area from before the Collapse, and sucked in a silent, steadying breath. From this angle, she could identify the spots of rust decorating the map's handwritten adjustments that marked the last seventy or so years of geographical change. When she was sure she wouldn't embarrass herself by gagging, she crouched next to Crane and braced her hand on a clean spot on the wall behind him.

Crane's head was turned towards her, his brown eyes filmy. Bloody streaks deepened the lines on his pallid skin and stained the mix of grey and white scruff lining his chin and jaw. The macabre details added decades to his features.

Mottling spanned one side of his face, and his lips bore multiple cuts as if something or someone had hit him repeatedly. "Looks like he took a few punches."

"They'd need a two-by-four to damage his thick skull." Boden stayed where he was and let her do her thing.

Gingerly she lifted Crane's left arm, and then turned it, examining the back of his hand. Sure enough his knuckles were scraped raw which meant he managed to get in a few hits of his own. But that wasn't what had her sucking in a sharp breath. "Someone took a souvenir."

Something scraped against the floor and then the light shifted as Boden came to a crouch on Crane's other side. "What the hell?"

She lifted Crane's wrist, exposing the man's mutilated hand. "He's missing his ring finger."

Fury eclipsed Boden's face. "Proof of a completed job?"

She set Crane's hand down and shook her head. "There's nothing unique about a finger."

"There is about Crane's."

That caught her attention. When he said nothing further, she pushed, "What?"

Boden rubbed his chin. "He had a tattoo, like a ring. Except his was some kind of bird." He grimaced. "Never paid much attention to it."

"Someone else obviously did." Her niggling instincts grew teeth. Unwilling to touch the body more than necessary, she studied the various wounds littering Crane's torso, including what appeared to be a graze left by a bullet along his right side. "Without stripping him, it looks like they nailed him a couple times. Could be lucky shots."

Unlike her, Boden didn't hesitate to pull back the left side of Crane's faded hunting jacket. "He took one to the shoulder. That one," he pointed out the second, small dark hole a bit lower. "Probably bounced off a rib." He let the jacket fall back in place.

She lifted the right side and found another hole. "Third shot down near the kidney. Just these three made him a dead man walking." Because Pebble Creek didn't sport anything close to the medical facilities found in the few remaining cities, instead they relied on the patch and pray philosophy.

Boden directed her attention to the deep cuts scoring Crane's lower stomach. "These wouldn't have helped either."

Good god, the old codger took a hell of a beating. There was one more thing she wanted to check. "Lean him forward, would you?"

Boden shifted around, managed to brace Crane's body, and create enough space to work. First, she ran her fingers over the back of his skull. Sure enough, she found a telltale lump just behind his ear. Since the wall behind Crane was saturated with blood, it was safe to assume he bled out under the counter.

"Go ahead and put him back," she murmured, thinking it through. "I'm betting the Raider behind the counter followed him in, nailed him from behind, thinking that's all he needed to take him down." She straightened and Boden did the same. She went behind the counter, stood next to the body with the dented skull pierced by the letter opener, and eyed the very long phone cord that was still plugged in. "Crane brained him with the phone, then set the knife in his skull to be sure he didn't get up. Unfortunately, with his back to the door, he missed the nasty duo coming in behind."

"I can see that," Boden said. "It also means they were watching for a chance to catch him alone, hence the firefight out front that kept everyone busy." He set Crane back in place and straightened. "And the finger?"

She stared at the missing appendage. *The cut was too neat.* "I think he was already dead when they took it."

"Which means they needed proof of death, then."

As the answer was obvious, she didn't bother commenting.

Boden wasn't done. "I bet the first three Raiders were sent ahead to take him down." He frowned. "And someone else came back in after the deed was done to get the finger."

Coming back to retrieve the finger indicated sloppy work. "Which makes zero sense." Boden grunted but didn't disagree with her assessment instead he pointed out, "Bounties aren't standard Raider behavior."

"True, so what changed?" She didn't expect an answer because there were still too damn many questions. She tucked her question away for later consideration. There was nothing more left to learn here. She headed for the door.

"Little hard to question the dead," Boden called after her.

She didn't bother responding, just kept going until she was back outside. Do her best not to be obvious about it, she sucked in crisp air to drive out the sourness left behind from the miasma of spilt blood and guts.

Boden came up behind her. "What the hell is going on, Charity?" He skirted around her until he blocked her way, his gaze dark and hard. "What kind of trouble did you bring me?"

If it was anyone else asking, she'd resort to the tried-and-true batting of eyelashes and clueless demeanor, but with him, it was a wasted effort. She rubbed the back of her neck. Since the moment she arrived, nothing had gone as planned. For someone in her position, that wasn't a good thing.

There were multiple reasons behind her seemingly impromptu visit, some she couldn't share with Boden, not unless he stepped into Crane's still warm boots. And this particular pair wasn't easy to fill. Crane's stabilizing presence was all that kept the two feuding west coast power players in line. Without Crane to run interference? The impending disasters didn't bear thinking about it. No matter how much she twisted it, she couldn't see her old mentor playing that tricky role. "Whatever trouble killed Crane, wasn't mine." So far as she knew. If she was wrong, well, that would make things … interesting.

Voices from those who survived the Raiders' attack called back and forth, the sound drifting in the air as background noise. Meanwhile, his face an implacable mask as her tension rose, her one-time trainer studied her, clearly unconvinced. "You're sure?"

"As much as I can be." She wanted to say more but couldn't. Not yet.

He finally shifted to the side with a muttered curse.

"Based on what happened in there—", she indicated the building behind them with her head, "—the Raiders weren't jacking around. That list of who had it in for Crane, you want to share names?"

He grimaced. "It could be any damn one, so long as they could pay up."

"Anyone with particularly deep pockets?" She fell in step behind him and together they moved towards the building normally used for social gatherings, but currently serving duty as a makeshift medical ward. Once upon a time, it housed some other, less serious purpose. Maybe to watch those movie things old timers sometimes mentioned.

Boden shrugged. "You think I have time to track that shit, girl?"

"You said there was a list."

"It's Crane we're talking about." He slanted her a look. "You know, it could just as easily be someone new crawling out of the pits."

Considering how fast the tides of influence shifted, he was probably right. She wanted to dig for more and unearth whatever bones Crane was messing with, but first things first. As they drew closer to the main social hall, the clamor of those helping the wounded was interspersed with broken moans and sobs from the injured and dying.

She stepped inside and blinked, trying to adjust her eyes to the dimness. Even the sunlight pouring through the windows and the thrown open exterior doors couldn't lighten the somber atmosphere. Her gaze swept over the rows of the wounded, neatly laid in the center of the room. "How many?"

Boden heard her soft question and answered just as quietly, "At last count, we lost four to their fifteen. Three more could go either way. The rest should make it."

Hidden deep where no eyes would ever witness, she flinched. Humanity's numbers were nothing like before, and in a mid-size rural community like this, that seemingly low number carried long-lasting implications. "You have enough antibiotics on hand?"

"Lucky for us, we just got a recent resupply." Movement caught his attention and his spine stiffened, then he was working his way across the floor, his goal a reed-thin woman currently directing the chaos. "Mandy."

At the sound of her name, the woman turned, and light glinted off the wire frame of her glasses. Brown hair was pulled back into a severe bun that only emphasized the exhaustion honing her face into sharp angles. "Boden." Her gaze flicked to the entryway before coming back to the big man in front of her. "Crane?"

"Will wait until later," Boden answered.

Correctly translating the unspoken answer, she muttered, "Dammit." Her mouth pulled down as her fist came up to rub at her chest and genuine grief shadowed her eyes.

Boden didn't waste time. "Updates?"

"The bastards took out one of the supply sheds with a Molotov cocktail. We lost a couple of shipments awaiting transport to the border, a couple of mechanicals in the midst of repairs, and overflow foodstuffs." She listed the damage in a hard voice. She shook her head and frowned. "Their timing was shit for them, but good for us. Since it wasn't a market day, most of our people were tucked away on their homesteads or deeper inside the town, away from the gates."

Charity added that nugget to her list of shit that didn't make sense. Raiders tended to attack when maximum damage could be inflicted, which made market days the perfect lure. Most settlements upped their guardsmen during those times. "Maybe they thought today was market day?"

"Not likely," Boden said before he snapped his mouth shut and his jawbone pressed white against his weathered skin. Despite the bandage wrapped around his chest, he folded his arms and asked Mandy, "Nothing critical?'

The other woman rolled her shoulders. "Not to us. But I'm not sure how understanding those waiting on the border shipments will be."

Possible scenarios spun through Charity's mind, some more paranoid than others, but that was the curse of experience. Her mental acrobats were about to leap into the ramifications of Crane's sudden demise when Boden asked the older woman a new question. "Anyone missing?"

Mandy took off her glasses, rubbed her red eyes, and then carefully resettled her frame, her careful movements tweaking Charity's curiosity. "Simon took off after two Raiders who bolted when it became obvious their friends weren't getting out alive."

"Simon?" Charity tried to put a name to a face and came up blank.

A cloud of worry settled over Boden's face as his question chased the heels of hers. "Did the hot-headed fool take any backup?"

Picking up on his uneasiness, Mandy's tired gaze sharpened. "Not that I know of, why?"

Boden spun on his heel and headed towards the main door without answering.

Charity chased after him. "Boden, who's Simon?"

He spared her a brief, undecipherable look. "Besides me? The only man stupid enough to be convinced to take Crane's place."

The pit in her stomach roiled. "You think the runaway Raiders are leading him into trap?"

"Don't think it, little girl, know it."

His response left her mentally spewing every nasty word she knew. They rushed outside only to be met by the distinctive rumble of motorcycles that pulled them both up short. Two unmistakable bikes roared into the open space, matte black and kitted out, the dust covered machines seemed familiar. When she realized why, she wanted to kick something.

Trouble, with a capital T, pulled to a stop in a cloud of dust. The low thunder of the engines drifted away as the two men dismounted. One was tall and whipcord lean, while the other could give Boden a run for his money on the brawler front. The taller one took point, and pulled down his dust-covered bandana to reveal a short dark beard. He stalked forward with a loose-hipped swagger, which might be interesting under different circumstances, and then met Boden with a manly arm grasp.

"Ruin," Boden greeted as he pulled the lighter man in and bumped shoulders.

"Bo-man." When Ruin stepped back, his friend came in and repeated the greeting.

"Havoc." Boden added a solid slap on the second man's back and got a silent nod in return.

Hearing the names cinched it for Charity. Ruin and Havoc, one-half of Fate's Vultures, a nomadic band of vigilantes with an ever expanding notorious reputation for brutal justice. *Fan-freaking-tastic.* She definitely picked the wrong damn day to visit Pebble Creek. Feeling the weight of a stare, she took her sweet ass time acknowledging it.

Ruin was staring. Maybe. Hard to tell since his eyes were hidden behind dark lenses. "I know you."

That deep voice sank under her skin and ignited a series of quakes. Temptation raised its troublesome head and licked its lips in anticipation. Determined to maintain control, she cocked her head to the side and used a finger to motion for him to remove the glasses.

His lips twitched, but he pushed them up over his barely restrained, wild tangle of hair streaked with burnished copper. Eyes the startling color of amber were revealed.

Every one of her nerve endings came alive, and that bitch temptation began to laugh. *Oh yeah, she was in trouble.* Years and years of practice allowed her to speak without revealing a damn thing as she slowly shook her head. "Nope. Never met."

Her answer got a long slow blink, and a speculative gleam, but no response. A little disappointed, she shoved a gag in temptation's mouth and tossed her ass into a locked room.

Ruin turned back to Boden. "What happened here?"

"Raider blitz attack." Boden didn't need to elaborate as a couple of the walking wounded dragged the last of the dead Raiders away.

Ruin's gaze swept over the area. "Where's Simon?"

Not the question she expected, but Boden didn't even bat an eyelash. "Chasing a couple of escapees. We were just getting ready to track his ass down."

Ruin frowned. His attention shifted to her, lingered, darkened, and then went back to the bigger man. "Mind if I tag along?"

"The more, the merrier." Boden turned to her. "Charity, catch them up on shit, I need to grab a couple of things before we head out." He didn't wait for her answer, but moved away, shouting at one of the men on the far end of the yard.

Her gaze collided with Ruin's and the merciless speculation she saw brought her earlier unease back with a vengeance. Unable to stop herself, she arched a brow in silent question.

His lips curved, but there was nothing friendly about it. "That shit include why no one's answering Crane's phone?"

Ruin's drawled question took her from wary to braced for impact as she finally figured out who Crane tried to call. Just to be sure, she asked, "Crane called you?"

"Not directly," Ruin said. "He called Holden."

Unwilling to follow Boden into a possible trap without a bit more backup, she turned and started to where her bike was stashed.

It didn't surprise her when Ruin kept pace, leaving his silent partner behind with their bikes. "We were there mediating—" the word carried a sneer, "—when it came in."

Holden ran a meeting place just north of what used to be Salt Lake City. It was considered neutral ground, the perfect place for mediations. If Crane called the Vultures in, it was because he knew he was in trouble. "Crane's dead." She wouldn't go into details, not her place. If Boden wanted to share, that was on him.

"Dead?" There wasn't much in Ruin's voice, making it hard to read.

Doing her best to ward off pesky questions, she said, "Yep."

They reached her bike, and she crouched down to unlock the custom storage compartment that held an old-style Glock 19. Ammunition was a bitch to get a hold of, but she made a point to have connections. Normally, her blades provided adequate backup, but considering the amount of brass littering the ground and the still stinging graze on her shoulder, the need for something more than a knife was painfully obvious.

Plus, she had no clue if the missing Simon, or the Raiders

he was chasing, were carrying. It would suck to walk into a firefight empty handed. She belted the leather holster around her waist and propped her boot on her bike's back tire as she tightened the thigh strap that would hold it in place. Tucking the Glock home, she made sure to grab the extra magazine as well. She felt Ruin watching her, his gaze taking on a tactile weight. An unsettling sensation, but considering her earlier reaction to him, not unexpected.

She turned and came face to face with him as he invaded her personal space. Used to the posturing alpha male routine, she folded her arms over her chest, and cocked her head to the side, not giving an inch. Despite what her body wanted, she wasn't here to play, so she attacked first. "What did Crane say that sent you rushing up here?"

"Didn't talk to him." The predatory light in Ruin's eyes made a lie of his lazy demeanor. "Holden answered, got an earful of screams before the line went out. That generally means trouble."

"So you just raced hell-bent for leather to dive right into that trouble?" Despite the temptation he presented, his arrogance nibbled at her patience and left her irritated enough to stay on the offense.

"Wanted to be sure that trouble didn't include Simon."

Simon? Not Crane? Interesting. "Why? Is he one of you?"

It was Ruin's turn to lift an eyebrow. "One of me?"

She waved a hand dismissively. "Fate's Vultures."

Male ego rose to the fore. "Ahh, so we have met."

Exasperated, she shook her head, pressed her palm against his chest, and gave him a light shove, a silent indication to back off. Despite his t-shirt, heat met her palm and her fingers flexed just enough for her nails to bite into his chest. "More like your reputation precedes you."

He held firm long enough to ensure she knew when he

stepped back it was his choice. "Nope, Simon's not part of us, but he is Crane's."

"And just like the Vultures, he answers to Crane." Even as he stepped back, his heat still seared her palm. Keeping her hand half-hidden by her side, she curled her fingers into a fist. "Correction, answered to Crane."

Ruin's expression didn't change, but there was no way to miss the rise of temper that flared in his eyes. "We don't answer to anyone."

Their conversation was interrupted when Boden came up behind him. He had a short-handled axe strapped to his back, the blade's head rising behind his shoulder. Ruin turned and moved to stand at her side, leaning down to keep what he said next between them. "Simon might not be part of the Vultures, but he is a well-valued friend."

His breath tickled her ear, and she fought her body's instinctive shiver. Unable to meet those sharp eyes, she muttered, "Must be a hell of a friend."

Ruin's answer was unexpected. "Closer than a brother."

Well, hell, that changed things. Because now the situation went from complicated to completely fucked.

two

An hour out, Ruin hit an isolated spot tucked in the mountains behind Pebble Creek and the end of Simon's trail. Motorcycles were useless on these narrow trails, which meant taking the slower option of horseback. As his mount blew out a soft huff, Ruin studied the smears of blood marring the trunk of a nearby tree and the brown drops decorating the surrounding bushes. Those weren't the only signs of a hurried passage. There was the scuffed dirt, broken twigs, torn leaves, and gouges where boots and blades had dug into the ground.

Ruin crouched, one hand on the reins, the other curled into a fist as he choked back the gnawing frustration edged with dread souring his gut. As the steepest and narrowest part of the trail it made for the perfect pinch point for an ambush, and Simon apparently waltzed right into the Raiders' trap.

"You stupid fuck," he muttered. *How many damn times had he warned Simon that his need to rush in would get him killed?* Ruin flexed his bloodless fingers as he considered his next steps. He crouched next to the torn-up grass and scanned the surrounding area carefully.

Strangely, the well-armed, blonde bundle of trouble behind him remained quiet, watching from her seat on the back of the sturdy paint. A distant part of his mind, not running through possible scenarios, was grateful she stayed out of his way.

On their way out of Pebble Creek, they were stopped by the sudden appearance of a scared out of his mind kid, who, seeing them approached, dropped to his knees. His normally tanned skin was leeched of color and streaked with blood and dirt. He was breathing so hard he could barely speak. Surprisingly, it was Charity who managed to calm him enough to get the story.

According to the boy, the Raiders, en route to Crane, decided to use the kid's family as a pre-party warm-up. The boy's homestead sat just outside of Pebble Creek and served as a homestead to multiple generations of the same family. While the Raiders did their thing, the boy hid with his younger siblings and cousins. The older family members fought back, but it didn't take long for the Raiders to guarantee there was no one left to raise the alarm before they hit the main settlement. The boy waited to ensure the Raiders wouldn't return, before he headed out on foot for help.

After the boy's story, a short conversation ensued with the growing group of curious, but clearly rattled residents and it soon became clear that leaving Pebble Creek without a de facto leader was just asking for more trouble. Boden agreed to remain behind while Havoc and a couple of medics headed to the boy's home in search of survivors. Which is how Ruin ended up with the woman, two horses, a hunting rifle, and a growing pile of rocks in his gut.

"Someone put up a fight." No longer on her horse, Charity approached and stopped next to him. Her ability to move so quietly spoke to a specific skill set he was innately familiar with and raised a red flag about her sudden appearance at Pebble Creek.

Guess she was done with being quiet. She was close enough a simple shift in his position and his shoulder would brush her thigh. The heat of her body left the hairs on his arm standing at attention. And that wasn't the only body part rising to the occasion. *Ain't lust an inconvenient bitch?*

"Not a surprise," he said. Between his unwanted attraction and his worry and frustration surrounding Simon, he felt decidedly on edge. The woman generated a list of questions that grew by the hour, but something warned him getting answers would require a creative approach. Good thing for her he didn't have the time to indulge in an interrogation session. Shoving the tangle of messy emotions to the back-burner, he rose to his feet. "Simon's not the type to go quietly."

A breeze drifted through the surrounding trees and danced through the sunlit strands of her hair, whipping them across her eyes. She hooked the flyaway strands with a finger and tucked them behind her ear, her gaze studying their surroundings. "Where did they go?"

Her muttered question echoed his. He did a slow pivot on his heel, taking in the knee-high grass and wind-bent trees, as his mind worked through potential options. The Collapse reconfigured the terrain of what used to be Idaho, Wyoming, and Montana until forests and lakes dominated the area. Viable routes through this area were few and far between, and it had been years since he traveled this one.

The narrow pass was caught between the sprawling stretch of Lolo Forest to the west and the treacherous terrain of Yellowstone to the east. It served as the only route between the two, with a straight shot to the Northland border. The mountain chain they were currently in consisted of several high peaks. Harsh and unforgiving, they weren't the best option for hiding but, as history proved, a determined individual, or the occasional lone hunter, desperate to remain isolated from what remained of the world, could make do.

His gaze narrowed on one of the nearby peaks where a strange, unnaturally wide swath cut through the trees. A long-ago memory whispered awake. He hooked a finger on the thin chain curled over his hip and attached to a belt loop before it disappeared into his front pocket and pulled. As he cupped the small but sturdy compass in his palm, he oriented himself. "My money's on the old Cammon place."

"How far away?"

"Maybe an hour that way." He tilted his head to the north. "It's a small cluster of old cabins tucked up by an abandoned ski resort."

Charity moved back to her paint before he finished. Moments later he led the way on the faint trail. With the compass in hand, he used his thighs to guide his quarter horse as he split his attention between maintaining the correct direction and any possible signs of Simon or the Raiders.

Thankfully, Charity wasn't a magpie, so other than the muted sound of hooves, and the occasional bird call, the silence was strangely comfortable and undemanding. She finally broke the quiet when the sun started inching its way towards the horizon. "Ruin."

"Yeah?" Without look back at her, he made another adjustment in their direction.

The current path was wide enough for her to pull her mount up alongside his. "Not to be a downer or anything, but are you considering this a rescue or retrieval?"

His already tight gut clenched a bit more, and he fought to keep his grip on the reins unaffected. "Simon's a tough ass bastard, so until I have proof otherwise, I'm aiming for rescue."

She didn't argue. In fact, she dipped that pointed chin in acknowledgement. "Then we need an infiltration plan."

Yep, definitely a woman of hidden agendas. "Got an idea?"

"Yeah, actually I do."

"How good is your crazy?"

There was a note in her voice that made him brace. He canted his head and took a moment to replay her question. "Come again?"

Those full lips twitched, causing his cock to do the same. "Time to let your crazy fly, Ruin." She didn't wait for his response. "You and Boden seem certain the Raiders were leading Simon into a trap. Add in the fact we're tracking them deeper in the mountains, I'm thinking we're about to be outnumbered."

A light touch on the reins brought his horse to a stop. "And?"

Charity's paint took another step or two before doing the same. She twisted in her saddle to face him, a dark mischief dancing in her electric blue eyes. Slim shoulders rose in a delicate shrug under the battered leather jacket. "Why go in hard, when we can go in soft?"

He touched his heels into his horse and nudged it forward. "I'm listening."

"This Cammon place." She held his gaze as he came up beside her. "How many people know about it?'

"Long-timers mainly," he answered, thinking of the eclectic individuals who haunted these mountains. "Some stay tucked up here for years on end."

"So if one of those long-timers happened to be a trapper calling it home?" Her horse held steady as his crowded close.

He caught a flash of heated awareness in her gaze before she doused it. Deep inside, under his wiseass persona, the hunter smiled in anticipation. *God how he loved a challenge wrapped in a puzzle.*

Absently he clicked his tongue and tightened his legs, urging his mount to hold steady, then filled in the blanks of her suggestion. "Crazy ass loner comes back from a hunt, his woman in tow, only to stumble upon uninvited guests."

She shifted in her saddle, touched the tip of a finger to her nose, and tapped twice.

Hmm, it might work.

"Guns or blades, you think?" It was a question he hadn't asked her earlier, too caught up in tracking Simon. Since she was there during the attack, she might have an idea of the Raiders' weapons.

"I'm thinking, both."

His gaze went to the gun strapped to her thigh. "You any good with that?"

Feminine arrogance straightened her spine, and her hand caressed the weapon. The real woman peeked out behind the alluring mask. "Wanna play target?" Her tantalizing lips curved into a wicked smirk. "I'll even give you a head's start."

There was a dangerous purr in her voice that he liked, but he ignored the implied invitation and raised an eyebrow. "Confusion will only work for a few minutes at most before they decide we're not worth the hassle."

An unflinching cunning and intelligence moved over her face and her gaze hardened. "Long enough to even out the numbers if need be." She leaned over and braced her hand on his thigh where his knives rested, her touch a hot brand that seeped through his jeans and skin to marked bone. "Then you can bring these boys out to play."

Her fingers brushed against the leather holding one of his blades and he locked her wrist in his grip, and tugged it away, forcing her horse to sidestep nervously. Dust and sweat couldn't drown out the delicate spice of her scent, so he gave in curiosity and used his free hand to capture her chin. Then he dipped his head until their lips were a breath apart. "No touching."

Her pupils flared with heat and awareness, but she didn't

fight his hold or jerk back. Instead, she held his gaze and remained still, waiting, watching.

Sexual tension rose in a fast wave and snapped into place with a disconcerting speed and strength that left him wary. He couldn't remember the last time he got hot and sweaty between the sheets. Not that this was the time, and she sure as hell wasn't the right woman, but ... he couldn't resist taking a taste and brushed his lips over hers. Her breath hitched and he drew back. The warmth of her lips lingered and turned his voice into a rough rasp as he brought their conversation back on track. "You got anything against getting dirty?"

She sat back in the saddle, red staining her gold skin, but her comeback was whip quick. "How dirty?"

Explicit images exploded in his head, but he stifled his grin before it could emerge. She was damn lethal, in more ways than one. He set his attraction aside for the moment and got down to business. "We need to look like we've spent weeks in the wild, otherwise we won't get past the tree line."

He put his heels to his horse and took lead. With his back to Charity, he attempted to shift his position, hoping to eliminate the possibility of permanently damaging his more important parts. "There should be a small creek out near Cammon. We can use the mud to help grunge shit up."

She made a soft clicking sound, then the soft thud of hooves followed. "It'd be better if we hit it closer to sundown."

He couldn't fault her logic as the evening shadows would mask their approach. "I agree."

A minute slid as he considered what needed to be accomplished in a short amount of time. To pull this off, they needed as many trappings of reality as possible.

Charity's voice broke into his thoughts. "We'll need to do some hunting."

It was eerie how close she followed his thoughts. Her detailed level of thinking was another indicator of how intelligent and dangerous she was. *Dammit, she was definitely trouble.* It would also give us a chance to scope out what we're up against."

"We should go in by foot."

Something he already considered as his mind picked apart their plan, piece by piece. "We can leave the horses down by the creek."

Another pause, then she said, "We could use the saddle blankets as ponchos and hide our weapons."

He grunted his agreement, but didn't say anything more and she let the quiet hold as they made their way to their target. As much as going into this situation with an unknown at his back sucked ass, he couldn't—wouldn't—fail Simon. His gut screamed that waiting for the other Vultures, Reaper and Vex, would guarantee Simon a hole in the ground. He knew damn well Charity had her own agenda, but as much of a crapshoot as this plan was, it was his best bet of getting Simon out.

Of course, if the woman behind him screwed him over, he didn't have issues adjusting his plan accordingly either.

three

Braced in the crook of a tree where a heavy tree limb met the thick trunk, Ruin used the artificial height and a compact pair of binoculars with night sights to scope out the Cammon place.

The field glasses, picked up a few years back when he stumbled upon a rare cache of military equipment stashed in a dilapidated barn, were one of his prized possessions. The small lenses painted the scene in shades of green as the sun ducked behind the mountains, allowing the shadows to take over. Mother Nature wasted no time in reclaiming the area, but the relics of what once served as a large sprawling central building lingered. Two scorched marked walls stretched towards the star dotted sky, their fallen brethren nothing but a pile of wood at their feet. Scattered across the open space, four cabins had managed to survive the combined assaults of nature and man, but each one was visibly on its last legs.

An expectant hush settled over the night, allowing the slightest sound to be carried through the quiet. In the thirty minutes since he and Charity had settled in, low tortured moans and choked, hoarse cries indicated Simon was alive.

At least for now.

Each time one of those nerve-shredding screams hit the airwaves, it was all Ruin could do not to charge in and wipe the bastards out. The only thing that kept him in check was the brutal lessons he learned about rushing into the unknown. It wouldn't do Simon a damn bit of good if Ruin got gutted before he made it through the door. And he knew exactly which cabin Simon was in because the fucktards holding him were sloppy as shit.

A sharp breeze came down from the peaks and whipped around the poorly covered window of Simon's cabin, ruffling the material, and exposing the interior light for a good five seconds. Just long enough to note at least three Raiders were moving around the interior and sharing a bottle of whatever the hell they managed to scrounge up. Then one of the dumb fucks refastened the tattered window covering.

Outside the cabin, the occasional orange flicker gave away the position of the one playing guard as he sucked on a cigarette. That tiny flicker acted like a bullseye.

Another cry filled the night and then morphed into a pain-filled groan. Ruin's jaw locked down so hard he wouldn't be surprised if his teeth shattered. He slid down the tree, and dropped next to Charity who waited below, her crouched figure merging with the tree trunk's shadows.

The mud from the creek mixed with a few leaves and handfuls of dirt turned her hair into a dull, dark, matted nest. A mixture of dust and dirt blurred the delicate edges of her face and left her looking sickly and drawn. She handed his saddle blanket over without taking her gaze from the buildings in front of them.

He pocketed his field glasses, and then wrapped the blanket around his shoulders, tossing one end over his shoulder so it covered his spine. His hair, now reduced to thick hanks covered in dirt, was tucked under a disreputable baseball cap Charity produced from one of the saddlebags. More dirt and mud, mixed with blood from the rabbits he managed to nab, coated their jeans.

To keep their shadows low to the ground, he crouched next to her. His nose wrinkled at the foul odor drifting from the blanket draped over her chest and shoulders. *Good god whatever the woman did to the poor blanket should be outlawed.*

Her gaze didn't leave the clearing, even as a soft metallic snick barely muffled by her improvised poncho sounded. She shifted her weight and tucked her gun away, most likely using the waist of her jeans to hold it in place since her holster was back with the horses. He hadn't missed the two wicked blades she stashed in custom hilts at her hips. Raiders would expect blades since they were the easiest weapons to get your hands on. Guns were a different matter.

After the Collapse, firearms became scarce, and ammunition was more coveted than food. But in the last few years, something had changed because lately he and the Vultures had their share of run-ins with well-armed idiots. Those clashes left Ruin with a few pretty pieces of his own. But his piece was back with the horses in case the Raiders got leery and decided to pat him down.

Another low groan was followed by a bark of cruel laughter that was quickly muffled and Ruin's patience came to an abrupt end. *Time to move.* "Ready?"

"Ready," was her quiet reply.

He grabbed the trio of dead rabbits, slung them over his shoulder, and straightened. With his first step he altered his posture, adopting hunched shoulders to minimize his height and adding a hitch to his gait, which created an awkward shuffle. The brim of his battered baseball cap was pulled low, hiding his eyes, and obscuring his face. What it didn't cover, his beard did.

Charity fell in behind him, her wrists wrapped in the

leather of one of the reins as it acted like a makeshift leash. She stayed to his right as they broke free of the tree line and moved into the open space. She shuffled along, her head lowered, her hair a ratty curtain hiding her face, and her dirt-stained fingers clutched the end of her leash as if it would keep him from dragging her along.

Ruin set his crazy loose and began to mutter, mimicking the distracted cadence most isolated long-timers adopted. "Dammit, woman, get yo' ass up here." He tugged on the leash, jerking Charity forward. "Ain't dealin' with yo' shite tonight. Got us a decent meal, you best not ruin, or I'll be sure yo' regret it, hear?"

"I hear ya'." The high-pitched whine was radically different from her low, sultry timbre. Then, under her breath she added, "Ain't deaf, ya frickin' moron."

He fought back his brief spurt of amusement at her sass just as the door on the occupied cabin was flung open. Light seared into the night before someone stepped into the frame, throwing a long, dark shadow. Pretending to be oblivious to their observers, Ruin kept up his act, lurching around to loom over Charity, and brought his free hand up in a visible fist.

Playing her role to the hilt, she cowered, curled her arms above her head, and whimpered. "Didn' do nothin'!"

"What the hell you doing here, old man?" The sneering question shot through the night as one of the Raiders stalked towards them, but he stopped just out of reach.

Ruin slowly lowered his arm and began to turn. He kept his head angled so the hat and shadows acted as a mask. "Who da hell are you?"

"I asked first." The juvenile response was accompanied by ink-covered arms crossing over a puffed-out chest that could benefit from a few push-ups. Despite the cool weather, the wanna-be big man wore faded jeans, a pocket-infested vest, and a thin, raggedy t-shirt.

"This here is my home." Ruin squinted, curled his lip, and scratched his ear. "Meybe I should be askin' you what da hell you doin' here, yeah? You tryin' to take my shite?"

Instead of answering, a sneer broke through the pock-marked face revealing a collection of chipped and crooked teeth. Add in the stubble covered skull, the various scars that showcased the vagaries of the Raider lifestyle, and it all added up to a hard casing. Still, it wasn't enough to hide the man wasn't that far into his twenties.

Another unmistakable low cry of pain escaped the open doorway and drifted through the night. Ruin turned towards the cabin. "What's that?" He shuffled a couple feet closer. "What kind of shite are y'all up to?" In full crazy loner style, he shook his head, and waved a hand. "Never you mind, I don' wanna know." He aimed a finger at the Raider. "Get yo' things and yo' gang, and head out. This is my home."

"If that's so, where you been?" The kid invaded Ruin's space, proving he was nowhere near the brains of this operation.

Time to bring the others out to play. "Huntin', ya blind idjigit." Ruin dropped his end of Charity's leash in an unspoken signal and then tore the dead rabbits off his shoulder. He shoved the brace under the Raider's nose, and closed the distance between them to mere inches.

The young Raider slapped at the carcasses. "Get that crap out of my face!"

"Gladly." Ruin pushed the rabbits into the fool's chest as his free hand disappeared under his blanket-slash-poncho, to grip his knife.

The kid's hands clutched at the furred bodies in an instinctive reaction to push them away.

Ruin drew his blade with one hand and used the other to clamp down on the Raider's shoulder and jerked him close.

Blade and skin met, the lethally sharpened metal sinking deep into the Raider's stomach.

The kid's eyes flew wide as a startled half cry, half gasp escaped, but Ruin didn't pause. He twisted his wrist and yanked upwards, the honed edge slicing through delicate stomach tissues before slamming against bone. He shifted the blade's angle and ran it along the rib's edge before ripping it free of the Raider's body.

As the mortally wounded Raider tried unsuccessfully to escape Ruin's grip, the harsh report of Charity's gun sounded. A burly shadow stumbled to a stop and collapsed into an unmoving lump on the ground. Bright flashes from the cabin preceded the deeper coughs of a rifle.

Charity's answers were spaced apart as a rage-filled cry came from Ruin's left. He turned to the incoming threat and used the dying Raider as a shield before sending his blade through the falling night. A grunt of impact indicated a hit, but it barely slowed the latest attacker down.

Under the combined weights of his dying human shield and the attacker, Ruin stumbled back and dropped to one knee. His attacker's bellows of rage continued unabated as the now limp body was torn from Ruin's grip and tossed aside. He braced his hands against the ground, and swept out with his leg, tripping the heavily muscled man. In a well-practiced move, Ruin rolled across the dirt and out of the way. When he came back up, his second blade was hidden along his wrist.

The bigger man fell to his hands and knees, but despite his bulkier frame, he took the fall in a controlled forward roll, coming up to his feet in a low crouch. "Ready to die?"

Ignoring the asinine taunt Ruin darted in. Sometimes being leaner and meaner was all it took to tip the scales in your favor.

They came together in a bone-rattling clash. Ham-sized fists targeted Ruin's ribs and stomach, but since the moron telegraphed his every move, Ruin danced clear of the most damaging hits. Adrenaline kept pain at a distance, leaving behind a ruthless calculation. Ruin countered the barrage of strikes with strategic cuts to vital areas. It wasn't long before those wounds began to weep red. As the seconds stretched into a minute, then two, the steady blood loss interrupted the bigger man's concentration. His swing faltered and went wide, tilting him off balance and offering Ruin the chance to bring this lethal dance to an end.

Not giving the Raider a chance to recover, Ruin snapped out with a kick to the giant's thigh, knowing the impact would deaden his opponent's leg. Ruin's ears ran with the resulting bellow and the heavier man crashed to all fours. Ruin snapped a vicious kick that cracked the Raider's head back. *Where the head goes, the body follows.*

The Raider collapsed on his back, beefy hands going to the crush throat, harsh choking noises emerged as he rolled from side to side.

Another rough scream tore through the night and jerked Ruin's focus from his fallen opponent to the cabin. Cold rage sank its claws deep and he slowly turned his head to glare at the man at his feet. With a callous deliberateness, he adjusted his grip on his knife and slammed one knee into the barrel chest, the bone audibly snapping under the impact. He grabbed a handful of the Raider's greasy, coarse hair, yanked hard enough to tilt the chin back, and ended the fight in a single, brutal swipe, carving a bloody slice from ear to ear.

four

Charity brought her gun up on the shadow rushing in from the right, as the boy Raider died on Ruin's knife. A caress of the trigger followed by the bite of cordite, and the shadow stumbled and fell.

Somewhere in the darkness, a rifle coughed. Fire sliced across the top of her injured shoulder. A flurry of curses rang through her skull and escaped on a muffled hiss. She dove behind the nearest tree stump. Unfortunately, it wasn't very tall, which meant she was hugging the dirt. She shifted around the broad base and scanned the night for the rifleman. She started with the cabin, where flickering light crept from the open door, but no more man-sized shadows broke the illumination. She tore her gaze from the weirdly mesmerizing dance of light and quartered the surrounding trees.

An enraged bellow erupted somewhere to her right, turning her attention back to Ruin. The Vulture was currently engaged in exchanging hits with a shadow that made her think of a bear. When Ruin scored three lightning-fast cuts to the bulky Raider's body, she knew he'd be just fine on his own, so she turned back to her hunt.

She cleared her mind on a silent exhale and let the sounds of the nearby fight fade into the black. Her body and instincts settled into a well-honed stillness, leaving only her gaze to move. Remaining still for hours wasn't a hardship, but she doubted she'd have to wait long tonight. Raiders weren't known for their patience.

Underneath her feet, the ground shook from a nearby impact, but her attention didn't waver from a patch of darker shadows she was certain wasn't natural. Inch by inch, she adjusted her aim. Sure enough, a piece of the darkness rose against the tree line. Moonlight glinted off the rifle's barrel, giving her a target.

When a scream escaped from the cabin, the shadow jerked, and the rifle's barrel started to swing around. She pulled the trigger, then added two more shots in close succession. *Better safe than sorry.*

Her first bullet shoved the shadow back a step. The next two sent it into a jerky dance. The rifle gave one last, desperate bark, its bullet disappearing into the night. Then movement registered on her periphery, and she turned to see Ruin racing towards the cabin. She was on her feet and in pursuit before the shadow dropped to the ground.

Dammit, Ruin was running right into death's eager arms.

The Vultures never forgive her if one of theirs got hurt. Even as her feet pounded in his wake, she scanned their surroundings, in case another Raider decided to pop up and join the party. Since Ruin too focused on his friend to think clearly, it was up to her to keep the vermin off their backs.

Instinct urged her to push harder, closing the distance between them and she was on his heels. The cabin's door was inches away when she grabbed the back of his t-shirt and yanked him off course. Her injured shoulder protested as she pulled him up short with her free hand.

Ruin spun around with a furious growl, slammed out an arm and dislodged her hold.

Undeterred by his ferocious anger, or the painful hit, she stepped in close and shoved the gun clutched in her fist, against his chest, hard, forcing his spine against the cabin's exterior wall between the window and the side of the door. When she had him trapped, she hissed in sotto voce, "Think, Ruin!"

He glared, but she was relieved to see rationale slowly shove aside his cold rage. He ran a hand through his hair, tugging viciously when his fingers tangled in the matted strands. Somewhere behind them his baseball cap and saddle blanket lay discarded.

She rose on tiptoe and flattened her empty palm against his chest for balance as she leaned in until her lips were close to his ear. "Let me clear the cabin."

She held his gaze and waited for his stilted nod before she dropped to her heels, gave a soft sigh of relief, and stepped back. It was time to worry if she was the voice of reason.

She put her back to the cabin and slid down into a crouch. She took a breath, braced the gun in her right hand with her left, elbows bent, finger hovering beside the trigger, and inched towards the opening. She went in low and to the right on a silent exhale, leading with her gun.

A deafening blast erupted from the dim interior, and the doorjamb inches above her head erupted into splinters, proving her decision to be wise. If she'd been standing, she'd be sporting a gory hole about chest height. Adjusting her aim, she returned fire.

A muffled grunt penetrated the ringing of her ears and indicated a lucky hit. So did the gun that skittered across the floor. She rose, her grip rock solid as she began to move into the cabin, her eyes peeled for any movement since she couldn't hear a damn thing.

Gunfire in enclosed spaces sucked.

There wasn't much to the front room. It shared space with the kitchen and was decorated in empty bottles, trash, and haphazard furniture. Over by the gun and slumped in the far corner by the window was a moaning Raider. Since he was busy bleeding out, she wasn't worried about him making a move toward the fallen weapon.

She glided closer and realized there was more to his injuries than her lucky shot. A poorly bandaged gut wound was stained crimson. Probably a souvenir from his run-in with Crane's people. Leaving him to Ruin, she continued down the short hall.

She cleared the noxious bathroom, shoved open a warped door that led into what once was a bedroom but was now missing most of one log wall. She backed out and heard a soft groan. She followed the sound down the hall to the last partially closed door. Dread pooled, but she nudged the door open with the gun's barrel.

"Oh dear god," she breathed in horror, as she tried to make sense of the scene before her.

A stone fireplace dominated one wall, but it was what was highlighted by a couple of lanterns and hung on the opposite side that had her yelling for Ruin. She tucked her gun in her waistband and rushed to the bloody man hanging on the wall.

Coarse rope wound around the man's wrists and ankles. More was wrapped around his neck, and the tail end was looped over a thick beam overhead. A couple of cement bricks on the floor held the longer end in place, its intended usage clear.

A makeshift hangman's noose.

She rushed to the battered body and gently pushed his chin aside, revealing the layered rope burns and cuts on his neck, indicators of repeated hanging. The faint brush of breath against her hand had her yanking her blade free. Since she couldn't reach the rope above his lowered head, she sawed through the tail end of it.

Dear god, how the hell was he still alive?

But that wasn't the worst of it. Thick nails ran in a haphazard line from palm to shoulder and foot to hip, impaling the tortured and nude body. One final hack of her knife and the rope split, the tail dropping to curl on the floor.

Breath coming hard and fast, she wrapped her shaking hand around the slick, blood-coated nail driven deep into his upper thigh. Praying it wasn't near anything vital, she gave it a careful tug, only to realize it was deeply embedded in the wooden wall.

The hard thump of running feet had her turning, an ugly and unfamiliar sense of uselessness tearing through her. "I can't get him down."

Ruin rocked to a halt in the doorway, his hands clutching the frame tight enough to turn his fingers bloodless. A mix of fury and horror paled his olive skin and darkened his eyes. "What the fuck?"

With no answers to offer him, Charity turned back and started searching for something to help get the man down. She took a step and stumbled over a pile of thick nails, and a discarded nail gun, its long barrel grip smeared with blood. She kicked it viciously out of the way and kept searching.

She spotted a stained canvas bag near a ratty mattress in the corner. Dashing to it, she dropped to her knees, her hands frantically pawing through the bag's contents. Knives, in all shapes and sizes, a couple of guns, a frickin' blow torch, hammers, rope, and finally, at the bottom, a pair of heavy duty pliers, the kind that just might cut through nails. The ends were deeply stained, and her stomach clenched at the whisper of evil as she pulled them out of the Raiders' torture bag.

She clutched the heavy-duty pliers, swallowed down her rising gorge, pushed to her feet and hurried back to Ruin. He stood next to the man, his voice low, soothing. The only sign of his carefully contained rage was the unearthly light in his eyes. Unable to hold his disconcerting gaze, she handed him the pliers. "It's the only thing that will work."

Ruin didn't say a thing as he took them. Instead, he moved in closer, cradling the man's face with his free hand and whispered something in his ear. When he lifted his head, his gaze zeroed in on Charity. "Find something to use as bandages before we do this."

This being the brutal task of cutting the nails from the walls because there was no way to pry each one out.

It was a relief to rush out of the room, but the image of what hung there would haunt her nightmares. She didn't want to think about how long it would take to cut through each of those nails, or what the ordeal would mean to the barely breathing man.

Or to the one determined to save him.

five

As Charity left him alone with Simon, Ruin choked back his rage. He was going to gut the asshole out front. Slowly, inch by incremental inch. First, he needed to get Simon down. The ropes buried in Simon's torn skin at wrists and ankles would need to be cut last, otherwise, his body weight would cause his flesh to tear free the nails. It left Ruin with two choices. Cut each nail close to the skin, then pull Simon free, or cut the nails close to the wall, and then dig out every piece of metal. Both options intensified the sickness roiling in his gut, but it wasn't enough to dim his determination.

There were very few individuals Ruin considered his—Vex, Havoc, Reaper, and Simon. No way in hell was he giving up. He eyed the spike driven through the center of Simon's palm and sucked in a bracing breath. He positioned the pliers as close to Simon's palm as possible and clipped the head of the nail. Simon's fingers jerked, and his head lolled to the side, as a low groan cut through the room.

"You hang on, Si," Ruin whispered.

Blood streaked Simon's dark skin, highlighting the cuts

and bruises inflicted by bare knuckles. One eye was swollen shut, and the other fluttered open, awareness flickering through the bloodshot eye. "Ruin?"

At the garbled sound of his name, a turbulent wave of relief threatened to bring Ruin to his knees. His shaken composure was reflected in his gruff voice. "Who else would chase your sorry ass?"

Simon's split and swollen lips twitched. He drew in breath to reply, except words never came, drowned out by a harsh, wheezing cough. The abrasive sounds a clear indicator of internal injuries.

Simon's obvious agony left Ruin gritting his teeth. He found an unmarred spot on Simon's shoulder and gave him a gentle squeeze. Lame ass comfort, but it was all he could offer. "Don't speak, just hold on a bit longer."

Simon's eye fluttered shut as Charity came to Ruin's side, hands filled with an assortment of cloths and a water-filled container. Uncertain how long Simon's unconscious state would last, Ruin shared his plan with her.

She didn't waste time asking questions, instead she tugged the ratty-ass mattress in front of the empty fireplace and laid out their limited first-aid supplies. While she was busy with that, he focused on cutting the nail heads off, and did his best not to think about the next step.

Ruin kept a steady pace, despite Simon's occasional moans. As the last piece of metal dropped to the floor, Ruin tossed aside the heavy pliers and stepped back. The weight of what he had to do next sat on his chest like a two-ton stone. He flexed his stiff fingers, absently noting the slight tremor in his hand. At the barest touch on his arm, his attention snapped to the woman standing steady at his side.

Her face was pale and carried a slight sheen of sweat, but there was a steely resolution burning in the stormy blue depths, darkening them from their earlier electric color. "Ready?"

Denial was lodged in his throat, instead of forcing it free, he managed a jerky nod.

Her jaw firmed at his assent and her spine straightened. "You brace his body, I'll pull him free."

He wanted to argue but her logic worked. Simon was almost as tall as him, which meant there was no way she would be able to keep Simon high enough to not add more pressure on the nails as they pulled him free.

"Okay." Charity positioned to his left.

Ruin stepped in close to Simon and used his body to brace Simon's against the wall at his back. Simon's head rested on Ruin's shoulder, his breath a faint tickle against Ruin's neck. He slid Charity a look. "Ready?"

"Ready." Her answer was soft, but she got close, braced her feet, and braced her feet slid one hand between the wall and Simon's hand, and then used her other hand to brace his wrist. "On two. One. Two." She pulled.

Simon jerked awake with a short scream. Ruin held his friend's head still with one hand, keeping it between his shoulder and neck. "Si, it's alright. Don't fight, let me get you free."

Ruin continued his muttered reassurances as Charity relentlessly continued her grisly work, her jaw getting tighter and harder with each removal. By the time both of Simon's arms were free, Ruin was more than happy to leave him in the minor reprieve of unconsciousness.

Charity wiped her bloody hands on her jeans, then pulled her knife free to work on the rope at Simon's wrists. She turned her head enough to confirm she had Ruin's attention. Silent tear tracks trailed in her grime covered face, but her hand was steady. "Brace." The harsh one-word warning was all he got before she cut through the rope.

He crowded in so Simon's torso slumped against his. He wrapped his arms around his friend's bruised and battered chest. Warmth seeped through his t-shirt and on some distant level Ruin realized it was Simon's blood. He continued to murmur to Simon, even after his voice grew hoarse. It didn't matter if Simon wasn't awake, no way was he letting his friend think he was alone in this.

Charity crouched at his side, her voice rough, "I've got to start at his feet and move up because I'll need your help with the nails in his hips and thighs."

He shifted until he stood between Simon's legs. With Simon in his arms, he couldn't see her, but he could feel the way her muscles bunched before each tug, and how she braced against his leg before she pulled Simon free. He dropped his head against the wooden wall and concentrated on her movements as she switched to his other side and repeated the process.

The minutes stretched out, but she finally rose and met his gaze, her concern evident in the lines around her eyes and mouth. "There are two nails on each side, high up on his thigh. I'm worried they're too close to the major arteries. If we pull him free, we could nick one."

Ruin lifted his head and his stiff muscles protested the change in position. "Can you cut between the wall and Simon?"

She grimaced and shook her head. "I don't think I have enough strength to cut through the metal at that angle."

"Then we trade places."

She studied him and Simon, then her gaze turned to the room, before coming back to him. "Hold him for just another minute. I think there was an old crate in the other room that I can stand on. It should put me high enough to take your place."

Not waiting for his response, she darted out. It wasn't

long before the sharp clatter of heavy objects spilling across the floor sounded. Then she was back, a weathered crate in hand. As awkward as it was, he was able to get her enough room so she could place the crate directly between him and Simon. Then she climbed on.

Despite the gruesome situation, Ruin couldn't ignore the faint scent of wildflowers buried under the sweat and dirt, or the warmth of her body as it inched its way through the tense chill of his. When she stood on the crate it put her almost even with Ruin. They were pressed so close together he could feel each bump of her spine and the shift of muscle as she got ready. She braced her feet, and slid her arms under his, prepared to take Simon's weight.

He kept his arms above hers and waited until he was sure she was steady, then, he asked, "You good?"

"Yeah." Her reply was a bit strained, but firm.

Taking her at her word, Ruin inched his arms away. The wooden crate creaked ominously under the additional weight but held strong. If he moved too fast, or Charity slipped, Simon's weight would cause his body to rip away from the remaining nails, causing catastrophic damage. Something Ruin wanted to avoid since the Raiders managed to do a fucktacular job all on their own.

Once he was certain she was good, he grabbed the pliers, crouched, and adjusted one of the lanterns so there was enough light to work by. "We need to angle him, otherwise this won't work."

Charity inched and shifted, her movements causing both her and the crate to wobble.

Ruin shot up, his pulse racing, and stepped in right behind her, ready to brace them both. "Got him?"

"Yeah." She adjusted her hold, keeping Simon at an angle. "Move fast."

Heeding her warning, he dropped back down, carefully

positioned the pliers, and snipped the two remaining nails. He braced Charity as she shifted before he repeated his actions on Simon's other side. Despite his occasional pained sounds, Simon remained blessedly unconscious.

Once Ruin finished his grisly task, he dropped the pliers and helped Charity move Simon's battered body to the nearby mattress. Together they laid him down next to the water and pile of neatly stacked cloth bandages, the material nothing more than cut pieces of clothing and bedding scoured from the cabin.

"We need a fire," she murmured. "And the first-aid kit." She started to clean the multiple wounds decorating Simon's shuddering body. "There was a wood pile outside to the left of the cabin and a kit in the saddlebag.'

"On it." He stood up and moved to the doorway.

"Ruin?"

He pulled up short at her call and looked back.

"Don't kill him."

The fact she felt the need to warn him off the piece of shit in the front room made him wonder how much of his rage was on his face.

Then she added a ruthless, "Not yet."

He watched the fragile movements of Simon's chest and clenched his fist. "Don't worry, I'll be sure to keep him around."

Charity gave a resigned sigh but said nothing more, clearly understanding where he stood. Which was good because he had no time to waste on pointless reassurances or unnecessary explanations.

He strode out of the room, his focus narrowing in on the muffled whimpers coming from the front room. With each step, the flint of his rage scraped against his need to exact revenge. *There wasn't a chance in hell he'd let the mangy excuse escape by dying so easily.* Not until he got the answers, he wanted on why his brother in all but blood lay dying in the other room.

Ruin entered the front room and the whimpers cut out. He deliberately ignored the pathetic being huddled in the corner. Stalked by what lay in the room behind him, Ruin stayed on task. He was almost to the door before the piece of shit decided to speak.

"How do you like our home improvements, asshole?" The question was wheezy, but audible, as was the phlegmy cough that followed.

Ruin froze as fury broke through his self-imposed lock and burned everything, including logic, to ashes. With deliberate menace, he slowly pivoted. His gaze zeroed in on the sweat-glazed visage of the man on the floor. Cruel pleasure curled through him when the fool's snarling defiance failed to hide the fear crawling underneath his pain. That defiance was stupid. The idiot was weaponless, and his lifespan could be measured in a handful of hours. Ruin withdrew one of his knives and played it through his fingers with deceptively casual ease as he stalked across the room.

The fevered gaze of the wounded Raider darted between Ruin's face and the knife in his hand. *Oh yeah, the dumbass was betting on a quick end.* Too bad Ruin's temper was made of much colder, crueler things.

His boots brushed the mud-covered soles of the Raider's. He dropped into a slow crouch, his knife still twirling in a mesmerizing dance of metal. The Raider tried to back away, a difficult feat when there was a wall at his back. Flickers of fear and panic chased each other across the Raider's face. It was like waving fresh meant before the vengeful beast pacing inside Ruin.

A distant part of him found the image amusing, but none of that was apparent in his voice. "Now, see, when it comes to home improvement projects, most people are all about the end results. They follow the step-by-step directions, believing that's the only way to get the desired results. But I'm not one for rules." His lips curled into a lethal grin. "I'm more apt to try my hand at unusual techniques. The end results are amazingly more exciting that way."

The blade came to a stop, the point resting just under the Raider's chin. He jerked his head back, even though the sudden movement caused an emergence of a new red stain lower down.

Undeterred, Ruin traced the blade's sharp point over the Raider's bobbing Adam's apple, bypassed the seeping gunshot wound up near the collarbone, and continued down his chest, leaving a thin red line in its wake. He stopped with the knife's point poised just above the crimson-stained hand trying to keep the Raider's innards in place.

He held the Raider's wide, horrified gaze. "Home improvement is a tiring endeavor, and I'm sure you want to call it a day, but I have a better idea." Ruin drove the point of his knife into the back of the Raider's hand, twisted, and then pulled it free, all in the space of a blink.

The Raider's pained cry was choked off when Ruin slammed his other hand over his mouth. The Raider's eyes bugged out as he tried to breathe around the tightly clamped hand.

Ruin leaned in and growled, "You sit here and decide if you prefer a tried-and-true approach before we chat, or we can try out a few of my more 'unusual' techniques." He yanked his hand back and wiped it on his thigh.

"Play with your chew toy later.'" The feminine admonishment came from behind him.

Ruin straightened, turned, and watched Charity moved into the pathetic excuse for a kitchen, her bloodstained hands holding the plastic basin of water. "Chew toy?"

She continued to the sink, tipped the container, and

emptied the stained water. "Did I stutter?" She pulled up the handle on the faucet causing the pipes to groan before spitting out water. A minor miracle that meant the cabin must have access to a well. She quickly rinsed and refilled the basin. "I need that kit. More to the point," she tilted her head in the direction where Simon lay, suffering, "he needs that kit."

Bossy little thing. But she was right. "I'm going."

Basin in hand, she turned from the sink and started to head back. She stopped at the beginning of the hall, and her gaze dropped to the Raider. An implacable hardness shirted her delicate features into a cold mask. She turned back to Ruin. "When you come back, make sure he talks. We need answers." Without waiting for a response, she continued down the hall.

We? Now wasn't that an interesting twist? Just what kind of answers was she expecting to hear?

His attention went back to the now silent Raider, and he wasn't the least bit surprised to find him staring back, all signs of his earlier defiance gone.

"You heard the lady." Ruin pivoted on his heel and went to get the first-aid kit and firewood. "Better make your decision fast, or I'll make it for you."

six

Ruin stormed out of the cabin and headed to the horses. He ignored the bodies, only stopping to collect his discarded cap and blanket, and then he led the horses back to the relative safety of the cabin.

While he took care of that, he mentally churned through the entire clusterfuck. Things didn't add up.

Crane created and held one of the most pivotal territories this side of the Mississippi. He established a ruthless reputation with Raiders decades before and ruled with an unforgiving fist. What would drive the Raiders to attack now? They tended to hit targets that guaranteed a sweet haul. Targeting Pebble Creek was like playing Russian roulette, with the lone bullet being a successful hit. The only thing that could encourage the Raiders to take on Crane would be the promise of a huge payoff. And the only power players with enough resources to afford that kind of payoff would be Michael and Lilith.

Between the collapsing infrastructure and the rising oceans that devoured the western coastlines and widened the inland rivers, the majority of what used to be the western states belonged to three people: Michael, Lilith, and Crane. Michael's reach extended from Washington through Oregon, and into most of California, while encompassing the Tahoe Forest. Lilith played queen over Colorado and what remained unclaimed of New Mexico and Texas, including both Albuquerque and the now coastal town of Houston.

That left Crane with Idaho, Utah, and northern Arizona. Unfortunately, after the Collapse, the Mexican Cartels had claimed Los Angeles, Phoenix, El Paso, and San Antonio, which forced the country's borders to shift. Then the dams failed, and the Free People reclaimed all Southwest water rights, and Nevada was abandoned, leaving the barren stretch of desert wide open for the Raiders to set up shop. The current territorial arrangement meant any kind of travel was treacherous and played havoc with the vital supply lines. A situation Crane took unfettered advantage of since he was the most secure bridge between Michael and Lilith's holdings.

Ruin tethered the two horses to a post set to the side of the cabin, and dug through the saddlebags on the paint, unearthing a thick first-aid kit in tough canvas. His movements automatic as his mind spun through scenarios.

Neither Michael nor Lilith would be stupid enough to upset the shaky peace by taking out Crane. *Right?*

They would if they could gain a huge advantage, a cynical voice piped up. Especially if they were desperate.

But there hadn't been any mutterings along those lines, not lately.

Normally when shit was about to hit the fan, he and the other Vultures tended to hear about it during their travels between territories. He made a mental note to double check with Reaper on the latest rumblings as he walked back into the cabin and rejoined Charity.

He found her bent over Simon, gently washing his bruised ribs. She didn't look up when Ruin crouched next to her. He reached around her and held out the kit so she could see it, not missing the sheen of sweat beading Simon's now ashy brow.

"About damn time," she muttered, snatching his offering before crossing her legs tailor-style.

"His ribs are cracked, not broken." She unzipped the case, and rummaged through it, pulling free a small paper packet.

"How can you be sure?"

She finally looked up as she tore the packet open with her teeth and dumped two pills onto her palm. "I'm not a hundred percent sure, but he's not bubbling up blood, which I'm hoping means he doesn't have any internal punctures."

And if he did, with no equipment and limited supplies there wasn't a damn thing they could do about it here. It also meant getting him back down to Pebble Creek would be tricky as hell, if not impossible.

"Fire." She reminded him.

He tipped an imaginary hat and dropped his relatively clean saddle blanket at the foot of the mattress. Then he turned, headed back out. He brought the wood back and went about setting a fire in the fireplace. He used a well-worn silver lighter, one of the few things he managed to hold on to from his father and set it to the tinder. *Here's hoping the chimney wasn't falling in on itself or they'd be smoked out.*

With his arms dangling on his bent knees, he watched the flames devour the wood. Their mesmerizing dance drew him away from the fury coiled inside him. Thankfully, the growing tendrils of smoke wafted upwards, showing no signs of returning. A soft touch on his shoulder brought him back to the here and now.

Charity held out a slender needle in silent question.

He took it and held it in the nearest flame, the heat sterilizing what it could. He handed it back, then straightened, his gaze going straight to Simon, holding tight to the slow, barely-there rise and fall of his chest. Despite knowing Simon's chances of making it through the next few hours were slight, it was enough to keep the ember of hope Ruin hoarded alive.

He could stay while Charity sewed Simon up, but it wouldn't get Ruin the answers he needed. Still, he had to ask. "Do you need me?"

She shook her head, the lantern's dancing light deepening the lines on her face. "No, I've got this." Her brow furrowed. "This will take some time." She slid a sideways glance his way. "You'll have plenty of quality alone time with your chew toy."

He folded his arms across his chest and cocked an eyebrow. "Won't need much."

A soft derisive snort sounded, before she resumed her spot next to Simon. She sorted the makeshift bandages, lines of thread, and a rare tube of antibiotic cream, arranging each with meticulous precision.

Taking in the items laid out, Ruin felt a rare burst of gratefulness that Boden packed a hell of a first-aid kit, especially since Simon's continued existence depended on what the woman could accomplish with it.

She didn't look at him as she warned, "If you don't get to it, there'll be nothing left to work with."

Since he had no intention of losing that advantage, he turned to leave. At the door, he stopped, gripped the doorjamb, and turned his head to the side. "Keep him alive."

With his back to the room, he couldn't see her face, but he heard her soft response. "No promises, but I'll do my best."

He ignored the lump in his throat, nodded, and left his brother in the hands of an unknown woman so he could rip the truth from the dying piece of shit in the front room.

seven

As Ruin's overwhelming presence moved down the hall, Charity let out a long, quiet breath. To still the fine tremors in her hands, she curled her fingers into tight fists. Her ragged nails bit into her palms as she took a moment to calm down. Her shoulder ached like a bitch but taking a painkiller was out of the question. The man on the floor needed them much more than she did.

She relaxed her hands, pleased to see them hold steady. Turning back to her patient, she studied his numerous wounds and pity welled. That he was still breathing said a great deal about Ruin's friend and his will to live.

That wasn't her only surprise here. Based on Ruin's warning as he left, it was obvious Simon meant a great deal to him. And that was intriguing. The stories surrounding Fate's Vultures portrayed them as a tight group, fiercely loyal to one another and beholden to no one. Which made their connection to Crane curious.

What had Crane offered that kept them at his side, even after his death?

Perhaps the answer lay with the man in front of her. A possibility she wouldn't get a chance to explore if she failed to save him.

She threaded the needle and went to work. Since there was no way Simon would stay under during the whole ordeal, she talked to him. Maybe if he knew the hands causing him pain were trying to help, he wouldn't come up swinging. Plus, it gave her something else to focus on instead of the fact she was setting tiny stitches into human flesh with the barest of medical supplies.

"You're a lucky man, Simon. Loyalty like Ruin's is hard to find. Not to say it doesn't happen, but I can count those who have mine on one hand. You know one of them. Boden."

Simon's breathing hitched and she paused when he winced.

She tied off the current stitch, grabbed the wet cloth on the side of the basin, and wiped his face. "Sorry. I know it hurts, but we can't leave you leaking. Just hang in there for me, yeah?"

She set the cloth aside and picked up the needle. "Okay, here we go again." She bent over Simon's arm and started stitching again. "How about I tell you how I met Boden?"

There was no response, not that she expected one.

"Maybe it'll give you some blackmail material for when you're back in Pebble Creek." Besides, it was one of the few things she could share without revealing anything important. "I was living in New Seattle. Correction, surviving in New Seattle."

It was an apt word choice, as the city was guaranteed to chew you up and spit you out if you didn't have the right connections. A truth she learned damn fast when her parents made a serious mistake and ran a grift on the wrong person.

Memories crowded close, but with the ease of long practice, she shuffled them back to the dusty confines where they belonged. "Anyway, I was heading back home—" home being a tucked away space in a crumbling building one good shake of the earth away from collapse, "—minding my own business, when this giant stumbles out of an alleyway. The fool was bouncing off the walls like a drunk rubber ball. Since it was the end of a craptastic week, I figured the appearance of an easy mark was the universe's way of ending on a high note. So, I made sure we ran into each other."

She finished the stitch and moved on to the next wound. "Unfortunately for me, he wasn't drunk, but he was quick. He managed to tag my wrist as I snagged my haul. Then something darted from the shadows and jumped between us. Next thing I know, I've got an armful of squalling fur while doing my damnedest not to lose my handful of city credits, and the giant is standing there glaring at me. Then he rumbles—," she dropped her voice to mimic Boden's deep tones and tied off another thread, "—'Hand 'em over, missy.'"

She felt her lip curl in a rueful smile as she started on the next cut. "Missy. What a way to piss off a teenage female. I refused, of course. Not very politely. No way was I handing over the credits or a defenseless cat when it was obviously running from him."

Discounting an animal's reaction to a human was a sure-fire way of getting your ass in trouble. When it came to humans and their intentions animals were near infallible indicators of intent. She went back to her story. "That's when the poor, abused cat decided to decorate my arms with her claws." She still carried the thin white scars from that little hellcat all these years later. "Boden went to help, me or the cat, I'm still not sure, but all I saw was a big man making a move. Instincts kicked in. The cat was on her own, and I managed to nail Boden in the balls."

Her brief amusement faded as she continued her work.

"Life on the streets teaches you to expect the worst and never hesitate." She noted the old scars decorating Simon's skin and added softly, "Something I'm thinking isn't news to you."

She fell silent as she maneuvered around a particularly deep tear. Simon's soft groan broke the quiet and his eyes moved under his lids, but he stayed under. Barely. "Shh, I know. I'll be as gentle as I can," she soothed. A tense minute or two passed before she dared to move on to the next wound.

She picked up the threads of her story. "It was raining—" because it was always raining in New Seattle, "—and despite my well-aimed kick, Boden managed to trap my leg even as he tried not to puke. That's when this crazy-assed woman decided to join our little party. She came out of the alley, practically nude, yelling at Boden about letting her precious Maddy-girl out in the horrible weather."

It had been one of the most surreal situations she'd ever experienced. Boden's grip on her ankle had been firm, but not cruel. He hadn't twisted it to take her to the ground in retaliation for picking his pocket or kicking him, and it had left her off balance, literally and figuratively.

"When Boden let me go, I was so caught up in the drama that I stayed to watch this itty-bitty thing, she couldn't have been more than five feet tall, in a wet, transparent robe, verbally rip a giant of a man to pieces."

Actually, she had been stunned that the big man stood there and took the verbal abuse, never once raising his voice or his fist in retaliation. Through the lens of hindsight, she wondered if Boden had been the first person to find her after her parents' death, who would she be now? Not that it mattered anymore.

Simon shifted restlessly and she stilled until he re-settled. "You should've seen it. You would've laughed your ass off." She went back to her painstaking work. "Her rant was cut short when the little fur menace decided to step up and get busy wrapping around its mistress's ankles. Boden's woman of the moment went from bitch to angel in seconds. She grabbed her pet, gave Boden one more accusing glare, and left." Years later Charity still shook her head over how things played out. "Me being me, I told Boden his skills with the ladies and their pussy cats was liable to get him killed."

That night, teenage bravado, and the need to disappear was all she had, and she used it. Except Boden was far from a fool, and under the violence-hardened exterior existed a cautious vein of compassion. "Instead of being pissed, he laughed. Standing in a stinking alley, rain pouring down, his chances of getting laid walking away, he laughed."

Her voice softened as she tied off another suture. "Old man takes pride in flaunting expectations, makes him hard to predict, even back then. Instead of demanding his credits back and kicking my ass, he fed me. He even offered to train me in hand-to-hand, saying if I showed potential, there might be a job for me. But I had other promises to keep first."

The past rose up and pulled her back. She fell quiet as her hands continued their work. At that time, consumed by grief and anger, her single-minded focus on revenge set her feet on her current path.

Luckily, Boden had never been one to give up easily. His offer—come train with him—hadn't come with an expiration date. Two weeks after that pivotal scene, when she finished her devil's bargain, she tracked him down and for the next three-and-a-half years she took him up on his offer. She trained, honing her innate skills, and strengthening the ties of their unusual friendship. In her deepest heart, she acknowledged that Boden stepped into the empty space left behind from her parents' violent death. Not that she ever told him that.

A harsh, guttural scream erupted from the direction of the front room. Her hand froze and her head came up. Another pain-filled cry followed, only to be cut short. She turned back to her task and concentrated on tying off the thread. "Sounds like someone's having fun," she muttered.

She reached for her knife to cut the thread and was unprepared for the fist that nailed her. In a well-practiced move, she dropped and rolled out of targeting range, but she forgot her injured shoulder. At least until she hit the floor. A sharp crease of fire made her hiss as she came up to find Simon awake, but not so aware.

Despite his battered body, he was half-turned on his side, his non-swollen eye locked onto her, bright with maddened pain. Unintelligible noises came from his abused throat as he tried to get to her. His jerky movements knocked the water basin over and scattered the supplies.

"Dammit." She scrambled to her knees, caught his flailing arms, and used her body weight to force his back to the floor. "Simon! Stop! Ruin's here!"

She gritted her teeth and put everything she had into holding him in place without causing further damage. She was breathing hard as she pinned his wrists to the floor, her chest pressed against his, and her face inches away.

Under her, Simon bucked, his head snapping up.

She jerked her head back to avoid a broken nose. "Calm, Simon!"

Warm wetness met her palms as they shackled his wrists, and her heart began to race. He couldn't afford to lose more blood. If he reopened her stitches, they were screwed. "If you don't calm down, I'll call Ruin in to knock your ass out. Do you hear me? Do you want Ruin to hit you?"

Whether it was the repeated use of Ruin's name, or Simon's sudden burst of strength giving out, his movements slowed, then stilled. Unwilling to take a chance on another black eye, she stayed where she was half-draped over his chest, all but eye to eye with him. She was so close she saw the moment awareness began to replace Simon's mindless fury.

A moan drifted from the other room, and Simon's gaze went to the door, then came back to her.

It wasn't hard to decipher his silent question. "Ruin's questioning the last breathing Raider, while I try to patch your sorry hide before you bleed out. Now, will you behave?"

She waited. Finally, he gave a tiny nod. She slowly uncurled her fingers and pushed off of him. "You need to lie still so I can see what damage you did."

A quick scan showed her stitches held. She ran a hand through her hair, forgetting about the blood on her hands until it was too late. Muttering another curse under breath, she re-gathered the supplies.

"You managed to dump out all the water." She grabbed a couple of cloth strips that managed not to get caught in the spill, and quickly bound his wrists to stop the bleeding. "Now sit tight while I go refill this, and we'll get back to sewing you up."

She set her hand on the mattress and went to push to her feet. Simon grabbed her wrist and brought her to a stop. She gave him her attention and waited.

Finally, he managed one croaked word. "Ruin?"

She gave him what she hoped was a reassuring smile, and then gently patted his hand. "He's pissed, but otherwise fine. He'll be back in a few minutes."

As if to emphasize her answer, a teeth-gritting whimper drifted down the hall. Simon's eye went to the door, then came back.

Carefully disengaging from his hold, she rescued what supplies she could. "Don't worry. Ruin's got it under control." Hopefully, better than she did.

Once things were safely set up again, she gathered the now empty bin and stood, trying not to wince as her head and shoulder protested the move. Between Simon's right hook and her fall, she was going to be feeling it for a while. She looked down and met Simon's gaze. "Do me a favor and don't try anything until I get back. I'm not sure we have enough supplies to re-do our Frankenstein work if you break open my stitches, understood?"

After receiving his nod, she left to refill the basin.

God, she really picked the worst day to visit Crane.

eight

R uin wiped away one last rivulet of cold creek water from his neck with his stained t-shirt. He pulled on a clean shirt and walked back to the cabin. He stopped at the dozing horses, balled up the trashed shirt, and tucked it deep in the bottom of the bag strapped to the back of his quarter horse. He took one last survey of the quiet darkness, then headed in, stopping just outside the open door.

The sickly sour stench of sweat-laced fear and stale copper hit his nose. Evidently leaving the door open as he cleaned hadn't been enough to air out the interior. His back and shoulders ached from hauling the Raiders' dead bodies into one of the abandoned basement rooms in what used to be the main building.

As difficult as it was to drag their dead weight through the collapsed passageways, it was easier than trying to dig a hole in the forest. Safer too. Didn't take much to send disease on a rampage anymore. The world being what it was, utilizing unusual dumping sites created by the Collapse was a necessary skill he often practiced.

Blowing out a tired breath, he moved inside, and headed straight to the kitchen.

He scoured the surviving cabinets and found an empty gallon tin can. He took it to the sink. A couple minutes later, all that was left of what Charity termed his chew toy, was a wet spot on the wood. With the Raider's gun tucked into the small of his back, the spent shell casings and remaining bullets stashed in his pocket, he finally went to check on Simon.

As he made his way down the hall, the silence crawled under his skin and raked merciless claws over his nerves. He kept his steps soft and stopped in the doorway, taking in the scene in front of the fireplace. Charity's dirty blonde head lay on the mattress, one hand rested on Simon's chest just above what Ruin recognized as his saddle blanket.

Her hand and his friend's chest rose and fell in a steady pattern. The mismatched cloth bandages decorated Simon's dark skin here and there, a few bore a brownish stain but not enough to cause Ruin concern. The tension that locked his muscles tight loosened, making room for exhaustion to take its place. "He's still breathing."

Without moving from her positions, Charity nodded. "Yep." Her response was muffled.

Judging the space between the fireplace and the mattress, he went over and started to drop into a crouch. The shift of metal against the base of his spine had him straightening back up. He removed the Raider's gun and set it on the roughly hewn mantle before resuming his position at Simon's side.

This close he could tell that not all the wounds were bandaged. Neat stitches sat under the gleam of antibiotic cream, the tiny sutures surprising him. "You have a careful hand at this."

"Practice makes perfect." Even with her head buried in an arm, he was able to make out her words.

"Must have been a hell of a lot of practice, sugar."

The hand on Simon's chest twitched, rose, and gave him the finger. Despite the grim situation, her unexpected reaction surprised a rusty chuckle from him. The sound made her shift, and she finally looked up.

A purpling bruise decorated her cheekbone and puffed the edges of her eye. His brief spurt of humor disappeared. He came around the mattress, caught her chin, and tilted her head until her face was in the light. "What the hell?"

She grimaced. "Your friend has a hell of a right."

"Should've ducked."

"Tried." She tugged free of his hold and turned so she could rest her back against the mattress. She drew her legs up and rested her arms on her knees. "Get anything interesting out of the roadkill out front?"

Mimicking her position, he sat next to her, their shoulders brushing as they faced the bloodstained wall, Simon, and the fire behind him. "Yes and no."

Her head tilted until she could see him. "Going to share?"

Now that things were relatively calm, he took a moment to really study her. Besides the obvious signs of exhaustion, there were traces of dust near her hairline, clearly missed in her earlier attempt at cleaning her face. They didn't take away from the thick lashes that veiled crystal blue eyes or the faint dusting of freckles that spanned her cheeks and nose.

Firelight played over her delicate jaw line, emphasizing the hollows, and adding a touch of mystery to an already intriguing profile. Her damn lush lips could lead a man into serious trouble. Little white lines of pain bracketed her sinful mouth. Probably from the shiner Simon inflicted, but there might be another reason.

She shifted under his regard, wincing slightly. A rust stain marred the right shoulder of her grimy shirt.

Yep, definitely more to it.

This close he couldn't miss her scent, a curiously

appealing mix of dust, dirt, blood, sweat, and wildflowers. "Share after you get cleaned up."

Her nose wrinkled in a strangely adorable manner, but he didn't miss her worried glance at Simon.

The telling action snuck under his guard and left his voice gruff. "I'll watch over him."

"Thanks." She pushed to her feet with a soft groan. Once upright, she pressed her fists to the small of her back and twisted her spine, eliciting a series of soft pops.

The action made it impossible for him to miss how her tits pressed against her shirt. For a small woman, she was blessed with serious curves. A very cynical voice that sounded just like his twin sister, Vex, wondered if the move was deliberate. When Charity dropped her arms and turned away without even looking at him, he decided probably not.

"I'll be back in fifteen," she warned, before she disappeared through the door.

He waited until the sounds of her moving faded into quiet and left him alone with Simon's breathing, and the fire's occasional snap. He eased down until he could stretch his legs out along the floor, crossed his boots at the ankles, and then his head rested on the mattress by Simon's side. "She's pure trouble, buddy."

Admitting it out loud didn't diminish his fascination with her, though. Something about her pulled at him. Maybe it was the combination of ruthless practicality evidenced in her behavior towards the Raiders, and the bits of compassion he caught when she worked on Simon.

Or maybe he just needed to get laid.

Whatever it was, Charity had the potential to be a problem because he wasn't an idiot, and her appearance in Pebble Creek as shit hit the fan posed all sorts of troublesome questions. Questions he had every intention of getting answers to.

"Ruin?"

The familiar voice, weak though it was, brought him up and around in record time. He hovered over Simon as his friend's eyes fluttered. Only one opened since the other was swollen shut. "Hey, Si."

Viable relief replaced the foggy comprehension. "Knew you'd come."

"I wouldn't leave your ass hanging. Besides, Vex would gut me if you got yourself killed."

That earned a twitch of lips. "Vex here?"

"She'll be here soon." He was willing to bet his father's lighter that his twin would arrive by morning. The bond they shared wouldn't let either of them leave the other in trouble. Reaper probably cursed the moment Ruin and Havoc's dust trails left home base, because Vex would ride Reaper's ass to make tracks behind them. It was simply a matter of time before his sister tracked Ruin to the cabin or showed up in Pebble Creek. Add in Simon's involvement and no way would his twin stay away. "How are you feeling?"

Sweat beaded Simon's brow and his tongue flicked over his dry lips. "Hurt like a bitch." He lifted his arm, his hand going to his neck.

Ruin stopped it before Simon could touch the brutally raw marks. "I bet."

He guided Simon's arm back to the mattress, then found a small cup with clean water. He supported Simon's head and put the cup to his lips. "Sips," he warned as Simon started to drink. When he was done, Ruin helped him resettle.

Simon closed his eye and breathed through his obvious discomfort his recent movements created. Eventually, he reopened his eye. "Crane?"

Ruin grimaced and shook his head. "Dead."

"Dammit." The word was soft. "Raiders?"

He went to say yes, only to realize he hadn't verified the

details with Charity. "I'm pretty sure, but we can double check with Charity when she gets back."

A frown creased Simon's forehead. "Charity?"

"That would be the blonde you decked as she was sewing your sorry ass up."

"Ah, shit." Remorse darkened his eye. "Guess I owe her an apology."

Ruin sat on the floor and faced Simon. "I think she understands."

Despite his pain-filled gaze, curiosity sharpened Simon's attention. "Who is she?"

Knowing his friend could be a little too perceptive at time, Ruin didn't dare look away. "Don't know, but I'll be finding out." Simon made a noncommittal noise that Ruin ignored. "So, you've never met her before?"

Simon carefully shook his head, paled, and then winced. "Nope. Why?" His question was squeezed out around gritted teeth.

"Found her at Pebble Creek, seems she knows Boden and Crane." Ruin found a scrap of unused cloth and wiped the sweat off Simon's brow.

Simon hissed, his eye squeezing shut as his jaw tightened. He visibly rode out a wave of pain that left his voice was breathy. "Met him in New Seattle."

Ruin waited patiently and stopped Simon's hand as it lifted again.

"She ... she talked when she was ... stitching me up." Pants broke up Simon's words. A few shallow breaths later, his eye reopened. "Something about a cat ... and an alley ... and a woman." His frowned deepened the existing lines on his face. "It's not real clear," he muttered. "But I remember... wondering what the hell Boden was doing ... in New Seattle."

"Take it slow, man." Ruin tucked the nugget of information away for examination later. He dipped the cloth into the nearby pail of water, squeezed it, and then laid it against Simon's brow. "Explains Boden, but what's her connection to Crane?"

"Not sure. Crane's been edgy last few days." Simon shifted restlessly, before stilling, his breathing heavier. "Kind of twitchy."

That didn't sound like Crane's normal rock steady behavior by any stretch of the imagination. Ruin's mind spun as Simon's breathing evened out and his jaw unlocked. The Vultures had joined up with Crane about a year ago. Then just over six months ago, a series of blitz attacks began hammering Crane's supply lines. There was no rhyme or reason to when or where they'd hit or what would be taken, but the frequency was ramping up at an alarming rate.

Losing shipments equaled losing customers, and Crane was pissed as hell. Then, a few weeks back, at Crane's order and under the pretense of handling disputes in the territory, Fate's Vultures hit the road determined to dig up who was screwing with Crane's supply lines. So far, they had come up with nothing but shit. "Any ideas why?"

Frustration and a grim anger settled Simon's face into a hard mask. "Yeah."

When that's all he said, Ruin prompted, "Care to elaborate?"

Simon shifted again, and a wheezing noise edged his breathing. "I need to sit up."

"You need to keep your ass still." Reigning in his concern, Ruin drawled, "You break open those stitches, and I'm betting Charity will deck you."

Simon's restless movements stilled and despite his battered face, there was no missing his quirked eyebrow. "Scared of her, Ruin?"

"If you weren't already laid up, I'd knock you one for that." Ruin pushed to his feet. "Hang tight while I find something so you can sit up." He left Simon alone for the minute or so it took to retrieve one of the saddles. He came back, positioned the saddle, covered it with one of the stinky blankets, and helped Simon to sit up, careful of the numerous stitches. When they were done, Simon's mahogany skin carried pale undertones, but his breathing came easier.

Simon took a minute to gather his strength before continuing their conversation. "Ever since the attacks, Crane had us riding the lines. A couple weeks back, we intersected an illegal transport." A grim shadow darkened his eyes. "Kids."

Ruin's gut clenched. "How many?"

Simon hitched a shoulder with an unconscious shrug, only to stop short with a muffled groan. When he spoke, his voice was harsh and tight. "Five. A boy and four girls, all under fourteen. Never seen Crane so furious."

Considering the rage simmering under Simon's pain, Ruin figured Crane hadn't been the only one. Not that he could blame either man on that. "Who was running them?"

"Was trying to figure that out when we got hit." Simon's mouth got tight, the lines around it going white, and he brought a bandaged hand to his ribs.

Ruin didn't miss the telling movement and kept a sharp eye on him. "Coincidence?"

"Not fucking likely," Simon muttered.

Yeah, Ruin didn't believe it either. "You think the hit on Pebble Creek is tied to the flesh peddler."

Even though it wasn't posed as a question, Simon dipped his head.

Feeling the weight of that acknowledgement, Ruin rubbed a hand over his face. "Shit."

He dropped his hand and fisted it as his side. He looked away, his mind shifting through the possibilities as he added Simon's story to the facts he pried from the Raider. He was about to share those facts with his friend when a sharp question came from the doorway.

"What now?" Charity stood there, obviously catching his last curse. She'd taken time to dress in a clean t-shirt, and her hair was a wet tangle about her shoulders. There was a slight bulge of a bandage on her right shoulder. She moved through the room to Simon's other side.

When she crossed in front of the fire and knelt to check Simon's wounds, the firelight took her t-shirt from thin to near transparent. The resulting surge of unwelcome lust reminded Ruin it was time to drag his brain out of his pants and cut through the bullshit. "Why were you in Pebble Creek?"

She lifted her head and narrowed her eyes. "Business."

Alarms bells clamored, drowning out the rising ache in his dick. "What kind of business?"

Her hands dropped from Simon as she held Ruin's gaze and lifted her chin. "The kind that involved Crane."

Her defiant and cagey attitude didn't do a thing to ease the warning itch under his skin. "Yet Crane's dead."

"And?"

"Who you planning on discussing your 'business' with now?"

Her gaze darted to Simon before she caught herself and needlessly straighten a bandage.

Not missing that tell, Simon's jaw tensed as he met Ruin's gaze, but he remained silent.

"I see," Ruin murmured, as he untangled her logic. With Crane dead, his territory and responsibilities would shift, either to Simon or Boden, or possibly both. And it appeared she was going to take advantage of her captive audience. No way in hell would he leave Simon alone with her now. "Since we're not going anywhere anytime soon, start talking."

Instead of the expected bristling reaction, the infuriating

woman smiled at him. But it wasn't nice. In fact, if he was honest, as he held her diamond hard, bright blue gaze, his balls whimpered. Her smile went from cruel to taunting. "Arrogant bastard, aren't you?"

Why tangling with her revved his engine, he couldn't say, but it wasn't going to stop him from pushing. "You wouldn't have me any other way." As tempted as he was to continue the lethal flirtation, his need for answers was a hell of a lot more important. "What did you need with Crane?"

As the seconds ticked by in silence, she studied him. Eventually, she reached some inner conclusion. "I share, you share. Deal?"

He considered what the Raider told him and weighed it against his unanswered questions. If did this with her, she might inadvertently fill in some holes and once he had those, it would be his turn to decide what got shared. "Deal."

She settled on the floor and brought one knee up to brace her arm. "I was looking for someone, and the trail led me north. I decided to swing up and see if Crane had heard anything."

She wasn't going to make this easy, was she? He stifled a sigh. "Who were you looking for?"

"A girl." She grimaced. "A child really. Her name is Tabitha. Her family asked for my help."

"Why you?"

"They know me and my reputation." There was no arrogance in her voice, she was simply stating a fact.

"Since I don't know either, enlighten me."

She tilted her head, her attention dancing between him and Simon, then back as she considered his request. Finally, she spoke, reluctance obvious in her stilted answered. "I'm rather good at finding lost things. Under normal circumstances, it's a simple transaction. If you offer me something of value, I will track down your lost item and bring it home."

Ruin's pulse spiked as a crucial piece fell into place. "You're a Bloodhound."

Bloodhounds, or 'Hounds as they were commonly called, were a select group of trackers who specialized in ferreting out information, individuals, and objects. Unlike the typical tracker employed by the Joe Shmoes, 'Hounds sniffed out significant pieces that could alter alliances and shift power. The cost of their services wasn't for the faint of heart, and neither was the job. Collecting and possessing that type of powerful information made you an unmistakable target. It was a dangerous profession, and most Bloodhounds maintained low profiles, which explained Charity's reluctance to divulge her personal agenda.

But something didn't add up. "What do you consider valuable enough to track down a missing kid?"

Ire sparked in her eyes and her lip curled, but she didn't take his bait. "In this case, I'm not collecting a fee. Her parents are frantic. Tabitha's a sweet kid and whoever took her needs to pay."

Despite the ring of truth in her words, he wasn't buying it. Talents like her's weren't normally wasted on missing kids. Not unless those kids belonged to someone important, or the payment was too good to pass up. Hell, 'Hounds tended to be leashed to seriously powerful individuals. *So who held Charity's leash?* "Tabitha must be a special kid to get that kind of commitment from a 'Hound."

A pitiless mask fell and wiped away every trace of emotion. The sudden change was all the more disturbing by her equally empty voice. "Tabitha isn't the first child to go missing. In the last two months, a total of nine have disappeared."

Ruin shared a silent look with Simon, who took the hint, and entered the conversation. "Did they all disappear from the same place?"

Her body shifted with a subtle tension. "Tabitha and one

other girl were taken from Boulder, the others were taken from elsewhere." She paused, and Ruin opened his mouth to interrupt, when she continued, "It's not just Colorado and Idaho who's missing kids. There were reports in Northern Colorado, eastern Utah, and southern Wyoming."

"Anything out of Arizona?" Ruin asked.

She gave an awkward shrug. "Not that I heard, but I didn't hit the Free People's territory on my way to Pebble Creek."

Simon's sweat-beaded brow furrowed at the news. "What age range?"

"The youngest was nine, the oldest thirteen." Charity's attention sharpened, like a dog coming on point. "Why?"

On top of the blanket, Simon's hand twitched. Ruin caught his wrist, stopping his friend from forming a fist and tearing the stitches in his palm. Simon blew out a harsh breath and relaxed under Ruin's grip before answering. "A couple weeks ago, we interrupted a small group of Raiders transporting on one of our routes." He shifted, bit back a groan, and struggled to catch his breath. "We confronted them, and when the dust settled, we had four dead Raiders and five traumatized kids."

Charity's gaze narrowed and the hand on her knee curled into a fist. When she spoke, her question carried the whip of anger. "Traumatized?"

Pity softened Simon's face. "They were in bad shape. Dehydration, malnutrition, signs of beatings, and worse." He shifted uncomfortably, his voice was grim as he shared, "One is catatonic."

Unbridled fury uncoiled in Ruin's gut and spread through muscle and tissue to emerge in a hissed, "Mother-fuckers."

On the other side of Simon, Charity shot to her feet, volatile emotions swirling around her like an invisible storm. As she paced, her hands tore through her still damp hair and curses flowed non-stop under her breath. When she finally stilled in front of the fire, she kept her back to them. "So the hit on Pebble Creek was retaliation for a lost flesh shipment?"

Ruin answered before Simon could. "Probably."

Her body swayed under the unseen blow, but she didn't turn around. "Not that I don't believe you, but Raiders don't stray far from Vegas unless there's a damn good reason."

Ah, but these were Raiders they were talking about. "If they're offered enough, they would," Ruin corrected.

"And it would have to be a hell of a lot for them to risk crossing Crane," Simon added.

At that Charity turned and propped her hands on her hips, a frown marring her brow. "Who the hell has enough influence to convince those roaches to run a suicide mission?"

Ruin took her question as his cue to uphold his half of the info sharing pact. "Reznik."

nine

eznik? The blast from the past locked every muscle in Charity's body tight. That wasn't the name she expected, but maybe, just maybe she should have.

"I see you know the name." Ruin's voice carried a razor edge that was anything but casual.

Dammit, this man was no one's fool. Something that would serve her well to remember. "You could say that."

She moved away from the fire, rubbed her arms against a sudden chill, and made her way around the end of Simon's mattress. Memories better left alone crowded close and threatened to set her mind into a tailspin. Nervous energy forced her to move. She paced the confines of the room, unable to stop despite the watching eyes of the too perceptive man and his friend. She picked through what she knew of Reznik, but no matter how she tried, she couldn't make the pieces work.

She stopped in front of Ruin. "What else did the Raider say?"

One dark brow rose. "Why?"

She choked back the urge to snap and kept her tone level. "Because this job doesn't fit Reznik's style."

"Care to elaborate?" The barely disguised order had her turning to Simon, who, despite his wan complexion, managed a formidable glower. He did a piss poor job of hiding his pain.

Since she didn't want to watch all her work go to waste, she refused to take offense at his tone. "He's a scum-sucking leech who gets off on playing king of the criminal element. Reznik is from New Seattle." A fact she knew all too well, considering how often she tried, and failed, to lure him outside the protection of his little kingdom.

"However, he stays in the city. It would take a shit-ton of incentive to get him to wander outside of New Seattle. Not only is he perfectly content where he is, but he's well-protected." A truth proven repeatedly over the years. She looked at Ruin, who got to his feet during her little rant. "What could he possibly gain by Crane's death?"

He studied her from inches away. "If he likes playing king, then it's all about power, isn't it?' His gaze was shuttered and dark, betraying nothing of what he was thinking.

"Even if he had the resources to pull it off, screwing with the supply lines is a stupid move," she argued. "In the hierarchy of power, Reznik would need a ladder to touch Crane's boots."

Ruin's voice was flat and icy. "Why do you know so much about Reznik?"

She refused to bow to his indomitable presence. Instead, she closed the small gap between them and went toe to toe with the coldly angry Vulture. "Because it's my job."

His lips curved, but his smile was far from friendly. "Really?"

Wherever he was trying to lead her, she didn't want to go, but it didn't stop her from answering, "Yeah, really."

He shook his head and leaned in. "Color me cynical, but I have a better answer. You've got a personal link with him."

She couldn't stop her instinctive flinch if she wanted.

And based off the satisfied gleam in his amber gaze, he hadn't missed it. "Oh yeah, you've got a hard-on for Reznik," he murmured. Then that satisfaction turned cruel and within the confines of his closely trimmed beard his lip curled. "What'd he do, hmm? You a woman scorned, Charity?"

The unexpected accusation brought her up short. "Excuse me?"

"C'mon, sugar," he drawled. "One of the most sure-fire ways of turning a woman rabid is to trade her in for a newer model. Is that what happened?"

She fought the urge to introduce her knee to his balls and slap the arrogance off his face, but that wasn't her best move. *At least not yet.* Instead, she settled for popping his overinflated ego with a piece of the truth. "No, dickhead, he murdered my parents."

It was Ruin's turn to blink and rock back on his heels. "Say again?"

She huffed out a breath and decided to elaborate. It wasn't as if her past was some deep dark secret. "My parents were grifters, damn good ones. Normally, they'd have no problems steering clear of trouble. They targeted the wealthy since the pickings were good, but then they ran a grift on the wrong man. When he figured out their con, he reached out to a friend of his. Unbeknownst to my folks, that friend was Reznik, who wasn't happy that one of his buddies got screwed over by some run of the mill thieves, especially if they weren't paying into his coffers."

The door on her memories cracked and released a bitterness grown brilliant with age. "He made an example of them, displaying his displeasure in bloody terms far and wide in case others were stupid enough to consider freelancing in what he considered his territory."

For a moment the only sound in the room was the dance

of the fire behind them, then Simon cut in with a soft, "You don't strike me as the forgiving type, Charity."

Oh, she wasn't. She peered around Ruin and gave Simon a toothy grin. "I'm also not stupid."

"So you let him walk away?"

Maybe Simon didn't mean to twist the knife in her soul, but it still shredded. "A fifteen- year-old street rat would end up smeared under Reznik's heel. Better to bide my time." And fortify her resources, which weren't quite on par with Reznik's, at least not yet. But, if things continued as planned, it shouldn't be long before that changed. She was careful not to linger on that thought because Ruin was too damn perceptive. "Besides, I've got more than enough on my plate right now."

Ruin crossed his arms over his chest. "Bide your time until when?"

"Uh-uh, your turn." She mimicked his posture. "I'm guessing Reznik's name came up when you were playing with your chew toy." A solid guess on her part and when he didn't refute it, she kept on. "You do realize that if someone's itching to share a name, in my experience the chances are pretty damn good it's not the right name." She cocked her head. "How sure are you that you're not being played?"

Ruin's expression was a weird cross between astonishment and offended dignity.

Simon gave a wheezy chuckle from his place on the mattress. "Ruin, I do believe she doubts your interrogation skills."

Ruin ignored his friend and kept his attention on her. "When you show a man his intestines, darlin', he gets highly motivated not to lie. In fact, he tends to spill his guts." His grin was all teeth. "Pun intended." His grin faded and was replaced by implacable lines. "The Raider was more than willing to share."

She stayed quiet, waiting for the rest.

He gave it to her. "Seems a few months back Reznik arrived in Vegas with four of his buddies in tow. The Raiders mistakenly thought them easy marks. After Tank's head, and only his head, showed up decorating the Tower, it didn't take them long to figure out who was the bigger predator."

She passed through Vegas once, and it was enough to sour her on a repeat trip. The place was crawling with Raiders, led by a giant bruiser known as Tank. Their goal? Terrorize anyone foolish enough to try their luck at passing through.

The Raiders nested in the crumbling remains of what one old trekker called the Strip. He'd shown her a tattered postcard filled with light-encrusted buildings that boggled the mind. Especially when compared to the desert-gnawed bones of what existed now. It was the strangest thing to recognize the Tower on the faded card. When she asked the trekker, he called it Eiffel, said it had something to do with Paris, which lay worlds away on the other side of the ocean in a land she'd never see.

Ruin wasn't finished sharing. "Once Reznik's posse managed to get the Raiders' attention, he made them an offer."

Unable to resist her curiosity, she nudged, "What kind of offer?"

Ruin grimaced. "We didn't get that far."

From the floor, Simon snorted, then cut off a moan. "What a surprise."

Charity took in the wounded man's drawn face and white-lined lips, dropped her arms, and shook her head. "Time for another painkiller."

She scanned the floor near the mattress and spotted the edge of the kit behind Ruin. She stepped forward and was unsurprised when Ruin braced. Instead of encouraging his tension, she put her hand on his hip and gently pushed until he moved back. Muscles shifted under her touch, and the heat of him burned her palm. As she crouched next to the kit, she surreptitiously curled her fingers over the lingering sensation before digging through the kit for the last of the painkillers. She worried if Simon took a turn for the worse over the next few hours, they'd be forced to dip into her stash of Mary Jane tucked in her saddlebag. Not that it would do a thing for fever, but at least he'd be able to ride above the pain.

A near palatable presence blanketed her spine and shoulders as Ruin crowded in behind her. He reached around her, retrieved the cup near Simon's saddle pillow, and then pulled it back. Still in her crouch, she half-turned and handed Simon the pills. Behind her came the sound of water being poured into the cup. Simon popped the pills in his mouth and reached for the cup Ruin offered, only to grimace as the move pulled at his wounds. Ruin quickly adjusted and held the cup to Simon's mouth until he could get enough to wash the pills down.

Charity settled cross-legged on the floor and rested her arms on the mattress. When Simon was done, Ruin settled at her side, placing the nearly empty cup on the floor. She eyed the injured man and knew it wouldn't take long for exhaustion and the pills to suck him under. Before that happened, she had a question for him. "The kids you rescued, are they still at Pebble Creek?"

Simon nodded. "We have them safely tucked away. Gives them a chance to recover."

The image of the stern-faced female in charge of the wounded at Pebble Creek rose and she took a guess at who was watching over them. "Mandy?"

Simon eyed her, clearly not expecting her question. "You met her?"

"Briefly." Something tight in her chest loosened, not relief exactly, but something close to it. "If I can, I'd like to talk to the kids when we get back."

"If you're expecting information from them," Ruin cut in. "It's a long shot."

"What he said," Simon added, his words starting to slur. "Besides, already tried."

She propped her chin on her palm and stared over Simon's torso, into the fire. "Not looking for information, just want to see if one of them is Tabby."

But if she was in the traumatized group, what then? If she took Tabby back to Boulder, it would mean leaving the Raiders to Ruin, and by extension, the Vultures. Not an option she liked, because if Reznik was behind this mess, then this might be her only real chance at payback. Not that dealing with Reznik was completely personal, not anymore. She considered it more akin to a mix of business and sadistic pleasure.

"Might not be her." There was a hint of kindness in Simon's voice, or maybe it was pity.

Whatever it was, it caused a lump to settle in her throat. She swallowed past it. "I know."

"If your girl is there—" Ruin's deep voice drew her attention, "—what's next?"

"What do you mean?"

"You giving up your piece of Reznik?"

There was no sign of judgement in his posture or tone, but she still frowned at implication. "Who said I was giving up anything?"

He didn't answer.

She shifted under his disconcerting gaze. "If she's with Mandy, I'll leave her there until this mess gets straightened out. If," she stressed, when guilt battled with duty while vengeance waited on the sidelines, "we prove Reznik's behind the kids' kidnapping and Crane's death, I intend to get my piece." When a hint of disagreement flashed in his eyes, she added, "But I'm not completely greedy. I'll make sure there's something left for you and your friends."

"Friends?"

His bland tone didn't fool her, and she was weary of playing the word game. "With the shape he's in, we can't move Simon." She turned back to stare at the fire. "I'm not stupid enough to believe the other Vultures aren't winging their way to you as we speak."

Simon's mumbled, "I can make it down the mountain," came from her right.

She stifled her sigh at having to handle yet another fragile male ego, and stared him down. "No, you can't."

He tried to argue but the painkillers finally kicked in and his one good eyelid fluttered closed and didn't lift.

With him safely asleep, she turned away. Without Ruin poking at her or Simon to tend to, she couldn't escape the aches and pains making a comeback. There was the way her shoulder ached like a bitch, how every muscle begged for sleep, and sand coated the interior of her eyelids. Unfortunately, sleep would have to wait, because now that Simon's body was more concerned about healing than breathing, chances were high he would spike a fever.

The second time she jerked herself out of a half-daze, warm, firm fingers tunneled through her hair, and pressed her head gently, but firmly against Ruin's shoulder. "Sleep, Charity, I got this."

"Just need a couple hours," she mumbled, blinking rapidly.

"Then take them." His voice was quiet. "If I need you, I'll wake you."

Reassured by the ring of truth in his voice, she allowed the last vestiges of her wariness to loosen. Some sixth sense told her she was safe. At least for now. She gave in to Ruin's urging and slid down until she could curl against the mattress' edge on her good shoulder.

As she laid there, her mind drifted, and from under her lashes, she studied the man next to her. With the fire behind him, his face was half-hidden in the flickering shadows. The way the light played over his hair, glinting off the strands of gold mixed in with the dark browns and blacks as it brushed his shoulders was mesmerizing. His neatly trimmed beard was a dark, appearing black, and emphasized the strong line of his jaw. The shadows that brushed along the straight blade of his nose left half of his face swathed in murky darkness.

But it was the unusual amber color of his eyes as he watched her watch him that captured her. Trapped in that startling intense connection, lust thickened her pulse and wound its way through her exhausted body. "You're danger-ous." The unchecked truth slipped out without warning.

"Very." His low rumble merged with the quiet night. "But so are you."

For some reason, his observation made her happy. "Does that worry you?"

His slow, sexy smile wormed its way below her lazy lust. "Nah." He traced the side of her face with his finger and tucked a strand of hair behind her ear.

The strangely intimate touch sent chills racing over her skin.

He leaned closer, his shoulder blocking out the light and leaving them stranded in shadows and unspoken expectations. "I've always enjoyed a little danger." His gaze drifted over her face, and his finger slowly, too slowly, traced its way to her chin.

She wasn't a naive daisy bell, but she was familiar enough with her body to know the difference between adrenaline-laced lust and something altogether different. This was a subtle combination of both.

"Be careful," she murmured as he curled a finger under her chin. "Don't underestimate me."

He closed the distance between them until his lips were a breath away. "Never." Then he kissed her.

It wasn't the hurricane of need and desire she expected. Instead, it was slow heat and slumberous want. A soft touch of lips, followed by a gentle glide of his tongue as it sought permission. Permission she granted when she met him, stroke for exploratory stroke.

They took time to learn each other's taste in lingering tangles. There was a faint hint of mint leaves under his uniquely masculine taste, a cool counterpoint to the heat. She circled his neck with an arm, burrowing closer.

He shifted positions, and the touch on her chin changed until he was cradling her face in his palms. His warmth seeped under her skin, switching her lust to hunger. As need began to overwhelm the strange dreamlike kiss, her soft moan escaped.

As if triggered by the, his kiss turned carnal, darker, more demanding. Instead of turning her off, his desire ignited a matching craving. Lost in the rising storm, she didn't realize he had her pressed against the mattress's edge until he moved from her mouth to her neck. The combination of his lips and beard over her the sensitive skin left a shivery heat behind.

She arched into the sensation and gasped at the feel of his chest, hard and hot, pressing against the sensuous ache in her nipples despite the thin barriers of their shirts. Her hands curled into his shoulders as his hand drifted to her chest, cupping and shaping her until her breasts ached for more. When he found a particularly sensitive spot where her shoulder and neck met, she couldn't stifle her, "Oh god."

With one last, torturous swipe of wicked fingers over her straining peaks, he lifted his head, his eyes glittering with lust and his lips swollen from bites she couldn't remember giving.

"Like I said—" his voice was rough with hunger, "—dangerous."

"Like I said—" his voice was rough with hunger, "—dangerous."

ten

Ruin completed another circuit around the cabin, as dawn slipped across the sky. He pocketed a few more spent shells from the gunfight and made a mental note to dump them in Havoc's hands later. He adjusted the rifle strapped to his back, courtesy of a dead Raider, and rapped his knuckles against the doorframe. He waited for Charity's faint answer before he led the horses to the creek.

Once there, he hobbled the horses and let them drink. He shifted the rifle's sling to his shoulder, leaned against the thick tree trunk, and tucked his hands in his pockets. Simon had survived the night, a feat Ruin owed Charity for.

Despite his casual pose, he didn't stop scanning his surroundings while guilt twitched in his gut. There was one tidbit of information garnered from the Raider's enforced confession that Ruin failed to share with Charity. The Raiders had a meet scheduled in Kennewick, one they were destined to missed since they were busy feeding the worms. A meeting he was betting would lead to bigger problems on the horizon.

Maybe he should've shared last night, but after that unexpected kiss, Ruin jumped at taking the first turn at watch, justifying his rapid retreat behind her exhaustion and his inability to know what the hell to say, even as his body clamored for more. When he got back, she was out like a light, and he figured he'd have more than enough time in the morning to ponder his decision.

Well, morning was here, and he still didn't feel like sharing. He had reasons, damn good strategic reasons, not to spill his guts to a woman he just met. First was her job as a 'Hound. Right behind that was the feeling he couldn't shake that there was something more to the girl's kidnapping that Charity wasn't sharing.

But logic wasn't easing his guilt. Poking and prodding at the uncomfortable sensation wasn't helping either, so he ignored it, and focused on the more immediate concern. Visitors. Not just the potential of more Raiders heading in, but there was a high chance Vex or Havoc, or both, would pop up at any minute.

In the branches above, birds chattered, their voices merging with the white-noise buzz of the insects below as the horses continued to drink. Then came a brief hiccup in the background choir. Ruin's muscles coiled in anticipation. Before he could react, one of the horses lifted its head and snorted. A familiar scent drifted with the shift of shadow and the soft whisper of leaves against cloth.

Ruin looked to his right and smiled in relief. "Took you long enough, sis."

"What the hell happened to Simon?" Forgoing a greeting, his twin stepped out of the dense foliage, her boots and the cuffs of her faded jeans stained with dirt. Vex came up to his side and folded her arms over her chest, her leather jacket creaking with the movement.

"He's alive." Only because she was his twin was he able to catch the subtle release of tension in her shoulders and jaw. He noted her worry in the bright gold of her gaze. "But getting him to Pebble Creek is going to be a challenge."

She turned away and bit her lower lip. Her hard-ass mask slipped, revealing a rare glimpse into the battered heart he loved. He leaned in and bumped her shoulder with his, mowing their version of a hug was all she would allow. He changed the subject. "Reaper and Havoc?"

"Waiting for us at Crane's place." Vex's weight settled against his side, and she rested her head on his shoulder, her thick braid brushing his back.

Heeding her rare, silent request, he wrapped his arm around her narrow waist and gave her a squeeze. "Simon will be back up and pissing you off in no time."

Vex said nothing, simply nodded.

They stood there in silence watching the horses, as Ruin gave his sister the time she needed to regain her balance. There was a slight hitch to her breathing.

The small, telling sound gave him hope. Maybe seeing how close Simon had come to dying would be enough to finally pierce his sister's well-protected heart and let her find some peace. He had no doubt of how much of that heart Simon held, but the problem was Vex. She was bound and determined to not let it matter, an attitude that sucked not just for Simon, but for her as well. Ruin tried talking to her about it, not that he had the patience for it, but he tried. Unfortunately, it was one topic Vex wasn't rational about. He sighed.

When she finally lifted her head and stepped back, her voice was husky. "Havoc said you got yourself a new friend."

Ruin shook his head, pushed away from the tree, and shifted the rifle until it was resettled across his back. "I'm not sure friend is the accurate term in this instance." He grabbed his horse's reins and started the trek back to the cabin.

Vex nabbed the reins of Charity's paint, sunlight glancing

off the sharpened metal tips of her gloved hand and followed. "Aww, Ruin, did someone stomp all over your precious ego?"

"No." He slid his sibling a narrow-eyed glare. "Brat."

Her habitual sneer disappeared as she laughed.

He turned serious. "I'm not sure what her game is here."

And wasn't that a bitch?

Because last night's kiss replayed in vivid detail and the memory of her taste, all heated spice, made it difficult to walk. *What the hell was he thinking kissing Charity?*

Not a damn thing.

He grimaced. That wasn't exactly true. His mind had been full of suggestions on what exactly to do with that armful of curves and heat. There was something about her that kept him hooked. Unwilling to go down that rabbit hole, he told Vex, "Her name's Charity, says she came to Crane's on the trail of a missing girl."

Vex made a noise in the back of her throat. "Missing girl? From where?"

"Boulder."

"And she followed a kid all the way up here?" Disbelief was clear in her voice.

Since all four Vultures lived and breathed suspicion, he wasn't surprised by her question. In fact, having his doubts reflected by his sister eased a bit of the guilt he carried. "Girl was the first of many." Knowing that wouldn't be enough for Vex, he clarified, "Charity's a Bloodhound." He took a few more steps before realizing his sister had stopped. He did the same and scratched the horse's nose so he could look over its neck.

Vex stood there, her forehead creased in a frown, and ignored the paint, who took the time to nuzzle her hair. "Who's the girl?"

He shrugged. "No one important."

"You sure about that?" Sarcasm dripped from her voice.

"You know the damn 'Hounds don't track out of the goodness of their hearts."

That they didn't, but ... "Sounds like it's personal. Charity has some sort of relationship with the girl's parents."

"Right." Vex looked away and stared towards the cabin barely visible through the trees. "If you believe that, I have a bridge to sell you." Her muttered phrase held traces of their old man. She gave a short shake of her head and turned back to him. "And Simon?"

"Simon was being Simon and ran straight into trouble." He started walking again and heard Vex do the same. "He trailed the surviving Raiders straight into the waiting arms of their buddies. They brought him here."

"Raiders don't come this far north."

"Not normally."

"Timing makes me smell a rat."

Since it coincided with the Vultures being on the road and not at Pebble Creek, he understood her concern. Still, he wasn't sold on the rat part. Not yet. "Maybe, but our absence wasn't a secret."

"Neither was Crane's anger about the missing shipments," Vex added. "What changed?"

He gave her another piece of the puzzle. "While running a check on the lines, Simon stumbled across a group of Raiders illegally transporting kids."

There was no missing Vex's sharp hiss of fury. "Kids? Since when the hell did Raiders start dealing in kids?"

He shrugged. "Don't have a fucking clue, but it can't be good. The kids were in bad shape." He caught her wince before she could hide it.

Her voice was hard and tight. "Where are they now?"

"With Mandy."

She nodded and they continued for a few more steps. Finally, she asked, "The Raiders dead?"

"Yep."

"Good."

His lips twitched at her grumpy tone. "Mad because I didn't leave you one?"

She gave him a mock glare. "Maybe."

He huffed out a low laugh. They continued on, the muffled sounds of the horses' hooves blending with the natural chorus of the forest.

Eventually, Vex called, "Ruin."

"Yeah?"

"Should we expect more company?"

Seemed his sister's mind followed his. "Maybe."

They broke through the tree line and started across the field. As they drew closer a shift of shadow from the cabin's doorway nabbed not just his attention, but Vex's. "That your new girlfriend?" The question held an equal mix of amusement and annoyance.

"Dare you to call her that to her face." He kept his voice low as Charity stepped into the doorframe, the muzzle of one of the rifles he retrieved earlier poking above her shoulder. She leaned against the frame with apparent casualness, but he didn't miss the fact no one would get through unless she let them.

"Might be fun."

He snorted at Vex. One of these days she would tip someone right over the edge and get pulled along for the fall before he could stop her. The weight of Charity's gaze followed him as he led the way to where they kept the horses hitched.

Yeah, he was dragging his feet on introducing the two women, but seriously, what guy wanted to be around for this get-together? The two might be completely opposite in looks, with Charity all sunlight and smiles, while Vex was shadows and hard-eyed stares, but under their masks, they were eerily similar. Dangerous and full of secrets.

With the horses secured, he unslung the rifle and slipped it into a loop on the saddle. Only then did he move towards Charity.

With a pleasant but empty expression, she watched them approach. Her gaze glided over him, and he throttled the urge to crowd her and provoke a reaction. Thankfully her attention shifted to Vex. At his side, he felt Vex stiffen under Charity's regard, and fought back a smile guaranteed to leave him a shredded bloody mess if either woman caught it. "Charity, Vex. Vex, Charity."

Neither woman moved, their gazes locked. For a moment he wondered if they were planning on standing here all damn morning.

Finally, Charity tilted her head in cautious acknowledgement. "Vex."

Vex bared her teeth. "Charity."

Without shifting from her position in the doorway, Charity deliberately dismissed Vex by addressing Ruin. "Is Havoc joining us as well?"

Before he could answer, Vex snapped, "Why? You got issues having us here?"

"Nope." Charity gave Vex a long look. "But then I'm not the one with an attitude problem."

Vex tossed aside the paint's reins, leaving Ruin to catch them. She stalked forward until she was in Charity's face. "Attitude problem?"

Charity didn't move except to shrug. "That or you missed your coffee this morning."

Her unexpected answer pulled Vex up short. It was comical to watch his sister torn between remaining pissy or laughing it off. "I'll be damned, little Miss Sunshine has teeth."

"And claws," Charity supplied unhelpfully.

Knowing what would happen next, Ruin lunged forward, but it wasn't fast enough to stop the impending cat fight.

"Like these?" Vex's hand whipped out.

The resounding slap of impact echoed through the morning air. Ruin blinked to make sure his eyes weren't playing tricks on him. In the middle of the doorway, Charity stood tall and unmoving with Vex's wrist locked in her grip. The metal tips of his sister's glove were less than an inch from Charity's face. From the flex of arm muscle, it was obvious both women were exerting pressure, but it was the knife poised at Vex's kidney that froze him in place. He watched Charity's knife.

"That wasn't nice." Charity's voice didn't reflect the strain of her hold.

"It wasn't meant to be," Vex snarled.

"You want in to see your man, you sheath your claws, kitty cat." Her wrist with the blade twitched.

Ruin growled a warning. "Charity."

Charity didn't shift her attention from Vex's threat. "Don't even think about interfering, Ruin."

With a twist of her arm Vex slipped from Charity's hold, or Charity let go, either way, Vex stepped back and gave him a disgusted look. "Really? I'm fine."

He pointedly glanced at the knife barely visible at Charity's side.

Vex snorted. "She wasn't going to cut me." Her brow furrowed and she turned to Charity. "Were you?"

Charity's smile was slow and disturbing. "Maybe."

Vex threw her head back and laughed. When she was finished, she glanced at Ruin. "I like her. You can keep her."

Charity's smile was replaced by a frown. "Not his choice."

Vex wiggled her eyebrows as she looked between the two, then she grinned. "Uh-huh, whatever." She pushed past her brother and headed for the cabin's door. "You going to let me through?"

Charity thought it over and eventually stepped back so Vex could brush by her and disappear inside.

His sister had no issue leaving him to fend for himself. *Ungrateful little witch. See if he'd play interference next time Simon picked on her.*

Charity left the cabin and came up to him. "Walk with me?"

It didn't take a genius to understand she wasn't asking, especially since there was no missing the bite in her voice. He stifled a sigh, looped the reins over the post, and fell into step beside her. It wasn't long before he realized she was doing a perimeter check.

It was only when she stopped at one of the other cabins that she finally faced him. "Besides your sister, any other friends of yours dropping by?"

Charity's assumption about Vex wasn't a surprise as their family connection was hard to miss when they shared the same space. "Why the concern?"

His provoking question earned him a glare that was equal parts frustration and puzzlement. "Excuse me?"

"Why the act at the door?" At her puzzled look he elaborated, "Not letting Vex inside." The itch of suspicion rode his spine. "What are you playing at?"

Red rose under her cheeks and her gaze narrowed. "I'm not playing at shit. I didn't bust my ass to keep your friend breathing, just to be blindsided by an unexpected visitor intent on finishing the job the Raiders started."

The ring of sincerity in her voice forced a sliver of remorse to work its way past his normal wariness, and he grudgingly admitted, "Probably not."

"Probably not," she muttered with evident sarcasm. She shook her head and turned, one hand going to her neck as she paced a few feet away. When she stopped, she kept her back to him and said, "We need to get Simon back to Pebble Creek."

"Thought you said he wouldn't make it down."

The hand at her neck dropped and fisted at her side. "That was before I found out we might end up with more company than we can handle."

"You think more Raiders are on their way?"

At his question, she finally turned back around and aimed a disbelieving look his way. "Don't you?"

It was a perfect opening to mention the Raiders' planned meet in Kennewick, but curious as to how she worked, he let it slip by. "If they were, what's your plan?" In a deliberate poke, he added a bit of derision to his voice. "Run away?"

Her jaw firmed and her eyes flashed. "You want to face another group of Raiders with what? Sticks and rocks?" Her lip curled. "Are you that eager to die?'

Her whiplash of contempt slipped under his skin and ignited his temper, incinerating the truth that he was playing the asshole in an effort to figure her out. Thinned by too little sleep, too much banked fury, and a side helping of lust, his control snapped, and he closed the distance between them.

She didn't budge an inch, simply watched him stalk forward.

When he closed in, he deliberately crowded her, his hands fisted at his side to combat the urge to shake the ever-living daylights out of her. He leaned in, his voice soft and deadly. "The only ones adding their bones to the ground will be Raiders, darlin'."

Charity propped her hands on her hips and tilted her head back until the sunlit strands fell away leaving her face exposed. Her pointed chin lifted, and she went on tiptoe until mere inches separated them. "No, darlin'—" Her mimicry of his endearment was full of scorn, "—it'll be Simon's bones littering the ground. Because once the Raiders have their fun with the bull-headed ass who mistakenly thought he was the shit, because he had—" her finger drilled into his chest with each word, "—no ... fucking ... weapons."

Lit by her fury, her bright blue gaze sparked with gold. Those fireworks fascinated him, so much so that his anger paused and gave logic a window. He held her furious gaze and muttered the first thing that came to his mind, "We have weapons."

Disbelief chased across her face as she dropped back down, took a step back, and canted her head. "Are you kidding me, Ruin? What weapons do you think we have?"

He opened his mouth to answer and never got a chance.

She waved an arm back toward the cabin, her voice sharp. "Did you get a good look at the bag those idiots left?" Again, she didn't give him an opening and continued to rant. "Because I did. What guns they have are corroded and more likely to explode in your face than fire. The knives aren't balanced for shit. I'm down to fifteen shots between my gun and the rifle, and you have what?" Her hand went to her hip, and she raked him with her gaze, her return trip slow and insolent. "A pocket full of shells?" Her lip curled derisively. "Gee, sugar, I'm feeling all warm and fuzzy about our chances of taking out another raiding party."

Even though he knew damn good and well this pointless argument was his fault, her barbs found their intended mark and left him gritting his teeth. Despite her shit-ton of snark, she had a valid point. There was no treasure trove of weapons lying around, and he was down to a handful of bullets for the rifle. But that didn't stop him from opening his mouth and pushing her right over the edge. "Don't need much to wreak havoc."

The noise she made was close to a snarl. She spun around, paced a few feet away, and fisted her hands in her hair as she muttered to herself. Unable to make out what she was saying, he waited her out, part of him amused by her temper.

Her temper tantrum didn't last long before she pivoted, nailed him with a glare, and stomped back, getting in his face. "What's more important here? Getting Simon back to Pebble Creek, or indulging in your bloodlust?"

He folded his arms over his chest and arched a brow. "What do you think?"

Her shoulders stiffened, her spine went ramrod straight, and her eyes narrowed as she studied him. Her reaction made him wonder if he overplayed his hand.

"I think,'" she started slow and soft, "that I'm done here."

Yeah, definitely overplayed his hand. He kept his face blank and hid his wince. "Done?"

She didn't answer, instead she turned and headed back to the cabin.

He called after her. "Charity?"

She didn't slow, didn't turn, didn't answer.

Ah shit. It was always a bad sign when a woman ignored you. He ran a hand through his hair, sent up a prayer for patience, and made short work of catching up to her. He wrapped a hand around her arm, being careful of her injured shoulder, and gently pulled her to a stop. "What do you mean, done?"

When she turned to face him, he recognized her default mask—an empty pleasantness, that pissed him off. Even her bland tone was irritating. "Between you and your sister, I'm sure the two of you can take care of Simon and whatever game you've decided to play here." She pulled against his grip. Unwilling to hurt her, he let go. She wasted no time putting deliberate distance between them. "I, on the other hand, need to get back to Pebble Creek."

"To find the girl you're looking for?" he asked.

She stopped moving and looked at him. "Among other things."

"What other things?"

For a moment, the predator she tried so hard to hide peeked out, giving her patiently false mask a dark edge. "Not your concern, Ruin."

"Now, darlin', that's where I have to disagree." He closed in, crowding her, unsurprised when she held her ground. "If Reznik is behind the Raiders, it most definitely is my concern. Mine and the Vultures."

A cold light entered her eyes, and she tossed his words from the night before back in his face. "Worried I won't leave you anything to play with?"

Enough was enough. He stopped his game and aimed for her jugular. "More worried about what part your sweet ass is playing in all of this."

Her head jerked back as if slapped. "My part?"

"Yeah, your part." The suspicions he harbored laced his voice with ice. "I don't doubt you're tracking your missing kid, but that's not the whole story on why you're here." He leaned in. "Is it, Charity?"

She crossed her arms, and he did his best to ignore what that move did to her chest. "You think I had a hand in what happened to Simon?"

Not really, but he held his tongue, more curious as to what she would say next.

"You are un-fucking-believable," she muttered. "Just so we're clear, Vulture, I had not one damn thing to do with Simon or Crane."

There was some note in her voice that made him push. "But?"

She considered him for a long moment before she admitted, "But you are right about one thing."

When she didn't say another word, he knew he was being led, but he still asked, "And that is?"

"Tracking Tabitha wasn't my only reason for seeking out Crane."

Adrenaline roared through him, and every hunting instinct he possessed went on point. *Finally, they were getting somewhere.* "Then what was?"

All business now, she said, "Something you aren't in a position to give me."

Stung on some inexplicable level, he snapped, "You sure about that?"

"Quite." Her smile caught him off guard. It was sharper than anything he'd seen and considering who his twin was, that was saying something. "Don't worry, sweetheart, I'm fairly certain that will change."

It sucked knowing he was being played, but he'd let her have this round. "And why's that?"

She made a soft hum, before elaborating. "Because I'm not done with you or the Vultures just yet."

eleven

Charity was pissed. Not at Ruin and his games. She expected those. Nope, all her anger was self-directed because she let a few hot tongue tangles and a case of raging hormones blindside her to who she was dealing with and that was not acceptable.

Nowadays, everyone had an agenda, and no matter how tempting Ruin was, she needed to remember his agenda could be just as dangerous, if not more so, than hers. That meant proceeding with caution, and not being sidetracked by a wickedly hot body and talented mouth. And the best way to ensure that was to saddle up and make tracks. The Twins of Trouble could deal with Simon all on their own.

Her exit strategy was derailed when Vex met her at the doorway with the order-bordering-on-threat to get her ass inside and help prep Simon for the trip back to Pebble Creek. If Charity hadn't spied the worry under Vex's bluster, she might have spent some time educating the other woman on why it was best not to threaten a 'Hound.

Instead, she silently fumed and chided her hormonally influenced brain, as she helped Vex prepare Simon for transport. Despite her teeth-gritting frustration and anger, she was careful to handle Simon as gently as possible. The poor guy didn't deserve to pay for his friend's crimes.

She and Vex bound his ribs, and then dressed him in one of Ruin's t-shirts and a salvaged pair of pants. When they finally got him to his feet, he was sweaty and pale. Between her and Vex, they managed to keep Simon upright during their slow journey to the cabin's doorway.

Outside, the sturdy, dust-covered beast Vex rode in on stood a few feet from the cabin's entrance, its reins in Ruin's hand. As she and Vex guided Simon into the morning sunshine, he dropped his head and a soft hiss escaped. His one good eye narrowed to a mere slit and his shoulders hunched.

Ruin held out his sunglasses. "Here."

Simon unwound his arm from Vex's shoulders, took the offering, and despite his shaky, bandaged hand, managed to get them on with a sigh a relief. "Thanks."

Vex slowly released Simon's waist and asked Charity for the fourth time, "You sure you've got this?"

Reaching for her waning patience, Charity smothered the urge to roll her eyes. "I've got him. Go, get up. Ruin and I will help Simon mount."

Vex waited for her brother to step in and take her place at Simon's other side, before mounting the horse.

Tightening her hold on Simon's waist, she asked him, "You ready?"

He eyed Vex and her horse, grim determination evident despite his washed-out coloring. "Let's do this before I pass out."

Taking him at his word, Ruin and Charity worked together, and with a minimum of curses, got Simon in the saddle behind Vex. Since they were heading back down the mountain, the decision had been made to have Simon ride behind Vex so he could use her as a brace.

Charity and Vex had both voiced serious concerns about the state of his ribs. Concerns, Simon was determined to ignore. As worried as Charity was about the toll this trip would take on him, there was no doubt Vex had her beat. It was strangely compelling to watch the kick-ass woman play mother hen.

Vex craned her head over her shoulder so she could see Simon, her face creased with a scary as shit frown. "You sure about this?"

Simon cautiously adjusted his seat in the saddle and tried to hide his wince. He failed. "Not like we've got much choice, doll." He gingerly wrapped his dark arm around her narrow waist, and Vex's hand immediately covered his.

Charity wondered if the other woman understood how much that one move revealed.

Simon leaned in and brushed his nose against Vex's jaw. "Let's hit the road. We need to get back." His comment was a clear indication Charity wasn't the only one feeling the itch of racing against an unseen clock.

Charity scanned the area one last time and checked to make sure there were no lingering signs of their stay. Well, except for the bodies Ruin stashed god knew where.

Behind her, she heard Vex ask, "Got everything?"

"Yeah," Ruin answered.

"Good, then mount up, and let's head out."

Ruin took lead as they headed down the mountain, leaving Charity to bring up the rear. Since sound carried, no one was inclined to chatter keeping conversation limited. Which left Charity with plenty of time to think.

Ruin's accusation that she had ulterior motives cut uncomfortably close to the truth. Unfortunately, there was more going on than he knew, but she wasn't in a position to share. Not yet.

That would change though. With Crane out of play,

Simon incapacitated, and Boden vehemently opposed to taking the driver's seat, it was a no brainer who would be running Pebble Creek.

Fate's Vultures.

She wasn't sure how to feel about that, or what it meant for her agenda considering how tight the Vultures were, with each other and Simon. On one hand, dealing with a group she held a healthy respect for wasn't a hardship. On the other, once they found out who sent her and why, they wouldn't be so keen on working with her.

And it wasn't like she could just say "Whoops, my bad," and leave. Not only because there was a little girl to rescue, but because there was still the business she originally intended to address with Crane. Business that required a certain level of discretion and trust.

She studied the two Vultures riding ahead and knew those two commodities would be in short supply. Granted, she might be creating problems where none existed, but she doubted it.

Part of her issue might be solved by placing a simple phone call once they hit Pebble Creek. Or at least give her a chance to explain before they booted her out of town. Except Crane's death turned her status report into something much more complex.

She blew out a quiet breath and ducked when her horse passed under low-lying branches. She was tempted to skip the check in. It wouldn't be that hard to blame it on a cut line. What was that old saying? Better to ask for forgiveness than permission? That sounded plausible, but no matter how her gut squirmed about the upcoming confrontation, and it would be a confrontation, she couldn't risk it. Not if that call would grant her the freedom to ally with the Vultures and hunt down whoever was behind the kidnappings. Besides, once she got Tabby home, she'd be able to ensure she wouldn't spend the rest of her life looking over her shoulder.

That's only if Tabby was one of the girls under Mandy's care, a little voice mocked.

Charity refused to think about the ramifications if Tabby wasn't with Mandy. Instead, she deliberately replayed her earlier exchange with Ruin, and tried to pinpoint why she was so pissed at him.

It wasn't his deliberate provocation. If she was honest with herself, she would have been disappointed if he hadn't tried such an approach. She scratched a little deeper only to find he'd hurt her feelings with his suspicions. Hurt feelings, what the hell was wrong with her? She winced just thinking the words. No way in hell would she ever admit that out loud. Talk about a childish reaction. Feelings would get her gutted faster than a Raider's knife.

Remember who you're dealing with, girl.

The old reminder was one she wished she heeded last night. It was better he considered her nothing more than a tool to be used, or a possible threat to eliminate, than something infinitely more damaging.

It was crystal fucking clear that he didn't trust her. Now that she had the distance and time, she picked through their conversation like a child with a troublesome knot—his phrasing, his expressions, the way he reacted—until it finally fell into place.

He played her.

Stunned by how long it took her to clue in, her frustration and anger peaked. Her head jerked up, and she glared at Ruin's back as it swayed ahead of her. "You bastard," she muttered under her breath.

Simon lifted his head from where it rested against Vex's shoulder. He tried to look back but barely managed to give Charity his profile. "Something up?"

His question had Ruin twisting in his saddle. Charity waved a hand at him to keep going, then she answered Simon. "Nope, just talking to myself back here."

"Might want to keep it down," Vex drawled, not bothering to look back.

Charity didn't snipe back because she was too busy reorganizing the pieces. Ruin's lack of concern about the possibility of incoming Raiders, his asinine argument about running away and the useless weapons, none of that fit with the highly intelligent hunter she knew him to be. There was only one explanation.

He knew no one was heading to the cabin.

What was his game?

Maybe he wanted to see how far he could push before she pushed back? Or maybe he hoped she would get so fed up, she would decide to bail? Hmm, maybe. Who the hell knew what went on in that disgustingly gorgeous head of his?

But if he knew no one was coming their way, why was he willing to risk his friend's health and book it down to Pebble Creek? Even Vex, who clearly had a thing for Simon, hadn't protested. Ruin simply had the horse ready and waiting when they brought Simon out.

So, if there was no incoming threat, what had lit a fire under Ruin's ass?

It had to be something his chew toy shared, something important. Say, like, where the hell the other Raiders were holed up? Or maybe a lead on Reznik? The more she turned it over, the more she was willing to bet one of her blades she was on the right track. And the more determined she became to stick like glue to the Vultures, and more importantly, Ruin.

Simon's condition slowed the trek down the mountain, and it was mid-afternoon by the time they hit Pebble Creek. Charity decided there was no point in confronting Ruin with her suspicions. As a 'Hound she understood the value of patience and timing.

Better for her to wait and see how things went with Reaper, the Vultures' de facto leader. There were rumors, many, and legion, about the man, which made it difficult to cull fact from fiction. The one thing that was certain, was that to be a leader of a volatile group like theirs, required the ability to weigh all options, and she was betting everything on Reaper's mind being more strategic than most.

As they approached the main gate, Boden's familiar form came into view, and he wasn't alone. Two others stood next to him, one was Havoc, and the other had to be Reaper. She took him in. Taller than Ruin, his inky black hair was pulled back, his dark brows matched his close-cropped beard, and it was finished off with the all-black outfit that covered an intimidating physique. He was the epitome of dark and dangerous. As she got closer, his glower hit her stomach with a lead fist, and her mouth dried up.

Shit.

Ruin pulled his horse to a stop, letting Vex move by him. At her back, Simon was barely conscious, his eyes closed, his body slumped and swaying with the horse's movements.

Havoc intercepted Vex, grabbed the horse's bridle, and brought them to a stop. His gaze swept over Simon and went back to Vex. "Medic."

Vex nodded and stayed mounted as she awkwardly braced Simon's body with an arm. Havoc led them, horse and all, hopefully to wherever Mandy waited.

Charity drew her paint to a halt a few feet back from Ruin's and waited while the Vultures got situated.

Boden walked over, stopped at her side, and kept his voice low. "Hey, little girl."

Grateful for a friendly face, she let her affection show. "Hey, old man."

He patted her mount's neck. "You get rid of the trash?"

She glanced at Ruin, who had dismounted and was talking with Reaper, then turned back to Boden, and matched his volume. "Some of it."

He frowned, but before he could press for more, Ruin called her. "Charity."

She looked over and found both Vultures staring. At her. Ruin simply beckoned her over. He didn't wait for her response, but returned to his conversation with Reaper, who continued to watch her. Despite the distance between them, a chill seeped into her bones, freezing her in place.

Forget culling fact from fiction or playing the odds, this man was beyond dangerous. And that left her in a precarious position. Seconds stretched as Reaper held her gaze. It was only when Ruin said something, that he finally, he turned away, releasing her.

She sucked a shaky breath into her aching lungs. A warm hand squeezed her calf and she looked down into Boden's battered but concerned face.

"Word of advice?"

She jerked her head in a nod.

"Don't play games."

"Wasn't planning on it." Especially not after that little look. She swung her leg over, slid down, and added a couple pats of her own to the paint's neck. Then she turned to Boden. "Is that phone working?"

His gaze sharpened as he gathered the reins. "Yeah, why?"

"Might need it later."

He shook his head, his exasperation clear. "Find me. I'll see what I can do." He led the horse away leaving her to face the two waiting men.

"Thanks," she called after him, before walking over to meet her fate. She did her best not to flinch under the disconcerting weight of Reaper's gaze. Next to him, Ruin waited, arms crossed over this chest, his face impassive. She came to a stop when only a couple feet separated them and waited, determined not to be the first one to speak.

That privilege belonged to Ruin who said, "Time to spill on why you're really here."

It wasn't easy, but she managed to pull off an unconcerned half-smile. "Already explained before, Ruin, I don't answer to you."

"You'd rather answer to me?" The question in the form of a low whip of menace snapped from the man next to him.

"Reaper, I presume?" It wasn't meant as a taunt, more as a way to buy some time, but when his eyes narrowed and the muscles along his folded arms tightened, she back peddled, easing the defensiveness in her voice. "I have no quarrel with you."

His lip curled in an obvious sneer. "You sure about that?"

Even though her legs turned to water, she dug around for her spine, found it, and held on for dear life. Her hands went to her hips. "What? No 'thank you' for keeping Simon breathing?"

Ruin's face darkened, but strangely Reaper's lightened, or maybe that was just her wishful thinking. "Thanks." It came out hard, and what followed was even harder. "Seems to me, you being reluctant to share why you're here, means I'm not going to like what you have to say."

Knowing it was in her best interest, she dropped her attitude. Not completely, but enough to be civil. "I don't know you enough to predict your behavior, nor do I know you enough to encourage me to share. Not to mention, it's not my decision to make."

Something she couldn't read flared in those dark eyes before he demanded, "Whose decision is it?"

Hard as it was, she held his stare, and kept mute.

It was Ruin who snapped the rising tension. His cool derision scraping like flint over her brittle temper. "If you want a chance to see if your girl is here, you might want to start talking."

Smothering the sparks of prissiness, she was uncharacteristically blunt as she decided to heed Boden's advice. This was not a time to play games, but clearing the air? Yeah, she could do that.

"You want me to start talking, Ruin?" She didn't give him a chance to answer but kept her voice low so those lingering nearby couldn't hear. "Unlike you, I have no problems sharing. How about we start with who put your ass in charge? Because last time I checked that position belongs to Simon, or Boden, or both. Or we can skip that part and move on to when I can see the kids, because until I know if Tabby is one of them, I'm not keen on telling you a damn thing."

A red tinge snuck under Ruin's arrogant mask. He dropped his arms, fisted his hands at his side, and closed in until they were face to face. "You want in on this situation, you'll share."

Guess she found the right button to push.

Undaunted, she leaned in and hissed, "Like you shared the real reason you decided to risk Simon's life by hauling ass back here?"

His gaze darkened. "Why the hell would I do that?"

"Maybe so you don't get your supposed best friend killed? Or, hey better yet, get your worthless ass shot down?"

His eyes narrowed. "I don't need you to keep breathing."

His contempt stung, but not for long. Red bled over her mind and vision. "Did you happen to forget that if it wasn't for me, you arrogant thick-witted bastard, you'd be pushing up fucking daisies?"

"Enough." The barked command snapped both of their heads around to find Reaper watching them. "Take her to Mandy," he directed Ruin. "If she's okay with Charity talking to the kids, let her." He turned to Charity. "If your girl is there, I expect full disclosure."

"If she isn't?" Strangely, the question came from Ruin.

Charity throttled back her volatile emotions and turned her back to Ruin as she held Reaper's gaze. Despite her discomfort, her voice came out even. "Even if she isn't here, let me use the phone for one call, and then I'll give you what I can before I head out."

Behind her, Ruin growled. "Where the hell do you think you're going?"

Paying him no heed, she waited for Reaper's decision, because he was the important one right now. Finally, he nodded, then pivoted on his heel, and walked away.

twelve

The damn woman was determined to drive Ruin nuts. Every time he thought he had her figured out, she went shady on him. Whatever it was she was hiding, he wanted to know it, because the not knowing was irritating the crap out of him. It was pure stupidity to consider hitting the road to Kennewick until he had answers. He grabbed Charity's arm and forced her to face him.

Her sharp hiss of pain came seconds too late, reminding him of her wounded shoulder. He barely dodged her incoming fist.

She snarled, "Don't touch me."

He ignored the flicker of guilt and didn't waste time letting her go. "Sorry." He raised his hands and took a step back. "Calm down."

Her eyes narrowed and her lips thinned. He braced for an angry outburst, but was thrown off guard when she ordered, "Just take me to Mandy."

"Not yet." Matching her attitude for attitude, he folded his arms over his chest. Time to start digging around and see what rose to the surface. "What the hell was that, Charity?"

She rubbed her shoulder. "What was what?"

"That." He waved a hand in Reaper's direction. "Your little rant about Simon, and who's in charge."

"What?" Thick mockery layered her question. "Am I not allowed to question the almighty Ruin?"

Her attitude, warranted or not, rankled. He looked away, clenching his teeth to keep his scathing response from slipping free. When he was sure it wouldn't escape, he blew out a hard breath. He caught sight of a young boy collecting Ruin's horse. It was a needed reminder that their fight was happening in the middle of Pebble Creek.

Sure enough, when he looked around, he discovered a handful of lookie-loos doing their best to appear busy but doing a piss-poor job of it. He and Charity needed privacy to hash this out. Plus, on the off chance he ended up throttling her, it was best if there were no witnesses.

Without a word, he turned on his heel and started for Grave Hall. A beleaguered sigh sounded behind him before Charity's light steps followed. The woman probably thought he was taking her to Mandy. Who was he to disabuse her of that notion? It was small and petty, but the sliver of childish satisfaction added a slight curve to his lips as he led her through the streets to where the Vultures normally stayed.

Before the Collapse, thousands called Pebble Creek home. Back then it wore a different name and a different face. After everything fell apart, and humanity reassembled, new towns rose, built upon the bones of the old. Now, less than a thousand called this settlement theirs. While large swaths of outlying areas had been stripped of usable materials and now lay in crumbling heaps, inside town, old structures, such as Grave Hall, found life in new roles. Whatever the Grave used to be, it now served as temporary living space for travelers.

He led Charity up the gently curving walkway of the single-story building and into the courtyard. Framed by a variety of greenery, the structure served as the connector for the two larger, four-story structures on either side. He pulled open the heavy door with an exaggerated flourish and waved her through. "After you."

Charity paused on the top step, her gaze sweeping over their surroundings before coming back to him. "The kids are staying here?"

Instead of lying, he wiggled his fingers, and indicated she head inside. She shook her head and stepped inside. Once she cleared the threshold, he followed, only to pull up short when she froze a few feet in. Stuck between her unmoving body and the closing door, he wrapped an arm around her waist for balance as the door pushed against his back.

For a searing moment, her every curve was pressed tight against him, bringing his slumbering hunger to roaring life. His arm at her waist tightened in unconscious reaction. Before she could snap his head off, or worse, he tugged her to the side so he could slide by, and then let her go. He throttled back his reaction and tried to see what was keeping her in place.

Grave Hall was an eclectic mix of comfort and practicality. Dining tables took up most of the space in the large room, some meant to accommodate cozy couples, while others could manage a bigger party of six or eight.

The back area doubled as a library. Stuffed reading chairs huddled together in strategic positions nestled between book-cases. Off to the side, away from the dining and reading areas, sat a broken in pool table and a well-used dartboard.

The only thing he could see that would cause Charity's reaction was the woman sitting at one of the tables. She was also the one person he hadn't expected to find here—Mandy. Looked like he would be postponing his chat with Charity.

Dammit it all to hell!

He stalked forward, and Charity trailed him. Mandy

watched them approach, her teacup poised halfway to her mouth.

"Doc," he greeted, unable to hide his impatience.

Mandy's eyes sparkled behind her lenses as she deliberately took a sip of tea. Then she settled the delicate looking cup on its equally delicate looking plate. "Ruin." His name carried a hint of humor. "Wasn't expecting to see you here."

"Yeah, same goes."

Mandy's attention wandered beyond him and stalled on Charity. She arched a dark brow. "Charity, correct?"

Charity moved to stand on the other side of the table and nodded. "Mandy, or do you prefer doctor?"

"Mandy's fine." The older woman waved Charity into the opposite seat. As Charity settled in, Mandy turned to Ruin. "You going to stand there and glare, or you going to join the conversation?"

He snagged a chair from a nearby empty table, swung it around, and straddled it, resting his arms along the back. "Happy now?"

Mandy leaned over and patted his cheek. "Very."

He allowed her the affectionate move simply because she was one of the few people in Pebble Creek who managed to make a spot for herself in his life. Probably because she spent so much time patching up his sorry hide.

Sitting back, Mandy studied him, a wariness lingering in her expression. "Did you bring Simon home?"

"A bit worse for wear, but yeah. Boden and Vex were hauling him over to the clinic earlier."

Relief gave her smile a bit more brightness than normal. "Kendra and Bryant are on, so he's in good hands." She made some minor adjustment to the teacup. "They'll come get me if they need me." Her smile slowly faded and was replaced by her normal stoic mask. "You took care of the Raiders, I presume?"

He understood her question wasn't prompted solely by

Simon's welfare, but a decade old scar rendered when her young family was massacred by a band of Raiders. "You presume correctly."

A flash of pain came and went. "Good." The word was soft. She cleared her throat, and the next part came out close to normal. "Were you two looking for me?"

Charity's 'yes' clashed with his 'no' and earned him a nasty look from the younger woman. Mandy simply raised an eyebrow in question.

Before an explanation could be offered a deep voice boomed through the large room. "Hey, Ruin!" A thick-chested man with a box in one arm and the other nimbly maneuvering a crutch, entered through a door in the back that Ruin knew led to a storage room.

Ruin stood up, took his leave of the women, and wove through the tables to head over to help. When he reached the man, Ruin took the box and set it down near a stuffed book-case. "Hey, Worth, how's things?"

The heavily tanned Worth offered his now free hand to Ruin for a quick handclasp. "Quiet. Not unexpected consid-ering some are still reeling from yesterday's attack." His atten-tion drifted to the two watching women, and his harsh face softened. "Mandy needed some peace and quiet, so I'm letting her do her tea thing here while I restock the reading supply."

Ruin grinned. "Mighty nice of you to allow her that." It was an open secret that Worth was sweet on the doc. Besides, the poor fool couldn't lie worth a damn.

Red rode the old man's cheeks, so Ruin figured his and Charity's arrival interrupted whatever plan Worth had set in motion. Worth's hand snuck out and flicked the back of Ruin's head. "Be useful and help restock the shelves, numbnuts."

Stifling his smile, Ruin crouched, grabbed a couple of books from the box at Worth's side, and handed them over, his arm brushing the empty lower leg of Worth's jeans. "Wouldn't want you to strain anything, old man."

Worth took the books and tucked them in on the shelf, shifting his weight on his crutch with the ease of practice. "Did you find Simon?"

Ruin rested his arms on his knees as Worth carefully positioned the books. "Yeah, he's going to be down for a bit." Once Worth finished fiddling with things, Ruin grabbed another handful of books and handed them over.

Worth took them, paused, and cocked his head, his dark eyes unfathomable as he considered the younger man. "You all sticking around for a bit then?"

"Not for long," he murmured, thinking about how soon he needed to hit the road. "But Reaper is stepping in to help Boden while Simon's recovering."

"Good, that's good." Worth set the books in line on the shelf. "Reaper's being here will keep the idiots in line."

And that was exactly why the Vultures' leader would stick around. His presence, alongside Boden's, would discourage anyone stupid enough to try and take Crane's place while Simon was out of commission. It also left the other Vultures, Ruin included, free to hunt down what triggered the Raiders attack on Pebble Creek.

In compatible silence, the two men continued to restock the shelves. Behind them the women's muted conversation continued in polite, stilted tones separated by long pauses. Once the box was empty, Ruin rose and followed Worth over to the women who were now quietly watching them.

Worth stopped behind Mandy's chair, his hand curling over the wooden back as he smiled at Charity. "Hello there."

Charity was all innocence and sweetness as she returned his smile. "Hello." She held her hand out to Worth as Ruin came up to her side and introduced herself. "Charity."

"Worth." The caretaker of Grave Hall released the chair,

reached around Mandy and over the table, to take Charity's hand. Then he brought it to his lips in an old-fashioned move filled with half-forgotten charm. Neither Mandy nor Charity batted an eyelash at Worth's over the top greeting. He let her go and settled back by Mandy's side. "A pleasure to meet you."

"This must be yours, I assume?" Charity indicated the room at large.

"Ah, yes." Worth managed a graceful pivot despite his crutch and missing lower leg. "Welcome to Grave Hall."

Charity studied the room as Mandy took another dainty sip. "Nice," Charity murmured, before her attention shifted to Ruin. "If the private rooms are as comfortable as this, it explains why Ruin calls it home."

Ruin managed not to wince at the underlying bite in her tone. Guess his scheme to get her alone was officially snuffed.

Ignorant of the undercurrents, Worth chuckled. "That, and because I don't mind running interference when he's keen on avoiding unwanted guests."

That earned Ruin a hard-eyed glare from the blonde, and an indulgent smile from Mandy. Worth sported a shit-eating grin. Feeling a need to mount a defense, Ruin changed the conversation. "Reaper's okay with letting Charity see the kids if you are, doc."

With carefully precise movements, the older woman set her teacup aside and focused her attention on the mundane task. Familiar with her eccentric mannerisms, Ruin gave her a moment to craft her response. No doubt the rescued kids had managed to kick Mandy's protective instincts into overdrive. Which meant she wouldn't be so keen on letting just anyone in to see them, regardless of who was asking.

Charity proved her skill at reading people when she didn't rush to fill the silence with useless words but waited for Mandy to take the conversational lead.

Finally, Mandy looked up and stared at Charity. Light

reflected off Mandy's lenses giving her a strange, alien appearance. "What the Raiders put those children through ..." She swallowed hard, her eyes bright with unshed tears, but they didn't fall. "We've barely gotten most of them back on their feet."

"I'm not surprised."

At Charity's softly offered response, Mandy arched a brow and tilted her head, as color rode under her skin. "Are you that familiar with the damage those beasts can do to the young?" An echo of the anger in her eyes, edged her question.

"Raiders aren't the only animals that prey on the helpless." Darkness swam through Charity's bright gaze.

Ruin was unprepared for the whisper of protectiveness that woke in tandem with an uncomfortable ache in his chest. As the two women continued their careful verbal dance, he absently rubbed at the discomforting sensation.

"Then you'll understand my reluctance to upset their environment."

"I do," Charity agreed. "I wouldn't ask if I had another choice."

Mandy studied the younger woman and finally made a decision. "One of the older girls is in a coma, but we were able to get a name from one of the two younger girls. It's not Tabby," she gently clarified when Charity shifted in her seat.

"The one in a coma, is she a redhead?" Charity's question came out strangled.

Mandy's expression softened. "No, but the younger girl who won't talk is." There was no missing Charity's flare of eagerness, and Mandy held up a hand as if it would hold her in place. "Be warned, neither her, nor the young man who stays at her side, have willingly said a word. They could be staying silent for any number of reasons, not the least of which is anger towards those who were supposed to protect them." Mandy's insightful comments served to remind Ruin there was more to patching people up than bandages. But Mandy wasn't quite finished with Charity. "How did they take your girl?"

Charity handled the question with better grace than Ruin anticipated. "I was out of town when it happened. I got back just after her family found her gone. They were frantic and desperate, so they reached out to me for help. When I retraced Tabby's movements, and found she left that morning to go to studies but never made it to class." Charity shifted in her chair, then winced, and absently adjusting her injured shoulder. "When questioned, her friends said they saw her talking to a guy. Not one they recognized, but they didn't think anything of it."

She shook her head, her exasperation obvious. "Kids being who they are, they saw Tabby talking, nothing overtly threatening happening, and shrugged it off. Tabby is known for being the type to help anyone in need, so if someone stopped to ask for directions, she wouldn't blink twice before offering help." She held Mandy's gaze. "This time, someone took advantage of that sweet spirit."

Mandy was quiet for a few moments and studied Charity intently. Ruin wondered what she saw because Charity wasn't giving much away. Finally, Mandy asked, "If her parents are so worried, why are you here and not them?"

When something too quick to catch slipped through Charity's gaze just before her lashes dropped veiling her eyes, Ruin's instincts woke. "My skills are better suited to tracking down a missing girl." Those long lashes lifted, revealing a steady and clear gaze.

Suddenly, the front door slammed open, sending dust mote-filled light to spill across the room. "Doc, you in here?" A dark-haired teen stepped inside, only to come to an awkward halt, his face turning beet red as the four adults turned to him. "Um, sorry?" He dragged a faded baseball cap from his head, releasing an influx of dark curls, and then proceeded to wring the cap into a twist of material.

The fumbling teen brought a welcoming smile to Mandy's face and chased away the shadows. "What do you need, Zane?"

The teen swallowed, his voice squeaking with nerves before settling down. "I was passin' by your place, and Liza asked me to remind you to stop by Crusty's to pick up her order."

"Thanks, Zane. I'd forgotten I promised to do that."

Zane dipped his head in a jerky nod, spun on a heel, and darted back out the door. Mandy turned to Charity, all traces of the warmth aimed at the teen gone, replaced by a core of determination. "The children don't react well to strangers." When she started to rise, Worth inched back, giving her room to slide her chair out and stand.

From his position, Ruin caught the subtle brush of Worth's hand on Mandy's spine as she brushed crumbs from her pants. The touch acted like a silent conversation because Mandy turned to him. Worth dipped his chin and Mandy's jaw firmed, but she blew out a breath and addressed Charity. "You're welcome to come and see if your Tabby is my redhead."

Next to Ruin, Charity stood, the scrape of wood over wood sounding. "Thank you."

"Don't thank me," Mandy warned. "The only reason I'm allowing you to see the children is because you helped bring Simon home." She moved around the table. "Plus, I won't be responsible for keeping those babies from their families."

As Mandy headed for the door, Charity bid Worth a soft goodbye. Ruin stood, then trailed Charity as she followed Mandy, who held the front door open, waiting for the two of them.

When Charity got closer, Mandy stepped in front of her, and brought the younger woman to a halt. "I'm not one to ignore my gut, especially when it comes to those in my care, so fair warning, Charity. You showing up on the heels of trouble doesn't reassure me of your intentions."

Standing behind her, Ruin waited for Charity's reaction. He expected her defenses to slam into place. Instead, she barely blinked at Mandy's comment. "My first priority is to find Tabby, not to court trouble."

Her dry response managed to get Mandy's lips to twitch, but it did nothing more to ease her formidable mask. "Courting it or not, don't invite it near those children."

thirteen

Warning delivered, Mandy led Ruin and Charity to a nearby bakery. She disappeared inside and returned a few minutes later with the promised delivery in hand. Silence accompanied the trio for the remainder of their walk to the doctor's house. With each step, Charity's nerves wound tighter and tighter. Anticipation of finally finding Tabby warred with the looming nightmares that lay in the shattered children under Mandy's care.

Close to fifteen minutes later, Charity entered the well-tended front yard of a sprawling ranch style home with a flat roof that doubled as a flourishing garden. Sitting among the pruned bushes off to the right was an updated rain collection system paired with an older cistern. To the left, beyond the storage area, the long blades of the wind turbine turned in slow, quiet circles as it provided power for the soft lights starting to glow in the late afternoon dusk.

It wasn't the only home in the neighborhood reliant on natural power. Other turbine blades rose like graceful herons between trees and flat, garden roofs. If Pebble Creek followed the same pattern of most rural communities, each home was served by similar arrangements for their water and power.

After the Collapse, rural areas learned to use what was at hand and turned to more natural sources for energy. Something the urban populations could now benefit from. Out here, no one could afford to rely on the rare fossil fuels used in the cities, because delivery, if it came at all, was spotty at best.

Mandy climbed the trio of stone steps, crossed the porch, and stopped with her hand on the doorknob. She half turned to Charity and Ruin, the bag from Crusty's bouncing against her hip. "Chances are Liza has the girls out back, in the yard. Ruin, you should stay inside."

At Mandy's implication, Charity's heart winced. No matter how much shit she saw, it made her sick to think of how much damage had been done for just the sight of a male to threaten these fragile souls.

Ruin's face darkened with grim understanding as he stopped at the foot of the steps. "You sure my being inside won't hurt things? I can always wait here."

The fact he was in tune enough to ask that question softened the edges of Charity's lingering resentment. Mandy worried her lower lip as she pondered his question. "Just stay at the table and try not to glare at anyone." Her admonishment earned a faint grin, that quickly disappeared. The doc turned to the door and disappeared inside, leaving them to follow.

Ruin waved her forward. Charity tucked her nervous anticipation away and steeled herself for possible disappointment. She followed Mandy through a simple, but comfortable, living room and into a huge, light-drenched kitchen where n influx of light funneled through the skylights. The wide entryway framed a deck that led to an expansive backyard. A refinished barn door hung next to the opening on a sliding system that made it easier to move the heavy door open or closed.

"Liza, I'm home with visitors." Mandy bypassed the battered table with eight spindle- backed chairs and headed to the counter and sink just to the side of the wide doorway.

"We're out back." When the woman who belonged to the voice stepped through the wide entryway, Charity was stunned by the young, dark-haired, delicate, and very much pregnant, Liza, who tucked a pair of garden gloves into her back pocket.

Charity came to a stop by the quietly humming refrigerator that sat just inside the kitchen. Ruin slipped around her and took a seat at the table, as far from the open doorway as possible.

Liza's smile was open and real as she nodded at Ruin and Charity before wrapping Mandy in a hug. "Did you get my bread?"

Mandy returned the affectionate squeeze and stepped back. "Yep, Zane found me. I'm guessing it's for Cody?" She handed over the Crusty's bag.

Liza took it and then bussed Mandy's cheek. "Of course, it is. He and Kyle love this stuff, and I promised them spaghetti and garlic bread." She took the bag to the large center island, opened a lower cabinet, and brought out a basket. As she began splitting up the bread, she kept talking. "Besides, Cody's been riding herd on Kyle for me for the last couple of days. I think that deserves a reward."

Mandy propped a hip against the cabinets by the sink. "So long as you don't overdo things."

Liza laughed, and the sound of pure joy unexpectedly charmed Charity. "I'm fine, Mandy." She rubbed gentle circles over her extended belly. "Baby and I are doing just fine. Besides we have a couple months yet before my toes disappear." She leaned against the counter's edge and eyed Ruin as he settled in at the table. "Ruin, right?"

"Yes, ma'am." Since Liza managed to rile Charity's protective streak, she was unsurprised by Ruin's switch from snarly and gruff to gentle and charming.

Liza's lips twitched. "Ma'am is for those much, much older than me. It's just Liza." Her gaze drifted to Charity. "You must be new."

"I am." Charity stepped forward and extended her hand to the young woman. "I'm a friend of Boden's."

Liza's mouth gaped open comically as she grasped Charity's hand in a firm grip, and she gave a dramatic gasp. "Boden has friends?"

Charity laughed, then raised a finger to her lips. "Shh, don't go telling anyone."

Mandy touched Liza on the shoulder even as her attention shifted to the backyard. "Are the kids outside?"

The bright humor in Liza's face dimmed as a somber awareness set in. "They are. Laura spoke today, not much, but enough to give me some hope." She followed Mandy's gaze.

From her position by the refrigerator, Charity couldn't see what, or who, they were watching.

"The other two aren't talking much and still refuse to give me their names." Liza rubbed her belly again and from the frown creasing her brow, Charity wondered if the action was Liza's comfort tool. "Our sleeping beauty is still dreaming."

Mandy went to the door leading to the backyard and propped a shoulder against the frame. "We take our wins where we can, and today you got four of them outside. That definitely goes in the win column."

Liza turned back to Charity. "Since Mandy dragged you home, I'm guessing you're here to see the kids?"

Once again, Charity explained her presence, but unlike with Mandy and Ruin, Liza barely batted an eyelash. Instead, there was no missing her spark of excitement as she grabbed Charity's hand and all but dragged her out the door. "Well, then, let's head out and introduce you. Maybe we'll be able to get one of these darlings back to their family."

They crossed the deck and headed into the yard. Well-established trees with foliage thick enough to provide a natural privacy barrier ringed the backyard. Plants in various colors exploded in a charming display of spring, and sitting areas were tucked away. One of which was half-hidden in shadows and was currently occupied by a young, dark-haired boy. He stood guard over a brunette in a pretty, floral shift, her thin arms wrapped around drawn up knobby knees, her chin resting on top, her gaze focused on the two similarly dressed girls currently kneeling among the flowers.

Sunlight brushed familiar burnished copper curls of one of the kneeling girls and Charity's heart lodged in her throat. For a moment, she fought back the tears that pressed hot and hard, and tried to speak around the weight settling on her chest. Her first attempt came out in a puff of air that Liza ignored as she pulled Charity along.

Only when they drew close did Liza finally slow, and let Charity go, before calling out softly, "Hey, kids."

Four pairs of eyes turned in their direction. It hurt to see the depth of fear and wariness painting their thin faces, but it was the one who paled and jerkily got to her feet that had Charity's legs turning to water, until she slowly sank to her knees, unable to stand.

"Aunt Char?"

It was barely a sound, but Charity heard it. "Tabby baby." Her voice was husky but audible.

As if flung forward, Tabby barreled towards her.

Charity caught the girl, holding the small, shaking body tight, her face pressed into the beloved copper curls. "Oh, Tabby love, we were so scared."

"I'm sorry," the little girl sobbed, her arms winding around Charity's neck in a stranglehold.

Without letting her go, Charity shifted until she was sitting on the ground with Tabby cradled in her arms. "Nothing to be sorry about, baby girl."

Tabby turned her head until her nose was buried next to Charity's ear and whispered, "Mom's going to kill me."

Charity closed her eyes and concentrated on breathing through the massive ache in her chest. She set her hands on either side of Tabby's head and carefully pulled the girl's face away until she could see the girl's green eyes. It was hard to witness the shadows slipping into what once shone with innocence.

Charity brushed her thumb over an escaping tear and rested her forehead against Tabby's. "Your mom may smother you with kisses, but she won't kill you. She's worried sick. We all were."

Tears welled as Tabby burrowed back in and clung like a monkey, her sobs, heartbreakingly quiet, rattled her entire frame. Liza gathered the remaining children and led them back inside, giving them privacy for their reunion.

Charity sat there, arms tight, rocking the little girl and making nonsensical comforting noises, all the while trying not to think about what Tabby endured. She compulsively traced the edges of the yellowing bruises marring the girl's arms, wanting to erase the signs of abuse.

The storm of weeping slowly passed, and Charity's shirt was left damp with spent tears. As the shadows around them deepened, Tabby lay in her arms, hands locked on Charity's arms, her eyes and nose red. Charity's rage and heartache fought for dominance and drowned her initial relief under her hardening determination.

The time for secrets was passed, and any doubts she harbored about the outcome of her upcoming phone call were shattered. She couldn't shake the haunting image of the four children's disquieting blankness when she first saw them. The stark evidence of what they endured triggered a visceral rage that would only be appeased when the ones who caused it lay at her feet, castrated and bleeding out.

At some point, Ruin slipped onto a nearby bench, a move Charity caught even though Tabby remained oblivious. With the other kids in the house, Charity's practical side understood his presence, but her protective side wanted to snap at him to leave. Perhaps it was best he stayed because it would be hard enough to get Tabby to share her story.

The sun dipped behind the horizon, and the small lights placed throughout the garden flickered to life when Tabby's breathing finally slowed and evened out. Charity ran a gentle hand through the soft curls, pressed a kiss into the top of her head, and then rested her cheek against the top of Tabby's head. "Tabby, baby, I need you to tell me what happened."

The young girl stiffened in silent protest. Charity held tight to her patience and continued her slow strokes, deliberately keeping her breathing steady, as she silently encouraged the child to speak. When Tabby finally spoke, her voice was shaky and barely audible, but little by little she started to share.

Much like Charity suspected, Tabby had fallen prey to the boy in need story. He introduced himself as Sean, new to town and lost. Tabby tried to be smart about it and agreed only to walk to a nearby shop in search of an adult that could help direct him. She thought if they stayed out in the open, nothing would happen. Not only did Sean have other ideas, but he wasn't working alone. It didn't take much for the two males to overpower Tabby, drug her, and then hit the road before anyone knew what had happened.

Tabby wasn't sure how long she was out, but when she woke, she was in a cage with three other girls and a boy. At first, they were held in the basement of a building, but then they were chained, gagged, locked in a box with air holes and moved.

"I fought, Aunt Charity." A fierce pride underscored Tabby's words. "I used the tricks you showed me, but—" her burst of pride faded, replaced by fear, "—I couldn't win."

Charity closed her eyes and fought not to react to the emotions in Tabby's voice. When she opened them, she had to clear her throat before saying, "Sometimes, sweetie, you fight not because you can win, but to let them know they won't break you."

Thin fingers curled into the back of Charity's t-shirt and griped it tight. "It didn't stop them."

Fury morphed into icy resolve, and Charity struggled to keep her voice even. "Tabby, I have to ask you something." Her stomach knotted as she wondered how to ask this beautiful child if she was raped. Somehow, she was able to force out the words, "Did they hurt you?"

She wasn't ready for Tabby's reaction. The girl unwound her arms and pushed back until she sat upright in Charity's lap. She lifted her tear-stained face until they faced each other. It was Tabby who held her gaze as she solemnly shook her head. "Not me, not like that," she choked out, tears welling even as her chin firmed. "They beat the crap out of me, and the others. Like they were bored or something. But the night before we were found ..." Her slender shoulders hunched, and her burst of bravery leaked away.

Fear at what would come next had Charity gathering her close.

Tabby collapsed into Charity's tight hold, her voice muffled. "The night before they were drinking. An argument broke out between Sean and one of the others. Geezer, the old guy, complained about how they weren't allowed any fun, but since no one was here, it wasn't like anyone would know. Sean warned him he'd know, so to stop being a dick. They fought while the others watched." The fact that normally reserved Tabby didn't even flinch repeating the crude word was yet another indicator of crushed innocence. The girl continued, "I think they were making bets."

Since Raiders were unconscionable assholes, it was a safe assumption.

Unaware of Charity's dark thoughts, Tabby kept talking. "When Geezer was done with Sean, he came after us. Katori, Katie, and me knew what was coming. We tried to protect the younger girls." The words started to fall fast and furious as if she was afraid to stop. "Geezer opened the door and leaned in. Katori, Katie, and me went after him at the same time. It was hard cuz of the chains, but we couldn't let him near the others. They knocked Katori out first, but Katie and me, we kept fighting."

Charity tightened her hold as the renewed shudders shook the girl and whispered, "You did good, baby, trying to keep them safe. That was brave, so brave of you."

Tabby turned her face against Charity. Over her head, Charity caught sight of Ruin and watched a gamut of emotions run through his face. Against her chest, she felt Tabby say something, but couldn't make it out. "What was that sweet pea?"

"I couldn't save Katie." The aching pain in Tabby's wail raked lasting wounds in Charity's soul. Images of what this child, who held a special spot in her heart, endured was killing her. Tabby's guilt spilled out as if lancing a festering wound. "Geezer dragged her out. One of the others dragged me out. They m-m-made me watch while they... hu ... hu—"

"Enough, Tabby." It took considerable effort to keep her voice from breaking, but somehow Charity managed. No way would she make Tabby relive the nightmarish details that would follow her for years, neither could she let Tabby drown in unnecessary guilt. She gently nudged Tabby until she was sitting up, and then held her gaze. This was too important to dare any misunderstanding.

Charity steeled her battered heart against the ravaged face and kept her voice firm. "You fought. You kept the younger girls as safe as you could. You and Katori and Katie did your best against full grown men who were bigger and stronger than you. It is not your fault that they hurt Katie."

"But—"

"No buts, Tabby." It sucked that Tabby had to learn this lesson at all, much less now. Yet no way could Charity live with herself if she didn't take this chance to erase the lingering touch of evil that threatened to dim Tabby's bright, brave spirit. "Even if you weren't chained, can you honestly tell me you could take out Geezer?" Tabby's lips thinned in a mutinous line, and the flash of stubbornness gave Charity a measure of reassurance. Still, she didn't relent. "What was the first thing I taught you about fighting those who are bigger and meaner?"

"Fight dirty."

She nodded. "What else did I tell you?"

Tabby's hands fisted in her lap, but she begrudgingly answered, "You won't always win, just make them hurt."

"Did you hurt them?"

"Not enough."

"Sometimes you can't ever hurt them enough."

"You could."

Tabby's obvious disillusionment made Charity want to rage. "Not in that situation." *Time for some cold, hard truths.* "The best I could do in the same situation is exactly what you did. Cause enough hurt to make them reconsider how much pain they wanted to endure before they came at me."

"They didn't hurt me!" Unprepared for Tabby's unbridled fury, Charity barely managed to dodge a wildly flailing hand. Child-size fists pummeled her chest and shoulders. It was as if

Charity's words had smashed through the door holding the girl's nightmare back. "They didn't hurt me. They hurt Katie. Nothing I did made them stop!" Tabby's voice rose until she was screaming, "Nothing!"

Charity weathered the storm, helpless to do anything but let the girl rage. If she could bring the Raiders back to life, she would. Then she'd take her time skinning them, inch by inch, until their vocal chords broke under their screams, exactly the way her heart was breaking under Tabby's.

Finally, the blows slowed to a stop and Tabby sat in Charity's lap, exhausted, her hands lying in her lap, her face red and tear-stained, and her eyes dull. "It should've been me."

Arguing with the child would gain nothing because Tabby was in no shape to hear her, but Charity had to try. She cupped Tabby's face and held her gaze. "Why?" When Tabby tried to look away, Charity held fast. "Why do you think it should've been you?"

Long, drenched lashes drifted down, then rose, and deep under the emotional fallout was an ember of anger. "Because Geezer said so."

Charity frowned. "I don't understand."

Tabby covered Charity's hands with her own, her ragged nails digging into Charity's skin as she leaned in, and with a furious hiss spat, "Geezer said the best way to f-f-f-fuck with Lilith was to f-f-f- fuck her daughter."

fourteen

The young girl's words echoed through Ruin and overrode his simmering frustration as he waited for Charity. He stood on Mandy's porch, his shoulder braced against one of the railing posts, and his arms crossed against his chest, as he stared unseeing at the star-studded sky.

Tabby was Lilith's daughter.

He hadn't seen that coming. The girl's parentage, or at least the maternal half of it, explained not only why behind the Raiders' choice to attack so close to home, but why Charity was so damn tight-lipped about who initially hired her. Not only was Charity the Rocky Mountain queen's damn 'Hound, but despite Charity's earlier evasive denials, there was the added joy of a family connection.

Son of a bitch, could things get any more convoluted?

Scratch that, best he not put that out in the universe to be answered.

Hard as it was to believe, it appeared the indomitable Lilith had a weakness, one she managed to keep buried for years. Based on his limited interactions with her, he was convinced such things as mercy, or a mothering nature, would be foreign concepts. *Guess he was wrong.* Absently he wondered if the father figure was around somewhere, or if Lilith had ensured the DNA supplier was also buried six feet under.

Once the existence of Lilith's daughter became public knowledge—because it was now a question of when, not if—the resulting shockwaves would curl through the ever-changing currents of power and shift the tides. And it wouldn't take long for the predators to rise to surface.

Hell, they were already circling. It didn't matter why Reznik hired the Raiders, only that he knew to target Tabitha. How had they known was the more disturbing question. Especially if Charity was to be believed and Reznik sat low on the power totem pole.

Images of the girl's tear-stained face haunted him, and pity welled. This fiasco marked the beginning of an unending nightmare for Tabitha. Those who lusted after Lilith's power would fight to use the one tool guaranteed to bring the most ruthless woman on the west coast to her knees. And it would, because if Tabitha didn't matter to her mother, her existence wouldn't be such a well-guarded secret or require the protection of a 'Hound.

Behind him a door opened, then closed, and that uncanny sixth sense he had whenever she was around kicked in with a vengeance, as he felt her come up behind him.

Think of the devil.

He didn't turn around, but he could stop his spine from straightening. Logic whispered the why Charity kept her connection to Lilith and Tabby quiet, but it didn't soothe his growing frustration.

She moved to the other side of the steps and stayed silent. He let the quiet stand because he wasn't sure what would come out of his mouth first—an accusation or questions he probably shouldn't ask.

"Go ahead, Ruin." There was a steely resignation in her voice, as if her time with Tabitha had worn away her earlier optimistic sheen and stripped her to grim practicality.

He tried not to think about how much the girl's tears and brutal retelling managed to scrape raw his hidden emotional spots, because that led to wondering how much damage it had done to Charity. *And why that should concern him remained a mystery.*

Without turning from his observance of the starry panoramic, he asked, "With what?"

Her sigh was soft, but there. "Fine. We'll do it your way, then." Her voice hardened. "Yes, she really is Lilith's daughter. No, she's not my actual niece, but I've known her since she was born. Yes, I lied to you about who sent me. No, I'm not going to apologize for keeping quiet about who hired me. Yes, I really came here for Crane's help. No, I didn't expect to walk into a blood bath. No, I didn't know you'd show up, any more than I knew the Raiders would take Simon, kill Crane, or turn out to be behind Tabby's kidnapping." She took a breath. "Did that cover everything?"

Stunned by finally getting some straight answers, it took him a moment to respond. "Nope." On that, he turned to face her. "But it's a good start."

She stared over the front yard as she leaned against the opposite support post, her arms folded across her chest, and her ankles crossed. Despite the soft porch light, she was difficult to read, and whatever was going on in her tricky head remained well hidden.

Considering who she was, he expected the emotionless mask she currently wore was more natural than anything she'd shown so far. Since she seemed to be in a talkative mood, he pushed for more. "You didn't wait for your phone call before sharing. Why?"

"What?" Her knee-jerk question was asked as she shifted

her gaze to his, lines creasing her forehead as she tried to decipher his hidden intent.

Since there wasn't one, she was bound for disappointment. He didn't repeat himself, simply waited.

Comprehension dawned, and she sighed before answering,
"Secrets have their place, but right now someone's playing a
dangerous game. If it's Reznik, we're better off pooling
resources to figure out his end game than trying to defend a
solitary position from multiple sides. Even Lilith can follow
that logic." She muttered the last part as if answering some
unseen naysayer.

"Multiple sides, uh? Thought you believed Reznik didn't
have the resources to pull off a power grab. You changing your
mind?"

She shrugged. "Hard to argue with the evidence."

He arched an eyebrow in silent query.

"Crane's death and the kidnappings," She explained
before cocking her head, a tell he was starting to recognize.
"Unless you think that was a coincidence?"

"Not any more than Tabitha being targeted," he shot
back. When she winced, he narrowed his gaze and snapped,
"What?"

Her shoulders lifted, and regret shimmered behind her
stubborn resolved. "Tabby wasn't the only one targeted."

Through sheer force of will he kept a tight hold on his
temper. "Explain."

"The boy, back at Mandy's? His name is Katori. He
belongs to Istaqa, the Southwest leader of the Free People."

Her revelation dropped and he lost it. "Oh, for fuck's sake,
Charity!" *What other potentially explosive secrets was the
woman keeping?*

Every time she gave him another piece, worry twisted his
gut. Each one was another layer of shit guaranteed to put the
Vultures' smack dab in the middle of the emerging political

cesspool, and potentially turning their lives to hell. Holding Pebble Creek together until Simon was back on his feet, was going to be rough enough, but this? Yeah, it was time to take this mess to Reaper.

Ruin closed his eyes in resignation. *Dammit, Reaper was going to have a fucking field day with Charity.* "You need to tell Reaper everything." He opened his eyes and pinned her in place with a glare. "And I mean fucking everything, Charity."

At his reprimand her eyes narrowed, and temper crawled under her cheeks as her mouth opened, likely to let loose a stinging remark.

"You said it yourself," he cut her off. "Someone is playing a dangerous game. He's going to be plenty pissed as is, don't add fuel to the fire by hiding shit."

"Unlike you, I'm not fond of games when lives of those I care about are at stake."

He stiffened as her barb, justified or not, found its mark.

She winced and lifted her hand only to drop it back to her side and curl it into a fist. "Dammit, that was bitchy of me, Ruin. I'm sorry."

He didn't think she used that word often. That she chose to do so now, had him offering a long overdue apology of his own. "The Raiders have a meet set in Kennewick."

She didn't hesitate before she said, "Don't think for a moment you're heading out by your lonesome. I'm going with you."

Still illogically pissed at her, he sniped, "Plan on carving your way through the Raiders until one of them squeals?"

She barely batted an eyelash and answered, "I have no intentions of letting you have all the fun. I'll be right next to you, knife in hand, taking my pound, or five, of flesh."

God, why did he find that ruthless streak a turn-on? He never realized what a glutton for punishment he was, or maybe it all depended on who was handing out the punishment. In the end it didn't matter, because only one person would make that call, and it wouldn't be either of them. "Only if Reaper allows it."

That got a low laugh. "Allows it?" She shook her head, eyes hard, and lips curved without amusement. "Reaper might hold your leash, but he doesn't hold mine."

He arched an eyebrow. "Maybe not, but I'm guessing Lilith's grip is just as tight."

Undaunted, she shrugged. "Considering the damage done to her daughter, do you really think anyone is going to convince Lilith to pull me off this hunt?"

No, not even Reaper would be able to keep Charity away from this now. Ruin pushed off the post and headed down the stairs, leaving her to follow. "Lilith's a long damn ways away, so it doesn't matter what you or I think. Only matters what Reaper thinks."

AFTER HER SHORT and decidedly private call to Lilith, Ruin took her back to Grave's Hall. Walt directed them to the isolated back room for the Vultures impromptu meeting. Vex was stretched out between two chairs, her boots on one, her ass on another, while Havoc took his customary post by the door, probably to ensure a quick escape if things got messy. Despite the tight confines, Reaper paced through the handful of mismatched chairs and a couple of tables as Charity brought everyone up to date on the situation with Tabitha and Katori.

In the stunned silence that followed Charity's big reveal, Reaper growled, "A daughter?"

As Charity faced the Vultures' obviously infuriated leader, Ruin stayed at her side in a silent show of support. He was reluctantly impressed with her unruffled composure because when Reaper was like this, most people cowered. Not Charity. She stood there, chin raised, hands on her hips, and wisely held her tongue.

Reaper continued to pace as he shot dark looks in Charity's direction. "What the hell are we supposed to do with Lilith's daughter?"

Funny, that wasn't the question Ruin expected. His was more along the lines of how the hell had Reznik known about Tabitha in the first place.

"The only thing Lilith asked was that you let Tabitha stay with Mandy until someone comes to pick the girl up." Charity's response was cool, crisp, and steady as if she wasn't staring down the biggest predator in the room.

Reaper prowled across the room and stopped directly in front of Charity, so close she was forced to crane her neck to hold his gaze. He leaned in and snarled, "Which 'someone' is her frickin' majesty sending?"

With her head craned back, it was easy to catch the movement of her throat as she swallowed. "Your guess is as good as mine."

"How come you're not taking the kid back?" The question was Vex's. Despite her casual pose, tiny indicators in the barely-there lines around her eyes, the hint of white around her lips, the constant flexing of her fingers revealed her tension. His sister was strung tighter than a bow, and his gut whispered there was more behind it than the current situation. But that was a problem for later. Right now, he had more than enough to handle, thank you very much.

Charity rocked back on her heels, forcing a few more inches between her and Reaper. Then she peered around him so she could see the other woman. "Because my talents are better utilized going after the one who sicced the Raiders on the kids, than providing protection for the journey home."

"She wants you to hunt Reznik." Havoc's voice rumbled through the room.

Charity gave the big man a nod. "Yep, she wants me to hunt."

Ruin noticed her avoidance of using Reznik's name, and he wondered if it was a deliberate omission or simple agreement?

"And you follow her orders without question." Reaper's comment cut through Ruin's musings and regained Charity's attention.

A flash of sympathy sparked in Ruin. It wasn't easy holding steady under a firing squad inquisition.

"Not always." Charity's answer surprised them all, but she wasn't done. "However, in this particular instance, yeah, I'm going to follow orders."

Vex sat up, dropped a foot to the floor, and zeroed in on Charity. "Got an appetite for revenge, Blondie?"

Charity met Vex's gaze. "This isn't about revenge. This is all about vengeance."

Vex smiled, not in amusement, but more a bearing of teeth. "There's a difference?"

"It's small." Charity held up her thumb and forefinger separated by the tiniest of distances. "Very small."

"Revenge," Ruin cut in. "Is to exact punishment for a wrong done to another."

Charity looked at him. "Vengeance is to inflict hurt and humiliation on one who has harmed another. Which do you think I prefer for Tabby?"

"Ohh, ohh, I know," Vex interrupted, waving her arm in the air as she got to her feet, waltzed over to Charity, and threw her arm around the shorter woman's shoulders. "Sweet, bloody vengeance."

Charity met Vex's crazed grin with one of her own and

bumped her hip against Vex's. "Sweet, bloody, *everlasting* vengeance actually."

Reaper eyed them both, his arms folded across his chest. "You two done with your girly bonding moment?"

Ruin dropped his gaze and tried to hide his wince at the bigger man's massive misstep. *You'd think after all these years, the man would know better.*

Sure enough, Vex's scuffed boots left Charity's side and moved to stop toe to toe to Reaper's. "Aww, Reapy-baby," her voice was syrupy sweet. "Are you mad that we're not properly cowed by your manly display of temper and alphaholeness?"

"Shit, Vex," Ruin muttered, not all surprised when she ignored his warning and continued to needle Reaper.

"Don't worry, we promise to clasp our hands in proper feminine amazement once you pull your head ou—"

Ruin wrapped one arm around his sister's waist and slapped his other hand over her mouth, cutting off the rest of her sentence as he wasn't keen on becoming an only child. "Enough, Vex." He dragged her back to her chair and forced her to sit back down. Then he pointed a finger at her, almost touching her nose, and snapped, "Stay put."

Familiar amber eyes fired, and her mouth opened.

"Shut it, sis." *God, her childish tantrums drove him nuts.* It didn't matter that he understood the whys, she was a grown-ass woman who knew better. "Not the right place. Not the right time." He held her furious gaze and waited her out.

It didn't take long. Her mouth closed, and her lips pressed into a mutinous line. She shifted her attention to Reaper, and Ruin was close enough to catch her flicker of remorse as she met their leader's gaze, then looked away.

Convinced Vex would zip it, he turned back to Reaper and Charity, highly aware of the uncomfortable tension now filling the room.

"Vex, girl," Reaper's voice was a low whip of sound. "One of these days, your mouth is going to get you killed."

"Likes to tempt death," Havoc added his pithy wisdom.

Vex stuck her tongue out at him but stayed silent.

Reaper ignored the byplay and focused once more on Charity and reset the conversation. "Lilith trusts you enough to send you out after her kid. Says something since she doesn't trust anyone."

That got a genuine smile from Charity, and she held up her right hand, palm out. "I swear on all that's holy, I am not any blood relation to Lilith."

"Thank god." Reaper waved her to a chair. "Sit." He ran a hand through his hair, crossed to one of the cushioned chairs, and dropped into it.

Charity took a seat and Ruin choose to keep his spot between the two and sat on one of the tables. He didn't give a damn what the silent move indicated. Reaper had his damn loyalty, but whether she admitted it or not, Charity needed someone on her side. Since she saved Simon, he owed her. Hell, all the Vultures owed her.

Reaper drummed his fingers against the armrest as the tick of a battered clock filled the quiet. Finally, he said, "You ready to put your cards on the table, 'Hound?"

Charity was no one's fool, and her nod was cautious.

"Good." The big man curled his hand into a fist, dropped it to his knee, and got down to it. "First, did Lilith send you to take out Crane?"

"No." Her answer was granite but based on the tiny frown lines in her forehead and the stutter tap of a finger against her knee, there was more behind her short answer.

Ever observant, Reaper demanded, "Give me a reason to believe you."

Her finger stilled. "Lilith had no reason to eliminate Crane because he was her information pipeline to what was happening in Michael's territory.'

"Doesn't mean much," Reaper said, clearly unimpressed. "Crane could just as easily have been feeding Michael the same on her."

Charity was shaking her head before he finished. "Not this time." She leaned forward and braced her arms on her knees. "You know that argument Crane and Michael got into about a year back?"

Ruin stiffened as Reaper's expression remained studiously blank. *How the hell did she know about that?*

Charity smirked, not fooled one bit by Reaper's deliberate non-reaction. "Right. While the details remain sketchy, whatever went down put a chink in their friendship."

"Working relationship," Reaper clarified.

"Working relationship," Charity repeated without breaking eye contact. "When Lilith caught wind, she decided to see if Crane was amenable to a new working relationship."

"And he agreed." It was hard to tell if Reaper, the cagey bastard, was asking or telling.

Charity nodded. "When Lilith got screwed in a weapons transaction six months ago after a seller tried to pass off junk as the real deal, she reached out to Crane with questions. Him being a new partner and all."

Sounded legit to Ruin. Crane oversaw most of the major trade arrangements and a transaction with Lilith would definitely count as a big-time arrangement. Screwing up a deal like that would garner serious questions.

"Unfortunately, Crane was unaware of the sale, nor had he heard of anyone interested in acquiring those weapons." Charity smirked. "But after a little judicious questioning, the seller admitted another unknown party contacted him, offered double the pay, and left with the weapons meant for Lilith."

"Bet that pissed her right off," Ruin said.

Charity grimaced. "Just a bit. Wasn't much left of the seller when she was done. Kind of a waste though because a couple months later it happened again. This time with a medical shipment."

Reaper shrugged. "Shit happens."

"Maybe, but Lilith's not one to wait for coincidence to make an appearance."

"So, she sent you out to find out if this was just bad timing or something altogether else?" Reaper pressed.

She nodded.

His gaze narrowed. "You went looking at Crane."

"He was the newest factor in the whole situation." She rubbed her chin. "So yeah, initially I took a serious look. But when I found a string of similar situations ranging from the Rockies all the way down to Houston, I went to ask him if he was encountering the same problem." She held Reaper's gaze. "He was."

"The raids on the routes." Vex shared a look with Ruin.

"Bet that was the first move," Ruin said. It was the string of botched deliveries that drove Simon and Crane to pull in the Vultures.

Reaper ignored the twins' side conversation and focused on Charity. "When you realized Crane was dealing with the same shit as Lilith, you crossed him off your list?"

She squirmed a bit and sat back. "Actually, I crossed him off fairly early, after I found out the targeted shipments shared a common trait."

"The shipments originated from Michael's territory." Reaper to put the pieces together quickly. "Let me guess," scorn edged his voice, "Lilith blamed Michael for her troubles."

"Right." A pained expression twisted Charity's face. "There's no love lost between Lilith and Michael."

That brought a harsh bark of laughter from Reaper.

"There is no one on this earth that Lilith hates more than Michael."

Charity winced, and then gallantly pushed on. "She wanted to know if Michael was facing the same challenges or if he was the one behind it, so she sent me to ask Crane."

Reaper obviously caught something in her expression that Ruin missed because he pushed, "Was he?"

She shrugged. "Don't know. Before I could hit the road, two things happened." She glanced at Ruin before continuing. "Lilith got an urgent message from Istaqa. He sent a picture of Katori with a request to send word if he was spotted. Then Tabby was taken."

A spark of relief hit Ruin when she took his advice to heart about giving Reaper everything.

"Istaqa prefers keeping his business within his borders." Havoc's distinctive rumble filled the spaces left behind Charity's answer. "Why is he reaching out to Lilith?"

"He was a parent with a missing child?" She rubbed her arm, just below the bandage, a small frown furrowed on her forehead. "I think he was desperate."

A pensive shadow crossed Havoc's harsh features, but he stayed silent.

Charity took it as a cue to keep sharing. "I wasn't expecting to find him here. Hell, I wasn't expecting to find a trail of missing kids, either. But Lilith felt that Tabby's disappearance hitting so close on the heels of the delivery fiasco was too big to be a coincidence. She just couldn't figure out why. Still, her biggest concern was Tabby, and that became my primary focus. When Tabby's trail went north, it seemed best to combine both hunts. I was hoping to touch base with Crane, see if he heard anything about Tabby's kidnapping, but we all know how that turned out."

Considering her initial dismissive take on Reznik's ability to marshal the necessary resources to pull off a coup, Ruin decided to re-test her conviction. "The kids' kidnappings, the Raiders' attack on Crane and the shipments. You're thinking they're all part of the same grand scheme?"

She didn't miss his skepticism and color rode high along her cheeks, but her voice remained steady. "Either Reznik is working on his own, or he's being played by someone we don't even know about. His aren't the only greedy hands looking to take what isn't theirs."

At her answer, something coiled tight in Ruin's chest loosened.

Reaper studied Charity, his mental wheels no doubt spinning at high speed. Eventually, he spoke. "If I send you after the Raiders with Ruin, you going to be focused on vengeance or power games?"

"Vengeance." Her answer was sure.

Doubt lingered in his gaze. "You admit to being Lilith's 'Hound. A dog can't serve two masters."

Ruin didn't miss Charity's minuscule jerk when Reaper's scorn hit her head on, but he was puzzled by Reaper's harsher than normal approach. *Granted, tact wasn't in the big man's vocabulary, but was he egging Charity to go for his throat?* He opened his mouth, only to stop when Vex gave a sharp shake of her head.

Instead of snarling back as expected, Charity gave an inelegant snort. "Seriously? That's the best you can do? Like I haven't heard that one before." She tilted her head to the side. "Guess I should be grateful you refrained from calling me a bitch."

Ruin silently applauded her response.

Reaper's lips curled up, but it was hard to tell if it was a smile or a sneer. "Give it time, I'm sure I'll get to it."

"Probably," she muttered.

All faint traces of humor disappeared, and Reaper's expression returned to his typical glower. "What guarantee do

I have you won't stab my man in the back, or sell his ass out if it got you closer to the information Lilith wants?"

"You don't, but if I had plans to go after you or yours, there were plenty of opportunities to cut his throat—" she jerked a thumb in Ruin's direction, "—or ensure Simon never made it back down the mountain."

Slightly affronted, Ruin protested, "As if you could."

Charity gave him a sidelong glare before turning her attention back to Reaper. "My focus is making the bastards who hurt Tabby pay. Whatever political or power games are being played can wait."

Reaper rubbed his jaw. "And if I decided you weren't going with Ruin, you'd just go out on your own."

"Not to brag, but tracking is my specialty." She waited a heartbeat, then two. "Look, I'm not sure how I prove I'm not trying to pick you off. Honestly, that's not my type of thing anyway. If Lilith wanted any of you out of the picture, she has other, better options than me for the job."

Reaper's dark gaze sharpened. "Is that job on her to-do list?"

"Not as far as I know," Charity said, then she added, "But then again, I'm no mind reader."

fifteen

After her pow-wow with the Vultures, Ruin escorted Charity, who promised Tabby she would return, back to Mandy's place. There, she spent the night fighting back the girl's demons. Charity waited to tell Tabby she was leaving until she had no choice, and when the time came, it didn't go over well. Once Tabby figured out tears wouldn't change Charity's mind, the girl switched to silent, mutinous anger, and refused to say anything. Charity hated to leave under those circumstances, but her need for retribution rode her hard.

When Ruin pulled his bike up to Mandy's house in the wee hours before sunrise, Charity had her saddlebags packed, and her weapons loaded and stashed. He didn't bother shutting his bike down, but simply waited, silent and grim-faced, for her to fire up her bike. Once her butt hit the seat, he tugged his bandana up over his nose, and without a word, took to the road.

He led her west for hours. One thing the long, arduous bike ride gave her was time to think. She picked through the known pieces, trying to determine if the threat was Reznik or someone bigger and badder. As the sun inched higher, her suspicions that Reznik wasn't working alone solidified. Whether Ruin or the Vultures agreed, she couldn't shake her belief someone was hiding behind the huge ass target Reznik presented. Hell, as arrogant as he was, Reznik was probably convinced it was all his idea, which left him in the perfect fall guy position. Which begged the question—who was pulling his strings?

While Charity knew the last thing Lilith would ever do was put Tabby in the middle, arguing that point with stone-faced Reaper was akin to hitting her head against a wall. If things weren't such a mess right now, Charity would consider that kind of stubborn refusal to listen as an invitation to go digging into secrets probably best left alone. *If* she was still breathing after this, which was an iffy outcome at best as Lilith was convinced it was Michael behind this, maybe she would.

Charity wasn't sold on the Michael angle. Not that she knew him or anything, but Lilith's depth of abhorrence for the west coast leader was a well-known fact. So much so, it worried Charity. If Lilith continued to be blinded by whatever fueled her hatred, it could cause lethal repercussions. While humanity's numbers remained a fraction of what they once were, so long as more than one person breathed the same air, schemes for maintaining and growing power were a guarantee.

Michael and Lilith weren't the only power players who shared this land, they were simply the two biggest targets on this side of the Mississippi. Even Istaqa, Katori's father, played an influential role. As the head of the Southwest tribes, who called themselves the Free People, he controlled the water rights that kept the desert livable.

Strangely, it was the Free People who managed to garner the combined respect of Lilith, Crane, and the Mexican

Cartels. An admirable feat, since water was crucial to all three groups in keeping their territories viable. For the children of two strong leaders to disappear, and then show up together, set off every one of Charity's instincts for trouble.

The answer of who was playing mastermind was up for grabs.

As far as the Vultures' were concerned, it was either Michael or Lilith, and they didn't care who ended up being the puppet master. But, by sending Ruin after the Raiders, the Vultures, who claimed to not want a role in this power game, took their turn at the board and threw the dice. They might not give a shit who their opponent was, but it was an in-your-face, ballsy move.

Reaper's decision made her antsy, especially when she preferred a stealthier approach. But this time she didn't have a choice—*thank you, Lilith*—as her orders were to find out who instigated the kidnapping and 'take care of it' by whatever means necessary.

Thanks to her position as a 'Hound, her worldview was broader than most, and that perspective warned her not to ignore the unknown possibilities. Unfortunately, working with unknowns had its own inherent problems, which left her mind clicking through the bits and pieces as mile after mile disappeared under her tires as they made their way to Kennewick. When her brain began to beat itself bloody thanks to the plethora of missing pieces, she finally gave up on solving the puzzle.

Ruin was hell on wheels, and pushed relentlessly onward, leaving her to concentrate on keeping him in sight. In the early afternoon, they took their one and only break to refuel. She was more concerned with gulping down water than talking. A position Ruin also took since he didn't say much.

Their destination was one of the few cities left between

Pebble Creek and New Seattle and sat in the Tri-City area of what once was Washington State. The Collapse left the label a bit of a misnomer, but the old title still stuck. Three robust town used to sit where the Columbia and Yakima Rivers met, and then rising sea levels bloated the rivers and flooded the surrounding area, birthing a massive inland lake and drowning the city of Richland under the newly christened Yakima Lake. To survive, the Tri-City population retreated from the flood-waters and set up residence just north of the Snake River, spreading to both sides of the Columbia River, and rebuilding on the bones of Kennewick and Pasco.

After ten hours of hard riding over broken stretches of asphalt and through rough off-road trails, Charity's ass was numb. The only thing on her mind was finding a room with a working shower, then falling face first into a bed. So, when the thick dual rivers of the Columbia and Snake came into view, she almost cried in relief.

As they got closer, Ruin dropped his speed and they merged with the evening traffic meandering between the flickering solar lamps that marked Blue Bridge's span at regular intervals. Off to their right and further downriver came the glow of lights from Cable Bridge.

They carefully wove their way through the late-night mix of pedestrians, couples and families on horse-drawn makeshift wagons, and single riders mounted on horses and bikes, both pedal-powered and motorized. Their passage earned a handful of glances that were quickly adverted. Nowadays, no one was eager to engage strangers.

Not that it bothered Charity. She was more concerned about finding a boarding house and prayed that was where Ruin was heading. Not that she knew for sure since the closed mouth bastard hadn't shared his lodging plans.

He took her down the wide main road, its sides lined with

a jumbled mix of massive storage containers turned living spaces, and old trailers, no longer mobile, but converted by judicious, and not so judicious, use of add-on structures into local eateries and shops that catered to the bustling community. Thankfully some were still open.

The seductive lure of fried foods and the hickory bite of barbecue woke her stomach with a vengeance. A cacophony of laughter, music, and spiced-laden air spilled out of a still-open establishment called Agatha's. Charity made a mental note of its location because she planned on returning, with or without Ruin.

Her frustration and hunger rose in equal parts as Ruin made a right off the main road and continued his slow and steady pace. Just as she was about to turn and head back to Agatha's and to hell with Ruin, he pulled into a wide lot guarded by a thick iron gate and two sentry posts. He slowed his bike to a stop next to the small enclosure on the right.

Wary, but sticking close, she scanned for some sort of sign to indicate where they were. She stayed behind Ruin, keeping enough room for a quick exit if needed.

As his bike's growl died away, Ruin kicked down the stand and stretched.

After a second or two of internal debate, Charity finally shut her bike down, but kept her hand near the gun holstered on her thigh.

As the rumble of their engines faded, the high pitch buzz emanating from the two security lights at the gate took its place. The obvious use of electricity set this place apart from the typical boarding house, but the bright lights made it difficult to make out the dark forms manning the dual sentry posts.

One of those shadows stepped out of the small shack and moved toward them. "Ruin?"

"Kayvao, my man, how's it going?" Ruin swung his leg over and walked around his bike, hand out.

Kayvao stepped free of the shadows and so did his four-legged companion. The two moved in tandem until the German Shepherd heeded the man's subtle hand movement and sat. A few inches taller and wider than Ruin, the man was dressed in fatigues, from jacket to pants, and the only break in the material's pattern was the light tan t-shirt underneath and his black boots.

The canine was just as intimidating, despite his lolling tongue, his gaze riveted on the visitors. One wrong move on her or Ruin's part and that dog would be at their throats. If that wasn't enough to remind visitors to watch their step, the human-shaped shadow lingering at the other sentry point was. Charity studied the dog's handler as she continued to straddle her bike.

Kayvao clasped Ruin's arm and dragged him in for a back thumping. "It's going." His voice was deep, steady. He stepped back, raised a hand to signal the all clear to the other guard, and then turned his gaze to Charity. "You brought a friend?"

Ruin stood side-by-side with Kayvao, his expression unreadable as he watched her. "You could say that." He turned back to his friend. "We're working on something for Reaper."

The bigger man smiled, his teeth a startling white against the deeper warmth of his skin. It was far from reassuring.

Charity's finger twitched against the butt of her gun, but she stilled it through sheer force of will.

Kayvao didn't look away from her as he asked Ruin, "Shy, is she?"

Was he for real? "Cautious is more like," she countered.

He chuckled at her snippy tone. "Cautious is good." He motioned her forward. "Get on over here. I promise I won't bite."

She deliberately looked to his furry sidekick.

He followed the direction of her gaze to the patiently waiting dog behind him and he grinned. "Fai will behave, she's working."

Charity consciously relaxed the last of her tight muscles and got off her bike. She took a moment to work out the pins and needles in her legs and regain feeling in her ass. The change in position played hell on her legs, and her first step was a bit shaky, but the second and third were smoother.

She stopped in front of the two men and offered her hand to Kayvao. "Charity."

He clasped her hand, careful of grip in the way big men tended to be. "Charity, nice to meet you." He let her go, stepped back, and turned to Ruin. "Let me guess." He set his fists on his hips, the move pulling the edges of his jacket back and revealing dark holster straps and the two guns.. "You're in need of a room."

Ruin's shuttered expression disappeared, replaced by a devilish grin. "You going to deny me?"

The other man snorted. "You going to leave trouble passed out in the shower at the pool house again?"

"Trouble follows me," Ruin drawled, his gaze deliberately sliding to her, before returning to his friend. "I don't go looking for it."

"Sure, man."

It was hunger, not jealousy, that twisted her stomach and forced Charity to redirect the conversation. "How long is Agatha's open?"

That got both men's attention, but it was Kayvao that said, "Based upon the amount of dust you're wearing, I'm assuming food is right up there with a shower."

Charity stifled her sigh, shifted her weight, and moved her hand from the holster to her hip. "You'd guess right."

He rubbed his chin, more to cover his grin than anything

else, she suspected, then he said, "Since it's not polite to keep a lady waiting, let's get you settled in. Cort will keep an eye on your bikes for now." The big man turned, flicked his hand at Fai, who stood and came to heel at the silent signal. "We're a bit booked thanks to the Spring Faire, so you're lucky your room is open."

Charity's mind stuttered over the singular use of room, but Ruin appeared unfazed as he lifted a hand in thanks to the other guard and fell in step with Kayvao. "Funny how luck is directly tied to the depth of Reaper's pockets."

Kayvao shrugged off the dig. "You know how it goes. Jack likes his creature comforts. Unexpected guests like you make it possible for him to indulge."

That earned a snort from Ruin. "Ain't that the truth. Anything worth checking out at the Faire this time?"

Charity did her best to ignore her mental hiccup of sharing a room with Ruin and fell in behind the two men as they conversed about the various vendors converging on the town. Twice a year, the Faires made the rounds of the mid-size cities, and the various vendors shared their eclectic mix of wares with the residents.

As the conversation flowed, Kayvao led them through a heavy metal door with solid security bars at the top and bottom. *Armed guards, electric lights, blast doors and security gates—this place was set to withstand a siege.*

Despite her reservations about sharing a room, the prospect of getting an uninterrupted night's rest almost added a skip to her step.

They crossed an interior lot that spanned both sides of the security gate. There was a hodgepodge of stables for horses and donkeys to the left, and covered spaces for mechanical transport to the right.

The cement walkways wound through a collection of smaller buildings to an eclectic array of hotel-like doors that surrounded the courtyard where a handful of private structures took up the middle area.

The big man stopped at one of the private structures tucked toward the back and some of Charity's worries faded.

Private meant more than one room, more than one room meant a possible couch.

At the door, the men came to a halt, and Fai settled off to the side, a prime position to keep an eye on all three humans. Kayvao turned and blocked the entrance, his gaze settling on Charity.

The light hanging above the entrance added a menacing touch to his shadowed visage, which matched the hard-ass tone of his voice. "Run down on the rules as this is your first time here."

He started listing them off, emphasizing each with a thick finger. "One, start a fight behind these walls and I will finish it. Two, if trouble follows you, be sure to lose it before you step through my gate, because if it inflicts damages to the premises and/or other residents, your rights to safe lodging are automatically revoked. Three, you assume all responsibility for your visitors and their ability to follow rules number one and two. Questions?"

Charity raised her hand. "Just one." When Kayvao quirked an eyebrow in silent question, she lowered her hand. "Any limits on hot water usage?"

"Keep it under twenty minutes and you should be good." With that, he moved to the side and directed his next comment to Ruin. "You have the combo?"

Ruin nodded.

"Good. You need me, you know where to find me."

Ruin took Kayvao's place at the door. "Thanks, man."

Kayvao nodded, and motioned to Fai, who fell in at his side. "I'd advise not leaving your bikes out front for long, too much temptation for the local street rats."

Since food was her main goal, she'd get in, throw some water on her face to remove her mask of dust, and then head back out to her bike. Her stomach emitted an audible growl of agreement, and Fai's ears perked in her direction.

Ruin shot her an amused look before telling Kayvao, "Sounds like we'll be back up in a few."

Kayvao grinned, pivoted on his heel, and headed back to the gate.

She watched his back disappear into the darkness and waited until he was out of earshot before she addressed Ruin without turning around, "Quite the place you picked out.".

"You complaining?" A series of muted electronic beeps sounded from behind her as he undid the door's lock.

"Nope." She turned at the sharp click of the knob turning.

He pushed the door wide. "Good." He disappeared inside.

She stepped in the doorway and leaned her uninjured shoulder against the doorjamb, as he cleared the room. "So, a standing reservation at a Guardian Lodge, uh?"

He emerged from the interior shadows and halted just inside the door. He braced one arm against the wall above her head and looked down into her face. "That a question?"

She tipped her chin and shrugged. "Maybe." She shifted her stance and ignored the pull of stitches at her shoulder. "A place like this, it's hard to get a reservation. The security costs alone tend to keep it out of reach for most."

"Fate's Vultures aren't 'most' people, darlin'." His damn sexy drawl was back in force.

She folded her arms and wrinkled her nose. "Oh, I don't doubt that, but it still doesn't answer what y'all did, exactly, to get such a benefit." And the curiosity was killing her. His answer might provide her a way to leverage the same benefit in her future. *You never knew when a girl could use a well-guarded bolt hole.*

Clearly following her logic, he leaned in, shrinking the

distance between them. "You'd have to trade for that bit of information." He held her gaze, a glint of temptation flickering in the amber depths. "You sure you're up for it?"

Part of her wondered what his game was, blowing cold one minute, hot the next. It was enough to give a girl a complex. Well, maybe not her considering she liked playing with dangerous things.

Her pulse tripped and picked up speed, her body uncaring of his mixed messages. Unfortunately, her mind wasn't too far behind. She shifted a fraction closer. "It's something I might consider."

His smile rode the edge of wicked enticement as he lifted his free hand and traced a fingertip along her jaw. "Is there something, in particular, that might tip the scales on your decision?"

The promise in his smile made it difficult to catch her breath or keep her attention on his face instead of other, more interesting parts. Too bad her mind was determined to ruin her sexual appetite by pointing out all the reasons indulging in Ruin was a very bad idea.

She fed just the tiniest bit of her craving by angling her head to deepen that feather-light touch and forced her lips to curve into an answering smile. "Feed me first."

His lashes dropped in a slow blink before he shook his head and dropped his hand. "One track mind."

She sighed. If he only knew how narrow that track was, chances were damn good they'd be skipping dinner.

He pushed off the wall and straightened, pulling her back from her lust-induced hysteria. "I'll go grab our bags and drop them in the room. Gives you some time to do whatever you need to before we head out to eat." He didn't wait for her response but slid by her and out the door.

She watched him walk away, her thoughts hazed with things better left ignored. "Food, Charity," she muttered, before turning away and heading in. "Eat first, and maybe your mind will get back on track."

She ran a hand over the inside wall until she found an actual switch and flicked it on.

One of the perks that came with staying at a Guardian Lodge was electricity. The bright lights sprang on, and illuminated the interior. Most businesses relied on solar or wick-fueled lanterns, but Lodges always used the best of the best, hence their hefty price tags.

She took her time and wandered around, checking out the unexpected luxuries.

The front room held a beautiful collection of hand carved furniture, the kind intended to last, even as it offered comfort to the weary traveler. A small kitchen sat off to one side, complete with an icebox and a two-burner hotplate. Should they decide to forgo the local eateries, there was a two-person table tucked near the wall.

Down the hall, she found the bathroom and used the sink to wash her face. She was rehanging the fluffy towel when she heard Ruin come back. She stood in the short hall and watched as he dropped his bags on the couch. Then, he crossed the room, stopped in front of her, and shrugged the saddlebags off his shoulder and handed them over. "Here, figured you'd want the bedroom. I'll take the couch."

If he thought she'd argue, he was in for a surprise. "Thanks." She took the bags and headed to the bedroom, haunted by the unexpected memories of the last hall she walked down. Resolutely she pushed them away, knowing the nightmares would return later tonight.

Ruin called out after her, "What? No offering to take the couch?"

"Nope," she threw over her shoulder as she entered the bedroom. A gorgeous quilt covered the large bed, the multitude of colors chasing away some of her road-induced exhaustion. She dropped the bags on the floor, and couldn't resist running a hand over the piece of art. The tiny, precise stitches revealed it was just as handcrafted as the furniture.

"You going to stay and pet the bed or come eat?"

She turned to find Ruin at the bedroom door. She forced her hand away from the quilt and walked towards him. "Let's go hit Agatha's."

He didn't move, blocking the way. "What's your fascination with Agatha's?"

She wrinkled her nose. "Saw it on the way in, about the same time my nose picked up the scent of barbecue. Ribs and a beer sound good right about now."

He shifted to the side with a mocking bow. "After you."

She shook her head, and led the way back out. She waited at the bottom of the steps as he reset the lock. "Going to share the combo with me?"

"Nope." He tested the door to make sure it was locked. "If I gave you the combo, then we'd have to change it after whatever this is we're doing."

Despite that being the answer she expected, she had to ask. "Then do me a favor and don't go looking for trouble this time around, okay?"

"Don't need to." He fell into step next to her as they headed back to the gates. "Got more than enough to keep me busy."

She gave him a narrow-eyed look. "You calling me trouble?"

"Aren't you?" His beard couldn't hide his teasing grin.

She huffed out a breath. "I think that's more your role than mine."

His grin went full bore teasing. "I beg to disagree."

Their conversation spanned two unmistakable levels, and despite the fun as she was having, she wasn't quite ready to dive into the deep end. "Whatever."

At the gate, Ruin lifted a hand in Kayvao's direction, and then they stepped through the blast door. After it closed behind them, Ruin said, "I'll follow you."

She nodded and got on her bike. *Time to go feed her hunger.*

Not that one, a wicked little voice whined.

She gritted her teeth and shot it a mental finger.

sixteen

Ruin tipped back his chair until only two of its legs touched the floor. He braced his shoulders against the wall and balanced a sweating glass of beer against his stomach. Sitting across from him, Charity shook her head. Belly full of damn fine barbecue, his mood was mellow as he surveyed Agatha's patrons. Kennewick might not be a hotbed of nightlife, but despite being long past the dinner hour, people were out and about.

Under the soft glow of solar-powered lights, locals and travelers mixed easily. Even with the irregular illumination it wasn't hard to tell which was which. The locals gathered in relaxed groups around various tables, engaged in low-key conversations. Visitors congregated near the bar, their interactions interspersed with the occasional overly loud laughter, earning jaded glances from the locals. It was a familiar scene and one he was happy to simply watch.

Too bad the jet-haired barmaid who kept his beer topped off wanted his participation in something more than talk. As if the very thought conjured her up, she headed over, working her exceptional body with undaunted confidence.

Kitty? Katy? —damned if he could remember—sidled up to the table. "Need another refill, baby?"

He hefted his almost full glass. "I'm good, thanks."

She managed an artful pout. "Well, just holler when you're ready for another."

"Karen, sugar," Charity's sweet as pie request came from across the table, "you mind getting me another?'

Ruin lifted his glass to his lips hoping it hid his grin. *Bless her heart, the woman could make nice downright evil when she wanted.*

For a telling moment Karen's pout tightened then smoothed into her professional service smile. "Of course, be right back."

She swiped Charity's empty glass with enough force to leave skid marks, then turned and stalked back to the bar. Her passage caught every male eye in her wake.

He gave credit where credit was due, her exit was fairly impressive. Sad as it was to admit, he couldn't muster an ounce of curiosity for Karen's luscious offer, when what he really wanted to tangle with sat on the other side of the table currently giving him her best smirk.

"Must be hard to be you." Between the murmur of conversations and underlying music from the guitar trio in the corner, Charity's voice was low enough to keep their conversation private.

He lowered his glass and arched a brow. "How so?"

Charity sat in her chair with her feet drawn up and legs folded tailor-style. Her elbows were braced on the tabletop, and she propped her chin in her hand. The tail end of her braid curled down her front and hovered just above a mouth-watering curve. She batted her ridiculously long eyelashes and adopted a breathless voice. "If there's anything, anything at all, that I can do you for—" another exaggerated blink, "—I mean do for you, just let me know." She wrinkled her nose, and her voice went back to its normal husky timbre. "Doesn't it get old?"

Hmm, was that a bit of green in her baby blues? Unable to resist poking at her inadvertent opening, he drawled, "Jealous, darlin'?"

She cocked her head, and a small frown creased her brow. "Why would I be?"

"Isn't that a normal female thing?" He got a kick out of the rising color in her cheeks and the sparks flaring in her eyes.

"What? Deliberately dropping IQ points to gain a guy's interest?" She waved her other hand back toward the bar. "You're free to take her up on her offer." She bit her bottom lip, slid him a sly look, and slowly smiled. "Just didn't think you were into pretty and deliberately dumb."

Meow. He liked her flash of claws and decided to play. "I think I've just been insulted."

She aimed a Cheshire grin his way.

He held her smug gaze and deliberately dropped his chair legs to the floor. He carefully set his beer to the side, folded his arms on the table's top, and leaned in, happy to see an edge of wariness creep into her bright eyes. "If you wanted to know what turns me on, Charity, all you have to do is ask." *Said the spider to the fly.*

Her tongue darted out to swipe over her lips, a small nervous tell that fed the prowling hunger inside him. "Why would I do that?"

He caught the underlying tinge of curiosity in her low questions and felt his pulse kick up. "Because part of you wants to play as much as I do." He didn't try to hide the hunger grinding against his control, the same hunger that whipped him from perverse curiosity to gnawing frustration to simmering anger and back in an infinite cycle. Slowly, he reached out and wrapped his hand around her narrow wrist, pleased when the butterfly beat of her pulse fluttered under his fingers. "Admit it. I dare you."

Proving the type of woman she was, she didn't pull back. "And if I did, what then, Ruin?" She uncrossed her legs and leaned in until their faces were so close to anyone watching they would appear to be deeply involved. "If I told you I wanted to strip you down and take my time with you, would you let me?"

"In a fucking heartbeat," he ground out as a sucker punch of lust ignited at the image her words painted. "Only a fool would turn down an invitation like that."

Her smile was full of female wickedness. "I'd need longer than that to get my fill, darlin'."

"I'm counting on it." Visceral satisfaction filled him as hunger and need rose in her gaze, but he wasn't done. "Because I have every intention of returning the favor, and fair warning, I'm extremely detail oriented in my studies."

Her breathing hitched and her tongue made a reappearance, but it didn't detract him from her quickly doused flash of uncertainty. "And when you've completed your study, what then?"

"Why? You looking for a lifetime commitment?" he growled.

Her laugh was soft. "No."

He shifted his hold, brought her hand up to his mouth, and nipped her fingers. "So, what's holding you back?"

She drew the fingertips of her free hand along the edge of his cheek and down his jaw, her nails scraping against his beard. "Did you happen to forget why we're here? We can't afford to be distracted."

There was a wistful note behind her words, but as she stepped into his seductive web, he felt the first vibration. "Chances are good that nothing much will happen until tomorrow, and I can't think of anything better to be distracted with. Can you?"

Her gaze dropped to where he slowly brushed his thumb over the inside of her wrist. Her answer was soft, "No." She visibly swallowed, lifted her gaze, and tried to pull back. When he refused to let go, she stilled. "I learned a long time ago, it doesn't pay to fuck someone you work with. It never ends well."

He wondered if she understood the challenge she presented. "Maybe you've been fucking the wrong people."

She blinked and her mouth opened, but whatever she planned on saying was cut off when a beer mug was slammed on the table between them. Amber liquid sloshed over the edges.

"You need anything else?"

Without releasing Charity, he turned his head to face a fuming Karen. "Not right now."

She stiffened at the edge of irritation in his voice, then, with a huff, turned on her heel and stalked away. A muffled snort from Charity regained his attention. "What?"

"Nothing." She patted his cheek, then twisted her wrist. He let her go so she could sit back. She drew her beer close. "If you're done flirting, how about you share your plan."

He'd let her believe she was shutting him down, for now. He reclaimed his beer and rocked his chair back into his previous position. 'Hounds weren't the only ones who understood the value of patience. "My plan?"

She pulled one leg up and used her knee to brace her arm. "Please tell me you have one."

He took a sip and avoided her gaze.

"Oh for the love of ..." She closed her eyes and grimaced, rubbing her forehead. Her lips moved but he couldn't catch whatever it was she muttered. When she opened her eyes, she pinned him with a hard stare. "Do you know where the Raiders are planning on meeting?"

He lifted his glass. "Kind of."

"You 'kind of' know where the meet is." Disbelief added a bite to her words.

Since she wasn't asking, he didn't answer, instead he explained, "Shouldn't take much to figure out where."

"Seriously? How do you figure that?"

"Because Kennewick isn't New Seattle. Options are limited."

"Not enough to pinpoint the spot by tomorrow." She blew out a breath. "Dammit, Ruin. Didn't your chew toy give you anything else?"

"Yep."

She waited. When he kept silent, she reached across the table and snapped her fingers in his face. "Spill."

Her frustrated frown was on the cute side, but he wasn't about to tell her that. Nope, he was an intelligent man. "He didn't have much but overheard someone mention Riverman and painted horses."

"Riverman and painted horses? That's it?" She dropped her head into her hands with a groan. "God save me from fools."

He caught her muttered comment and his temper flared. *Did she really think he was stupid?* He wouldn't have hauled ass to Kennewick unless they had a damn good chance of taking those bastards out. Not when shit was serious in Pebble Creek. "Charity." He set his beer on the table hard enough to bring her head up.

She sat up, her gaze watchful.

"Look around. How well do you think Raiders would blend in here?"

She surveyed the other diners, realization dawning. "They timed their meet with the Faire."

"To give themselves a thin layer of anonymity," he agreed. "But it won't be enough." He watched her think it through and it wasn't long before she connected the dots. If the Raiders showed up, they would stick out like a sore thumb. So much so that whispers of their presence should already be wafting through the seamier side of the city. Ruin and Charity just needed to ask the right person the right question.

She traced the rim of her glass. "You won't find information here."

"Nope," he drawled. "But you wanted to eat."

"Didn't hear you complaining," she muttered ungraciously. She worried her bottom lip, and he could practically see her mind spinning. "I've got an idea."

He raised an eyebrow and waited for her to share.

Instead, she raised her glass and downed a healthy amount. When she set it down, she pushed back from the table and stood. "Make sure you give Karen a decent tip."

So, no sharing then. Good thing he didn't have any issue tagging along. He drained the last of his beer and rose. "Why?"

Charity shot him an exasperated look. "Because I don't want her spitting in my food when we come back."

Hmm, good point. He tossed down some credits and followed her out of Agatha's.

Outside, instead of heading for their bikes, Charity stopped on the sidewalk and looked around.

Curious, Ruin asked, "You looking for someone?"

"Yeah," she answered absently. Then she must have spotted who, or what, she was looking for because she said, "Wait here. I'll be right back."

Before he could respond, she was approaching a lanky kid hanging in-between Agatha's and the shuttered building next door. As she closed in, the kid straightened, but didn't bolt. There wasn't enough light to make out his features, but that didn't stop Ruin from watching the unfolding discussion.

Not that Charity couldn't take care of herself, but it didn't hurt to have her back.

Charity said something. The kid shook his head. She asked another question, got an answer, then nodded and pulled something out of her pocket. She held it out and the kid's hand shot out, grabbed whatever she offered, and then he followed her back to Ruin.

Charity stopped at his side and waved a hand to indicate the kid behind her. "This is Sam. He's going to watch our bikes."

He eyed Sam, noting the traces of dirt along the kid's hack-job of a haircut and the worn state of his mismatched, too large clothes. "Watch or strip?"

"Gave my word." Teenage bravado screamed to the fore as Sam's chin jutted out. "Promised the chick here I'd watch for two hours, then I'm out."

Ruin shifted around Charity, and crowded Sam, forcing the man-boy to look up. He gave the kid his best hard-ass stare, the one he learned from Reaper, and kept his voice hard. "Find out your word is shit, I'll hunt you down and take the price of my bike in body parts. Clear?"

He gave the kid credit. Sam paled but didn't back down. "Clear."

Behind him, Charity said, "Two hours, Sam. Rest of payment then." She leaned around Ruin. "If the bikes are in the same shape we left them, I'll get you a bonus."

Sam nodded.

Ruin stepped back, giving Sam room to sit on the edge of the sidewalk between the two bikes. Once the kid was settled, Ruin lengthened his stride to catch up to Charity who was striding off. "You sure our bikes will still be there?"

Completely unconcerned, she said, "Yep."

They strode down the street, passing others on their way to whatever they had planned for the evening. He kept his attention on those they passed, as he continued their conversation. "Why?"

She gave him a look. "Instinct."

Disbelief brought him to an abrupt halt. "Are you kidding me?"

A few steps ahead, she stopped, turned, and retraced her steps until she stood directly in front of him. They were close enough to ensure privacy, but her voice remained razor sharp, "In case you forgot, I grew up grifting, a lifestyle that relies on finely-tuned instincts, especially when it comes to people. And mine are telling me Sam will watch over our bikes for two hours. Since we're on a clock, get your ass in gear."

Undaunted he snapped back, "One scratch on my bike and when I'm done with Sam, I'll be taking it up with you."

"Whatever." Undaunted, she turned on her heel, and headed back down the street. "Keep up, Vulture boy."

He followed, grumbling under his breath about stubborn females and the accompanying pains they brought the entire time. She led him through what constituted Kennewick's main drag, a snaking road of cracked asphalt. Both sides were lined with storefronts, ranging from The Burnt Pipe, a smoke shop offering a wide selection of traditional tobacco or narcotic herb, to Montestreso Outfitters, showcasing clothing displays in darkened windows protected by sturdy iron bars. There was even a library tucked between a strip club and an antique store. Funny how a city's main street evolved when you needed to set up shop out of the hungry river's reach.

Wherever Charity was headed, it wasn't in the nicer part of town. The further they went, the grimier and sketchier the neighborhood became. After about fifteen minutes, she slipped into a narrow alley between a shuttered bar decorated with graffiti and what appeared to be a burnt out abandoned storehouse.

A crawling sensation crept along his spine, and he slid one

of his knives free, holding it along his side, out of sight. The familiar hilt's weight against his palm eased some of the spidery feelings at the base of his skull.

Charity continued about halfway down the dark passageway and stopped under a feeble blue light. He came up behind her as she faced a rusted door bearing a yellow, hand painted image about eye level. It resembled a solid circle missing a pie-like portion. Puzzled, he looked to Charity. "What the hell is this?"

She pounded her fist against the door three times. "An underground arcade den."

"Guess you've been to Kennewick before," he noted.

A small square in the door slid back and a pair of eyes stared through the small opening. Charity ignored Ruin and said, "Julia Angwin."

There was a grunt, and then the opening disappeared. Within moments dull *thunks* sounded, indicating interior locks being thrown, then the door swung wide. Charity stepped through, and he stayed on her heels.

Red light and the dull haze of smoke hit them full force as they moved deeper into the narrow hall. He tried not to cough at the smoky assault, and when he looked back, the door was closed and a lanky form was trying to squeeze by. He shifted so the stranger could pass and caught the impression of dark hair cut close to the skull, the brush of a flannel shirt, and the unique, overwhelming scent of patchouli mixed with someone who didn't like showers.

The guy moved in front of Charity, waved his hand forward, and headed down the hall that disappeared in the uncertain lighting. Charity followed. Ruin brought up the rear, and tried to breathe through his mouth to spare his nose.

The narrow hall abruptly opened into a vast space crowded with people and machines. Their mute guide waved them forward, then turned, and returned down the hall. Ruin took in the scene.

Old-style arcade games were clustered into groups and formed strange pods in the middle of the floor. Booths were tucked along the walls, each one featuring either a laptop or desktop computer. The exterior walls were painted black and laced with snaking wires and cables. Illumination was limited to the screens and clusters of strung lights. The din of computerized warnings of imminent attack and high-pitched beeps competed with shouts and groans from those either playing or watching the screens.

Ruin tucked his knife away, and leaned over Charity's shoulder, putting his mouth close to her ear so he could be heard. "Where the hell do they get the electricity from?"

She turned her head just enough to answer, "They steal it from nearby businesses."

"And they haven't been shut down?"

She grinned, her teeth overly white in the dimness. "Nope, because they have under-the-table deals with various powers that be.

"Figures."

"Come on." She grabbed his hand and dragged him across the rough cement floors.

Surprised by her unexpected move, he held on, not wanting to lose her in the crush. There was no straightforward path thanks to the tangle of cords snaking across the ground. But it didn't take Charity long to find an empty booth. She scooted across the bench's cracked fake leather, and brushed a hand over the crumb strewn tabletop, knocking wadded napkins to the ground. She settled in a spot in the middle. "Sit, Ruin."

He slid in next to her, but it took a few minutes to find a comfortable position where he could stretch out his legs, instead of bumping his knees against the underside of the battered tabletop. Next to him, Charity dragged over the booth's laptop, the security cord trailing along, and started typing away. He let a minute pass, wondering if she planned on explaining what the hell they were doing in a place like this, because there was no way a Raider would show up here. When she continued to type, he asked, "What are we doing here?"

Her fingers flew over the keyboard, and she didn't look up from the screen. "Waiting."

"For?"

She hit a few more keys and finally gave him her attention. "Echo."

Above them the lights flared bright, then settled back into their sub-par glow. A sharp curse erupted from the booth behind him and drew Ruin's attention. He twisted to look over his shoulder, and found an older couple huddled around a monitor with disgruntled expressions. Since the monitor faced him, he could see the blue screen filled with a jumble of white text.

There was a shift of weight, and then a warm press of a hand against his shoulder. He turned and found Charity kneeling next to him. "Bet the power surge fried their motherboard."

He lost her touch when she resumed her previous position, so he resettled and laid his arm along the back of the bench above her shoulders. "Who's Echo?"

"Echo's how we find the Raiders."

"You're using a code monkey to track down Raiders?" He shook his head. "Hate to break it to you, but it isn't the early 2000's anymore. Using antiquated technology to track someone's movements is virtually useless."

A round of cheers from the cluster of gaming consoles interrupted him.

He flicked a hand towards the group of backslapping teens. "This is what technology has devolved into, stealing electricity to play video games. Hell, there isn't much of a—what do you call it? Interweb?" Her mouth opened but he talked over her. "Whatever they called that electronic network, for them to even tap into anymore."

She shifted until she faced him, amusement evident in her voice. "First, it was called the internet. Second, you may not have noticed, but underground clubs, like this one, have managed to rebuild a fairly large network despite having to syphon off their surrounding communities. Third, contrary to the obvious appearance, it's not all about video games."

She grabbed his chin and directed his attention a few booths down in the corner where a woman, wearing red-framed glasses strewn with rhinestone and elaborate pigtails animatedly talked to a burly man in a cotton button-down shirt with matching tie. The computer sat off to the side, unused, yet the mismatched couple continued what appeared to be a very serious conversation.

Even from here, Ruin could see the frown creasing the man's face as he furiously wrote on a notepad in front of him. Only when the woman said something did his frown disappear, to be replaced by a relieved smile. Charity's fingers let go, and she said into his ear, "Watch."

The man made a few more notes, adding the occasional nod. Finally done with his writing, he set the pen down, and offered his hand to the woman. They shook. The man gathered his notebook, set something on the table, and gave the woman another smile before disappearing into the gloom of the room.

Charity was so close her breath brushed against his ear, the intimacy of it leaving chills to race over his skin. "Untraceable information is why we're here."

He turned his head and opened his mouth, only to forget what he was going to say when he came face to face with Charity.

Their gazes caught and held. She was so close he swore he could feel the heat of her blush as it crept over her cheeks. Her bright gaze drifted to his mouth, and her tongue darted out in that nervous tell he was beginning to crave. His earlier hunger roared to the surface with a vengeance. It wasn't his brain doing the thinking when he lifted his arm from the back of the bench to curl around her, or when his hand slid under her braid to cradle the base of her head and slowly brought her those last few inches closer so he could kiss her.

Her balance compromised, Charity's hands flattened against his chest as her gaze centered on his mouth. She didn't fight his hold but leaned in. He accepted her unspoken invitation and captured her lips with his. He took advantage of her small gasp, and his tongue breached the unintended opening and made the most of it.

God, her taste! Intoxicating heat edged with an exhilarating bite, much like the woman herself. It didn't matter who she worked for, why she was there, why he was there, all that mattered was gorging on this delectable feast she presented.

Trust for Charity, the operator, might be in short supply, but when it came to Charity, the woman, he found he craved something more. Maybe, if he could feed this damn hunger that gnawed its way into his very bones, he'd be able to think again.

He nipped and teased, grateful when she met him stroke for stroke proving this desire between them was far from one sided. Some faint part of him noted the bite of her nails against his chest as her hands curled into his t-shirt and pulled him closer. Her hand drifted down his chest to rest tantalizingly close to his aching dick. He refused to stop kissing her but growled low in his throat in a wordless command. Just in case she missed it, he covered her hand with his and guided it where he wanted.

Before he could get her on target, someone cleared their throat. Loudly.

He squeezed her hand, then let her go, but took his time pulling back from the scorching kiss.

A beleaguered sigh sounded behind him.

Not to be rushed, Ruin slowly uncurled his hand from Charity's hair, deliberately stroked along her jaw, and brushed his thumb over her kiss-swollen lips.

Amusement and lust glittered in her eyes as she held his gaze and eased back, but she didn't break eye contact as she addressed the person waiting behind him. "Took you long enough."

"I see you decided to give the club a show."

seventeen

Charity finally shifted her gaze from Ruin, looked at the woman standing at their table and felt Ruin do the same. "Jealous, Echo?"

"Yeah, maybe." There was a trace of truth in the grudgingly given reply.

"Sorry, sweets, still not leaning that way." Charity grinned. "Promise you'll be the second to know if I do."

"Promises, promises," Echo chided as her brightly painted lips formed a moue of mock disappointment. She sent Ruin a wink from behind her garish glasses and then slid in on the table's other side, smoothing her skirt under her as she sat. Her elaborate pigtails swayed with her movements. "Who's your friend?"

Charity waited for the other woman's shrewd gaze to come back to her answering. "Ruin met Echo. Echo, Ruin."

An eyebrow rose under the precisely cut dark bangs as Echo studied him. She made a *tsking* noise. "Not your normal type, Charity."

Charity gave an amused snort. "I don't have a type."

"I beg to differ." Echo rested her elbow on the table and

one teal blue nail, filed into a sharp point accented with a winking faux diamond stabbed the air. "Rough-edged." Another finger rose. "Silent and broody." A third went up as she openly leered at Ruin. "Built for dirty, dirty deeds." She dropped her fingers, set her chin on her palm, and shifted her speculative gaze back to Charity. "Hate to break it to you, honey, but that constitutes a type."

Charity's imagination was tangled up in Echo's 'dirty, dirty deeds' comment, yet by some miracle she managed not to squirm or look at Ruin. "Not here to discuss my personal life."

Echo sighed dramatically. "Sadly, you never are." She twirled the end of one pigtail around her finger. "Since you won't indulge me, why don't you ask me for what you need?"

Not fooled by Echo's flippant demeanor because past transactions had proven the calculating mind beneath the glitzy demeanor, Charity braced and asked, "What's it going to cost me?"

The hair twirling stopped mid-spin and, like a shark scenting bloodied water, Echo flipped the switch from flirtatious to business. "Normal scale applies. The more likely I am to get burned for sharing, the deeper you'll be digging into your pockets." Her attention flicked to Ruin and returned, predatory interest vying with an edgy curiosity. "Is this personal or professional?"

Charity leaned back and the weight of Ruin's arm curled around her shoulder. *A silent warning on oversharing, maybe?* Not that it was needed since she had no plans to give Echo any more than the barest of details. Still, to throw Echo off the true nature of their business, she shifted until she was tucked against Ruin's side, creating the image of a united couple. "Does it matter?"

As much as she enjoyed witnessing Echo's internal struggle between her need to pry and her love of payment play, Charity had no doubt of the eventual outcome. Echo never snubbed an opportunity to line her pockets, be it with city credits or favors owed.

Sure enough, Echo gave in. "Fine, keep your secrets. I'll give you two questions."

Ruin shifted against the cracked upholstery but didn't let Charity go. "What does painted horses mean to you?"

Puzzlement swept over Echo's face. "You have a fetish for decorating poor, dumb animals?"

"Let me rephrase," Charity clarified, "If you were visiting from out of town and wanted to stay off the grid, where would you go?"

Echo frowned in thought. "I could bring up a fairly long list using those two criteria alone. You need to narrow the parameters."

"Maybe a place a visitor could find without relying on the locals for direction? Private and out of the way would be non-negotiable." Because whoever the Raiders planned to meet, wouldn't want to be seen with them. "Easily accessible and defendable."

Echo shook her head. "Not enough, need something more."

Frustration and impatience clawed at Charity, but she dug deep. "Could be the name connects with painted horses? Maybe some sort of statue or carving? An old street name? Something that used to be known for horses?" The last was a stretch, but the wider their net, the more likely they were to actually catch a damn clue.

Echo stilled for a moment and stared into space. "Maybe."

Her pensive answer ignited a familiar buzz of anticipation in Charity's gut. "Maybe what?"

Echo sat back, the move turning her glass lenses under the string of decorative lights. She nabbed one of the unused napkins on the table and started shredding it into confetti.

"It's a damn long shot," she said, reluctance clear in her voice. "But maybe the Carousel."

"Carousel?" Ruin's question shot out like a bullet.

Echo gave a slow nod, absently arranging the napkin shreds into a neat pile. "If I remember my history right, it was some lame attempt at bringing tradition back to the area." Her nose wrinkled as she shook her head. "Not sure how erecting an amusement ride in the middle of nowhere generates tradition, but then again, a lot of decisions made before the Collapse don't make sense. I mean, really? Who, in their right mind, thinks creating super viruses, or dumping tons of poison into the air is a bright move?"

"The Carousel, Echo?" Charity decided to cut in before the other woman got lost in one of her well-known rants on the idiocy of society before Mother Nature and natural consequences bitch slapped humanity back into line. '

"Right." Echo's nervous movements stopped, and she blew out a breath. "Talk about a throwback. That place was ransacked decades ago. It sits out on the other side of the river. Not like there was much there to start with. Some buildings, fields, and I think there used to be one of those shopping center monstrosities. I mean, it's in the middle of nowhere, so it fits some of your criteria."

It did, but Charity banked her rising excitement. "Anything still standing out there?"

Echo shrugged. "Dunno. Haven't been out there in years. Last I remember there were a few buildings that might pass for usable. If you're desperate enough."

Depending on the payoff, the Raiders wouldn't care if they were meeting in the middle of hell.

Ruin leaned in. "Anyone using them?"

Echo's attention sharpened. You mean like street rats?"

He nodded.

She took a moment to think it over. "It's possible. It's far enough outside the city limits no one would give a damn who crashed there. Plus, anything of value was stripped forever ago so it's not like it's on anyone's radar."

"You got directions?" When Echo nodded, he grabbed a napkin and shoved it at her. "Map."

Surprisingly the other woman didn't protest his bossy demand but slipped her fingers under the edge of her top, pulled out a pen, and started sketching out the directions.

Guess that was as good a place as any to stash your writing utensils. If this Carousel place was such a relic, then the good news was there shouldn't be much in the way of security. Which just left the bad news. Under the protection of the table, Charity squeeze Ruin's thigh in warning. "Riverman mean anything to you?"

Echo's pen stilled before resuming its scratching over the paper, but Charity didn't miss the minute shift in her posture or her quick swallow. "Riverman?"

Oh yeah, it meant something. Charity waited her out.

Echo tucked the pen away, flicked the paper toward them, braced her forearms on the table, and lowered her voice. "Considering how long we've been business associates, Charity, may I suggest you and your man be careful where you toss that name at?"

Charity's stomach knotted at the unsettling seriousness on the other woman's face. She ignored the 'your man' part as uneasiness replaced her earlier anticipation. "Why do you think we're talking to you?"

Charity's respond eased some of the tension in Echo's expression. "Always knew there was a solid brain in that skull of yours, girl."

"You're stalling," Ruin cut in, earning a glare from Echo but he was undaunted. "Who is he?"

Her mouth pressed into a mutinous line, and on the table, her hand curled into a fist, then slowly relaxed. "He is River

Man." She separated the name into two parts. "It's the only name used around here. Mainly because those who go fishing for more end up face down in the river."

Charity kept her mocking quip about obvious naming conventions to herself.

Next to her Ruin tensed, but his question was deceptively casual. "What's his specialty?"

"He's a Broker."

Again with the emphasis? Echo wasn't normally this much of a drama queen, especially when it came to business, yet the name scratched at Charity's memory. "Who does he broker for?"

"Nope." Echo shook her head. "No more. I gave you your two answers, and I like breathing." She shifted forward, her face and voice hard. "Pay up."

Despite the flash of fear Echo tried desperately to hide, Charity took her time pulling away from Ruin so she could reach into her pocket. She dug out the agreed upon payment and held the two thin squares of credit between her thumb and forefinger. The other woman's arm snaked out and latched on, but instead of letting go, Charity held on and kept her voice low. "What does he broker, Echo?"

Echo tugged unsuccessfully on the credits, the flash of fear morphing into a resigned panic. "Anything, if you can afford it."

Charity let go.

Echo yanked the credits back and added, "But rest assured, even you can't afford him." On that parting shot, she got out of the booth, tucked her payment away, and smoothed down her skirt. Then she found her footing, in more ways than one, and some unreadable emotion slipped through her wary gaze.

"*Raid!*" The shout cut through the electronic din just as her mouth opened, and hit the room like a bomb. Gamers scattered like rats on a sinking ship, abandoning their electronic conquests as they raced for exits.

Ruin slipped out of the booth and offered Charity a hand. Echo's attention was on the entrance hall, but Charity couldn't see who or what she was staring at because the club's lights started a seizure-inducing dance. What she could see was Echo spinning on her heel, her intent clear—escape.

She snagged Echo's wrist and pitched her voice to be heard over the racket. "Exit?"

Echo yanked free and headed for the back wall. With Ruin's hand in hers, Charity followed, determined to keep the other woman in sight. Knowing Echo wouldn't want to be 'detained' by whoever served as the local authorities any more than they did, Charity trusted her to lead them out.

They reached the back wall, where Echo ran her hand over the surface. A section slid away, exposing a dark opening. They followed Echo into the narrow space. Charity stepped into the shadows and immediately hugged the wall as Echo, who waited until Ruin ducked inside before closing the escape hatch behind them.

With the opening sealed, the darkness was complete. Normally comfortable in the dark, the suffocating confines gave Charity the willies. Even Ruin's solid presence at her back could hold her shiver back.

There was the sound of something scraping over wood and then a sharp snap. A feeble greenish glow sparked, and added a macabre cast to Echo's face. She raised the glow stick above her head and pointed beyond Charity.

Charity turned to face the unrelenting darkness. *Guess they were going forward.*

She looked back over her shoulder, just as Echo squeezed by Ruin, who was hunched over, his shoulders skimming the sides of the escape tunnel. Charity sucked in her stomach and pressed hard against the wall as Echo slid by to take the lead.

"Here." The word was a bare whisper.

Charity took the unbroken glow stick. Echo didn't wait and kept moving. Charity snapped her glow stick awake and turned to Ruin. Before she could say anything, a muffled shout seeped through the wall. Charity scrambled after Echo, leaving Ruin to follow.

It wasn't long before the narrow passageway came to an end what resembled a metal shaft. Raising her glow stick, Charity turned in a slow circle, searching for a ladder or another door. *Nothing.*

She turned to Echo, only to see the other woman steadily crawling up the sheer wall. She got within inches of the wall and discovered there were shallow depressions staggered up the side. *A haphazard, built-in ladder. Lovely.*

She put the glow stick between her teeth, and tested the first handhold, unsurprised when she found only enough room to curl her fingers over the edge. She looked over her shoulder at Ruin, dropped her gaze to his booted feet, and frowned.

Those were big damn feet and getting them to fit into the narrow depressions was going to be iffy at best. A touch on her chin brought her eyes to his.

"Go," he mouthed, then motioned her to hurry.

She turned back and started to climb.

Long minutes passed, the quiet broken only by their breathing and the soft sounds of their climb. When Echo finally stopped, Charity's fingers were going numb. Not wanting to stare up Echo's skirt, for any number of reasons, Charity twisted her neck to find Ruin grimly clinging to the wall a step or two below her.

The scrape of metal sounded and was followed by a breeze. Charity looked back just in time to watch Echo disappear through an opening. With an end to the muscle-seizing climb in reach, Charity scrambled up. At the top, she forced her aching arms to lever her body out of the opening. She rolled to her back on what appeared to be a roof of some sort and sucked in deep breaths. She took a moment to flex her fingers and toes in an effort to restore feeling and blinked at the cloud-draped night sky.

There was a masculine grunt as Ruin joined her. Instead of lying back, he remained on his hands and knees next to her, his face above hers.

She shifted her head just a bit to see his face. "That was fun."

His amber eyes glittered in the night, and there was a flash of white as he grinned.

Their moment was interrupted by another scrape of metal and a dull thunk as Echo closed the hatch. Charity rolled over and up into a sitting position. "Thanks."

Echo brushed off her skirt and gave her a glare. "Working with you is a pain in the ass, Charity."

Deciding to take that as a compliment, Charity grinned.

Echo shook her head, her disgust evident. "I'm out of here."

"Where is here?" Ruin asked, as he shifted to sit next to Charity.

"Just south and east of where you started." Echo straightened her shoulders and started walking in the opposite direction. "Next time you need information, hit up someone else." With that last sour warning, she slipped over the roof's edge and disappeared.

Ruin turned to Charity. "I'm assuming she doesn't fly."

Charity shook her head. "I'm betting she'll use a neighboring roof as her exit."

"Interesting friends you have."

"More of a business acquaintance than a friend." She pushed to her feet and wandered over to the edge where Echo disappeared. Sure enough, the neighboring building's roof was close enough to jump to, and she'd bet there was an access door just on the other side of that section on the left. Nice escape route, but not one she wanted to follow.

She walked in the opposite direction, ignoring Ruin as he sat and watched her. After peering over the edge, she realized they were on the roof of the graffiti-covered bar. Ruin came up beside her and together they watched as the local militia hauled out a handful of teens from the front of the burned-out warehouse and sat them on the curb.

"Looks as if some didn't run fast enough," he noted.

"I wouldn't be surprised if they were paid to be caught."

"Seriously?"

Ignoring the weight of his stare, she nodded. "It gives everyone else time to get out of the zone."

"Huh," he sounded thoughtful. "Not sure anyone could pay me enough to take the heat for someone else."

Good to know. She pushed away from the edge. "Well, shall we make the most of their sacrifice?" Together they went to the roof's backside, as far as they could get from the activity out front.

"We jumping?" Ruin stood at her side, his dry amusement evident.

"Yep." Thankfully, in this area, the buildings were all but stacked on top of each other. The distance from the bar to the building behind wasn't more than six, maybe seven, feet. The jump was still nerve-wracking, especially considering if they missed the other ledge, the resulting drop was a good thirty feet.

"I'll go first," he offered.

"Okay." It was logic, not procrastination dictating her answer, despite the clammy sweat rolling down her spine. If she misjudged the distance, with his longer reach, he was more likely to make it.

They picked a starting point far enough back to give them

the speed they needed and got ready to leap. Ruin grabbed her hand, squeezed, then let her go. "See ya on the other side, sweet cheeks."

He was gone before she could respond, racing over the roof and launching his body into the air. As he hung in the air, her breath caught. When he landed in a forward roll, air escaped her lungs in a rush.

She tried to settle her breathing and pulse, but it was useless. "Suck it up, Charity," she muttered under her breath as Ruin waited on the other side.

She gritted her teeth, sprinted forward, and picked up speed as she raced over the roof. Her foot hit the ledge and with every ounce of strength available, she launched into the air, her stomach free-falling as she stretched towards Ruin.

Her heart seized as her body began its decent. *She wasn't going to make it.*

Panic clawed for a foothold. She focused on Ruin, who leaned forward with his hands out, reaching for her. She twisted, stretched, and strained, connecting in a hard sting slap of skin. Ruin's solid grip on her wrist came first. Quickly followed by the scrape of brick under her other palm as she desperately clung to the edge of the building. Her body slammed against the wall, and her lungs stalled at the impact.

Ruin didn't give her a chance to relearn to breathe before he hauled her up. Her shoulder screamed, but between his hold and her grip, she finally managed to make it up and over.

Once safe, she collapsed to her ass. Her chest ached as she sucked in air and waited out the shakes, staring at the raw, seeping scrapes that marred her palm. The screaming pain of her shoulder slowly dulled, and tomorrow her wrist would carry bruises from Ruin's unrelenting grip.

Ruin crouched in front of her. "You okay?"

Before she could guess his intentions, he caught her hand and turned it palm up under the feeble moonlight. His thumb absently stroked over her pulse, which responded by picking up speed.

Swallowing against her suddenly dry mouth, she croaked, "Oh, yeah."

"When we get back, clean this." He only let her go once she nodded, then he settled in next to her, their backs braced against the low edge of the roof.

She took advantage of their momentary respite and waited until she was certain she could stand without her legs collapsing before saying, "We better head back."

Ruin got to his feet and offered her a hand. "If that kid stripped my bike, I'll have his ass."

She managed a grin and gave him her undamaged hand so he could help her up. Thankfully, her legs held. "We still have twenty minutes before our deadline." They crossed to the roof's access door. "Our bikes will be fine."

He yanked the door open and waved her through. "You sure about that?"

She stopped in front of him, so close the feel of him, solid and strong, calmed the last of her tremors. "Positive."

Riding high on adrenaline-laced hunger, Ruin stared back. "Willing to offer your ass in his place, darlin'?"

His husky question triggered a startling deep vein of lust. *Who knew cheating death was an aphrodisiac?* Caught in the mesmerizing glow of desire kindled in his amber gaze, she willfully tempted the burn. "That all you want?"

His gaze darkened and his voice deepened. "You temptin' me, Charity?"

Uncharacteristically emboldened by her near-death experience, she answered, "Yep."

He dipped his head, nipped her lips, and whispered, "Then let's see how far I can fall."

eighteen

As they wove their way back to Agatha's, Ruin forced his thoughts away from the hunger running through his veins. It wasn't easy, but at least he managed not to incur life-altering damage to an organ he considered vital to his future plans. When he discovered their bikes were still in one piece, he wasn't sure if he was disappointed or not. He double-checked the bikes as Charity paid Sam. After checking the fuel lines, he straightened and watched Sam dart into the night, payment locked tight in his clutched fist.

Charity came over and gave him a cheeky grin, the heat from their earlier exchange still simmering in her bright eyes and heated cheeks. "Can I say it now?"

He knew damn good and well what was coming, but he played along. "Say what?"

She stepped in close, close enough her scent wrapped around him, undoing his previous good intentions. Her voice was husky as she said, "I told you so."

Before he could give in and drag her back to finish what they started on the roof, she spun away, her grin grew wide, and straddled her bike.

Her teasing lit a strange, but not uncomfortable ache in his chest. He absently rubbed his knuckles over the phantom sensation.

Charity kicked her bike to life and twisted the grip for a bit more fuel, only to wince. She released the throttle, shook out her palm, and gingerly replaced it. When she caught him watching, her expression turned rueful. "It'll be fine until we get back and I can grab a shower."

Images crowded his brain and rocketed straight to his dick. Which, based upon her obvious amusement, was the evil woman's intent. "Dammit, woman," he muttered over her chuckles as he mounted his bike. "Teasing a man before he gets on his bike is just cruel."

"Aww, poor baby. I'm sure you'll survive." With that, she started walking her bike back.

They headed to the Lodge without incident. A fact Ruin was grateful for as his focus continually drifted to how he planned to fill the next few hours with the woman riding at his side.

When they approached the gate, he lifted a hand to Kayvao. The gate rolled back, and once they were inside, the gate's heavy locks fell into place with resounding thumps that merged with the fading rumbles of their engines.

Late as it was, light rimmed a couple of curtained windows, but no-one lingered in the courtyard. Once they had their bikes stashed for the night, they headed towards their room, walking side-by-side, so close their arms brushed. Neither one spoke, but the air between them sang with erotic awareness.

At their room, he unlocked the door and cleared the interior while she leaned against the doorjamb. He didn't bother with talking, simply took her hand, pulled her inside, and closed the door. A lone lamp bathed the front room in a cozy glow, but it was enough to illuminate her face as he crowded her against the door.

Her hand rose in a lame attempt to hold him at bay, and unmistakable lust shone bright in her eyes even as her nose wrinkled. "Whoa, buddy. Shower, remember?"

He braced his hands on either side of her head and trapped her without actually touching her. "Mmmm." He dipped in and nuzzled a spot just below her ear. "Not sure I want to risk you changing your mind."

A soft moan escaped her parted lips and her fingers tangled in his t-shirt as she tugged him closer. "Who said I would?"

He nipped along her delicate jawline and followed each tiny sting with a soft brush of lips. "Better safe than sorry."

She tilted her head and bared her neck, causing his beard to rasp over her skin. She gave a full body shiver at the sensual contact.

Male satisfaction filled him at her telling reaction. *Oh yeah, he wasn't the only one revved and ready.*

Her gaze drifted to his lips, and she drew her free hand up his arm to trail over his shoulder. She didn't stop until her fingers curled in the gathered hair at his nape, then she gently pushed at his neck at the same time she tugged his shirt.

He gave in to her tandem nudges and brushed his lips with hers. Her husky, "Knew you were smart," made him smile just before he caught her mouth in a scalding kiss that burned everything away. The delicate brush of her tongue drew him deeper, giving her equal access.

As if it was the signal she was waiting for, she grew bolder, adding in teasing forays and taunting nips designed to drive him out of his fucking mind.

It worked like a charm. Caught in her spell, he let her lead, for now, curious to see how far she'd take them both. *Her taste. Damn, it was better than any whisky and dangerously addictive.*

He fell deeper and deeper into the inferno, barely noticing when her head fell back.

A feminine gasp escaped, followed by a breathy, "Ruin."

With his ability to speak all but gone, he managed a rumbled growl and kissed along her exposed neck.

"Ruin, shower." Her gentle protest buzzed against his hunger, and only when her hands drifted to press against his chest, did her words penetrate.

He lifted his head.

Her face was flushed, her gaze dark and slumberous. She tried again. "Shower?"

He watched her lush lips form the word. "Right, shower."

His voice was rough, and his body ached. It didn't help that her hands kept moving, roving over his chest before dropping lower. At her touch, he groaned, his stomach muscles contracting in anticipation.

He covered her curious hands with one of his, pressing her palms flat against his stomach, and rested his forehead against hers. It was the perfect position to observe the intriguing rise and fall of her chest.

Fucking beautiful.

"Ruin?" There were traces of laughter in her voice.

"Yeah?" Under his hand, hers flexed, but he refused to let her go.

"You with me?"

So much it hurt. "Yeah, just trying to decide if it's worth it."

She stilled and feminine outrage added a bite to her voice. "Worth it?"

Unable to help it, his lips twitched. He lifted his gaze and straightened slowly. "If moving is worth the risk of damage to my dick, darlin'."

Answering humor lit her eyes. "Will it help if I promise to kiss it better?"

The idea of her lush lips wrapped around his cock just about dropped him to his knees and he groaned. "You're a cruel, cruel woman."

He grabbed her wrist and led her down the hall to the bathroom. Her soft laugh ran down his spine and seeped under his skin.

Once in the tight confines of the bathroom, he turned on the shower, toed off his boots, ripped off his t-shirt, and unbuttoned his jeans. Only then did he turn and saw that Charity was way ahead of him. Her boots were by the door, and her shirt was gone, leaving her in nothing but a cropped, thin camisole and skin. Her head was bent as she undid her pants.

Wanting to unwrap all that was her, he brushed her hands away and took over. He eased her zipper down, and loosened the material enough to slide his hands in. Heat and whisper-soft cotton met his touch. He slowly sank to his knees as he drew her jeans down, his attention riveted on what he exposed.

Itty-bitty pieces of material rode over luscious curves and highlighted taut muscles and acres of skin that begged to be tasted. She was the ultimate in temptation and he sure as hell wasn't strong enough to resist.

Not that he wanted to. He leaned in and pressed a soft kiss just above the edge of her panties. Teased by a hint of cinnamon-spiced honey, he followed with a delicate swipe of his tongue. *Mmm, warm and sweet.*

Her hands sank into his hair and pulled it free. "Focus, Ruin." Her husky command was followed by a gentle tug on his hair.

He took his time acquiescing to her demand, his gaze leisurely drifted up until it met hers. "I'm so fucking focused."

Without breaking eye contact, he stroked up those toned legs and over the globes of her ass, pulled her close, and drew his tongue along her stomach, going higher, his ultimate goal unmistakable. Her hands slipped from his hair, soft sounds escaping, and clutched his shoulders as he took his time tasting her. He relished the sexy noises and feel of her nails digging into his shoulders as he indulged.

Even better was witnessing how lost she was in the rising storm. Passion colored her face and left her lashes at half-mast as her chest rose and fell, all visceral evidence of her need. When that damn tongue of hers darted out and her white teeth caught her lower lip in a vain attempt to stifle her hungry sounds, he was truly lost.

Using his hold on her ass, he dragged her close until her knees buckled, and she slid down to meet him. The feel of her, hot and soft, had his dick demanding freedom. He forced his hands to release her plump curves and stroked his palms along her spine.

His caress caused her to arch closer and press her gorgeous chest against his. She writhed against him, and the sensation left them both groaning in unison. He tore her thin camisole up and off and cupped her breasts.

The feel of the warm, luscious weight against his palms made his mouth water. His thumbs brushed the sides and came perilously close to her sensitive tips. He bent down and captured one berry-colored nipple with his mouth and fed.

Her fingers tunneled into his hair and gripped. "Ruin."

Her husky groan was music to his ears but making out on the bathroom floor wasn't going to cut it for him. Not when his body was straining at the bit. He curled his tongue over her nipple for one more taste, then lifted his head.

He stared into her dazed expression and noticed the glistening drops of sweat on her brow. It hit him that the room was filled with steam from the damn shower. *Right, focus.* He growled, "Shower."

He didn't give her a chance to respond, simply stood, and brought her with him as he turned and opened the shower door. "Get in."

She leaned into him and pressed a series of open mouth kisses against his chest. "You joining me?"

He stroked a hand down her braid and gave it a gentle tug. "Hell, yeah."

Her hand caressed his ribs and drifted lower before curling over the edge of his waistband. His stomach muscles contracted as she popped the top button on his jeans. "You forget something?"

He stifled a groan at her teasing touch against his bare skin. "Nope, just making sure you get that damn shower you want."

Her smile was full of sin and temptation. "Now who's teasing?"

Her devious fingers dipped further until her touch burned like a brand, their path forever seared into his skin. Strangely, the concept didn't bother him. Instead, it felt right.

As she explored, he lost his train of thought. Every synapsis fired under the onslaught, and shot his concentration to hell, until all that was important was getting more of her touch. His hips surged forward in demand as her feather-light brush against the sensitive skin of his groin seared straight to his dick.

It took an insane amount of effort to fight free of the lust-filled fog conquering his brain. He gave her ass a sharp slap and grinned at her undignified squeak. "Get in."

With a huff, she gave him her back and stepped in. He made quick work of his jeans, grimacing a bit when they snagged on his cock, but finally, he was naked. Charity still had her back to him and was undoing her braid when he stepped in the shower's tight confines. Water fell over them and did nothing to ease the fire raging between them.

He grasped her hips and pulled her back until the feel of her ass against his dick had his eyes crossing in sheer delight. He wrapped his arms around her waist pulling her so close not even air could get between them. "God, Charity, you make me ache."

Her hands went to his and her head fell back against his shoulder. It gave him an unobstructed view the water sliding down her beautiful curves and beading over her tightly furled nipples. He shifted his grip, glided his hands up until he could capture her breasts, and played with her until she undulated against him, her hands locked behind his neck leaving her vulnerable to his touch. It was a surrender that ratcheted his hunger to a new level, where only sensation existed.

She let him indulge for a few heart-pounding minutes before she turned in his arms and blinked water-tipped lashes. "My turn."

As if he'd argue.

She started her exploration with butterfly tracings that soon escalated to a more tactile mapping. Every nerve ending ignited as she learned what made him tick, and she was a damn quick study.

It wasn't long before she wrapped her hand around his dick. He groaned, his hand guiding hers, showing her what he liked. She followed his lead but leaned in to lick and nibble at his chest, which added to his torment.

But he wanted more. He buried his hands in her hair and exerted slow pressure to get her luscious lips where he wanted them. When her wicked mouth covered the head of his straining dick, his knees almost buckled.

She played her tongue along his aching length, teasing and tormenting with relentless pleasure. It was all he could do not to drag her to the floor and gorge on what she offered.

Not wanting it to end in the next few seconds, he breathed through the ravaging hunger and carefully pulled her off him. Ignoring her disappointed whimper, he drew her back to her feet. Drowning the need to sate his hunger, he managed one word, "Bed."

She tilted her head in silent offering and he captured her mouth in a kiss that rivaled the heat of the falling water. Her hot little hands left his dick and ran over his bare chest. It took a tremendous amount of restraint to lift his head and free her lips.

He breathed through the storm of brutal lust and reached over to turn off the water. She took advantage of his inattention and pressed a series of open mouth kisses at the base of his neck. Her unerring accuracy left chills dancing over his skin.

She caught his reaction and flashed a wicked smile. "You like that."

Instead of answering, he shoved open the door, grabbed the towel hanging to the side, and wrapped it around her. If he didn't get them out of here, he was going to fuck her against the tiled wall. "Out."

She followed his command and stepped out. He snagged the other towel, did a quick pass, and then stepped out. He dropped it and in front of him, she did the same. As he barreled down the road in the wake of sensual temptation, sweet words fell by the wayside leaving him with limited options. He cupped her ass. "Up."

She braced her hands on his shoulders as he lifted and wrapped her legs around his hips. Taking advantage of her new position she slid her wet warmth against his dick. At the slick feel of her he just about blew. Instead, he groaned, not at all surprised when he felt her smile as she continued to kiss him. She showed him no mercy. Her mouth and hands were determined to drive him over the edge.

It hurt to walk, but with the end goal in sight, he was

determined to make his goal. As soon as he reached the bed, he bent forward, one hand holding her against him, the other braced on the mattress. She continued to cling to him as her spine hit the bed, and he followed her down. With her sprawled out like some decadent feast, he took a breath to appreciate the image of her lying there, watching him as avidly as he watched her.

She didn't hide her anticipation or her need. Her hair, turned dark from the water, spread around her. Her lips were swollen, her skin rosy with heat.

He crawled over her, until he surrounded her. He leaned in, his hair falling forward and shutting them into an intimate cocoon. He studied her expression as he brushed his thumb over her lips. When a sweet vulnerability drifted over her features, his heart clenched.

For a moment the raging lust was lulled by an unknown peace. In the strange quiet, they traced each other's faces, their gazes locked, and their touch sharing unspoken words. Her hands cupped his face and tugged him closer. As the familiar insatiable hunger started to reclaim its dominant position, he sealed their unexpected moment with a gentle kiss.

Their lips touched and clung, as the stunning realization dawned that despite the ache and burn of his body, this, with her, would not be satisfied with a one-time thing.

He lifted his head, stretched out beside her, and gloried in her heated gaze as it devoured him. Lying on his side, he propped his head on one hand and smoothed his other over the feast before him as she turned to mirror him.

His imagination hadn't even come close to reality. His palm drifted over one leanly muscled leg as it flared into a mouth-watering curve that led to a tucked in waist. Tempted by the enticement, he continued his exploration, brushing teasing fingers through the neatly trimmed patch at her core. As he played, her legs shifted restlessly, granting fleeting access.

She wasn't a passive partner, something he was extremely grateful for because the feel of her hands roaming over his body stoked the fire to a combustible level. Determined not to miss his chance, he left her wet heat and continued to caress over her trembling stomach to the straining tips of her tits.

Cupping her, he dipped his head down as he brought her flushed flesh to his mouth. As he licked and sucked at her sweetness, her fingers clutched at his scalp, holding him close even as she arched back. With her encouraging low cries, he continued his sensual assault.

She pushed him to his back and straddled him, teasing her heated core against him. Unable to resist the deliberate provocation, he tightened his hold on her curves, and thrust his hips until his dick could slide through her damp, welcoming center. Her nails bit into his chest as their groans sounded in unison.

"Fuck, Charity."

She bent in, nipped his lips, and answered his plea with a mischievous grin and a husky, "Please do."

Taking her at her word, he grabbed her waist and reversed their positions. One more hard kiss to keep her distracted, then he reached over her to the table by the bed and fumbled the drawer open. When he found one of the condoms conveniently supplied by the Lodge, he snatched it up and muttered a triumphant, "Yes!"

Charity took it with a sexy laugh and wasted no time covering him. "We owe the maids a huge ass tip."

He recaptured her wicked hands, locked them in place by her shoulders, and took her mouth again. She shifted restlessly against him, and he lifted enough so she could widen her legs, making a place for him in. He lowered down, released her hands, and drew her thigh over his hip so he could take his time and tease them both.

It wasn't long before she bent her other leg and braced her

foot against the bed as her hips rose and fell. He released her leg and used his hand to position his cock against her wet heat. Slowly, with deliberate intent, he dragged his aching length along her center. She gasped and her spine bowed, trying to bring him in.

"Patience, baby." It was sweet torture to deny them both, but if he let the leash slip, he wouldn't last long.

"Maybe next time." Frustration was evident in the bite of her response, but she gripped his arms and flexed her hips in unmistakable feminine demand.

It proved to be too much. He caught her mouth in another hot tangle of tongues and plunged forward. Their mouths broke apart as she cried out and he groaned as they came together in a flash of fire.

The feel of her so tight and hot, was like being wrapped in living flames. Caught in the wildfire, he couldn't slow to enjoy the journey, he could only tumble headfirst into the storm.

They moved together in a breath-stealing race towards the looming peek. Her soft cries mixed with his groans as their bodies strained under the relentless whip of desire. The fire between them raged, turning their world into a white-hot inferno. Then, as one, they crested and broke, free falling into a beautiful oblivion.

Ruin lay there, his hunger briefly sated, and anticipated the next go around. With the clawing need held at bay, this time he would go slower and spend his time delving into the fascinating spell of the woman who still trembling beneath him. Being with her, like this, felt familiar and right, a fact that should alarm him, but all he wanted was to spend the night indulging in his brand-new addiction – Charity.

RUIN WOKE with an arm full of feminine curves and a smile on his face. Charity was sprawled across his chest, her blonde tresses clinging to his beard. He curled one silky tendril over his finger and savored the unexpected peace of the moment.

Bit by bit, the truth eroded his calm. He was in trouble here. Somehow, someway, Charity managed to sneak in and carve out a soft spot in his heart. At the thought, he stifled a groan. Vex would laugh her ass off about this—him being done in by a blonde bundle of trouble in such a short time, yet he couldn't rouse much concern.

Charity was unique. Behind her guileless blue eyes and blonde hair existed layer after layer of fire, spice, and a bit of deviousness. The woman was a never-ending puzzle. Each time he figured out a piece, she revealed another clue that drew him deeper, until she sank into places he hadn't known existed. Ripping her from those spots would leave scars.

Not to say that keeping her wouldn't cause more, but even knowing her loyalty rested with a woman Ruin wouldn't dare trust, couldn't stop what was happening.

What would it be like to be that important to someone?

That depth of commitment was admirable and enviable. Granted, the Vultures would always have his back, but having a woman like Charity in the same position wasn't a bad thing. In fact, it was one of the many reasons he was so attracted to her. Granted, she could lie with the best of them, but for the most part, she played it straight—no bullshit. Nor did she take his, which was refreshing.

A demanding pounding at the door interrupted his self-analysis.

He frowned. *Who the hell was at their door?*

Next to him Charity shifted and woke. "Who is it?"

"Don't know, babe," he murmured, untangling from her.

He grabbed a knife from the nightstand, strode naked and barefoot to the bathroom to snag a damp towel. He wrapped it around his waist as another impatient demand pounded against the door. Even though there were only a few people who could make it passed the Lodge's gate, Ruin wasn't about to play it stupid. He stopped well away from the door and snapped, "What?"

A soft rustle had him turning to see Charity coming up behind him, a blade in one hand, her other tugging his t-shirt down over her hips.

"Ruin, man." Kayvao's voice was muffled by the door. "Got a message for you."

"Hang on." Ruin crossed the remaining distance, grateful when Charity stayed close, but not too close. He opened the door.

The bigger man tagged Ruin's present state of undress and Charity behind him, and smirked. "Sorry to interrupt."

"Bullshit." Ruin's retort held no heat. "What's up?"

Kayvao handed over an envelope. "Delivered by some kid named Sam, said you'd want it."

Ruin frowned, handed Charity his blade, and took the letter. He opened it and scanned the three lines, while Charity read over his shoulder. He met her gaze. "Well, damn, that changes my plans."

nineteen

"You know this is stupid, right?" Charity tightened the thigh strap on her knife sheath as she braced her bare foot against the bed's edge. Despite the intervening couple of hours after the message's arrival, her irritation crowded out the occasional twinges from their earlier activities. *The man knew how to leave a lasting impression.*

"Got a better idea?" Ruin mumbled around the hair tie in his mouth. He pulled his hair back, took the tie, and secured it.

No, she didn't, dammit. She dropped her foot and stifled a sigh. But she couldn't ignore her clenched gut either.

"Besides," Ruin started to gather the weapons spread over the rumpled bed. "You're the one who asked Sam to keep an ear open." He slid his collection of blades into various spots on his body.

"Yeah, but having him and Echo both come up with the same name? It's too easy." And in her book, easy generally equaled a set up. "Besides, the way Echo talked about River Man ..." She wasn't sure how to put her worry to words.

Ruin tucked a blade into his boot, tugged the leg of his pants back into place, and straightened. "She was scared."

True. Charity sat on the edge of the bed and pulled on her boots. "Beyond the normal level of 'he's a scary ass dude' scared."

Ruin went and sat next to her, eyeing her closely. "And?"

She thumped her heel twice, sat back up, braced her arms on her knees, and met his amber gaze. For a moment her mind blanked, and all she could think was, *God, he's stunning.* It was more than the outer package, it was everything—his humor, his temper, his mind, his touch.

Hell, his touch was seared into her very bones. Instead of taking the edge off her desire, last night had honed it to a delicate finish. She wanted to ignore this crap and play some more. A soft tap on her nose made her blink.

Amusement lit deep in his eyes. "And?"

Her face heated. "And," it came out husky, so she swallowed. "And I don't like going into a situation blind."

"Understood, but it's happening today." His amusement faded as he studied her and was replaced by a calculating seriousness. "We've narrowed down the location. Thanks to what Sam picked up on the street, we have confirmation that whatever is happening definitely involves this Broker, River Man, whatever name he goes by, and the dung-shit Raiders that made it back. One way or the other, we'll get our answers."

Maybe. "And if it's a trap?"

Instead of laughing off her paranoia, his voice hardened. "The Vultures and Lilith were the only ones who knew we were heading this way." His affable mask slipped, revealing the battle-scarred warrior beneath. "I know who has my back, can you say the same?"

She grimaced. "It's not Lilith, or your friends, that worry me."

"Then who?" He cocked his head, his eyes narrowing. "Reznik?"

"Told you before, he's a bully, not a strategist." She shook her head. "He wouldn't risk whatever the hell this is by showing up."

"You sure about that?"

Was she? With her stomach in knots, she wasn't sure of much right now. "No," her uncertainty drew the word out. "Right now, I'm not sure what the hell is going on." *And that was what was keeping her on edge.*

"Well, then." He flashed her a devilish grin and slapped his thighs. "Let's go find out, shall we?"

IN THE PRE-DAWN HOUR, the ride out to what was left of the Carousel took Ruin and Charity a solid twenty minutes. They stashed their bikes in a dilapidated shack half collapsed under a slowly dying tree in the remains of what used to be a well-planned neighborhood. They took the last mile by foot and made their way through the overgrown remains of houses and old paved streets.

Charity's spine itched the whole damn time.

Crawling through virtual ghost towns never failed to creep her out. She swore the ghosts of those who once called places like this home, lingered like poisonous mists, just waiting for their chance to add another soul to their collection. Since Ruin displayed no such misgivings, she figured the hang-up was purely hers.

Luck made an appearance when they discovered a partially erect structure positioned just across from their target location. At one point in time, it stood higher than its current couple of stories, but it still provided enough height to get a prime vantage point. As they settled in among the rusted rebar, crumbling cement and torn metal, light was sneaking across the sky.

On what was left of the top floor, they cleared out a spot in the corner. Then they took turns at the empty window frame and used Ruin's binoculars to study the structure across the way.

There were two buildings, one long and rectangular, half of its roof gone, and behind it, a round building, its roof pitted with holes. Even with the brightening light, it was hard to make out much more than shadows.

Minutes ticked by, and stretched into an hour before Charity, handed the field glasses back to Ruin and broke the quiet. "If any street rats are holed up in there, they aren't moving."

"Maybe they aren't morning people," he murmured as he scanned the area.

Maybe, or maybe they'd been run off. She slumped down below the window frame. "We need to get inside."

"Know that darlin', but not keen on getting my throat slit before noon."

"Then you might want to be careful where you point those things." She motioned to the binoculars in his hand. "The sun's up. You misjudge the angle, and you'll lead them right to us."

He pulled the binoculars down and frowned. "Know that too."

At his grumpy tone, she sighed.

Debris crunched under his boot heel when he turned, sat next to her, and nudged her shoulder with his. "Thought you 'Hounds were all about patience."

She picked up a pebble and tossed it, listening to the tiny pings as it disappeared amid the rest of the rubble. "I don't like it here."

"Why?"

She met his gaze. "Because if I was up to no damn good and wanted to hold a meeting in the middle of nowhere, the first thing I'd do is scout the surrounding areas for any unwelcome visitors."

"Raiders aren't exactly known for their brains."

Yeah, but what was that old saying? Something about assuming and asses? No way she wanted her ass hanging out there. "Maybe, but it's not making my itch go away."

He sighed. "Don't need you breaking out in hives." He got to his feet and offered his hand.

She took it, let him pull her to her feet, and said with saccharine sweetness, "You're so thoughtful, Ruin."

He tucked the binoculars into one of his jacket pockets and then headed back the way they came. He looked over his shoulder as she followed and winked. "Don't let it fool you, sweet cheeks, your itch is contagious."

He disappeared through the opening and left her shaking her head.

They made it to the scattered remains of the long, rectangular building undetected and slipped in through an empty doorway. Once inside, they picked their way through collapsed roof beams, piles of trash, broken tables and chairs, and curtains that were now nothing more than rags.

There were torn up mattresses tossed aside, who lost the battle with field mice, and the floor was marred with signs of old fires. Graffiti and scales of peeling paint lined the water-damaged walls as sunlight drifted through the missing roof to mix with dust motes, layering the interior in a hazy glow.

Following Ruin's carefully chosen path, she was grateful for the whisper of an occasional breeze that played through the desiccated remains. Not only did they lighten the heavy air, they broke the waiting silence and muffled their passage.

Halfway across the floor, Ruin lifted a hand, signaling her

to stop. She stilled, her hand hovering over the hilt of her knife as she scanned their surroundings.

Ruin crouched next to what appeared to be a pile of wood shoved against a wall. He lifted his arm, palm flat and, keeping an inch between him and the wood, brought it slowly down the uneven side. Then he turned and kept his voice low, "Come help me with this."

She went to his side and tried to see what caught his attention. When cool, ghostly fingers whispered against her face, she realized what the debris pile hid. "Is that a tunnel?"

He nodded and rose. "Grab that end. If we shift this piece, we can squeeze in."

It didn't take them long to expose the opening. She stared at the half-hidden entrance and the itch at the back of her neck increased. "You sure about this?"

"Nope."

Right then, that was comforting. Not.

Together they shifted one of the longer pieces of wood, and when a cloud of dust drifted up, she tried to stifle her sneeze. Ruin brought out a small flashlight from his pockets-of-plenty and aimed it into the opening.

From where she stood behind him, she could identify the graffiti that covered the rough walls. She didn't need his admonishment of 'Stay close' since there was no possible way she wanted him out of her sight. She gripped the waistband of his jeans as he stepped into the tunnel.

They crept down the relatively clear passageway for what felt like forever, but was more like ten minutes, before the darkness ahead started to lighten. Ruin slowed and she let go, needing her hands free, just in case. He clicked off the light and she blinked a few times until her eyes adjusted.

Ruin hugged one wall and she mirrored him on the other side. The edge toward the opening, and she let out a little, surprised gasp. Ruin frowned at her in silent reprimand. She shut her mouth and continued to stare at the strange sight.

The tunnel dropped them into the smaller round building. Early morning sunlight fell through the arched openings that ringed the high, domed ceiling. In the middle of the vast room, under a canopy of shattered remnants of light bulbs, stood a collection of animal statues held in place by poles evenly spaced on a faded red, circular platform. The surreal sight was a visual explanation of the Carousel moniker.

There was a large cat, its mouth opened in a ferocious growl. Despite its faded colors, the details were disturbingly real. Next to it, a regal horse in dusty white with dull gold detailing was frozen in mid-stride, neck arched. *Who the hell put an amusement ride in the middle of nowhere?* She wondered at the logic used by those of the past, because for all their advancements, they seemed enamored of useless shit.

A soft hiss brought her attention back to Ruin. She followed his hand gestures and slipped out of the tunnel. They split up and made their way around the opposite sides of the merry-go-round.

She passed a door blocked by a floor to ceiling pile of rubble. Ahead there was another door, this one usable, but the tunnel was the easiest route between the buildings. She tried to ignore all the glassy, staring eyes of the painted animals, but couldn't shake the weird feeling of being watched. It left her wired.

When Ruin slipped up next to her, she started. He shook his head, his face carved in lines of frustration.

She mimicked him, indicating the same. There wasn't much more to the room, but she could see why it would be the perfect place for a meet. No one could approach without being seen. It also meant that finding a concealed spot to spy from would be a challenge.

Ruin was apparently following the same logic. "Well,

shit," he kept his voice low so it wouldn't carry. "Not much we can use."

She turned away from the staring, inanimate herd, and scanned the interior. There had to be some sort of concealment around here. She looked up and studied the domed ceiling. Lined with planks, it was bare of any usable light fixtures or crawl spaces. In fact, their only option was the stupid carousel.

She glared at the ridiculous thing, taking in the high curlicues that ringed the top and framed various scenic paintings, each one topped with – *were those grapes? Seriously?*

She continued her examination, determined to find something that would work. No way was she missing out on this damn meet, not if it got her closer to those who had targeted Tabby.

She left Ruin standing there and stepped onto the platform. When it shook under her feet, she grabbed the nearest pole. A groan of protest drew her gaze up. The pole was hanging on by a screw. She let go, frowned, stepped off the platform, looked up, and then back under the roof, an idea sparking. She backed away and eyed the grape-topped crown. "Ruin."

He was at her side in moments. "What?"

She pointed up. "We can hide up top."

He eyed the monstrosity warily and raised an eyebrow.

She grabbed his chin and lifted it.

He followed her direction and frowned.

Exerting patience, she explained, "If we lie down, we can stay behind those edges. They're high enough to hide us from those below."

He hopped up on the rickety platform and considered the ceiling. "If it holds our weight, it could work." Before he stepped down, a muffled thunk drifted from the tunnel and caught their attention.

They turned towards the opening as more sounds drifted over. There was a rattle of pebbles underfoot, a muffled curse abruptly cut short, and then the unmistakable sound of heavy footsteps coming closer. Her pulse raced and her nerves stretched into razor wire.

Ruin snagged her hand and dragged her to the back of the carousel, keeping kept the contraption between them and the tunnel's entrance. Once out of sight, he grasped her waist and all but threw her up. Her hands caught the scalloped edge of the ride's crown and the carousel rocked with a soft groan of wood under her weight.

She gritted her teeth, ignored the dull throb of her shoulder, and pulled herself up and over. With time running out, she did her damnedest to move soft and fast, not wanting the thing to shake apart.

Thankfully, as she climbed up, the structure remained fairly level, lessening its shimmy. Even better was discovering the roof was constructed of metal sheets, not the same dried wood as the edges, which drastically lowered their chances of crashing through the weakened roof.

Ruin swung up behind her and dropped flat next to her. Lying side-by-side, they stilled as the sounds drew nearer. She stared at the back of one of the panels and concentrated on slowing her breathing.

A touch on her arm brought her head around to see Ruin motioning for her to move towards the front. She raised an eyebrow in silent question. Correctly interpreting it, he motioned to the other side and then leveled both hands, shifting them up and down.

She got it. If they laid on opposite sides of the roof, their weight would be more evenly distributed, and it would keep the roof somewhat level, eliminating any possible signs of their presence. She dipped her head and he inched carefully back and headed for the far side.

Once he was far enough back, she inched into position on her side. The metal under her stomach vibrated faintly as he did the same on his side. The sounds of someone approaching became louder, hopefully drowning out any noises Ruin's movements caused.

Lying hidden behind the large arching panel to the left of center, she kept her body relaxed and angled her head to the side. Under her, the carousel slowly stilled as Ruin settled in place. She rolled her eyes up and saw Ruin lying in a similar position on the other side. Just in time too.

The sounds disappeared and she didn't need a visual to know that whoever arrived was studying the room. It was there in the expectant silence that crept through the room. She didn't dare move and continued to hold Ruin's gaze.

Normally, in a situation like this, she was on her own. Yet staring into his steady gaze, she found a soothing sort of calm. It wasn't until his lips formed the word 'breathe' that she realized she was holding her breath. With a slow blink, she let out a silent exhale and turned away.

Below them, their unseen visitor must have finally decided it was safe because the crunch of gravel turning underfoot broke the quiet. She closed her eyes, pressed her cheek against the cool metal and listened to him move around.

An ear-piercing squeal of metal over cement cut through the room, followed by the clatter of wood.

"Watch it, asshole!"

"Fuck you, dipshit."

A harsh grunt followed the witty conversation, and suddenly the carousel rocked. Unprepared for the movement, Charity's cheek slammed against the roof with bruising force. She bit her lip to keep her pained yelp silent and her watering eyes flew open, her hands scrambling for a non-existent purchase on the metallic surface. Somehow, she managed to brace her palms and toes against the high edge and the center drum. Spread-eagle, she tried to become part of the roof.

"Ow! What's that fer?" The whiny question came from idiot number one, AKA Dipshit.

"What? I need a reason to dump ya on your ass now?" answered idiot number two, or Asshole.

"What the hell's this anyways?" Dipshit's question was full of youthful disdain.

"Don't know, don't care," growled Asshole. "But if ya don't shut yer piehole, I'll shove a pole up yer ass and add yer squealing carcass to whatever the hell it is."

Catching the hard, mean tones, Charity made a note to watch herself around that one.

The structure rocked again as heavy soled shoes—probably boots—hit the platform creating a dull echo. "Looks like the shit back home."

Charity didn't need to see young Dipshit to follow his path as he wound through the painted animals, his footsteps easy enough to trace. So were his grumblings. "When we going home, Pit?"

"When we're finished," Pit the Asshole snapped.

Another thud sounded almost directly below her. "Hate hiding out in the damn boonies." The complaint was followed by another thud.

"Stop kicking shit." Heavy footsteps drew close, then landed on the platform below.

She wrinkled her nose in silent protest of the sour stench wafting up from below. It was familiar, carrying the combination of sweat, dirt, unwashed bodies, stale blood, and rancid sourness that mixed in eau de Raider.

Ignoring the threat in Pit's voice, the kid kept whining, "Don't know why we can't check shit out in town. Ain't nobody know who we are."

"Shut. Yer. Trap."

A squawk came from below, then the carousel rocked in tandem with three solid thumps and a protesting groan of metal. The thud of a body hitting the ground was accompanied by a harsh, choking gasp.

"Stop yer damn yammering and get yer ass outside and make sure no-one's around."

The sounds of scrambling were followed by the rapid beat of running feet. Guess Dipshit didn't want to stick around. She didn't blame him. Pit's threat chilled even her blood.

She listened to Pit move around and vented, "Gonna make them pay fer saddling me with some dumbass who don't know shite. Should've gutted him before we got here, saved me a damn headache."

The Raider continued his rampaging monologue and she flinched when wood splintered against a wall. Finally, he wound down to the occasional curse.

"Considering your behavior, should I be concerned?" The casual question snaked into the room like a well-honed blade, smooth and lethal.

Curious as to who had joined their little get-together, Charity carefully shifted her head until she found a gap on the panel. It wasn't much, just a minor break between boards, but it gave her a slender sightline to the tunnel's entrance.

From her limited position, she made out an average frame in dark clothes. Facial features were blocked by the edge of the carousel's roof. If she wanted to see more, she'd have to move. Hopefully, Ruin had a better angle.

The newcomer stuck close to the walls. Despite the morning light that seeped through empty window frames high in the ceiling and stretched in from the doorways, his dark clothing blended with the shadows. A trick Charity was familiar with, considering she used the same one, once or twice.

Pit stomped over and into her line of sight. Built like a

cage fighter, the Raider was big and solid. From her vantage point, she could see ink crawling out of the dingy color of his shirt and up the base of his shaved skull. *What the hell did they feed Raiders to get them that size?*

"Nothin' fer you to be concerned 'bout, River Man," Pit snarled, closing in on the newcomer.

"That's close enough." The ice-cold command was followed by the soft click of a gun's safety being released.

Pit rocked to a halt, his fists going to his waist. "Gonna shoot me to get out of our deal?"

"No." River Man remained unruffled. "However, I have no problem putting a bullet between your eyes if you come any closer."

That got a harsh bark of amusement, but Pit held his position. "Ya sure your employer—" the word was sneered, "—would like that? He didn't strike me as the forgivin' type."

Coldly confident, River Man said, "He trusts me to protect his interests, which is why you are dealing with me, instead of him." The smaller man's head canted to the side as he lowered his gun. "Of course, if you would rather deal with him directly, I'm sure it can be arranged."

There was something disturbing in his voice, something even the thickheaded Pit didn't miss, because he lost some of his bluster and muttered, "Don't need no personal meetin'."

A flash of teeth emerged from the pulled-up hoodie as River Man's gun disappeared into a pocket. "Yes, well, considering how things played out with Tank's personal meeting, I'm sure that's a wise decision."

That earned a low growl from Pit.

Charity's body stiffened at the subtle confirmation of Reznik's role with the Raiders. Despite her self-directed disgust at overlooking Reznik's hunger for power, she stayed focused on the conversation below.

River Man kept talking. "Why don't you bring me up to

date on where things stand with our last order? I do hope you have better news for me."

From her spot she watched Pit's jaw flex as he gritted his teeth. "Ain't our fault Crane's people attacked us."

"Isn't it?" Disdain dripped from the question.

Pit stared him down. "Your man was supposed to keep 'em busy. Obviously, he didn't do so good with that."

Great, add one more thing to worry about. There was a mole was somewhere in Pebble Creek. Ruin would be foaming at the mouth to let the Vultures in on that tidbit.

Now it was River Man's turn to be pissed. "And your men were supposed to bring those kids here, not stop on the way to get their rocks off." He kept his voice low and whip sharp. "My employer is not pleased, not pleased at all. You losing those kids screwed his plans."

"Since Crane's guts are decoratin' his office," Pit snarled, "your boss got one of his wishes, so you best pay up."

River Man stiffened and never took his attention from the burly Raider. "My proof?"

Pit dug a meaty hand into his pocket, pulled something out, and tossed it to the Broker, who caught it.

"What's this?" River Man held up the small, wrapped package. Duct tape circled stained paper.

Charity had a sudden thought of what lay inside, and her heart winced.

"Yer proof." Sure enough, Pit's cruel amusement confirmed her guess. "Crane's finger, the one he inked with that damn pansy ass Mick design." Pit folded his arms over his chest. "Go ahead, look fer yerself. I promise to stand right here while ya do."

Seconds ticked by as River Man unwrapped the grisly package. For once, Charity was grateful she couldn't see the details.

Obviously impatient, Pit broke the silence. "That work?"

River Man took his time re-wrapping the Raider's proof. "It's acceptable." The package disappeared into another one of the Broker's pockets. "Were you able to remove the Vultures from the picture?"

"Vultures weren't anywheres around. Lest not close enough to stop us," growled Pit. "It was just Crane, his pansy-assed second, and the other big idjit."

"I assume you mean Simon and Boden." Whoever the Pebble Creek mole was, they had a direct line to Crane's operation.

Pit shrugged. "Yeah, sure. 'Cept you don't haft to worry about Simon. I'm pretty damn sure he ain't breathing no more."

Strangely, River Man snapped, "Explain."

"When I left the others, they were busy nailing his hide to a wall." Pit's dark chuckle grated over Charity's skin and left her fighting back images of Simon's impaled body. She breathed through her fury and refocused on the conversation below.

Suddenly River Man moved into her line of sight and despite the concealing edge of the hoodie, Charity made out a square jaw and pointed nose, but not much else, before he crowded into Pit's personal space and forced him to take a couple steps back. "Excuse me?"

Confusion melded with Pit's mulish expression. "We followed directions. We hit Pebble Creek, took out Crane, and made sure to leave 'em scrambling. But we was leaving and he was doggin' our heels, so we took care of him."

"That wasn't part of your assignment," the smaller man hissed, his displeasure clear.

Pit stopped his retreat and faced down River Man, his fists clenching and unclenching at his sides as if it took everything he had not to wrap his thick hands around the other man's neck and squeeze. "Meybe not, but the fool followed us out. No way was he gettin' a chance to go back and set those damn Vultures on our asses."

"You sure he's dead?"

That question told Charity whoever was spying for Reznik hadn't checked in lately, otherwise River Man would be taking a different approach.

"Yeah, I'm sure."

River Man held still and stared at the Raider. "For your sake, you best be damn sure."

"The agreement was takin' out Crane, not the Vultures." Pit put his face close to River Man's. "We don't want the trouble they bring."

"Then your fellow Raiders will not be pleased when you bring that trouble to their doorstep."

The burly idiot shook his head. "Ain't no trouble followin' me."

The Broker cocked his head. "You sure about that? Where's the rest of your crew?"

Pit glared. "They be here in a few hours."

River Man studied him. "You better hope so, because if the Vultures catch the barest hint you had anything to do with killing Simon, you've got a shit-ton more than trouble on your asses."

"Whadda ya mean?"

River Man stepped back and shook his head. "I don't have the time nor inclination to explain it to you." He turned back and started for the tunnel's entrance. "Tell the others we'll have the agreed upon payment ready and waiting."

"Hold on, you little sh—" Pit's words cut off as a bloody hole blossomed between his startled eyes. He weaved like a cut tree before his knees collapsed and he toppled forward.

The sharp echoing crack of a long-distance shot bounced around the room and Charity winced. Stunned by the sudden addition of a sniper, she froze. Only when Ruin's barely audible oath whispered her way, did she angle her head until their gazes met and held.

The faint call of "Pit?" drifted from outside. Then came a second shot, followed by the dull thump of a body hitting the ground.

Charity turned back to the room.

River Man uttered a vicious curse and dove headlong into the tunnel, just as another shot ricocheted off the wall where he once stood. Noises drifted from the tunnel as he ran away, eliminating his chance of becoming the third body to drop.

Seconds stretched by as she waited for another shot, but all remained quiet. She stared down at creeping pool of crimson haloing the now dead Raider crumpled on the ground. It seemed someone was determined to tie up loose ends.

A touch on her arm jerked her attention to the fact that Ruin had crawled closer. "We need to follow him."

Him being River Man. She managed a jerky nod, knowing if they didn't get to him before the shooter, they could kiss their chances of getting to Reznik goodbye.

She followed Ruin to the back of the carousel, both being careful to stay low. She strained to hear over her thudding pulse, but her ears could only pick up the occasional breeze. No revving engines or running feet joined the morning.

At the back edge of the roof, as far from the sniper's sight as possible, they slid down to the floor. She grabbed Ruin's arm and kept her voice soft. "We can't go back out the tunnel or we'll cross his sights." And become new targets.

He shook his head. "Don't have much of a choice. Plus, I think he's already gone, probably trying to do the same thing we're going to do."

She gathered her disjointed thoughts and muttered, "Track down River Man."

Ruin nodded. "Ready?"

Not really, but she wasn't about to sit here and wait to get shot either. "Yeah, let's do it."

twenty

They made it back to their bikes without spotting a single hair of River Man or their mysterious shooter. Ruin's frustration rose as their cautious exit was further delayed when Charity dug the slug from the third shot out of the cement wall. Not only did it give their prey a huge head start, what did she plan to gain from a clump of mangled lead?

He didn't get a chance to ask, because once at their bikes, a half-assed plan was put together to head back into Kennewick so Charity could reach along her web of contacts to find out who had put the hit out on River Man.

With the Raiders dead, and River Man in the wind with a big old target on his ass, their next steps were limited. Use the Broker to get to Reznik. Unfortunately, chances were high their shooter was doing the same thing.

Ruin brooded over the conversation at the Carousel as he led Charity back into Kennewick. Even if he added in the new pieces to his patchy puzzle of what the hell was going on, he couldn't avoid the fact that their problems were piling up fast.

First and foremost was the Broker's unintended confirmation of Reznik's role in this mess. Charity's belief that Reznik couldn't manage something this big had bothered him from the beginning. Like an itch in the middle of his spine, forever out of reach. It got more irritating the longer he worked with her, because she had a knack for reading people. Except, it seemed, when it came to the New Seattle crime lord. At this point, it wouldn't surprise him to learn the shooter was hired by Reznik to tie up loose ends. *No honor among thieves and all that shit.*

Then there was the latest bombshell. There was a traitor in Pebble Creek. And if that wasn't enough to make him long for a straitjacket, the singular interest in the kids twisted his guts into knots. He had to find a phone quick because Reaper needed to watch his back and keep a close eye on those kids.

And the icing on the cake? River Man was on the run. It wouldn't be long before he started to question who wanted him dead, and the Vultures would no doubt top his list since the Raiders had fucked things up in Pebble Creek with Simon. The whole thing stank to high heaven and added credibility to Charity's assumption that something bigger was at play.

Going back to the Lodge was out because if River Man didn't know a Vulture was in town circling, he likely did now as the more questionable members of Kennewick all but pissed their pants at his name. That same fear left Ruin holding little hope Charity's upcoming search would produce viable results.

They hit the more populated edges of Kennewick and Charity took the lead. It was late morning, and the roads were busy. He followed her twists and turns as she headed into the older section of the city, in the opposite direction of the Lodge. The crowds thinned and buildings grew more and more decrepit. The echo of their passage was overly loud as they steered down alleys so narrow his shoulders nearly brushed the walls.

The hair at the back of his neck rose and stayed there,

quivering. He scanned their tight surroundings and various openings, catching the shift of shadows that indicated they were being watched.

Charity stopped in front of a scarred metal garage door that guarded a loading dock attached to an equally timeworn building. She left her bike running, hopped off, and slipped inside through the fire-scorched side door. The protesting creak of metal joined the grind of heavy chains as the loading dock door slowly rose.

As soon as it was high enough to clear, he drove in and turned off his bike. He dismounted and took her place at the chain, as Charity ducked back outside. Once she was back inside, he lowered the heavy door in place. The solid thunk as it touched down echoed through the cavernous space.

He pushed his sunglasses up and looked around the dim interior as Charity shut her bike down. Sunlight forced its way through grimy windows illuminating cobweb shrouded bare bulbs hanging from long wires along the center beams. A stack of boxes and piles of barrels lined one wall. Here and there, thick chains draped the beams and long tables with scattered, rusted tools sat under them. There were a couple of sections partitioned off, decorated with faded, curled posters of long-gone cars and partially nude women displaying their assets.

Interesting decor.

Charity wheeled her bike toward the back area. "We need to move the bikes."

He grabbed his bike and followed. When she disappeared around the corner, he realized a hidden back room sat behind the partition.

She positioned her bike in the center of the oil-stained floor and motioned for him to do the same. "Park it here." When it was in place, she led him back to the wall where an old electrical box sat. "Now watch." She opened the panel, flipped a couple of switches until a motor ground to life and the floor under the bikes started to drop.

"Nice." Color him impressed. "Yours?"

Charity shook her head. "Way out of my price league."

"Let me guess," he drawled. "Lilith's?"

"Bingo." She kept an eye on the lift as it dropped into place.

He studied her profile. "You sure that shooter didn't belong to her?"

She wrinkled her nose, but her answer was solid. "Wasn't hers. Too messy, and River Man's still breathing."

Which reminded him... "Why dig the bullet out?"

The lift hit bottom with a muffle *thud* and she answered absently, "Snipers tend to use unique ammunition."

Right, Havoc mentioned that once. Skilled shooters were notoriously paranoid about their bullets and tended to personally hand-pack their ammunition. And anything hand-made carried unique traits. "You're thinking it might be a way to trace the shooter?"

She shrugged. "It's a long shot." She flipped another switch and what looked like a replica of the earlier floor section slid close with a solid click, hiding the bikes. "If we strike out here, it's one I'm willing to try."

"You sure it won't lead back to Lilith?" The minute he asked, he knew he was reaching.

So did Charity. There was a cynical twist to her lips when she met gaze. "She wouldn't want their end to be that quick."

Of that he had no doubt, but he couldn't shake his displeasure with Charity's connection to Lilith. Since that wasn't going to change any time soon, and they needed to work together, he needed to set aside his personal hang-ups. He followed her back out front, determined to do just that and get back on track. "Can you get me to a phone?"

She worried her bottom lip and then gave a slow nod.

"Yeah, but it'll take a bit." She stopped by one of the tables, leaned a hip against it, and folded her arms over her chest. "You sure you want to call in now? It's not like we've got much to give."

He raised a brow and opened his mouth, but before he could answer, she cut him off with a raised hand. "I get there's a mole, but we don't have a name, or anything, to go on."

True, but... He rubbed the back of his neck. "It's more than that, it's the threat to the kids."

Her expression softened. "I don't think anyone's getting past Mandy, and that's if they make it by Reaper first."

He matched her pose and considered her point. With Lilith coming for her daughter, Reaper would have those kids locked down tight, but that wasn't enough to keep Ruin from giving Reaper a head's up. "How sure are you that you'll find a hit on River Man?"

A minute ticked by as she seriously considered his question. "Fairly certain. A job like that requires specialized skills."

"Which means a limited pool of options."

She nodded.

Curious, he asked, "So what's the plan? You're going to reach out and just ask who's got a hard-on for River Man?"

She rolled her eyes. "As if that would work. You saw Echo's reaction. If she's running scared of him, no way in hell I'm getting anyone else to 'fess up." A tiny frown furrowed her brow. "I need more subtlety than that."

Something about that frown got to him. Unable to resist, he reached out and used his finger to smooth out the lines. Her breath caught and he kept going, drawing that light touch down to her chin. With a gentle nudge, he tipped her chin up and caught the assessing gleam burning deep in those blue depths.

His gaze drifted over her flushed features, only to stop on her lips. It was tempting, very, very tempting to kiss her, instead, he clawed his lust back, dropped his hand, and cleared his throat. "Your plan?"

"I'll put out word that Lilith has a job open." Her response was equally husky and went straight to his dick. Then again, since last night, pretty much everything she did invoked that reaction.

He forced himself to step back, putting space between him and her sensual pull. "We don't have much time to waste on chasing dead ends."

"We won't have to." She straightened. "I'll make it a time sensitive job, give enough details to keep it close to the hit we just witnessed. Between that, and the specific skills set required, we should have a name or two to check out by tonight, giving you something solid to share."

Holding off a few more hours shouldn't hurt, but... "Won't your request be obvious, coming on the heels of what went down?"

She shrugged. "It's a chance worth taking." She cocked her head. "Unless you have a better idea?"

"Not yet, but I'll let you know if that changes." For now, he had no choice but to utilize her skills as a 'Hound for his answers.

She laughed at his obvious disgruntlement, her face lit with genuine amusement, and the momentary beauty of it left him stunned. She brushed past him and teased, "Gee, don't get too excited."

"Too late," he muttered, as he tried to clear the dazed fog from his mind. He straightened and followed in her wake.

"Hurry up," she called without looking back. "The longer we take, the deeper he'll go."

twenty-one

By late afternoon, thanks to the copious amount of home-brew that Ruin had sucked down, his feet were nothing more than a dull throb kept in check by his boots. Charity's version of 'putting out word' equaled his version of bar hopping.

Watching her work was pure hell. He spent most of his time hanging back and gritting his teeth as drunk and not-so-drunk bastards risked their lives by putting their hands on her. He didn't know if he wanted to shake her or bend her over the nearest surface and stake his claim in the most basic way possible. It was so far from his normal love- 'em-and-leave- 'em attitude, that his temper teetered on a dangerous edge honed by, he hated to admit, jealousy.

Despite his primitive response, he couldn't deny she was fucking brilliant at what she did. Every time she slipped into a group, she morphed into whatever personality fit best. A crucial skill in her line of work, but worrisome, nonetheless. Instead of outright interrogations, she finagled information with an easy laugh and encouraging smile. For the harder customers, her smile gained a sharper, hungrier curve, and her laugh left a few sweaty, pale faces behind. Either way, each time she walked away with more information.

As they headed towards yet another damn bar, his glare was focused on her ass that swayed in front of him. He wondered how much longer he was going to last before he lost it and gave into the hunger clawing under his skin.

He forced his gaze away from her curves and scanned their surroundings. Maybe he'd get lucky, and another dumbass would try to tail them. So far, he had run off two, but it wasn't enough to put a dent in his roiling frustration. Maybe a third time would be the charm.

A soft weight landed on his chest, and he pulled up short. He blinked and looked down to find Charity standing in front of him, her eyes narrowed.

"Is there something wrong with my ass, Ruin?"

His mind and tongue got tangled, but he finally got out a, "What?"

"You've spent the last few minutes singeing my ass with your glare." She leaned in and her voice dropped to a near purr. "So, is something wrong with it?"

His control slipped at her feminine challenge, and he cupped the back of her head, dragged her close, and used his other hand to squeeze the ass in question. He relished the press of her curves against his aching body for a few seconds before giving her a quick, hard kiss. Not enough to satisfy, just enough to soothe the jealous beast inside.

He lifted his head but didn't release her. "Not a damn thing. In fact, instead of hitting another dive, I have a better idea."

Her lips twitched, and she rubbed her hard little nipples against him in a slow drag. "Do you now?"

"Mm-hmm." Unable to resist, he took another taste, this one a little deeper.

Her body shifted against his as she gave as good as she got, before she slowly pulled back. "Thought you wanted to use a phone?" There was a hint of breathlessness to her question.

"Right." He rested his forehead against hers and fought to regain control. His dick ached, wanting nothing more than to stay right where it was, pressed up against her heat. He sucked in another deep breath, forced himself to let her go, and step back. "This time, I want food."

She laughed, and then the tease spun away, leaving him to follow her into yet another dive.

At least this one appeared to be a step up from her previous choices. The bottles behind the bar appeared grime free, the noise level was tolerable, and the air wasn't thick with smoke. Even the middle-aged bartender was an improvement, the man more likely to be in a community school than a bar.

Ruin's tension eased as he settled into a seat next to Charity at a battered, but clean table.

Within moments, a kid just out of his teens laid thick paper menus in front of them. "Hey, Charity."

"Hey Max." She gave the kid one of her rare, but real, smiles. "How's it going?"

"Busy with the Faire and all, but worth it." Max followed the menus with two glasses of iced water.

"Good tips?"

"Hell, yeah." He jerked a thumb over his shoulder towards the bar. "Dad managed to talk Mom into investing in some of the good stuff. Want some?"

The bartender raised a hand in their direction.

"Tell your dad we'll pass." Charity wiggled her fingers back. "Hey, is your mom free?"

"Let me check in with a couple of tables and then I can go let her know you're asking."

"Much appreciated."

"No problem." Max rapped his knuckles against the table. "Need some time?"

"Please."

The kid gave her a nod and left them alone.

Ruin picked up the menu and scanned the short list of offerings. "You think we'll get any bites from our fishing trip?"

"Maybe." She propped her chin on her hand and frowned. "If nothing else, we should get nibbles on who the shooter's identity. Especially since it's a well-known fact Lilith can afford the best."

Too bad he didn't share her optimism. "And if our bait catches the wrong attention, or worse, no attention? You got a plan for that?"

"Maybe."

He arched a brow and reached for his water. "Going to share?" He lifted the glass and took a long swallow.

Her gaze drift to his throat and stayed. "We corner Echo and force her to give up what she knows on River Man." She lifted her eyes to his, the hard, unforgiving bite in her voice at odds with the heated perusal in her bright blue eyes.

The strange combination fascinated him. He set his glass down. "And that wasn't your first choice, why?"

Her gaze didn't waver. "I prefer my lines of communication remain undamaged as long as possible."

That made sense considering where those lines might lead. "About finding a telephone."

She shifted in her chair and sat back. "I thought you were hungry?"

He gave her a mock glare.

She laughed. "Max's mom has a working phone."

Knowing that meant she was more familiar with Kennewick than he suspected. Add in the friendly reception, and he couldn't stifle his curiosity. "How often are you here?"

"I stop in whenever work brings me by." Her humor faded and was replaced by a careful wariness. "Max's family are good people."

A note in her voice indicated a story existed there. "Do they know who you work for?"

Her lips twisted with self-directed mockery. "Working for Lilith causes people to pay attention."

Ah. "So, your reputation precedes you."

A bit of color drifted over her cheeks, her gaze skittered away, and she reached for her water, mumbling, "Something like that." Then she took a drink.

He waited until she set her glass back on the table. "Tell me something."

Caution tightened her expression, but she met his eyes and said, "Depends on what you're asking."

Fair enough. He asked her the one question that had haunted him. "What did Lilith do to gain your loyalty?"

She went to answer, but before she could, Max was there. "You two ready to order?"

Ruin shook his head and picked up his menu.

Charity ordered. "I'll take the BLT."

"Want a side?"

"Apples and peanut butter, if you have it."

Max nodded, then turned to Ruin, and waited.

Ruin said, "Make it a double."

The kid collected the menus. "Mom's dealing with a delayed order, but she said she'd stop by when she's done."

"Thanks, Max." Charity flashed a smile.

Max flushed, nodded, and turned away.

Ruin gave a silent snort. Looked like someone had a crush going on. Once they were alone again, he turned to Charity, determined to resume their conversation.

Correctly interpreting his unspoken demand, she held up a hand and said, "I'll make you a deal, my story for yours."

Surprised, he considered her offer. It was tempting as hell, especially since his curiosity was burning bright. Besides, it wasn't as if he had any deep dark secrets hidden away. "Deal."

"My parents bounced around a bit, mainly sticking to the west coast territories, following whatever grift was working at the time." She twisted the sweating glass of water in a slow circle. "We landed in New Seattle about a year before I lost them. Things were good then, which is probably why they got sloppy. One night..." She trailed off and visibly swallowed, before continuing. "One night, I wanted to go out with some new friends, but my parents said no, so I snuck out." Her shrug was awkward. "When I finally got home, I walked right into Reznik's version of payback."

Despite her flat words, he caught the flashes of pain her memories invoked. He could imagine just what kind of nightmare a younger Charity had walked into and it left him heartsore. He kept his voice gentle. "Rough scene for a teen to walk into."

Her faint smile was filled with a rueful sorrow. "Yeah, rough's one way to put it." Her lips turned down, and she went back to studying the table. "Afterwards, I wasn't in the greatest of shape."

"No surprise there, darlin'." It was a lame attempt at comfort, but it was all he had to offer.

She sighed, sat back, and dropped her hands to her lap. "After their death I became rather obsessively focused."

Yeah, he could see that.

"Unfortunately," she continued. "I was so keen on taking out Reznik, I made a stupid mistake, and ended up in the wrong place at the wrong time." She finally met his gaze. "I went to where I thought Reznik had a deal going down, instead I stumbled into a transaction between one of his lackey's and Lilith. My sudden appearance in the midst of a delicate deal left Reznik's man jumpy." She winced at the memory. "Lilith talked him off the edge and managed to get what she needed. No harm no foul."

Somehow, he doubted that. "What? She just let you hang around while she finished up with business?"

That earned him a dry chuckle. "Nope, she nailed me a good one that left me seeing stars and meeting the pavement up close and personal. Then she put her knife to my throat and told Reznik's guy she didn't appreciate him trying to fuck her."

Charity's fingers drifted to a small scar on her neck, then fell away as she shook her head. "He was so worried she'd turn on him, he all but pissed his pants trying to convince her that he had no idea who the hell I was, or why I was there. When he finally left, it was my turn to answer her questions. She was quite explicit about what would happen if I didn't. Since I had no intentions of ending up in bloody pieces or bound in chains at Reznik's feet, I answered."

"I'm surprised you're still breathing." God knew Lilith wasn't one to take interference lightly, intentional, or not.

"Me too." Charity's brow wrinkled as if she was still a bit puzzled by Lilith's behavior all those years ago. Then it disappeared and her voice returned to its normal even keel. "In the end, instead of turning me over to Reznik, she offered the one thing guaranteed to get my attention."

"Revenge." It wasn't a guess.

She nodded. "In that brief time, watching her was a revelation. The way Lilith worked and went about getting what she wanted. The woman has mad skills." There was no mistaking the admiration in her voice.

It rubbed Ruin the wrong way. "She's also a cold-hearted, calculating bitch."

"Yes, she is." Charity's grin was cheeky. "But the things I learned from her were worth every terrifyingly wonderful minute."

Belaboring the point would be ridiculous, so he shifted

the conversation. "Explains why you stayed, but not why she didn't dump you."

Charity eased back in her chair, her expression contemplative. "Initially I think she took me under her wing because she viewed my obsessive need for vengeance as a potential tool against Reznik's games."

Considering the fact that it was easy to see how Charity's tenacity would go a long damn way if channeled correctly, he had to agree. But now she was a world away from that enraged teen. "And now?"

"Now she finds my skills irreplaceable. Her words, not mine." Unapologetic confidence swept over her expression. "I've worked hard to be who I am and I'm damn good at it." She leaned over the table as if to share a secret, a hint of mischief in her eyes. Unable to resist, he leaned in, and only then did Charity add, "Plus it's fun."

"Fun?" He held her sparkling gaze across the mere inches separating them and his voice was low when he asked, "You admitting to getting off on danger?"

He didn't expect her to reach out and tap his nose, but she did. "Don't you?"

He blinked and gave her question due consideration. Since he currently sat across from a woman guaranteed to blow his world to smithereens and had no urge to walk away, maybe it was his turn to admit his adrenaline addiction. "Is this where I do the 'danger is my middle name' shit?"

Her smile bloomed slow and sexy.

A plate hit the table and was accompanied by Max's squeaky, "Here you go."

Ruin slowly sat back as Max set another plate in front of Charity with more finesse. While the little shit managed to sneak a glare or two Ruin's way, the kid could barely look Charity in the face.

Ruin stifled a sigh and hoped Max hadn't spat in his food.

When Max left, Charity nabbed an apple slice, swiped it through the generous side of peanut butter, and took a bite.

Ruin picked up half his sandwich and took a healthy bite. His stomach rumbled with appreciation. They continued their meals in companionable silence as they filled their stomachs.

When he was down to just a few apple slices and a plate covered in crumbs, she finally broke the quiet. "Your turn."

"Don't remember much of my mom except that we lost her when Vex and I were about five." He nudged his crumb splattered plate to the side and sat back. "Know her death was hard on our old man. He wasn't much for kindness or smiles, but after Mom died, they became even more rare. He was a hard ass, but solid, and gave us a good life."

"Where did you live?"

"Outside of Portland, on the edge of the Dalles."

She propped her chin on her hand. "Been through there, it's beautiful, all those waterfalls and gorges."

Yeah, the land was wild but gorgeous, and sometimes he missed it. There was a simplicity to his life before things went to shit, but he was old enough to recognize that what seemed great to a kid, wasn't the same when viewed through adult eyes. "Just before winter, when we were about ten, he went out to hunt. He didn't make it back."

Catching the sympathy darkening her eyes, he forced an unconcerned shrug. "It took a bit before we finally admitted something bigger and meaner got a hold of him, but it left us on our own."

That first winter had been hell, and there were quite a few times he wasn't sure if he or Vex would survive until spring, but by some miracle they did. "We knew we couldn't stay put, so we headed out on our own. Eventually, we made it to Portland. We ended up joining one of the street gangs and ran wild for a few years. Eventually, a bigger group moved in and our little ragtag gang was given a choice."

"Join or die," Charity stated.

He nodded and his voice flattened. "We liked breathing, but as things do, it didn't take long before shit went south."

"Let me guess." Charity's expression darkened, adding an unmistakable edge of menace to her face. "Whoever ran things decided Vex was more valuable as a commodity."

Even years later, as old memories of what almost happened to his twin flooded back his gut soured. He swallowed hard, shoved the sickness back, and gritted out, "Sounds like you know the feeling."

Her lashes came down, but not before he caught a glimpse of the same nightmare he saw reflected in Vex's eyes all too often. "Yeah, seems as if females hold only one value on the street." She paused, both of them caught up in things better left alone. "So, how did you hook up with Reaper and Havoc?"

Grateful for the conversational shift, he latched on to it. "We fucked up. The head of our gang decided to send Vex and I over to repo their bikes."

Her eyes narrowed and her head tilted. "His way of eliminating problems?"

Ruin shrugged. "Probably, but in the end, it worked out."

"How so?" Genuine curiosity colored her question.

"We weren't as smooth as we thought we were." He scratched his chin, his lips curving slightly as he remembered the outcome of their failed robbery attempt. "After we picked our asses up, Reaper offered us a choice—go down with the gang or make amends."

"Wait, let me get this straight." Charity blinked in clear disbelief. "You joined the Vultures as penance?"

When she put it like that ... "Yeah, seems that way." He paused, then said, "Tell me how you met Boden."

"Didn't Simon share?"

"He said something about a cat, and alley and a woman."

"That about covers it."

"Really?"

She blew out an aggrieved sigh. "Yeah, I was heading home and ran into him— literally—as he was out in the rain looking for his current lady friend's pussy ..." She deliberately paused and aimed a wicked smile in his direction, then finished with, "cat."

He chuckled at her wit. "Chasing pussy's a bitch," he drawled.

Heat and carnal knowledge crawled over her face, leaving her flushed. "You'd know all about that, wouldn't you?"

The male beast inside him sat up, enjoying the hint of jealousy in her voice. "I know how to make one purr."

The flush in her skin deepened, but she picked up the last slice of apple, dragged it through the peanut butter, then offered him a bite. When he leaned in to take her offer, she issued a husky warning. "Best be careful, Ruin, some of them come with sharp claws."

"Screw being careful." He savored the sexual byplay and nipped her fingers. "Told you, I enjoy the added kick of danger."

Her low laugh was throaty as she drew her fingers back, brought them to her mouth, and licked away the traces of peanut butter.

Damn tease.

"That explains it."

He wiggled his eyebrows. "Don't knock it, babe, you're just as addicted."

She was all mock innocence as she deliberately twisted his words. "Hate to shatter whatever fantasy you've got going, but as I told Echo, women aren't my thing."

He snapped his teeth at her. "Not what I meant, and you know it."

Caught in the light-hearted moment, their gazes locked and something indefinable passed between them. Their smiles faded until they simply stared at each other, neither one able to look away.

Finally, Charity whispered, "Told you before, you're dangerous for me."

He gently stroked a finger over the back of her hand fisted on the table and was deeply pleased by the faint tremble that followed. "Yet you're still here."

She tilted her head and whatever thoughts chased through her head were hidden behind an impenetrable mask. "You expecting me to run for the door?"

Actually, he hoped for a different outcome. As unsettling as the thought was, it didn't stop him from taking the risk. "You willing to see how far this goes?"

Her gaze searched his as if she could see deeper than he liked. "I could ask you the same."

"Think I can't?" Whether she meant it to or not, her response came across as a challenge. One he refused to back away from. *Come on, darlin', I dare you. Take a risk.*

She narrowed her gaze. "Think you won't."

Three words and he knew he had her. Now it was just a matter of keeping her. "Going to be fun proving you wrong."

twenty-two

Charity perched on the edge of the desk in the bar's back office as Ruin filled Havoc in on the latest. She couldn't shake Ruin's warning and it was definitely a warning. Since denying her feelings would lead to dangerous things, she acknowledged it wouldn't take much for her to fall hook, line, and sinker for his improbable promise.

It wasn't just his screw-the-devil attitude that rivaled hers, it was how she felt with him by her side. Since losing her parents, a hollow ache had settled deep in her soul, cold and unforgiving. It was what kept her from fully embracing the emotional ties offered by Boden and others like him. Even Lilith and Tabby couldn't breach the wall.

She always held a piece of herself back as she waited for shit to fall apart. At first, her fury at what Reznik did to her parents kept it in check, but lately the numbness had spread, thinning those personal ties, and shoving her closer and closer to a line she never wanted to cross. Nothing and no one managed to tempt her enough to fight free.

Until Ruin.

Like some world-altering wildfire, he seared her reservations to ash and dared her to dance in the flames. Hell, she was so twisted up in him now, she didn't want to consider how much worse it could get.

She tried fighting his pull with logic—once this mess was cleaned up, they'd part ways, and with the antipathy the Vultures held for Lilith, Charity's job would be problematic. But with the Vultures acting as Crane's de facto heirs, they wouldn't be able to avoid dealing with Lilith, regardless of their personal reservations. And it wasn't like she could stay in Pebble Creek, not when her home was in Boulder. Everyone knew long distance relationships were doomed from the start.

What if there was a chance to stay close to Ruin? Say, like being a much-needed liaison between Reaper and Lilith?

She tried to ignore the hail-Mary suggestion, as her mind stuttered, then took a sharp right. *Oh, dear god, was she really considering the 'r' word in connection with Ruin?*

Ruin set the phone back in its cradle with a muttered curse before she could face the answer. Grateful for the distraction, she half-turned as he leaned back in the chair. "What?"

Ruin rubbed the back of his neck and blew out a breath. "Havoc's a stubborn ass."

"Tell me something I don't know."

He pushed to his feet. "Havoc and Vex are already heading in, they should be here late tonight."

Okay, that's wasn't relief loosening her chest, right? "How late?"

He came around the desk and stood next to her. "Some time between midnight and two."

"I thought Reaper wanted them to stay while he got things handled?"

Ruin folded over his arms over chest and leaned against the desk's edge. "He's claiming it's under control."

Sounded as if Ruin thought differently. "You don't believe him?"

He grimaced. "I believe he believes it, but ..."

When he trailed off, she finished, "You're worried there's another strike coming?"

He glared at the space in front of him. "You heard the same things I did. Someone is determined to keep us occupied."

She understood his 'us' meant Fate's Vultures.

He turned to her, the skin around his eyes drawn tight. "Having Vex and Havoc on the road doesn't sit well with me. Neither does leaving Reaper holding the fort on his own."

She recalled his sharp responses on the call and pointed out, "Didn't sound as if they shared your worries."

"That's because they're idiots." He pushed off the desk and paced the small space.

Maybe, maybe not. She bet the reason Vex and Havoc were rushing to Ruin's side was because Reaper didn't want to leave his boy hanging with an unknown. "Or they have concerns of their own."

He paused and looked at her. "Maybe, but I can handle myself."

She refused to let his temper ruffle hers. "So can they."

He spun on his heel to resume his restless movements. "Doesn't mean I have to like it."

"Nope, it doesn't." She shoved away from the desk and walked over to the door.

"Where are you going?"

She didn't bother to look back as she pulled the door open. *Time for a little tough love.* "I'm not wasting time listening to you bitch about your friends." Plus, they had things to do. "There are a couple more places I want to stop by, then we need to find a new place to sleep since I'm not about to piss Kayvao off by bringing trouble his way." She headed back to the front of the bar.

He stomped in her wake and grumbled, "I'm not sleeping in a dump."

Some of her tension eased as she hid her smile. Determined to shake him free of his grumpiness, she teased, "Don't worry, princess, we'll find you an appropriate bed to lay your little head on. Wouldn't want to bruise your delicate flesh."

When his hard arm wrapped around her waist and dragged her back against a hard chest, she bit her lip to stifle her laugh. He nipped her ear and warned, "Can't make you the same promise, you wicked wench."

A sharp elbow to his ribs loosened his hold, and she stepped free with a husky, "First you have to keep up."

When they stepped outside the sun was starting its descent. They left the bar with a wave for Max and his dad. Charity stayed at Ruin's side as they casually made their way through the evening foot traffic. They made it about four blocks before Ruin wrapped an arm around her waist, drew her close, and nuzzled her ear. "We're being followed."

Not a surprise since she picked up their shadows' movements about a block back. She didn't turn to look, just returned Ruin's embrace as she scanned their surroundings. To anyone watching they were just another couple walking down the street. "I'm counting two behind and a third coming up from the other side."

Up ahead two men made their way through the other pedestrians who instinctively gave way, their hard stares locked on to Ruin and Charity.

"Six o'clock," he warned.

As the bigger one knocked into a passing bystander, she caught the flash of metal. "Blade Men," she muttered, barely moving her lips.

Ruin gave her waist a quick squeeze of acknowledgement. He bent his head as if completely caught up in her. In complete contrast to his actions, his voice was hard as he ordered, "Take it off the street."

Her hair caught against his beard as she gave a slight nod.

When a rather boisterous group erupted from one of the more questionable clubs, they used the distraction and darted into the narrow opening. Together they ran down the alley, the sounds of their feet hitting the ground echoed in the small space. When more joined in, she kicked it up a notch, and Ruin kept pace.

They took turns when they could, weaving deeper into the mismatched collection of buildings. They were running out of options when she spotted a low roof structure that would allow them a chance at the roofline. "There."

She didn't slow as they closed in, but took a running jump and grabbed the edge of what looked like a haphazard addition. Thankfully it was wood, so her palms gathered splinters instead of cuts. When the shaky overhang swayed, she held her breath and scrambled up with Ruin hot on her heels. Wood groaned under their combined weight and a sharp whistle raised the hair on the back of her neck.

She recognized the sound for the signal it was and sure enough, to their left, at the roof's edge, two heads popped up. She and Ruin went right, leapt over the two-foot space between buildings, and kept going, aiming for the far side of the roof. The next jump dropped them onto the corrugated metal roof with a dull thud. Her pulse kicked up as she realized they were out of buildings.

She searched for a ladder or fire escape, something that would take them back down and came up empty. Then, before panic could grab hold, Ruin snagged her wrist and pulled her to the far right corner. As they pounded closer, she caught the dark outlines of a ladder's rails. A shout went up behind them and was soon followed by another series of sharp whistles.

She slipped over the edge and grasped the ladder's rough metal rails. As the rough edges cut into her already scraped palms, she wished for gloves. She looked across the roof and saw four figures heading their way. With nothing for it, she gritted her teeth and scrambled down until she could drop the last few feet.

As she rolled with the fall, survival instincts screamed, and she pulled her blade free. It proved to be a good decision, because as she came up out of the roll, she caught the attacking Blade Man by surprise. She sliced out.

He yelped and jumped back, a red line appearing over his torso. "Bitch!"

He had no idea.

She darted in, not giving him a chance to regain his footing and keeping him on the defensive. The move also served to give Ruin a chance to get off the damn ladder. She went in low and mean, determined to even their odds.

But Blade Men weren't standard street thugs. A point proved as he parried and his blade nicked her flesh. No stranger to knife fights, or the inevitable fact that she'd be cut, she didn't let the initial sting slow her down. She ignored the burn, blocked his next swipe, and use the blade in her other hand to slice across his femoral. It wasn't about keeping him back but keeping his ass down because she and Ruin were about to be severely outnumbered.

He yowled and stumbled back, fury twisting his face. He lunged back in for more and his strikes took on a vicious edge.

She caught the moment he realized he was bleeding out, that spark of fear behind his rage. She distantly registered the sound of Ruin's boots hitting the ground as he dropped from the ladder and the rush of running feet coming closer, but her focus stayed on the threat in front of her.

She ducked under another wild swing and let the edge of his blade cut a line of fire along the back of her arm. She snaked her arm around his, locked his wrist and forearm in place and sank her blade up and under his ribs.

Her ears rang from his agonized bellow, but it didn't stop her from twisting the blade embedded in his chest. She forced her weight against his trapped arm until bone snapped. She yanked on her blade and at the same time released his now broken arm. The combination sent the sharp edge of her blade slicing through his heart. She pulled her knife free and shove her attacker. He staggered back, dropped to his knees, and fell face first to the ground.

She turned to help Ruin, only to take a solid kick to her back. She stumbled forward, and struggled to find her breath as searing pain tore through her lower side.

Son of a bitch.

Her only warning was a change in the air behind her. She dropped to her shoulder and rolled out of the way of the next hit. Being on the ground wasn't smart, but neither was taking another mind-numbing hit. She came up in a crouch, her back against the wall.

A thick-chested man with arms as wide as her thighs stood in front of her. He gave her an evil grin as he uncurled a length of thick chain and let it hang from one meaty fist.

She forced her attention away from the chain and focused on his chest. When his muscles twitched, she low to the ground and to the left. The chain whipped over her head. Hampered by the ache in her side, she wasn't fast enough to escape the stinging bite of the chain's tail end. A sharp hiss escaped. It got lost in the pained grunts and male curses coming from her other side where Ruin fought to hold his own.

The chain wielding fiend brought his metal back to heel and prepared for another strike. Trapped as she was between him and the building, she had two options—use her arm to tangle the chain, which would break it, or do the unexpected.

Since fighting with a broken arm was out, she pushed off with her toes and aimed low, slamming her shoulder into the behemoth's gut.

The impact streaked her vision white and despite her now numbed shoulder, she wrapped her arm around his waist. She tucked her head and used the blade in her other hand to awkwardly stab his back wherever she could reach.

The vibration of his pained howls reverberated through her aching shoulder. Under the combined onslaught of her knife and body weight, he stumbled back. He tried to use his fist to knock her away, but most of his blows landed along her back and shoulders. His weight shifted and he started to fall back.

She didn't hesitate to drill her blade in one last time, then tore it free and stumbled back. A right hook clipped her jaw and sent her careening off balance. It was followed by another fist that buried itself in her stomach. Agony tore through her as she bent in half, but she kept her blade.

She used her other hand to shackle the wrist attached to the fist in her stomach and dug her fingers deep into pressure points. The hand spasmed and she captured a finger, jerked it viciously back at an unnatural angle.

An angry roar erupted, and the finger's owner tore free of her grip.

Unfortunately, her reprieve didn't last long.

An arm wrapped around her neck. The hold bowed her back and brought her up on her toes as her abused stomach and ribs protested. She shifted the hold on her blade and stabbed backwards. The chokehold loosened. She dipped her chin, grabbed the thick wrist at her shoulder and raked her booted foot down the leg behind her.

She twisted free, bloody knife in hand, and her instincts screaming to protect her exposed back. It was too late. A stunning kick to the back of her thigh sent her to her knees.

Her hands flew forward, one flat, one holding the knife, and she barely managed to not smash her face against the ground.

A heavy boot stomped down on her wrist and ground down. She grunted at the bruising force, and her hand, the one miraculously still holding the knife, spasmed. Her blade fell away.

Someone grabbed her hair and yanked her head back. As cool metal kissed her neck she stilled, silently cursing a blue streak as she was hauled to her knees.

The sounds of pained grunts and the muffled impacts of fists on flesh continued somewhere out of her visual range. The hold in her hair shifted and fetid breath washed across her face. "You might wanna tell your boyfriend to give it up."

She suppressed her urge to gag, rolled her eyes up, and curled her lips into a sneer. Between her angle and the fading light, it was hard to make out much. Acne scars, small eyes under a heavy brow, overly large nose, cracked teeth – it wasn't a pretty picture.

Scar Face's eyes narrowed to mere slits, and he spit, "Do it!"

"Fuck you."

He looked up and gave a short nod.

A fist landed in her stomach. Her restrained position made the pain of the hit worse, but she fought her way through.

Dimly she heard the slimy voice say, "Ain't dicking around, bitch. I'll let my friends gut him. Technically, he'll still be breathing when we deliver your asses, so it counts as a live retrieval."

Under the haze of pain, she focused on the fact someone wanted them alive. It might be enough for a slim chance of escaping this mess.

"What's it gonna be?"

Slim was better than none. Swallowing hard, she called

out, "Ruin, stop!" She almost choked on the words, but she wasn't stupid.

The sounds of fighting continued and the grip in her hair tightened until she hissed. She didn't need Scar Face's glare to try again. She steeled herself and sucked in air, then she screamed, "Ruin!"

The sounds stopped.

Held as she was, she could only watch Scar Face's expression as he looked to somewhere in front of her. "Let him go."

"You first." The growl belonged to Ruin.

The knife at her throat pressed deeper, stinging as the edge bit. "Not a chance."

"Then I guess we're at a stand-off, asshole."

Scar Face's hand twitched and the blade sank in a bit more. *Dammit.* She didn't want her throat sliced because someone got nervous. "Ruin, they only get paid if we're delivered alive."

Seconds ticked by in the heavy silence, and then it was broken by the sound of a blade hitting the ground.

Above her, Scar Face smiled. "Get him."

twenty-three

Scar Face dragged Charity up by the hair as footsteps rushed pass. When she caught his smirk, she wanted to claw it off his ugly mug. As soon as she was on her feet, he twisted her arm up along her spine, and held the knife poised at her kidney. The only good thing was he let go of her hair, which gave her one weapon, her head.

Before she could use it, he hissed in her ear, "Try it and I'll let you bleed out."

She ground her teeth and stayed still. As two of the Blade Men took Ruin captive, frustration crawled through her veins like bitter acid.

As soon as they had his hands bound, the bigger of the two men, who sported a hell of a shiner, took his fists to Ruin's gut with rapid fire precision. Pained grunts escaped his clenched jaw, but his gaze didn't waver from hers.

Forever seemed to pass before Scar Face snapped, "Enough. Let's move."

The big man sank one more vicious gut shot, then turned away and headed straight for her. Determined to slit the bastard's throat, she memorized his face.

He caught her staring at him, and his smug grin faltered. "Whatcha looking at, bitch?" he growled.

She let the promise of his impending death shine free, but her voice was harder than diamonds. "A dead man walking."

He spat at her and turned away. The mercenary group dragged Ruin and Charity through the maze of Kennewick's seamier side, and Charity wasn't surprised by the lack of witnesses. In fact, she didn't miss the muted sounds of doors quickly being shut and shadows ducking back behind dark windows.

Yep, no one would risk their necks for two strangers.

She took inventory of the aches and pains radiating through her battered body. There was at least one, maybe two, cracked ribs, not to mention her already wounded shoulder, and the deepening ache in her side. In a day or so, if she was still breathing, her body would carry a map of bruises from head to toe.

She studied those around her and figured her injuries weren't too shabby considering between her and Ruin, they managed to cull the herd in half. Her gaze slid to one of the men who was currently being half carried by another. Based upon the amount of blood turning his dingy shirt into a macabre abstract, she amended her tally to four with a small, evil grin.

A shove to her back sent her stumbling forward. Next to her Ruin let out a low growl, but she gritted her teeth and kept her mouth shut. Talking was pointless. At least until they knew where they were going.

Blade Men were glorified bounty hunters and easy hires, but once transacted for a job, they completed it. Just not always the way a customer expected. Which meant whoever hired them was desperate, most likely working against the clock, and that made her think her bait was well and truly taken.

Ruin limped alongside her, his hair tangled around his bruised face. There was a seeping cut above his eye and his face was a stone mask. Occasionally he turned his head and spat. The red tinge left behind on his lower lip worried her. When he caught her look, he gave a slight shake of his head.

She forced her attention away from him and took note of their surroundings. The dank odor of wet, churned earth filled her nose and the soft shushing rush of water hit her ears. They were down by the river.

She looked around but found nothing but a jumble of old shipping containers. Some were stacked on top of each other, others lay as if tossed by some careless hand. The light was fading fast, leaving the place draped in various shades of grey and black.

She picked out a couple of shadows tracking them from the container roofs. Since Scar Face didn't seem concerned, she figured they were lookouts. Her assumption proved right when Scar Face raised a hand in a silent signal. One of the sentries took off, disappearing over the top of the containers.

Scar Face led the motley band down a twisty route through the narrow openings before finally stepping into one of the stacked containers. As she was shoved inside, she realized someone had changed the container into a two-level building by cutting the roof of one and floor of another in half. Propped against the far edge leading up to the second floor was a rickety set of stairs.

Scar Face headed over and Ruin and Charity were shoved along behind. She followed Ruin up the steps and noted the lack of railing. She made a mental note that a solid shove halfway up would result in a splatter pattern on the floor.

The weathered wood creaked under booted feet, and the tang of rusted metal replaced the faint traces of wet earth. At the top, another sharp shove from behind caught her off guard. She managed to regain her balance on the top step, but growled, spun, and drove her knee straight into the balls of her tormenter.

Her unexpected hit sent the bastard back a step or two. When his back foot slipped, he wobbled. A mix of fear and anger washed through his face just before he tumbled off the side of the staircase.

She barely got to appreciate her work or the resulting sharp crack and pained bellow as he smashed to the ground because the dick hidden behind him backhanded her. Her head slammed into the wall and left her vision wavy.

Someone barked, "Enough!"

It barely cut through the ringing in her ears. The idiot who hit her grabbed her arm, spun her around, and shoved her into the open space of the second floor. She ran her tongue along the inside of her cheek and tasted copper. She turned and found furious muddy eyes staring back. Unable to resist, she bared her blood-stained teeth in a macabre grin.

"I thought you were smarter than that." The droll comment came from behind her.

She turned back to see who had spoken but couldn't make out much. Two lanterns hung on either side, but their reach didn't touch the edges of the room or the unknown speaker.

"Perhaps my information was wrong."

Muddy eyes gave her another shove and she stumbled against Ruin. His, "You good?" was low and quiet.

"Just peachy." She straightened carefully and stood next to him, so together they faced the room.

Whoever waited for them stayed near the back wall where the light didn't reach. When he didn't step forward, Charity continued to scan the room. Her attention halted on a huddled form on the floor.

When a familiar gaze stared back from behind crooked rhinestone frames, Charity sucked in a breath. She took a step forward and was brought up short by cruel fingers that dug into her arm. She jerked free of the hold but didn't move forward. "Echo?"

The battered mess gave a wet laugh. "Fancy meeting you here, girl."

Seeing the normally outrageous woman reduced to a beaten pulp, ignited a cold fury. Charity turned her glare to the mystery figure coming up behind Echo. "What do you want?"

He stepped forward and Charity got her first good look at River Man, aka the Broker. "Shouldn't I be asking that question since you're the one looking for me?"

She wasn't impressed. His frame wasn't the only average thing about him. Brown hair cut short matched equally brown eyes set in a face neither attractive nor ugly. If she passed him on the street, she'd never guess at what lay under the skin. Thing was, after watching his interaction with the Raiders and seeing his handiwork with Echo, she wasn't about to underestimate him.

He stopped and brushed a hand over the tangle of Echo's dark hair. Her resulting flinch coiled like a vicious poison in Charity's gut as he smiled. Even River Man's smile was fucking average. "Echo here, has been nice enough to inform me you were recently asking questions about my business. Business that took a nasty turn this morning." The hand in Echo's hair clenched. "Something I explained to our mutual friend here, I wasn't happy about."

He shoved Echo with a viciousness that sent her sprawling. Her pained groan was muffled but River Man didn't shift his shark-like gaze from Charity. "In fact, I'm quite curious as to who invited you to what was a private meeting."

It struck Charity that River Man hadn't taken her bait, instead, he had gone the same route she did when she hit town —hit up the one person who knew the comings and goings of Kennewick – Echo. That meant he had no idea of who she or

Ruin were. If anything, he probably assumed they were the sniper team sent to take him out. It was too soon to decide if that was a good thing, or a bad thing.

Unfortunately, before she could say anything, Ruin cut in. "You did."

That took River Man by surprise. "Excuse me?"

Shut up, Ruin! She silently screamed the warning, wishing she had the ability to gag the idiot. Instead, she could only stand there, hands bound, teeth gritted, head aching and glare as he dug his own grave, and likely hers.

Ruin's bloodied lips curled into a sneer. "You should choose your business associates, with a bit more care. They got greedy."

Recognition struck and brown eyes widened. "Fuck me, you're a goddamn Vulture."

"Not my type, but I'm sure Reaper will make an exception just for you." His disdain struck deep.

She made a near-hysterical mental note to never get on the receiving end of Ruin's fury, but as a threat it worked because River Man's face lost a bit of color.

But it didn't take long before he reclaimed his arrogant mask and turned his attention to Charity. "And you?" Clear calculation seeped into his flat gaze.

Again, Ruin spoke first. "A fun piece to get to that one." Ruin lifted his chin towards Echo. "They've done business before, so I used her to get me in."

As much as she appreciated his attempt to keep her out of the line of fire, she wasn't comfortable with him playing her shield. Unfortunately, he wasn't giving her a choice.

When he refused to acknowledge her glare, she fought to keep her churning emotions from her face and turned her anger towards River Man. She held his reptilian gaze with a disdainful sneer.

His cold smile made her uneasy, an instinctive reaction to

an unknown threat. "Well then, I hope you enjoyed it while you could as I'm afraid your fun has come to an end." His attention shifted to behind her. "Gil, Bo, bring him along."

Scar Face and Muddy Eyes slithered up to Ruin, grabbed his arms, and dragged him back towards the stairs.

Fear seared through her turning her heart to ice. She went to follow, only to be yanked back by River Man. "Where are you taking him?"

His smile was merciless in its cruelty. "Whereas your worth is minor, as a Vulture, his is much, much more. Enough that I may yet be able to salvage the transaction you two cost me." He tossed her towards Echo and sent her to the unforgiving floor with bruising force.

With her hands bound, she could only twist to take the impact on something besides her face. Pain, bright and sharp, lanced over her hip and shoulder, and grayed the edges of her vision.

She tried to catch a breath and dimly heard him giving orders to the guards on the bottom floor. "Keep them here. I'll be back soon to get them ready for delivery."

She dropped her head to the floor, swallowed against the choking dread and prayed for a fucking miracle.

twenty-four

Another fist slammed into his already sore ribs and Ruin couldn't hold back his groan. He wasn't sure how long he hung here, playing punching bag for the two ham-fisted dick weasels intent on getting their rocks off. No doubt he'd be pissing blood for a week when he got out of here. And it was definitely a question of when, not if.

Shackled by the heavy links coiled around his wrists, his arms were chained above his head and the toes of his boots barely brushed the floor. He twisted his head to the side, spat another mouthful of blood, and waited for the next punch. When none was forthcoming, he lifted his head. His right eye was swollen shut but his left worked well enough to make out the man standing in front of him, arms crossed over his chest, his reptilian gaze centered on him. River Man.

Unfortunately, the bastard was smart enough to stay far enough back so Ruin couldn't kick him. He knew the Broker held no intention of killing him, but it hadn't stopped the fucker from beating the shit out of him once they arrived at wherever the hell they were. *Because River Man was a fucking sadist.* A fact proven when he shared, in perverted detail, the plans he had in store for Charity and Echo.

When their eyes met, River Man asked with fake solicitousness, "Feel like talking now?"

Ruin forced his abused lips into a fierce smile and held his silence. He figured out quick that the one thing guaranteed to get under River Man's skin was to say nothing. The ego-driven sociopath just couldn't resist bragging. Granted, Ruin's rebellion was petty as shit, but since all he could currently do was hang around, he'd make it work.

River Man considered him for another long, tense moment, then surprisingly, changed tactics. "Here's the thing, you and I wouldn't be here if Tyke employed a better caliber of talent. The directions given were simple, remove Crane, keep the Vultures busy. Yet the fuckwits decided to improvise. I'd offer my apologies on your friend's death, as I'm sure their choice of amusement was rather brutal, but I've a feeling you wouldn't take it. Not that I blame you. Of course, now that I have to clean up their mess, I'm tempted to set you loose on them. Save me the trouble of doing it later."

Finally, they were getting somewhere. "Feel free." His voice was rough. "I'd be more than happy to take out your trash."

River Man's smile didn't reach his eyes, but he wagged his finger. "Mm-mm, no, I'm afraid it's too late for that. Instead, I'm going to hand you over to someone who has a better use for you than I do."

It was time to wipe that smug-ass grin away, so Ruin decided to play his ace and drawled, "You mean Reznik?"

It worked like a charm. River Man's face wiped blank, and a slow tide of anger seeped in before he managed to resume his sneering mask. He tried to cover his momentary slip, but it was too late. "And who is Reznik?"

"Don't play stupid, it doesn't look good on you." Ruin

turned his head and sent another mouth full of blood to the stained floor. When he turned back to his tormentor, he gripped the chain between his wrists with numb fingers. "Reznik is the one pulling your strings."

He decided it was time for a little manipulation of his own. He manufactured a combination of pity and contempt as he stared down River Man. "And he's not one for loose ends either." He lifted his aching shoulders in a shrug and did his best to ignore the resulting flash fire of pain ripping along his nerve endings. "You're a lucky bastard, you know. If you hadn't dived for that tunnel this morning, there wouldn't be any loose ends to worry about."

As taunts went it was lame, but it did its job, because River Man spat, "You trying to get me to believe Reznik mad a deal with you?" He dropped his arms and his hands curled into fists. "A fucking Vulture? Why the hell would he do that?"

He wouldn't, and anyone with a working, non-paranoid brain would know that. Thankfully River Man's grey matter was jumpy as shit and susceptible to mind games, which gave Ruin a chance to buy time. "Not privy to the deets. I leave that political shit up to my man Reaper."

River Man inched closer his face dark with doubt and resentment. "The Vultures are loyal to Crane."

"Wrong." Ruin took a risk and leaned, the chain creaking with his movement. "The Vultures are loyal to the Vultures, everyone else can fuck off."

A crafty confidence bloomed in River Man's slow smile. "Except Simon," he taunted.

Just play along, Ruin.

The harsh reminder didn't do much, but it did allow him to choke back his snarl of fury and stifle the urge to do something stupid. "You said it yourself," he bit out. "The Raiders are fuckwits. When they killed Simon, they fucked with our plans. That kind of fuck-up earns a death sentence, for them and the one holding their leashes." River Man couldn't hide his flash of fear and Ruin enjoyed the savage it brought. "Mistakes are bad for business."

"Yet you're threatening to turn on the one you're supposedly working for?" There was an uneasy note in River Man's blustered question.

"Wasn't Reznik's hand on the Raiders' leash." Ruin forced his muscles to uncoil, bared his teeth in a feral smile, and delivered one more psychological cut. "It was yours."

River Man's dawning confusion snapped to wariness. "See, that's where you're mistaken," he said. "I didn't orchestrate Simon's death. I simply relayed Reznik's orders. The Raiders' decision to go after Simon rests on them. Feel free to wipe them out. I'm sure Reznik will be thrilled with their removal. It's one less loose thread he has to snip in the end."

In the end? What the hell did that mean?

Ruin studied his opponent and knew it was useless to pursue that angle. No way would he possess the real game plan, but he might hold clues to part of this mess. However, if Reznik truly didn't give a damn about wiping out the Raiders, he wouldn't blink at eliminating someone like River Man, which left Ruin an angle to exploit. "See? I think you don't give the Raider dogs enough credit. Taking them off the board plays hell with Reznik's kid snatching business, but taking your ass out, well that just leaves empty air. Easy enough to find another blowhard to take your spot. Hell, maybe I'll volunteer for it, might make for an amusing distraction."

When River Man's jaw clenched so hard the bone pressed against his skin, Ruin wondered if he finally managed to tip the asshole over. His hope was dashed when the River Man spat, "Those kids are more valuable than—" he stopped short, his lips compressing into a tight line. "Never mind. This is getting us nowhere." He spun away.

Which was Ruin goal. If he could give Charity, or Vex and

Havoc, enough time, there might be a chance to get out of this mess. He just had to hang in there. Messing with the little shit's mind was a bonus. *Time to go balls to the wall.* "Had Reznik's permission to put you in the crosshairs," he called after him.

His taunt not only stopped River Man's retreat but brought him back that final fucking step. Ruin grabbed the chain between his hands, whipped his leg up, and nailed the toe of his boot under River Man's chin. The impact snapped River Man's head back and a pained roar erupted as he stumbled and fell to his back on the floor, his hands covering his face.

The noise brought two others running in. Ruin managed to keep them at bay with a series of vicious kicks, but it was a losing battle. Their fists managed to connect more and more often, until he could only hang there and endure as the pain wrapped tighter and tighter coils around his mind. There was a lull in the pummeling, and something wrapped in his hair and yanked his head back with vicious intensity.

"Open your fucking eyes." The sibilant command penetrated the fog of screaming aches. "Open them or I'll cut off your balls, you bastard."

Yeah no, he had plans for his little buddies. He groaned but forced his heavy lids up. He managed to get his left eye open only to have River Man's blood-coated face take up all the space. *Well now, that was a thing of beauty.* The distant thought made his lips twitch, which sent an arrow of fire across his face.

"Think that was funny, fucker?"

It took effort, but Ruin got his tongue to work. "Fucking hysterical."

That got another jerk on his hair and sent knife-like pain radiating up his neck. "Let's see if you can keep laughing."

With that parting shot, the hold on his head reversed and slammed his head forward, sending his body swaying in the chains. The fists returned and it wasn't long before the sounds of his pained grunts filled the air.

Well, shit.

twenty-five

Charity rolled over with a soft groan and blinked up at the swaying play of shadows on the roof. She kept her voice soft, aware of the guards below. "What the hell happened, Echo?"

"Warned you." Echo's answer was a croak.

"You gave us up."

Echo's laugh edged close to a sob. "I like breathing, Charity."

Yeah, so did she. The ringing in her ears started to recede, and her headache stayed bearable if she didn't move. She stared blindly up at the ceiling wondering how long their two guards would stay away.

Worry for Ruin clawed at her, shredding the calm she relied on to tatters. *The stupid, thickheaded idiot. Giving himself up like that! Dammit.*

River Man would turn Ruin over to Reznik. The sleazy ass crime lord would take great pleasure in making an example out of one of the infamous Vultures. Granted he'd do worse to Lilith's top 'Hound, but it didn't soothe her worry or erase one iota of her guilt.

"Think we got time before he gets back?" The question drifted up from the bottom floor, courtesy of one of their guard dogs, and snapped her out of her pity party.

"Maybe," drawled a second one. "We can wait a bit, jus' to be sure he ain't coming back any time soon."

Next to her, Echo stiffened, but before the other woman could do much more, Charity shifted her leg and kicked Echo's ankle in warning. No need to cue in the moron twins that the two women were listening. Charity stayed still and kept her breathing shallow, grateful when Echo did the same.

"I need a piss."

"Yeah, I need a damn drink."

"We can't both leave at once," the first one whined.

"Where the hell they gonna go?" sneered the second. "Only way out is through us."

Charity let her lashes drift almost closed, anticipating what would come next. Sure enough, feet thudded up the steps and over to her, accompanied by the stench of body odor. "Bitches are out, they ain't going anywhere."

"You sure?"

It took everything she was not to brace for the kick that landed in her stomach. Instead, she doubled over the foot with a stifled groan, and mentally ripped him a new one.

The clueless motherfucker spat, "See? Out."

"Fine," the first one sniveled, then the two idiots clomped down the stairs.

She waited until the conversation downstairs resumed before whispering, "Echo?"

"What?" There was a snap of temper in Echo's response.

Reassured, Charity asked, "You up to fighting?"

"There's like two of them, maybe more, and I'm beat to shit if you haven't noticed."

So was she, but it wasn't enough to stop her from getting to Ruin. "Doesn't matter. They just sent one out to run sentry. If we do this right, they won't catch on until it's too late."

"I'm going to regret this," Echo muttered, but she rolled over to face Charity. "Now what?"

She took a quick inventory of Echo's battered body and sent up a fervent 'thank you' when she noticed Echo's swollen hands were bound in front of her. "I need you to get the blade out of my boot so we can cut these damn ropes."

Echo's bruised eyes drifted down Charity's legs. A glimpse of her normal irreverence appeared. "It took getting beaten near death to finally get my hands on your body."

Charity heard the fear under the false confidence and gave her a tiny grin. "Cheeky bitch."

The two carefully shifted their positions until Echo was at Charity's feet, her fumbling fingers at her pant leg. Seconds ticked by each one another lost moment.

When a soft, frustrated sob broke, Charity murmured, "It's okay, Echo, deep breath, you can do this." Finally, Charity felt her blade slide free.

"Okay, got it." Echo's voice was a mere whisper.

Charity forced her sore body around so Echo could cut the rope binding her hands. The harsh bark of male laughter brought their furtive movements to a stop, neither one daring to breathe until they were certain no one was coming back up.

Charity knew their luck wouldn't hold much longer. She strained her arms and kept tension on the rope. When the last strand snapped, the rush of returning blood reignited nerve endings, and she bit her lip to keep her painful yelp quiet.

As soon as she could, she rolled over, took the blade from Echo, and sawed through the other woman's bindings. With their hands free, they both sat up, their attention focused on the stairs, and ears strained to catch what was happening below.

Echo leaned in and rasped, "Now what?"

"Now we get our clueless duo back up here. Maybe draw the others out while we're at it."

Echo looked at her. "How do you plan to do that?"

"Give them every man's fantasy."

Her answer left Echo blinking. "Honey, I'm really not in the mood."

Charity snorted. "Not that, a cat fight."

Understanding lit Echo's eyes. "Got it."

And with that, they rose stiffly to their feet.

Charity's world dipped, then steadied, and her chest ached like a bitch, but she was upright and breathing. She shook out her arms, and although it worked, the hand crushed under the boot was slow to respond.

Echo did her own inventory and then gave her a nod.

Charity sucked in air and yelled, "You stupid bitch! I'll gut you for giving us up!"

"Giving you up?" Echo screamed back. "You still fucking owe me for the information. I'm not willing to die for you and your bastard boyfriend."

A shout from outside drifted upstairs and was soon followed by the pounding of feet rushing inside the bottom floor.

One of the guards shouted up, "What the fuck is going on up there?"

Charity ignored his demand from below and kept ranting at Echo. "That bastard will hang your ass high."

Echo grimaced but played her part. "He doesn't stand a chance against River Man. Besides, it'll be hard to do from the grave, you dimwitted twit."

Their screaming match drew the guards up the stairs. Since their only weapon was Charity's thin boot blade, she motioned Echo back to the side, took her position at the top of the stairs and crouched.

The first guard's head and torso emerged from the top few

steps. Charity darted in and sliced her blade up his chest before she shoved her shoulder into his gut and shoved him into the idiot coming up behind him.

The rear guard got his hands up in time to shove the wounded one off of him so he wouldn't stumble back down the stairs. His instinctive move sent the wounded guard off the rail less stairs and careening to the floor below. His scream cut off with a dull thud.

"Bitch."

Was that the only word these idiots knew?

Charity bared her teeth and backed away, aiming for the center of the room. First things first, she needed to even the odds. The man grinned, his intent to hurt clear in his brutish expression. Except Charity had other plans for him. Like the stairs, there was no railing at the edge of the cutaway floor, so she just needed to make sure the advancing guard took the express exit.

As he stalked closer, she wasn't surprised to find another chain wielding asswipe right behind him. Chain Man stopped at the top of the stairs, and dragged the heavy links across the floor, the threatening noise echoing through the space. *Good, one less to hunt down later.*

Both men seemed to have forgotten Echo as their focus remained on Charity, which worked for her. Thankfully it didn't take much to keep the guard between her and Chain Man. The hardest part of her plan would be right about … now.

Charity, her blade low and hidden, held her position as Guard Guy rushed her. At the last minute, as he rushed in, she slipped under his outstretched arm and spun away, her knife opening a wicked line across his stomach and along his side.

She blocked his wild hit with her free hand, trapped his wrist in an arm lock, and jerked back, forcing his spine to bow in a painful arc. She reversed her blade and slammed it into his kidney, then yanked it free. She braced her spine against his, and pulled her legs to her chest and rolled out of the way of the snapping chain. Instead of curling around her legs, the thick metal coiled around the injured moron and slammed him face down against the floor.

Charity landed in a crouch perilously close to where the floor fell away and sent a fierce grin to Chain Man who was desperately trying to free his tangled weapon. With an enraged bellow, he dropped the chain and charged.

She danced out of reach, knowing if he caught her, she was in trouble.

Intent on taking Charity down, he never saw Echo. On a shrill scream, she slammed into his back. As the big man lost his balance, Charity threw herself to the side. Echo slid down his back and her hands clawed at his legs.

He kicked out and missed Echo's head by a hair, but it was enough. With his balance shot to hell and positioned too close to the edge, he stumbled back into nothing and disappeared. The entire structure shook when his body hit the ground.

Charity rolled over as Echo remained on all fours and looked down to the two bodies below. The first guard was sprawled face down in a widening pool of blood. Nearby, was Chain Man. He managed to twist mid-fall and landed on his back. If his spine survived the impact, the unnatural angle of his leg would keep him in place.

Since she had some questions to ask, she needed to make sure he was breathing. She gathered her waning strength, shoved to her feet, and stumbled towards the stairs.

Echo lifted her head. "Going so soon?"

"Got to find out where Ruin is." Charity braced a hand against the wall as she didn't want to tempt fate and repeat the previous exits.

She was halfway down when Echo appeared and followed her down. When her feet hit the bottom floor, she blew out a relieved breath and made her way to the crumpled heap of flesh. Part of her was thrilled to see the rise and fall of the massive chest.

She got closer and noticed one thick arm was caught behind his back and based on the angle, was most likely dislocated. A wispy groan sounded and the other arm started to flail. Charity pinned his wrist under her boot and ground down. His eyes fluttered open and fear seeped through the pain. His mouth opened as he continued to struggle, but his movements lacked strength.

"Uh-uh, think again." She kept her foot in place, sank into a crouch, and laid her knife against his throat. "Don't."

Echo approached and his gaze flicked to her, then back to Charity. Panic widened his eyes, his struggle increased, but when his body failed to respond, whimpers fell from his mouth.

"Yeah, you took quite a little tumble there." Without moving her blade, she turned to Echo. "Need you to head to the Guardian Lodge with a message."

Echo looked to the door and then back to her. "Did you forget about the sentry?"

Charity curled her lip. "You telling me you can't slip by one measly little shit for brains?"

"Normally, piece of cake." Echo waved a hand over her battered body. "Like this?" She shook her head.

Charity's patience died a quick death as minutes slipped by, minutes where she didn't know where Ruin was or what was happening to him. Her voice was stone cold. "Do it, Echo."

Heeding the icy command, Echo checked her attitude. "Fine. What message?"

"There's a guard there, named Kayvao, knows Ruin. Tell him he's got Vultures incoming. Then you stick around and wait for those Vultures to land and bring them here."

Echo's eyes narrowed. "You'll owe me."

Charity held her resentful gaze and stated with lethal certainty, "No, you owe me."

Tension stretched between them, then Echo swallowed and her gaze skittered away and came back. "When this is done, we're even."

Charity studied the other woman for a long moment and then finally nodded.

With that, Echo made tracks and slipped out the door, leaving Charity with her very own chew toy.

Time was tight, but not so tight. It was time for answers. She turned her attention back to the man spread out before her. She smiled.

He paled.

"Playtime."

twenty-six

Ruin's world narrowed to enduring the next bruising impact. Each one left his battered body swinging from his aching shoulders and all but numb wrists. He was reduced to shallow inhales because those didn't cause his ribs and diaphragm to seize in protest. He lost track of time as it warped and curled in strange ways under the unrelenting abuse.

He wasn't sure when he first realized the beating had stopped, but when he finally surfaced, he didn't dare give away that he was awake and aware. He kept his eyes closed and head down and concentrated on the nearby sounds.

There was the creak of somebody's weight settling into a chair. The scuff of a boot against the hard floor proceeded a muttered curse. A bark of dark laughter followed, and then the metallic groan as a door was forced open despite its protesting hinges.

A cool breeze crept in, carrying a combination of spiced foods and ammonia. That last chased away the fetid odor of pain-laced sweat, the coppery bite of spilt blood, and other things best left unexplored.

"Drop him."

It was his only warning before rough hands yanked him around, the move twisting the chains and wrenching his shoulders. A hard arm wrapped around his bruised stomach and lifted, easing the tension on the chain. He couldn't stifle a couple of groans, but they were drowned out by more clanking and then the snick of a lock being released. The pressure on his shoulders disappeared and he dropped like a stone.

The only thing that kept his face from smashing into the unforgiving ground was the small mercy of the restraining hold at his waist. His sore stomach endured further punishment as he was haul over a thick shoulder. His arms hung down, all but numb, the heavy chains still attached and trailing along noisily, before he was dumped on the ground. He lay there, his head spinning, and grit his teeth against the agonizing sensation of blood returning to his abused limbs.

A hand gripped his hair, yanked his head up and shook it. "You alive, Vulture?"

Damn ass was going to snatch him bald. Since that wasn't a good look for him, he forced his one working eye to open.

Crouched in front of him was River Man, a smirk riding his lips. "Yeah, you're still there." His reptilian gaze roamed over Ruin's battered face, and savage delight dawned. "Not such an arrogant prick now, are you?"

Ruin maintained his baleful glare and kept silent.

His minor rebellion bounced right off the dickless wonder's ego. "You just sit tight." River Man patted Ruin's cheek, the slapping sting blending in with the existing aches. "Reznik's looking forward to talking with you." With that, he tore his hand out of Ruin's hair, got to his feet, and headed to where his sidekicks waited. "The two of you go make sure things stay clear."

The two men Ruin had dubbed the Bookend Bullies,

stared balefully back. The one with acne scars jerked a thumb in Ruin's direction. "What about him?"

"He's not going anywhere." River Man looked over his shoulder, his smile all teeth. "Are you, Vulture?" He didn't wait for answer but turned and walked away, then the unholy trio disappeared through the opening.

When they were gone, Ruin let his eye close and laid there as his mind scrambled for options and found nothing but the slippery slope of doubt. Unfortunately, River Man was right. He was in bad shape and his time was running out. Once Reznik arrived, all of Ruin's bullshit bluster would be blown away, leaving his ass exposed.

Where the hell was Charity? Or better yet, Vex and Havoc?

He clawed his way free of the dark thoughts inexorably sucking him under and concentrated on unraveling the puzzle pieces at hand.

While it was surprisingly easy to get under River Man's skin, proving yet again there was no honor among thieves, Ruin wasn't sure it would be enough to tip the scales in his favor. Pitting the puppet against the puppet master was a damn long shot.

And there was something else going on, something he couldn't quite make out, but it involved the kids. Reznik kidnapped not just Lilith's kid, but the son of the Free Nation leader, which suggested the crime lord was looking at leverage.

But for what?

Could Charity be right? Had the hit on Crane been an opening move in a much more deadly plan? And if so, what did Reznik gain by forcing the Vultures to play? Since River Man wanted him alive for his master, a more pertinent question would be why? Why would Reznik target them? As far as Ruin knew none of them were involved in a personal vendetta. Poisonous doubts slunk closer, and he wondered if Havoc or Reaper were keeping secrets from him and Vex.

He almost laughed, but since it would make his ribs scream, he choked it back. *Of course, Havoc and Reaper had secrets. Every-fucking-body had secrets. Even him and Vex.*

Hell, their childhood was littered with nasty choices, because in the end it came down to survival. No way was he hanging that sin-stained laundry out any damn time soon. And he knew, down to his bones, if Havoc or Reaper thought something of theirs factored into this mess, they would have spilt to spare Vex and Ruin.

The one who liked her damn secrets was Charity. Yeah, she had her reasons, but it made it hard to trust her intentions.

"Where are you taking him?" The echo of her last desperate question to River Man and the banked panic in her gaze as she tried to follow, snuck into his dark thoughts. Those weren't the words, or the actions, of a woman intent on betrayal. Those belonged to a woman worried about her man, and that solid nugget of realization shored up his shaky resolve.

Lying there battered, bruised, and heartsore in both body and mind, he clung to the nascent tie that anchored him to Charity and waited for his house of cards to be ripped apart. He found strength in how she stood at his side, coolly eliminating the Raiders as he ran hell-bent for leather to get to Simon. Her care as she dealt with Simon's injuries, and her determination to do whatever she needed to keep him alive. The heartbreaking pain and fury on her face as she held a broken little girl close. How she fielded Vex's snarling barbs with her own, only to team up with his twin later as they took on Reaper.

How she stuck with him, no matter how hard he tried to shake her. The feel of her, soft and heated, under him. Her quick wit. Her passion. Her strength of will. Her courage to share her past with him. The flash of uncertainty when he told her he was keeping her. The sense of pride and the lessening in the hollow spots of his soul when she accepted his challenge.

It was all that and more, that fueled the searing fear and violent protective streak that made him lose his mind and offer his ass to River Man. Because the thought of her near a monster like Reznik made him sick. More, it made his fucking heart break.

Son of a bitch, he was in love with Lilith's 'Hound.

twenty-seven

Charity lowered the lifeless body of the sentry to the ground and warily watched the approaching shadows. To her left was the doorway to the bi-level container, but she slipped around the corner to her right and waited to see who was coming. When the familiar features of Vex and Havoc emerged into the light spilling from the entryway, Charity's legs shook. She braced the hand still clutching her bloodied blade against the container's side and moved out of the shadows.

Her voice was rough as she dealt with her unexpected relief. "Welcome to the party."

Vex raked her glittering gaze over Charity from head to toe and snarled, "Where the fuck is my brother?"

Charity crouched, used the sentry's pants to wipe her blade clean, and then tucked it away. This once, she'd let Vex take that tone because she got it. *Boy, did she get it.* The choking mix of fear and worry was nothing compared to the ache in her heart. "River Man took him."

Her answer did little to soothe Vex. "What the hell happened?"

"Let's take this inside." She didn't wait for Vex's response, but pushed off the side, stepped out of the shadows, and headed for the entry.

Havoc took in her battered appearance with a severe frown. "Not looking so good, girlie."

"Not feeling so good," she muttered and limped inside. She waited until both Vultures cleared the door before asking, "How's Echo?"

Vex shot her a dark look. "You mean the punching bag you sent back to the Lodge?" She stomped past, her attention riveted on what lay on the floor. "She was barely staying upright, so Kayvao stashed her in an empty room." Vex stopped next to what was left of the chain wielding bastard and used the toe of her boot to nudge his thick arm. "What happened to him?"

Charity leant against the wall just inside the door because she didn't want to fall on her ass and met Vex's challenge. "Me."

Havoc roamed the edges of the room and stepped over the body by the stairs with a soft grunt.

The other woman made an indistinguishable noise, then dropped into a crouch next to the body. "Tell me you got something."

Watching Vex study her handiwork, Charity answered absently, "Yeah, I got something."

Vex lifted her head and aimed a hard ass stare her way. "Gonna share?"

Havoc completed his circuit and stood off to Charity's left, doing what he did best— playing silent witness to the drama.

Since shit would hit the fan once Ruin's twin learned why River Man took him, Charity really didn't want to share. Unfortunately, not answering wasn't an option. Reluctantly she said, "River Man's got him stashed about a mile up the shore at a private home."

Vex's gaze narrowed. "So why the hell are you still hanging here?"

"Because if I rushed to his rescue, neither one of us would be walking away."

Vex straighten and slowly stalked towards her. The clip of her boot heels added a sharp counterpoint to her low, venomous tone. "Exactly why does my brother need rescuing, 'Hound?"

And here came the shit part. It wasn't easy but Charity held that unflinching regard, knowing she couldn't afford any sign of weakness. She needed Vex thinking, not reacting. "He told River Man he was a Vulture."

A sudden, shocked silence filled the space, and Charity held her breath, waiting for the explosion to come. It didn't take long.

Vex rocked back on her heels, a riot of emotions sweeping through her face before settling on livid, gut-clenching fury. "Why the hell did he do that?"

Charity straightened and moved away from the wall. If, *no when*, Vex attacked, Charity needed the room to maneuver. "You tell me." She wasn't being flippant, she truly wanted Vex to explain it. Because Charity still couldn't wrap her brain around why Ruin basically offered himself up in her place.

A hair-raising growl escaped Vex and she lunged, only to be pulled up short by Havoc. He slipped between the two women, his big body blocking her access to Charity. He folded his arms over his chest and gave Vex a one-word order. "Calm."

Vex's growl was louder this time, and she slammed her hands against Havoc's chest, the sharp smack echoing through the room. "Fuck calm, Havoc."

Charity flinched when she heard the fear under Vex's anger.

"She dragged his ass into trouble and now she's left him hanging for her." Vex's accusation layered another caustic cut to Charity's lacerated conscience.

"He didn't give me a choice, Vex." Knowing what she risked, Charity stepped around Havoc's back and snapped back. "I warned him about playing games with Reznik, but did he listen? No, he didn't." Her temper rose, propelled by her worry of what might be happening to Ruin even now. "Instead, he opened his big, dumb mouth before I could get a word in and basically handed his ass right on over to Reznik's minion. He's your twin, so you tell me, why the hell would he do such a dumbass thing?" Fear, anger, and frustration boiled over and she stepped into Vex and snarled, "Why?"

Gold shot amber eyes that were achingly familiar and dark with indiscernible thoughts, studied her. Strangely Vex's anger edged back, until a disconcerting scrutiny took its place. She shook her head and backed off.

Vex's unexpected reaction threw Charity off balance. "What? What do you know?"

"Nothing." Before Charity could press for more, Vex switched lanes. "Fill us in."

Charity brought them up to speed as both Vultures had been long gone when Ruin called back to Pebble Creek with the latest developments. She finished with, "We crashed the Raiders' meeting with a local information broker known as River Man. Seems both the Raiders and River Man answer to Reznik."

"Whose decision was it to go after Simon?" Vex pressed.

"That was solely on the Raiders. They figured since Simon stuck to their mangy hides like a tick, Reznik wouldn't mind if they picked him off."

Before Vex could comment, Havoc cut in. "Crane's death?"

"Courtesy of Reznik," confirmed Charity.

Vex followed the natural course. "Reznik is making a play at the trade routes."

Charity nodded. "And has some grand plan in the works that involves the kids, hence their kidnappings. Unfortunately, before we could find out more, someone decided to take out the Raider and his mini-me with well-placed bullets, then tried to remove River Man."

"Obviously they didn't succeed since you said he has Ruin." That observation was Havoc's.

"Right." Charity rubbed her neck and tried to ignore the uneasiness crawling under her skin. "River Man plans on handing Ruin over to Reznik."

Vex's hands curled into fists, but her voice remained deceptively calm. "You got a plan on how to get my brother back?"

It was Charity's turn to growl, but instead of continuing to claw at Vex, she pivoted on her heel and stalked over to the dead man. She stood over the body and dragged a hand through the tangled mess of her hair as she stared unseeingly at the bloody mess at her feet. "For the most part."

Havoc went and stood on the dead man's other side so he could face her. "Lay it out."

She met his unreadable regard and winced. "You won't like it."

He grunted. "Will it get Ruin back?"

"That's the goal."

"Then get it on with it."

"Right." She blew out a breath and reached for a calm that kept slithering away in tandem to the sound of seconds ticking by.

While the two Vultures listened, she laid out her plan. It

was a hell of a long shot, but if it played out right, all the Vultures, including Ruin, would walk away.

When she was finished, both Vex and Havoc studied her with matching blank masks. It made her antsy. "What?"

"You going in planning to die?" Havoc's question was strangely gentle.

Stunned, she blinked. "No." But even as she answered, she ignored the burning certainty that if it came down to it, she wouldn't hesitate to step in front of Ruin and take a blade to the heart. She wasn't ready to face the real reason why it was so important Ruin survive. Not yet. Maybe later. She needed to focus on freeing Ruin and permanently removing the threat of River Man and Reznik.

Havoc watched her and said nothing, but it was Vex who took her by surprise. "Better not be lying, Charity, because I got a feeling if you are, it'll just piss my brother off. Ruin ain't nice when he's pissed."

Temper shot to shit, Charity snapped, "Think you're a little late with that warning."

Vex gave her a fierce smile. "Probably, but at least I can tell him I gave it."

ROUGHLY FIFTEEN MINUTES LATER, Charity led Havoc and Vex along the shore where a battered wall kept the undesirables from a three-story home. The stately old beauty managed to survive the widening reach of the Columbia, but not the greedy hands of a family with ties to New Seattle's underworld.

Chain wielding bastard did his best not to share, but she finally got him to squeal. Since the family split their time between their place in the city and here, River Man had an agreement that allowed him use of the family's home for business transactions when they weren't in residence. Even better, Reznik was expected to make an appearance sometime between two and three this morning. It was roughly two-thirty, and she hoped they weren't too late.

Predicting Reznik's behavior was a years' long obsession for her and in this instance would come in handy. Like the fact the paranoid weasel would bring in his standard six-person team to watch his back. Add in the two River Man took with him that she named Scar Face and Muddy Eyes, it brought their grand total of targets to ten.

Charity's font of reluctant information admitted there would only be a few sentries posted as River Man didn't like to make his business public. In this case, it meant less numbers for the Vultures to carve through while Charity kept Reznik, and River Man occupied.

The wall didn't last long and gave way to the heavy cover of old-growth trees. Charity's goal was the far corner of the property where foliage and shadows made it difficult to see, but easy to slip in. She scaled the walls using the rough surface as make-shift finger and toe holes. Her body protested with a series of aches and pains that she deliberately ignored.

At the top of the wall, she used the overreaching branches to make her way further into the property. She didn't wait on Vex or Havoc but picked a spot where she could monitor the house and any movement.

She straddled a thick branch and gave her body a break as she scanned the roofline. She quickly identified two sentry positions, one on the roof and one walking rotations on the ground. The split coverage upped her chances of gaining access without unwanted attention.

The tree swayed as Vex used a different branch to come up beside her. Charity's hand braced against the trunk, her body moving in sync with the tree. When everything settled, Vex's voice drifted over. "I'm counting two."

"Leaves at least another four inside," Charity confirmed.

"We hope," came Havoc's contribution from the nearby tree. "Time?"

"Four minutes." Charity's goal was the small third level window in what she hoped was an unused bedroom just above the back porch. According to her now dead informant, that particular window was left unlocked so River Man's minions could sneak a smoke.

She studied her intended path and did her best to mute the ticking clock in her head. The trail of overlapping branches stopped just short of the low porch roof on the second level. Thankfully the other larger nearby windows were dark. "' I'm going to need a clear shot to jump from the tree to the roof without being seen."

Vex was all business. "We'll take care of it."

Charity got to her feet and moved as carefully as possible over the branches. Years of sneaking into forbidden places took over, her pulse held steady, her head stayed clear, and it was all about the next step. Soon she was out of the tree and facing the gap between nature and architecture.

As the mental timer in her head counted down the last few seconds of her allotted time, a sharp crack sounded, muted shouting followed, and then came the rush of feet.

Trusting the Vultures to do what needed to be done, Charity took her chance and jumped. She landed with a soft thump and held her breath as she watched the windows for signs of detection. When nothing happened, she shimmied up one of the rounded pillars that supported the porch and grabbed the edge of the overhang.

She gritted her teeth against the screaming protest of various body parts and pulled herself up. She cleared the roof and rolled to her back, blinking away the sting of annoying tears. She sucked in air, rolled to her side and up to her feet. Mindful of the narrow ledge, she crept towards the dark window.

The window opened with a soft click, and she sent up a quick prayer of thanks for idiots and their addictions. She slipped inside, and the tension riding her ass eased as she sank into the dubious protection of the house. Once the window was closed, her nose was assailed with the mix of stale tobacco and the hushed mustiness of a shuttered room. She crouched under the windowsill and waited, letting the feel of the house settle around her.

In a strange occurrence that she never tried to explain because it barely made sense, her body tuned itself to the surrounding atmosphere until her presence and the house's blended into one entity. It made it easier for her to slip around the inhabitants unobserved.

This house carried a sense of quiet pride, the kind found in families who could trace their blood back through generations. But there was an insolent vibe to the pride, probably a recent addition from its new owners.

Charity used the ambient light to move soundlessly to the door. She waited to ensure no one lingered on the other side, then, standing off to the side, slowly pulled it open. The cooler, cleaner air danced in and spun the older air back into the hall. Charity followed in its wake.

She picked her way down polished wooden halls, her knife held close and out of sight. The top floor appeared empty and getting to the second floor was simple. But once there, she exercised more caution. Lights burned along the halls, and she strained her ears for voices. Silence answered.

There was no sense in checking the rooms on the third or second floor, because no matter how tight your ties to the criminal elements, those who lived like this abhorred blood on the hardwoods. That left her with the basement.

She bypassed the stairs leading to the ground floor and with a faint hope pushing at her, decided to risk checking the last rooms at the end of the hall. The hall light was dark, and her quick scan noted a burned out bulb. The first door revealed a book-lined room with a couple of couches. At any other time, she would have checked out the titles filling the shelves, instead she closed the door and moved to the next room.

Draped shapes indicated a storage area. She closed the door, backed to the middle of the hall and caught her shadowed reflection in the hanging wall mirror. Covered in dust, it turned her reflection into a ghostly apparition. Under the mirror, on a marble top entry table with delicate legs, was a dried flower arrangement. But that wasn't what caught her attention and drew her closer.

No, what sent anticipation humming through her veins was the curled leave that danced across the top. What appeared to be a sunken linen closet was actually a narrow servants' staircase. She did a mental victory dance. Not many surviving structures had one anymore, but this house had been around longer than most.

She crept down the claustrophobic passageway, and when voices drifted up, slowed to a stop a few stairs from the bottom. The tickle of ammonia hit her nose and she stifled an unexpected sneeze. Someone had been doing some serious cleaning.

"Where's Larson?" The whip of command indicated the voice belonged to whoever considered themselves in charge.

"He and Stig are doing the rounds outside."

"I'll send Baylor up to switch positions with Larson in fifteen."

"Yes, sir."

These disciplined men must be Reznik's because they were a far cry from the morons River Man hired.

"Anything comes, notify me. I'll be downstairs," directed the head honcho.

"Yes, sir."

She listened as the order giver moved away, then a heavy door opened, releasing a rush of damp, earth filled air. The corresponding shush of it closing was followed by a poorly stifled sigh and then lighter steps moved away from her hiding spot.

Charity palmed her knife and decided it was time to give a few orders of her own. Like, *sit. Stay. Roll over.* And her favorite, *play dead*.

She crept down the last few steps and peeked around the edge of the thick, hand carved post that marked the end of the cabinets concealed the stairway.

The man wandering the spacious kitchen and going from window to window was dressed in black, the standard mercenary uniform. Even his dark hair was shorn short.

The kitchen was open, cabinets, appliances and the sink lined three of the walls. The wall nearest her was an arched entryway into the main living spaces. The door she wanted was across the way, next to a huge ass refrigerator, a relic from before the Collapse.

Sheesh, it was big enough to stash a body.

The thought made her pause, then grin. First, she needed to catch the watcher off guard. She clicked through a few options before finally settling on one. It wouldn't work for long but should be enough for her to get close.

She moved out of the stairwell like a silent shadow and slipped along the wall of cabinets, her goal just inside the entryway, where the cabinets ended. She leaned against the side of the arch as if she had snuck in from outside. She brought her blade out and deliberately played with it.

The motion caught the guard's peripheral attention and

he spun around, menace dropping him into a prepared crouch, a blade in his fist.

She continued to play with her blade, flashed her craziest smile and didn't move from her purposely unconcerned pose. "Hiya, soldier boy."

He watched her for a few tense seconds, trying to judge the threat. "What the hell are you doing here?"

Using her blade, she aimed the tip at her chest and affected a mock pout. "Me? Why, sugar, I'm one of River Man's guards."

He slowly straightened and narrowed his gaze. "You weren't here before."

She shook her head in time with her blade. "Don't go gettin' yo'self all worked up there. I'm just reportin' in, followin' orders and all." She cocked her head to the side. "You know how it is, dontcha?"

"Yeah." His grimace was proof he was buying her act. "No one said anything about late comers."

"Oh don't fret, sugar." She took advantage of the small opening, pushed off the wall, and sauntered over to him. She dropped the hand with the blade to her side and adding extra swing to her hips.

Sure enough his gaze dropped, then stuttered back up.

She got close her voice husky with temptation. "I promise you won't get in trouble for my being here."

Proving that even the best-trained man could be blinded by hormones, he put his blade away, then folded his arms over his chest. "You going to guarantee that?"

She took the last step that put her inches away, then leaned in, laid one hand on his chest, petting it through his t-shirt, and tilted her head back.

At her unspoken offer, he lowered his head.

She bunched his t-shirt in her fist and whispered, "Yes, sir."

She pulled him down, her lips smothering his gasp, and stared into his widening eyes as she sent her blade slicing up and under his ribs. She finished with a quick turn of her wrist.

Moving his dead weight without removing her blade was awkward, but she didn't want to risk leaving a blood trail. As fun as it would be to test her theory about stashing a body in the fridge, it would take too long to make room in the thing. And time was one thing she was short on.

Instead, she dragged him into the oversized pantry. Judicious removal of some potatoes and other bulk staples gave her enough room to stash him under the bottom shelf.

She pulled her blade free, then re-arranged the items in front of him. Not the best solution, but by the time his blood made it out the door or someone stumbled across him, she'd be done.

She made a beeline for the heavy door, gripped the cool handle, and took a deep breath. This next part sucked because chances were high that her entrance would catch someone's attention. Hopefully, Vex and Havoc managed to remove the two outside.

She pulled it open.

twenty-eight

"**I**'m not happy." The cultured tones contained a lethal sharpness guaranteed to make a person bleed.

Not that the man the voice belonged to needed the help. As far as Ruin could tell, the bastard got off on watching others suffer. Not enough to do it himself, but having someone else do his dirty work? Oh yeah, that was working like a fucking charm for Reznik.

And didn't that prove Charity right?

In front of him and to his left Reznik was bitching to River Man. Once again Ruin was hanging from the damn chains. Another hit sent an agonizing burst tearing through him. It jerked his thoughts off-kilter and left him fighting back the darkness that beckoned.

"Making an example out of one of Fate's Vultures can't hurt," cajoled River Man.

Under the overhead lights, the classic lines of the crime lord's face took on an ominous edge. "If I wanted to make examples out of them, I would have directed Tyke's people to do so," he snapped. "I believe my orders were to wipe them out if possible. The only thing you've accomplished is directing the Vulture's attention to my doorstep."

"You can offer him to—"

"Who the hell are you?" A rough bark cut off River Man's suggestion.

"Back off unless you want to be wearing your intestines as a necklace."

Everything in Ruin stilled as the icy response slipped through his pain-filled haze. *She wouldn't fucking dare!*

"And I promise you, Reznik wants to see me." Feminine arrogance coated each word.

Ruin forced his head up and around to watch in furious shock as Charity backed Reznik's man down the stairs, her knife held at the ready. Reznik and River Man both turned at her appearance, but Ruin could still make out their faces.

Reznik's was cold and calculating. River Man's was dark with fury.

"You bitch." That endearment came from beside Ruin. Scar Face stepped away from Ruin and slid around Reznik, inching closer to her position.

"Uh-uh. Back off. Not here to talk to you or the flesh bag you call boss." She didn't take her gaze off the other man she was stalking. "I'm here to talk with Reznik."

"And you would be?" Reznik's question cut over the stuttering protests of the two hired Blade Men, and the strangled growl coming from River Man.

"An opportunity you don't want to miss."

"You'll have to give me more than that, my dear." Reznik's false charm provided a thin veneer for his calculation.

"I have an offer from Lilith."

And just like that his blonde bundle of trouble snagged her prey and made herself an irresistible target.

Ruin forced back a litany of curses through sheer will and the judicious application of his teeth to his tongue. Despite his impaired vision, he tried to look around without being obvious.

Reznik was in front of him to his left, River Man on the right. Behind him to his left Reznik's man and Charity were engaged in a stand-off at the base of the stairs. Scar Face and Muddy Eyes played witness from the far side, where Reznik's other man stood, still and silent.

He twisted to look to the staircase and prayed to see movement. When the shadows remained shadows, his gut clenched. *For all that was holy, please don't let her be here alone.*

"Let her through, Jonas," Reznik ordered the man on the other end of Charity's blade. When his man held his position in silent defiance, the crime lord snapped, "Now."

Jonas stepped back with obvious reluctance and allowed Charity the room to move around Ruin's left and into the room, which put her right in the middle of the pack of hyenas.

With each step she took, tension rose. Only after she put distance between her and Jonas, did she finally look at Ruin. Her cool arrogance never faltered, but Ruin caught the flare of fury in her eyes before she let her lashes drift down. She shifted her attention to River Man and used her mocking faux disappointment like a poker to his ass. "I'm surprised you're still breathing."

River Man snarled and went to lunge for her, only to be brought up short by Reznik's raised hand and Jonas's responding movement. It was like watching feral dogs be restrained by an invisible leash.

"Why's that?" Although Reznik's question seemed harmless enough, there was too much of his inner corrosion to hide his soulless heart.

Charity gave him a smile wrapped in condescension and threats. "I heard you don't tolerate incompetence, but maybe I misheard."

"You didn't."

"Then—" she circled her blade in River Man's direction, "—why?"

"You don't throw away good tools."

She laughed. "No, you don't really believe that."

"I don't?"

"Nope. If you did, then you wouldn't have put him in the crosshairs this morning." Her smirk suggested a cat with a mouthful of canary. "Granted, it does seem like an adequate repayment considering how badly he and the Raiders bungled your grand plan."

With his up-close view of both men, Ruin caught the moment River Man eyed Reznik and shifted his earlier anger to a new target.

Something Reznik missed as Charity chattered on. "Because that was your doing, wasn't it?"

"You ordered the hit?" River Man's question lashed out, like the warning flick of a whip, and he completely forgot the man at his back.

Reznik gave him a dismissive glance, turned away with a careless shrug, and directed his next comment to Charity. "Mistakes happen."

Charity didn't miss a beat and added more pressure to the fissure between the two. "Yeah, and your man and his flunkies tend to make quite a few, don't they?"

Her question swung River Man's head around and his gaze narrowed as he searched for her trap.

She kept the pressure up. "I have to wonder whose decision it was to approach the Raiders because they don't seem like your first choice when looking to shake things up."

That earned River Man a hard-eyed glance from Reznik, and Ruin stopped worrying about Charity pressing her luck and instead started listening. Here was the infamous 'Hound at work. The little manipulator was skilled at teasing out secrets. God knows she managed to get enough from him. Hopefully she knew her targets' limits, otherwise, things could go sideways quick. And since she dominated center stage, he used the respite to carefully position his body and will for whatever opening came his way.

"Let's review." Charity started ticking off an imaginary list. "First, the Raiders' hit and run approach fails to pull Fates' Vultures far enough away to leave Crane swinging in the wind. Then the Raiders managed to lose your cargo in Crane's front yard, which meant sending them in before you were ready."

She inched closer. "Now granted, they managed to check off one item on their to-do list, but not before they decided to improvise. Which nabbed attention from the one group you were hoping to avoid—our not-so-forgiving Vultures. They didn't take long to track your Raider buddies back here, and when they start picking through the rotten meat, they found River Boy. Which is where it really turns to shit."

Apparently fascinated by her, Reznik murmured, "Do tell."

Yeah, please do. Because Ruin was curious as to what held this together for her— knowledge or guesswork. Knowing how her mind worked, it was probably both.

River Man's face was white with fury as he slowly inched his way toward the stairs, and Ruin worried if Reznik failed to keep him leashed, Charity would be gutted and breathing her last at his feet.

Seemingly unaware of the danger she was in, Charity continued her game. "Your man had in his possession a very valuable, influential treasure that might just help you get to where you're going. Instead of recognizing what he had, he was more interested in making a quick buck with the flesh peddlers and stroking his bruised ego." She shook her head with mock pity. "It's so sad to see a good tool break with the first hit."

"You bitch." River Man's voice was rough with anger.

"Told you to be more creative." She wagged a finger. "That name is getting old.'

"Your grasp of information is astonishing, young lady," Reznik cut in. "But I fail to see how your presence is more beneficial to me than the Vulture behind me."

"Well for one, I'm not bleeding out on your floor," she drawled.

"I can fix that," River Man offered.

She ignored him and her free hand went to her hip. "And two, my grasp of information should be damn astonishing otherwise I'm not doing my job properly."

Ruin didn't miss the subtle shift of Reznik's pricey shirt as his shoulders stiffened. "And what job would that be?"

She touched a spot on her chest, just above a bloodstain, in an exaggerated show of surprise, complete with an over dramatic flutter of eyelashes. "Oh, did I forget to introduce myself properly? Let me rectify that." She bent in a shallow mock bow and never broke eye contact. "I'm Lilith's 'Hound."

Her announcement produced a momentary explosion of strangled sounds as River Man desperately tried to put words together, only to fail miserably. And Reznik? Well, his interest was firmly locked on Charity.

Meanwhile Scar Face used the unfolding drama to creep closer to Charity who was so focused on the bigger threats, Ruin was worried she wouldn't see him until it was too late. Before Scar Face could act, Reznik's other man stepped out of the shadows and brought Scar Face to a full stop.

Reznik straightened a tailored cuff, the light winking off the cufflink. "That would explain how you came about your stories, but it doesn't prove your authenticity."

She arched a brow and matched his pompous tone. "What kind of proof do you require?"

A condescending smile twisted his thin lips. "If you're a 'Hound, I'm sure you can come up with something."

"Hmm." She tapped her finger against her lips as she casually moved forward, knife at her side.

If you didn't know her, you might miss the baleful light in her eyes, the one that warned you were on dangerous ground. She inched closer to the two men, who seemed to have dismissed both her and Ruin as a non-threat. Their mistake, and Ruin was certain it wouldn't be their last.

"Why don't we go back a few years to when you were trying to impress the heads of New Seattle's underworld?" Charity's voice hardened. "You held one of your flashy little gatherings, the kind meant to intimidate and impress. And it did a bang-up job."

Seeing how Reznik was completely focused on her, Ruin figured the man knew exactly what she was talking about.

"Until a couple of grifters made the mistake of fleecing one of your private investors." She didn't wait for the crime lord's confirmation, but simply rolled along. "Not wanting to lose face, you decided to make an example out of them. You started with the woman first. You had your guard dogs play while her partner watched, unable to stop you or your men. You sat there, the uncrowned king of crime, and watched until her screams died with her. Then, you turned your attention to the man. You had fun with him."

Hurting for her, Ruin hoped he was the only one who caught the slight tremor of her knife against her thigh.

She inched closer, but those around her, caught in her story, didn't notice. Her voice dropped into the Arctic region. "Since he threatened your image, no sense in letting him off lightly. Nope, you drew it out, one slice at a time, until he was nothing more than meat. Then, to be sure others would think twice before crossing your line, you dumped them both in their home. Right where everyone could be sure to see your handiwork."

Darkness crawled through her face and matched the silky menace of her voice. "Just as you intended, your message spread like wildfire." She held his gaze with her burning one. "Proof enough?"

He dipped his chin in acknowledgement. "You disagree with my actions."

"I disagree with a great many things you've done," she said. "They make me wonder."

"About?"

She didn't answer straight away. "Once upon a time, you barely tolerated the most minor of infractions. Now?" Her gaze touched on River Man and her shoulders shifted with negligence. "You seem to tolerate third rate talent. It makes me wonder how you ever thought Lilith would consider working with you."

Reznik flicked his hand, and all hell broke loose.

Jonas stepped out of the shadows behind River Man, yanked his head back, and with a quick, brutal swipe slit his throat. On the other side of the room, Reznik's silent guard caught Muddy Eyes by surprise and slid his blade over the stunned Blade Man's throat. The only one not hampered by surprise or shock was Scar Face, who charged Charity in lethal silence.

Instinct had Ruin jerking forward, only to be pulled up short with a rattle of chain. He locked his muscles and shook with enraged restraint as he held tight to a desperate mantra. *Charity was lethal as shit.*

Warned by instinct or luck, Charity shifted to the side and deflected Scar Face's initial swipe. Ruin's gaze remained glued on the blur of blades. Blood spattered across the floor as pain-filled hisses intermixed with grunts and growls accompanied the brutal dance. As emotion fueled Scar Face's strikes, they failed to connect, and the control of the fight shifted to Charity.

The sickening dread riding Ruin's ass backed off when Charity's plan became clear. She lured Scar Face in with a deliberate feint that appeared to leave her exposed. Blinded by arrogant fury, the Blade Man committed to his strike, but Charity had already moved.

She stepped in under his raised arm and in a devastating burst strike, slammed the blade in her fist into his chest. At the same time, she used her other hand to block, then trap his knife hand in an arm lock. Twisting his trapped arm, she nailed his vulnerable areas with a series of debilitating knee strikes.

The sound of bone snapping preceded his high-pitched scream. Scar Face dropped to his knees, head back, his broken arm trapped. Charity didn't hesitate. She yanked her blade free and swiped across his exposed throat. She stepped back, her chest rising and falling, but her gaze remained on Scar Face. He held his gruesome kneeling position for a moment or two longer before pitching forward and ending up face down in his own blood.

"Messy but effective." Reznik's comment cut through the tension-filled aftermath.

Charity blinked, shook her head once, then crouched to clean her blade against Scar Face's shirt. She looked at Reznik. "I guess that's one way to rectify your mistakes." Without leaving her crouch she pivoted, her blade hand resting on her knee, her other braced on the floor behind Scar Face. "What's your follow up here?"

"My follow up?" Reznik repeated.

She nodded, pushed to her feet, and took a step forward, only to stop when Jonas and the silent one stepped closer. She caught their silent threat and gave Reznik a half-smile. "You finally tied up your loose ends, so what do you plan to do next?" Her hands went to her hips. "Let me guess." She caught her lower lip with her teeth, tilted her head to the side, and pretended to ponder. "Ah! I know." She dropped the insolent pose. "You're going to offer me something in return for my glowing recommendation to Lilith."

Reznik's evil chuckle made Ruin's balls shrivel. "Oh no, dear. That's too easy."

Charity barely blinked and simply continued to watch.

"Did you think I'd miss your little longing glances at what's hanging here?" The cold- hearted bastard made a *tsking* sound, then strode over to eye Ruin, giving Charity his back. He stopped just out of reach of Ruin and turned to face her.

Charity's gaze shifted to Ruin, and he caught a shadow of regret, there and gone, but her eyes were cold when they traveled back to Reznik. "You think I'm tangled up with him?"

"You're not the only one with access to information." Reznik pivoted so he could see Ruin and Charity at the same time, then he motioned to Jonas, who came up on Ruin's left. "Add in the disheveled state of the bedroom at the Lodge, and I'm going to have to go with—how did you put it?—oh yes, that you are well and truly tangled up with him." Reznik eyed Charity. "I think it's best if I send Lilith my condolences on the tragic loss of her 'Hound, lost in the crossfire when River Man betrayed me." A charming sincerity replaced the monster. "I was so impressed with her attempt to protect me, I had to personally deliver the news."

"Oh, Reznik," Charity purred. "You're such a man."

Her dismissal made Reznik flushed. "Excuse me?" Ice dripped from the two words.

She stepped forward and Reznik's silent guard dog did the same, gliding around Muddy Eyes' body at his feet. She stopped, lifted both hands, her blade still in her right hand, and shook her head. "Haven't you heard? Torture isn't always necessary to get what you want. You get more bees with honey than vinegar, and I can be sickeningly sweet when needed." Her shoulders rose in a graceful shrug. "Besides, sometimes a girl has to have a little bit of fun."

There was enough truth in Charity's voice that even Ruin, who knew it for a lie, had a niggle of doubt.

Reznik studied her carefully in an obvious attempt to gauge her sincerity. He turned his head to Ruin, who shoved his raging emotions deep where they couldn't be found. Ruin held that creepy ass gaze for what felt like an eternity. Reznik turned back to Charity, sighed, and moved towards her. "Well then, we'll just tidy up one more loose end then, shall we?"

Now or never. Ruin gripped the chain and drew up his legs, ignoring the pain that threatened to white out his vision. He lashed out, not expecting to hit Reznik, but prayed it was the distraction Charity needed.

At Jonas' warning shout, Reznik stumbled back from Ruin, which put him within Charity's reach. Except she wasn't looking at Reznik or the silent guard sneaking up behind her. Her attention was on Jonas who lunged for Ruin.

A roar erupted from the staircase as a small mountain barreled down the stairs. At the same time, Charity's knife flew through the air and sank into Jonas' shoulder with enough force to jerk him off course. Havoc finished the job and tackled Jonas to the floor.

Fury whipped through Ruin, and he struggled against the damn chains, desperate to get free. But he was too late. The silent guard dog took a now weaponless Charity to the floor. Ruin lost sight of them when Reznik turned and stalked forward, his face twisted into a nightmare, his lips drawn back from his teeth.

Vicious joy lit Reznik's features as Ruin continued to twist and turn in a futile struggle, and he dodged Ruin's desperate kicks.

A line of fire seared across Ruin's leg, and only then did

Ruin realize Reznik had a blade of his own. *It fucking figured.* Ruin did his best to time his kicks to avoid being hamstrung, but his strength was quickly taking a hike.

"I'm going to enjoy gutting you," Reznik taunted.

Ruin leaned forward and ignored the bite of strained muscles. "Bring it, asshat."

Reznik's growl was cut short, and he stopped mid-step, his eyes widening in shock. A familiar face appeared over Reznik's shoulder and Ruin didn't stop his fierce grin.

"Actually," Vex snarled. "I'm going to enjoy gutting you." She jerked her blade up along his spine, a move Ruin recognized by Reznik's jerky dance.

To add insult to injury, she put her boot in Reznik's ass and sent the crime lord to land face first at Ruin's feet. She stepped over the dying man and took in Ruin's battered appearance. "I leave you alone one fucking day and look at the mess you got into."

His relief was short-lived as he tried to see what was happening behind his twin. "Leave me and help Charity."

His beloved, but irritating twin, snorted. "She'll be fine."

Bombarded by unfamiliar emotions he lost his shit and yelled, "She threw her fucking knife away!" *And sacrificed herself to save him.*

He wasn't sure what to do with that. Later. He'd deal with it later. Perhaps after he paddled Charity's ass red for scaring the shit out of him.

Vex worked the chain's lock and turned to look back. "Well, looks like she found another one, so chill." She turned back and as the lock gave way, braced him with an arm around his waist.

He gritted his teeth, forced his legs to hold his weight, and tried to wrench free of Vex. "Let me go, dammit."

Vex's hands caught his face. "Fucking chill, brother." A

miasma of worry and love filled her eyes and he stilled, held by the plea in her gaze. "Please, Ruin."

The last was so soft he almost missed it. He closed his eyes, dropped his forehead to hers, and let her brace him while he fought to find his footing. On his second breath he heard, "Ruin?"

Vex kept her arm at his waist but shifted so he could finally see beyond her. And when his bloodstained blonde shuffled towards him, he could barely get her name around the choking tightness in his throat. "Charity?"

Then she was there, and despite Vex's presence, Charity's hands were busy running over every cut and bruise, her gaze frantic, her voice higher than normal. "You're okay, right?"

"Yeah, babe, I'll be fine." He lifted his still bound hands, dropped them over her shoulders, and pulled her close despite his body's various protests. He needed to feel her in his arms, just for a minute.

She settled against him, her face pressed against his chest, her arms slipping around him low in deference to his ribs.

He rested his cheek against her sweat-dampened hair and found Vex watching them with a rare, soft smile, one he hadn't seen in years. "Thanks," he mouthed.

Vex rolled her eyes, cleared her throat, and glowered. "You okay if I let your little girlfriend hold you up? I need to make sure Havoc's done playing."

The two women shifted around him, Vex stepping over Reznik's body as Charity took her position, then started unwrapping the chain from his wrists.

Vex didn't have to go far because Havoc came over. A bruise darkened his cheek, and a cut marred his forearm, but otherwise he appeared unharmed. "Finished."

"Good." Vex took in the carnage-strewn room, and propped her hands on her hips. "Well, that was fun. We should do this more often."

That earned a snort from Charity, who let the chain drop to the floor. "Next bloodbath, I'll be sure to send you an invite."

Ruin carefully moved his arms, wincing as his shoulders screamed. Then Charity's hands were there, helping to ease the ache.

Vex turned her way and winked. "You do that."

A groan at Ruin's feet drew their attention. Charity stared down at a still breathing Reznik and her hands stilled.

Vex's lip curled. "What do you know, he's still alive."

"I can fix that," Charity offered.

Without a word Havoc handed a blade, hilt-first, to Charity. She met the big man's gaze and took it. "Thanks."

He let go with a nod.

When looked back to Ruin, he caught the wild emotion in her gaze. It didn't take a psychic to understand the internal storm ripping through her at having her parents' killer at her mercy.

He dipped his head and calmed the small tremor of her lips with a soft press. When he was done, he lifted his head and muttered, "Do your thing so we can get the hell out of this town." Then he shuffled back as Vex and Havoc stepped in to make sure he didn't fall.

Charity used her foot to shove Reznik to his back, then crouched at his side. She tapped Havoc's blade against Reznik's cheek. "Wakey, wakey."

His lashes fluttered then lifted. As recognition filtered through his pain, his face twisted. "F-f-fucking 'Hound." The last came out on a pain-filled wheeze.

"Pay attention, little man," she crooned as she dragged the knife's tip through the no longer pristine shirt. Buttons fell away under the knife's edge and the material parted, leaving his throat bare. "I want you to hear this."

He open his mouth to respond and a rattling cough

emerged. When he was done with his coughing fit, his lips were blood-stained.

Charity watched dispassionately, slowly moving the blade back and forth over his throat. "You remember that story I told you? Do you know who that couple belonged to?" She leaned in, pressed the blade's edge against his throat, and put her mouth near his ear. "Me."

She pulled back. Reznik's face filled with horror and anger as he realized his since had come home to roost. Then it didn't matter because Charity's hand moved and Reznik died.

twenty-nine

When Charity finally resurfaced, it took her brain a few moments to kick into gear. Her body was stiff, and everything ached—ribs, knee, hands, shoulder, and spots she didn't know could ache. She didn't dare move for fear of setting off a boatload of bodily protests.

Instead, she relaxed deeper into the pillow where Ruin's familiar scent dominated. She was in Ruin's bed at Grave's Hall in Pebble Creek. And she wasn't alone. She stroked the arm lying over her hips but didn't open her eyes. Not yet. There was time enough to face what waited. For now, she wanted to enjoy the feel of Ruin, alive and breathing. Her heart clenched, and she forced her thoughts to veer away from the nightmares that chased her dreams.

The trip back to Pebble Creek was a blur of teeth-gritting endurance, one she didn't want to repeat any time soon. By the time they made it to Pebble Creek, she was barely upright and vaguely remembered Reaper's deep voice rumbling at the others. She didn't even remember making it to Grave's Hall.

But neither she nor the Vultures had wanted to stick

around Kennewick. Especially after they left the mansion behind as it burned in a massive bonfire that body disposal so much easier. Besides, there was no sense in hanging around waiting for trouble to find them, not when there was more than enough waiting for them back here.

The heat at her back shifted and the hand on her hip gently tugged her to her back. She gave in and rolled, blinking her eyes open to find Ruin staring down at her.

His tousled hair provided too much temptation, and she stroked her hands through his hair. He had a hell of a shiner, but at least it wasn't puffy. He leaned down and she helped by meeting him halfway for his kiss. Something she feared she would never get again.

Their tongues tangled and stroked, neither one in a hurry. The now familiar hunger rose and drowned out her lingering aches and pains. He trailed soft kisses over her chin and sucked gently at the base of her throat.

She arched her neck on a soft moan that morphed into a hiss as a muscle twisted wrong. She was tempted to keep going, but Ruin pulled back and narrowed his gaze. "We'll pick this up later."

She licked her lips. "Promise?"

Something hot and wicked turned his amber gaze gold. "Hell, yeah." He stroked her face, his touch curling her toes. "Right after I tan your ass."

It took a second for his words to sink in. "Excuse me?"

He caught her face between his hands and forced her to meet his gaze. She was stunned by the depth of worry and anger that underlined something she wasn't ready to name.

"What the hell were you thinking coming in on your own like that?"

Her temper flared into a wildfire at his reprimand, and despite his restraining hold, she got in his face, her fingers clutching his shoulders. "As if I'd leave your sorry ass hanging out there!"

"My ass was just fine," he shot back.

"Are you kidding me?" She jerked back with a huff. "What was your plan? Wearing out their fists?"

"Do you think you would have made it until Havoc and Vex arrived?" His grip shifted to her uninjured shoulder, and he gave her a short shake until she set her nails into his skin in protest. "I didn't want them focused on you."

"Boo fucking hoo, Ruin." She grabbed his hair and pulled him in until they were nose to nose. "I wasn't leaving you." The truth of her words tore through her heart with stunning force and left it raw.

Still propped above her he froze and searched her gaze with his. "Neither was I."

She recognized the wary hope that stared back, and because it existed in her, she accepted the inevitable. She was in love with this idiot.

God help them both.

Unable to outrun her battering flood of emotions, she swallowed around the thick knot in her throat. "I can't lose you."

His wicked, wicked smile returned. "You planning on ditching me now that you got what you wanted?"

She didn't miss the shadow of real worry under his teasing question. She cupped the side of his face, leaned up and pressed a soft kiss to the side of his mouth. When she drew back, she whispered, "Who said I got what I wanted?"

His smile softened. "You looking for something more?" Something in her expression must have given away her thoughts because he brushed her lips with his and whispered, "Yeah, me too."

Three words shifted her world and when it righted, it resettled at a whole new angle. "Well, shit."

Ruin threw his head back and laughed.

AFTER A SHARED SHOWER, Charity followed Ruin into the back room of Grave's Hall where reality waited for them. It was crowded.

She gave Boden a quick hug, and then moved towards one of the mismatched chairs. She considered sitting but decided against it. It would take too long to get back to her feet.

Ruin slipped around her and went to exchange a high five with a wan-looking Simon who was situated in a comfy, easy chair. Male greeting complete, he bumped fists with his twin.

Behind the table, Reaper watched his Vulture's entrance from behind the table. He stood against the wall, arms crossed, and a glower darker than pitch on his face.

What the hell crawled up Reaper's ass now? She got her answer when she caught sight of the stunning redhead sitting at the end of the table. She grinned. "Hello, Lilith."

Lilith rose with a smile and came over to give her a hug, her hold mindful of Charity's battered body. "Glad to see you upright." She stepped back, her sharp gaze taking in everything, including how Ruin came to stand at Charity's side. Instead of commenting, she simply raised an eyebrow, a mocking light in her jade eyes.

Ignoring her silent question, Charity asked, "How's Tabby?"

It was startling how fast the lazy humor turned into a chilling hardness. "Dealing, but she'll be better knowing you're okay."

"You need to keep a better eye on the girl." The growled comment came from Reaper.

Lilith's lips tightened, and her spine snapped ramrod straight before she turned with a predatory deliberateness. "My daughter, my concern, Vulture, unless you've changed your mind?"

Reaper's pissy mood downgraded to foreboding.

Charity braved the icy tension. "Changed your mind about what?"

Surprisingly it was Simon who answered. "I asked Reaper to take Crane's place."

Charity didn't like the smug curl of Lilith's lips.

Obviously, neither did Reaper because he spat, "Temporarily."

"Until we figure out what the hell is going on," Simon agreed, his attention on both Reaper and Lilith.

Reaper pushed off the wall and stalked to the table. He laid his hands flat against the surface, leaned in, and aimed his glare at Simon. "What's going on is we're being played."

Lilith crossed her arms, her smile replaced with her normal unreadable expression. "I'm not playing you, Vulture."

He turned his head slowly. "What the fuck do you really want, Lilith?"

Undaunted by the man's temper, she said, "I want you to prove me right."

"And if I prove you wrong?"

She shrugged. "Will it matter? In the end you'll know exactly who set Reznik loose."

Whatever private war Reaper and Lilith were engaged in, there was one thing that needed an answer. "I'd rather know why he targeted Tabby and the other kids."

"If we're taking a vote on this," Vex cut in, "so do I."

"Me three," Ruin added.

Even Simon nodded.

Reaper's gaze went to Havoc, who dipped his chin. The

Vultures' leader pushed off the table and straightened, his arms crossing over his chest as he stared at everyone gathered. Everyone but Lilith. "Fair warning. We start turning over rocks, we're liable to uncover a shitstorm."

"What else is new?" Ruin asked.

Reaper turned to Boden. "You sure you're okay with this?"

Boden looked to Simon, then back to Reaper. "As long as Simon is, I'm good."

"Fuck me." Reaper paced along the back wall.

Charity almost felt sorry for him. It sucked to be in charge of something you didn't want, and Reaper was obviously ambivalent about this.

Finally, Reaper stopped at the other side of the table and faced Lilith. "I'll fucking honor Crane's deal with you, but only until we figure out who was pulling that shit's strings and why he targeted the kids. When it's settled, Pebble Creek goes back to Simon."

Satisfaction lit Lilith's face. "Fine," her tone was regal. "Until then, I want to know what your birds find out.'

"Fine," Reaper snarled.

She inclined her head. "I'll take Tabby back to Boulder."

"I'll ensure Katori makes it to his father." Havoc offered unexpectedly.

Reaper nodded. "Take Vex with you."

Vex stirred but settled under Reaper's hard look.

Lilith turned to Charity. "For the foreseeable future, I need you here, keeping an eye on my—"' she smirked, "—partner. They'll need your expertise to decide the next step."

There was only one answer to give, so Charity nodded.

"Good," Lilith said. "That's good." She gave Charity one last hug, then sauntered out without looking back.

"Fuck me," Reaper muttered again, his attention on the now empty doorway as he shook his head.

Ruin braved the waters. "Guess we're working with Lilith now?"

Reaper wrapped a hand around the back of his neck and grimaced. "For now."

Charity dropped her gaze to her boots and hid her grin. *That had to hurt.* When she was sure her smile wouldn't escape, she lifted her head and came face to face with Reaper's dark gaze.

His attention drifted between Ruin and Charity. "You two head to New Seattle. Find out what you can about what that fuckwit was involved with, then get your asses back here."

"Hear that?" Ruin wrapped an arm around her waist and brought her into his side. "We get to take a vacation."

A resigned disgust filled Reaper's face. "Seriously? Like I don't have enough crap to deal with between Vex and Simon? Now I have to deal with you two?"

"Hey!"

"What the hell, Reaper?"

Vex and Simon's unified outrage stumbled over each other, but they subsided when Reaper shot them a hand.

The intimidating leader of the Vultures stared at Charity. "Your expertise extend to dealing with the Queen Bitch?"

"Don't worry, Reaper. I promise to share the secrets on how to deal with Lilith." She settled deeper into Ruin's hold as anticipation and happiness filled her. "It's a well-guarded secret, but because I like this guy, and he likes you, I figure it's worth it to keep you breathing to keep him happy."

Faint humor at her teasing crept into Reaper's dark gaze. "Bitch."

Her smile grew. "See, told you you'd get around to calling me that."

Ready for more? Then find out what happens when stoic and sexy Havoc crosses path with an enigmatic assassin on the run in BEG FOR MERCY.
Now available at your favorite bookseller!

the collapse:
fate's vultures

Meet a new breed of warriors, Fate's Vultures, a mercenary band who live by a code in a world gone to hell — loyalty to each other, but for the right price, they'll be the shield for those without. In the ravaged aftermath of the post-apocalyptic these evocative couples will stop at nothing to claim their future.

Binge the world of The Collapse, now available at your favorite bookseller!

LYING IN RUINS

Charity & Ruin

On a shared mission of vengeance, what will destroy them first—their suspicions or their enemies?

BEG FOR MERCY

Havoc & Mercy

Will an assassin and a mercenary find their balance on the thin line of loyalty, or will it snap under the weight of their wary hearts?

CAUGHT IN THE AFTERMATH

Vex & Math

*Caught between a looming conflict and the fallout of a brutal betrayal,
will they survive vengeance's aftermath?*

FEAR THE REAPER

Reaper & Lilith

*Two adversaries must navigate a minefield of past betrayals and
broken promises to defeat a common enemy before it all turns to hell.*

about the author

"This story is an emotional roller coaster, from betrayal, anger, fear, love..." —InD'tale Magazine

Jami Gray is the coffee addicted, music junkie, Queen Nerd of her personal Geek Squad, Alpha Mom of the Fur Minxes, who writes to soothe the voices crammed in her head. Her series combine high-stakes urban fantasy and edgy paranormal romantic suspense into books you don't want to put down. Buckle up and get ready for a wild ride through the fascinating worlds of the Arcane, the Kyn, the PSY-IV Teams, and the Collapse.

Come visit Jami's website at **https://www.jamigray.com** and stay up to date on what kind of trouble she's getting into and when you can expect to join in.

amazon.com/author/jamigray

instagram.com/jamigrayauthor

facebook.com/JamiGrayWriter

threads.com/@jamigrayauthor

goodreads.com/JamiGray

bookbub.com/authors/jami-gray